NOW AND FOREVER

A Novel

Anita Stansfield

Covenant Communications, Inc.

Published by Covenant Communications, Inc.
American Fork, Utah

Printed in the United States of America
First Printing: January 1996

01 00 99 98 97 96   10 9 8 7 6 5 4 3 2
ISBN 1-55503-910-3

To my sisters, Janet and Suzie.

"Thank you. Thank God for you, the wind beneath my wings."

It was nothing.

ACKNOWLEDGMENTS

A special thanks to JoAnn Jolley, my editor and friend, for humoring my eccentricities, and for the way you make a good book better. And to all the people at Covenant, for treating me so well. Also, to Colleen Saxey, for your medical expertise. And to Betty Haden, the sweetest Australian I've ever met. To my parents for all the babysitting. To Dennis, for some answers. To Nathan, for some genius. To my friends—you know who you are—for being there. And to all of you readers who love Michael and Emily almost as much as I do; thanks for the cards and letters. You've made it all worth it! And I can't forget the Independent Booksellers . . . for the votes. And last but not least, to my husband and children, for your love and support.

Oh, and. . . Cindy, I love you.
Your day in the spotlight will come, as surely
as you're reading this.

PROLOGUE

Jess Michael Hamilton married Emily Ladd Hall eleven years after he had originally planned. Michael, an Australian, had always wanted to attend college in the States, and it was at Brigham Young University that he met Emily. He knew from the moment he saw her that they were meant to be together. But it wasn't until he lost Emily for a decade that he figured out he needed to make some changes in his life before he could be worthy of her love.

Emily had left Michael, a nonmember, to marry Ryan Hall in the temple. Despite the struggles and disappointments in her marriage, only after Ryan's unexpected death was she willing to put them behind her and begin a new life with Michael. And Michael knew it was divine inspiration that had led him to join the Church before he even realized Ryan was gone.

It took time and effort to cope with all the changes that had occurred during their years apart, but their love and commitment were strong enough to overcome any earthly struggles. Emily had been willing to leave her life behind and join him in Australia, and Michael had wholeheartedly taken on her three daughters to raise as his own.

Eventually, the past fell behind them. They had two sons, and the children all blended together into a loving whole. The girls adapted to their environment as if Australian soil was in their blood. Married eight years, it was difficult to comprehend that Michael and Emily had not always been together. Life was good, better than it ever had been. Michael had no reason to believe it would not always be good.

CHAPTER ONE

South Queensland, Australia

Emily waited, staring through the darkness toward the ceiling. It seemed she was always waiting. Her body felt so exhausted she wanted to sink into oblivion for a day and a half. But her mind wouldn't allow her to rest—not until she knew Michael was safe.

She glanced wearily toward the clock. Red digital numbers glared at her through the darkness. 12:18 a.m. What could possibly be keeping him? Emily reminded herself that Michael was seeing to the Lord's work. But having a husband who was president of a branch that covered over a hundred square miles was not exactly easy. There were many needs among the members, and it was typical of him to be gone several hours at a time for two or three evenings a week. But she couldn't recall him ever being so late.

Emily finally convinced herself to call one of his counselors and find out when he'd left. She'd barely picked up the phone when she heard the familiar hum of Michael's plane, circling low over the house, as if to tell her he was all right. Emily sighed and rolled over, attempting to relax, but a familiar reminder of pregnancy urged her to the bathroom. She returned to the bed and tried again to relax, but the only position she found comfortable was on her back.

Pressing a hand over her slightly rounded belly, a new worry filled her mind as she continued to stare upward into the darkness. Perhaps it was time she admitted her fears to Michael, rather than keeping them to herself. She glanced at the clock. He would be here in less than half an hour. She had the time it took him to land the plane and drive in from the hangar down to a slim twenty-seven minutes.

In an effort to make the time go faster, Emily turned her thoughts to the child within her. Perhaps if she concentrated hard enough, she could will it to move. The faint fluttering she felt a couple of weeks ago had been right on time, but she'd felt nothing since. After bearing five children, she now had to admit that something was not right. The trouble was admitting it aloud; perhaps hoping that if she kept silent, the worst possibilities might never come about.

Emily heard footsteps in the hall and felt a quiver of anticipation. Nearly eight years of marriage had not lessened Michael's effect on her when he walked into a room. She watched his shadow as he closed the door softly and sat down to remove his boots. He was in the bathroom less than three minutes, but Emily lost track of the time while he knelt beside the bed in silent prayer.

When Michael finally crawled into bed, Emily eased close to him, urging his head to her shoulder.

"Emily," he sighed, reaching out to her. "Did I wake you?"

"How could I possibly sleep?"

"I'm sorry. I wanted to call, but honestly I didn't get a chance."

"Anything you can tell me about?" she asked gently, sensing the concern in his voice.

"Nothing confidential about this. Stewart Tres was killed earlier this evening."

"Oh, no." Emily raised herself on one elbow. "How?"

"He was electrocuted on a job site," Michael reported soberly. "It's not worth repeating the details. I had to identify the body. Nellie was already in shock."

"Who's with her now?" Emily asked.

"The Relief Society was quick to take over. Everything is under control for the moment, but Barry and I are going back to check on them tomorrow."

Michael pulled Emily closer. The toneless quality of his voice didn't fool her. He was upset and she could tell.

Nothing more was said, but Emily recalled the bishop who was there when her first husband had been killed. It made the hours of waiting for Michael seem insignificant.

Michael kissed her quickly on the mouth. "How was your day?" he asked, settling comfortably beside her.

"Nothing compared to yours." Her voice betrayed a compassion for what he had witnessed.

"Tell me anyway."

Emily sensed his need for distraction and began a brief report on the status of their children. Seventeen-year-old Allison was still impatient about getting away to college. Since her cousin Stacy had left for BYU a few months earlier, there had been no living in peace. Ten-year-old Amee was still fighting almost constantly with nine-year-old Alexa.

"And," she said with a little laugh, "Jess Michael Hamilton the fourth is about to drive me over the edge. Your mother swears you were that difficult to keep up with when you were six, but I'm not certain I believe her. If that child brings one more lizard into this house, I swear I'll . . . Michael, are you listening?"

"Of course," he answered groggily. "And how about James? Is his cold getting better?"

"He's not so stuffed up. He's saying new words every day. I don't recall the girls learning to talk like that before they were two."

"I do," he said through a yawn. "And how are you?"

Emily hesitated. "That's something I've been meaning to talk to you about. It hasn't been so long since I was pregnant, but sometimes I wonder if I remember correctly, or if I'm worrying for nothing. Perhaps if I—"

She stopped when Michael began snoring softly. At first she was tempted to wake him and finish her thought, but she knew how tired he must be. Surely it could wait one more day. After another quick trip to the bathroom, Emily nuzzled close to him and finally drifted to sleep with a firm resolve to discuss this first thing in the morning.

Emily woke up alone and wondered where Michael might have gone so early. She hurried to get dressed, hoping to find him still at breakfast. Then she heard the plane. She threw a pillow at the door in frustration, then sank into a chair and cried.

While she was making the bed, Emily found a note on his pillow. He loved her. He didn't want to wake her. He would be home for dinner. Emily tried not to feel put out, but the simple truth was that she needed her husband.

After choking down some breakfast, Emily tried to escape to the sitting room to paint. Toying with the oils was often a worthy distraction, but every few minutes Alexa or Amee came running to her with some complaint about the other, or Emily had to get up and cross the hall to break apart a playroom brawl between Jess and James. After so many interruptions, she gave up. She took the boys outside for a walk and tried to enjoy herself, but a heaviness settled into her lower back that she didn't want to think about. If only Michael would come home so they could talk about this! As the day wore on, the heaviness became more evident, and twinges of cramping forced her to face a hard reality. This baby was not going to make it.

Leaving the children in Mrs. Pace's care, Emily lay down, hoping the reality would go away. She'd never lost a baby and had no desire to do so now. Knowing it was common didn't make it any easier. She'd only been resting for a few minutes when LeNay peeked into her room. "Are you all right, love?" she asked. Michael's mother seemed to have a sixth sense about the happenings beneath her roof.

"No," Emily had to admit. She had to tell someone. LeNay hurried to the bedside and took her hand.

"What is it? Are you ill?"

"I think . . . I'm losing . . . the baby." Her words pressed out with a breathy sob.

LeNay gave a soft cry of empathy and wrapped her arms around Emily. "Are you having pains?" she asked.

"More a . . . heaviness, and cramping. But I haven't felt it move for over two weeks. I'm so scared." Emily put a hand over her mouth and squeezed her eyes shut.

LeNay's sigh told Emily the evidence was not good. "I know well how you feel, love," she said gently. "I only had two children, but I was pregnant six times."

"Six?" Emily pulled back, surprised. "You never told me."

"Oh, yes. I believe these days they call it RH factor. But when I was having babies, they had no cure. I lost a baby between Katherine and Michael, and three after he was born."

"That must have been horrible," Emily murmured.

"It's not an easy thing." LeNay pressed a comforting hand over hers. "But we'll see that you're cared for. I'm going to call the doctor."

Emily nodded gratefully, trying not to think about the full spectrum of what this meant. The reality sank in further as LeNay repeated her conversation with the doctor. He suggested waiting to come to the hospital until natural labor began, which he believed would happen soon enough according to her symptoms.

LeNay left Emily while she went to check on the children and see how supper was coming. As Katherine quietly came to take LeNay's place, Emily thought how grateful she was to be sharing this huge home with Michael's family. And having Mrs. Pace here to help with the children was such a blessing.

"Mother told me." Michael's sister sat beside the bed and offered an empathetic smile. "I'm so sorry, Emily. Really I am."

"Yes," Emily tried to smile, "so am I."

"How long have you known?"

Emily admitted reluctantly, "I've feared for a week or so that something was wrong."

"And you didn't say anything?"

"I didn't want to face it, I suppose."

"I'm surprised that Michael didn't say anything. He's—"

"He doesn't know," Emily interrupted.

Katherine was obviously surprised but didn't say anything. Emily sensed she was upset, but nothing more was said before Katherine went down to supper. LeNay brought Emily a tray but she felt little appetite. "Has Michael come home yet?" she asked, though she knew he hadn't because she'd not heard the plane.

"Not yet," LeNay apologized. "I wish he'd hurry, for your sake as well as his supper."

"Don't tell him," Emily pleaded. "I should be the one—"

"I understand," LeNay agreed. "I'll pass the word to Kate."

The children were in bed before Emily heard the plane. Katherine looked up from her book as if she could see him through the roof. "It's about bloomin' time," she muttered. Emily was too distracted by grief to comment.

Twenty-seven minutes later, Michael pushed open the bedroom

door. "What's wrong?" he demanded.

"What makes you think something's wrong?" Katherine responded sarcastically.

"Mother said I should hurry upstairs and—"

Katherine stood and slammed her book closed. "This is a fine church you belong to, Michael. If you're not working, you're out playing hero to everybody else in the world, while your wife suffers in silence."

"What's wrong?" he repeated, hurrying to Emily's side.

"Your priorities are screwed up," Katherine said on her way out the door. "That's what's wrong."

Michael ignored his sister and turned his full attention to Emily. "Are you ill?" he asked, touching her face as if to check for fever.

"No, I'm not ill," she stated. "I tried to tell you last night, but you fell asleep and . . ."

"Tell me what?" he urged when she hesitated.

"I felt the baby move, just a little, over two weeks ago, but . . ." She bit her lip in an effort to keep her emotions in control. "I haven't felt it move since."

Michael attempted to push aside the problems he'd been dealing with all day and approach this rationally. "Perhaps it's too soon yet," he said gently, "or maybe—"

"Don't you dare patronize me, Michael Hamilton," she snapped. "I spent ten years of my life with a man who ignored and patronized me. I don't need it from you."

Michael was stunned. "I merely suggested that—"

"Don't suggest anything to me when you have no idea what's going on around here." Emily knew her anger was blown out of proportion, but there was no denying her frustration. "If you were around more than five minutes a day, I might find the time to tell you how I feel."

Michael was stunned into realizing she was right. "How *do* you feel?" he asked humbly. Putting all the clues together, he could see that something was terribly wrong.

Emily hesitated to tell him, realizing it was as much her fault as his that he didn't know. She was contemplating an apology when he spoke again.

"You're angry with me," he said. "Do you want to tell me why?"

Emily sighed. "I'm sorry, Michael. I should have tried to talk to you about this before now, but it seemed there was so little opportunity. I know your work in the Church is important, and I don't want to take you away from it. But there has to be balance, Michael. Do you know how long it's been since you've shared family prayer with us . . . or sat down to dinner with us . . . or . . ." She looked up at him, tears glistening in her eyes. "You have a wife and five children who need you, Michael."

Michael laid his hand against her belly. "Six," he corrected, showing a gentle smile that he hoped would ease her anger.

Emily shook her head slowly. Michael's smile faded as he tried to absorb what she was implying. He wouldn't even consider the possibility of what crossed his mind, until she said with a shaky voice, "Only five, Michael."

Michael stared at her, attempting to rationalize away the heated tears in her eyes. "Just because it hasn't moved," he finally said. "Maybe it's—"

"Listen to me, Michael," she cried. "I'm bleeding. I'm cramping. This baby is not going to make it."

Emily hung her head and cried while Michael held her hands so tight they hurt. "But it can't be," he protested. "We're supposed to have this baby. I felt it. You felt it. We talked about it . . . prayed about it . . . and we knew that . . ." His futile reasoning dissipated into tears as Emily crumbled in his arms.

In the silence of the night, Michael sat near the window, his forearms leaning against his thighs, his head hung in disbelief. Attempting to shake off a foreboding chill, he glanced up occasionally to gaze at his beautiful wife. She rested quietly in the midst of white bed linens, illuminated by the subtle glow of a bedside lamp. He knew she couldn't sleep, but he'd insisted she try to rest to keep up her strength. He glanced at the clock. 2:37 a.m. He still couldn't believe this was happening. There was a numbness blanketing the pain that he dreaded parting with. And if the realization that they were losing a baby wasn't bad enough, he had to admit that his sister was right. His priorities *were* screwed up. Emily had said he needed balance. She was obviously right. He had been cautioned by his Church leaders when he'd accepted this calling that he must not let his family suffer for the sake of others. But that was a hard line to draw when so many people were in need. Obviously he'd not drawn it in the right place. He was blessed with the means to help others a great deal, but perhaps that in itself had contributed to his loss of balance.

"Michael." Emily's voice startled him and he looked up abruptly. She was sitting on the edge of the bed, putting on her shoes. "I think we need to go now."

For a moment Michael tried to figure what she meant. He nodded slowly as he perceived it. Reality had to be faced.

"Do we need to take anything?" He stood up and stretched.

"Mother helped me pack a bag." She nodded toward it as Michael put on a jacket. He picked up the bag and she added, "Could you help me with my sweater?"

Michael set the bag on the bed and held the heavy black cardigan as she slipped her arms into it. Hesitantly he moved in front of her and pulled the sweater together, allowing his hand to linger against her slightly rounded belly, as if he could say good-bye to this child they had created. In response to the pain in Emily's eyes, he put his arms around her and held her almost fiercely.

"We've got to go," she whispered. The tone in her voice caught his attention, and he realized she was hurting.

Michael drove through the night in silence, holding Emily's hand tightly in his. He kept glancing at the clock in an effort to gauge the miles behind them. A formless urgency broke the silence as he admitted humbly, "You were right, Emily. I should have been around more. I should have sensed long before now that something wasn't right. There are so many needs out there. But I've got to remember that I can't do everything for everyone, and your needs are my most important stewardship."

Michael let her hand go and touched her face gently. Compassion filled him as he realized she was in pain but doing her best to conceal it. "You've always been so strong that sometimes I think you can handle things fine without me. But if you need me half as much as I need you, then I can see that's not true."

Emily kissed the palm of his hand. "You are my strength, Michael. I *do* need you." She grimaced slightly then took a deep breath. "I know you're trying to do what's right, Michael, but. . ." Her words faded as the contraction worsened, then gradually eased.

"I will be there for you, Emily. I promise."

"I'm not asking you to ignore your responsibilities as branch president or—"

"I know that, but I will strive for more balance. I will."

Emily smiled through the darkness. "I believe you, because you've never left the sink dirty."

"What?" he laughed.

"In college, when I was trying to find something wrong with you, I told you that you didn't clean the sink after you used my kitchen to cook. You've never left a sink dirty since."

"I wouldn't want you to think I don't care."

"I love you, Michael."

"I love you, too," he replied, and silence fell again.

A few minutes later, Emily asked with distress in her voice, "How much longer?"

"Thirty minutes or so," he replied, then added with an edge of panic, "Why?"

Emily gave up trying to be brave as the tone in his question shattered every nerve of self-control. "I didn't think it would be . . . this bad," she admitted.

"How bad?" His voice deepened with dread.

"I don't remember labor being any worse."

For the next several minutes, Michael heard more than saw the signs of increasing pain. Emily sank low in the seat and gripped the armrest on the door as if it might save her. When he tried to hold her hand, she snapped at him with a firm, "Drive, Michael. If you don't get me there alive, there's not much point in going through this."

Michael kept both hands firmly on the steering wheel, hoping she wouldn't notice how fast he was driving. His knuckles turned white and his heart beat into his ears. "I feel so blasted helpless," he muttered.

"That makes two of us," she managed to say before her breathing became so sharp he feared she'd hyperventilate.

The miles seemed endless, and Emily felt sure she couldn't bear this. If the physical pain wasn't bad enough, she had to keep reminding herself that this was for nothing. She would not be going home with a baby. A part of her flesh and blood was tearing itself away, and every contraction tore at her heart. As the pain reached what she knew was transition, Emily began to fear they weren't going to make it to the hospital before this happened.

When they finally arrived, everything blurred around her. Her keenest awareness was Michael's hand in hers as the bed beneath her was rolled down a hall and into a room with bright lights and a sterile aroma. Emily was vaguely aware of monitors being attached to her, clothes being removed, needles being inserted. But the center of everything was the pain. Just before she blacked out, the only words she recognized over a blur of voices was a frenzied, "She's hemorrhaging!"

Michael felt confidence when they arrived at the hospital and everything seemed routine and under control. Then suddenly that confidence waned as the medical team surrounding his wife dispatched into an orderly chaos. He was forced away from her and then forgotten.

With a fist pressed to his mouth, Michael became aware of a fear so intense he would have never thought it possible. Overwhelmed by the blur of activity, the tubes, the needles, the blood, he chose to concentrate on the little light that was monitoring Emily's heartbeat. He could almost feel his own heart beating in time with the up-and-down rhythm that assured him she was still alive. He studied it with such intensity that it began to go in and out of focus. He had to blink several times to be convinced that the loud beep he was hearing was connected to the straight line now running across that screen. In one blinding instant, he realized what had happened. A distant voice confirmed it. "Her heart stopped!"

Every grain of logic told Michael to force his way through the crush of people and medical equipment and take hold of her. The only thing that kept him from trying was the hard realization that they could save her and he couldn't.

"Please, God," he muttered aloud, "don't take her from me. I beg you. Please!" Michael didn't realize he was crying until he felt tears soak into his collar. He wiped his hands over his face and bit into his knuckle to keep from screaming. He winced with every effort they made to shock Emily's heart into beating. His mind raced across the evidence of death he'd dealt with earlier in the Tres home. But that had been a detached kind of pain. This was as if a part of his flesh and blood was being torn away. He thought of the children, and of the fact that he could be facing another forty years without his wife. Then he recalled, for the first time in years, that Emily was not sealed to him. It felt like a slap in the face. Was her first husband waiting on the other side to take her back? The thought filled him with such a raging desperation that he might have forced his way to her side if it had not been for a noticeable change of activity in the room.

She's dead, he thought as he watched the medical team relax and ease back. Then his eyes shot to the monitor, and he realized that her heart was beating again. He wanted to just curl up on the floor and bawl like a baby. The relief was as intense as his fear had been, and he began to wonder if he could remain standing any longer.

As Emily's condition was declared stable, Michael's presence was noticed and he was gently ushered to a waiting area with the assurance that everything would be fine. He sank weakly into a chair and pressed his forehead into his hand. "Thank you, God," he breathed. "Thank you."

CHAPTER TWO

Sunlight filled the small hospital room, illuminating every detail of all that was needed to feed life back into Emily's frail body. Michael studied the blood dripping systematically into a tube feeding her arm. Other tubes of clear liquid flowed into her veins, while monitors informed him that all was well. He had been assured she was out of danger, but he knew those monitors were being read down the hall, and any sign of trouble would bring help immediately.

Michael wearily leaned his chin on the edge of the bed and studied Emily's peaked face. It was so close to the color of the pillow that he feared she might break if he touched her, as easily as over-baked porcelain.

Michael knew he should try to sleep, and he'd been offered a place to rest more than once. But fear kept him by her side, as if losing consciousness would somehow take her away from him forever. The horror of nearly losing her played over and over in his mind until the reality couldn't be denied. Had they been five minutes slower getting to the hospital, Emily could well be dead.

The fear woven into that possibility pushed pain intensely between his eyes until he had no choice but to bury his face in his hands and cry. He wept without restraint until an emotional exhaustion left him quietly holding her hand, watching her face with his head against the bed. When he saw her brow furrow and her eyelids twitch, he raised his head to watch her. A faint smile touched the corners of her lips, and he realized she was dreaming. Before he had a chance to wonder what her dream might be, she spoke in a weak but clear voice, "Don't leave now, Alexa, I want to ask you if . . ."

Michael unconsciously squeezed her hand, then regretted it when her words stopped and an expression of confusion came over her countenance. She opened her eyes and looked at him as if she was disoriented. After a long moment she said matter-of-factly, "It's all right, Michael. Your great-grandmother was here. She's going to take care of the baby until . . ."

Emily saw tears rolling over Michael's cheeks. She paused to wonder why he might be crying when she felt such peace. In an effort to find the answer, she turned to look around her and reality descended.

"Michael," she whimpered, and he thought his heart would break. Her hand went instinctively to her belly and the emptiness became evident. "My baby." She looked to him with a question in her eyes, and he swallowed hard.

"It's all over now," he whispered, pressing a hand to her face.

Emily squeezed her eyes shut and tears trickled into the hair at her temples. Michael stood and leaned over the bed, holding her as close as possible under the circumstances. They held each other and cried until a nurse came in to check on Emily. Michael moved away and she gave him an empathetic smile.

"Seems you're doing much better," the nurse observed while she checked Emily's temperature and looked over the monitor printouts. "Your doctor just called. He'll be in to see you in an hour or so."

"Thank you," Michael said, and they were left alone again. He stuffed his hands in his pockets and watched Emily as she looked over the contraptions attached to her. Just to see her move, her eyes blink, seemed such a miracle that he was in awe. She turned to him with a quizzical expression as the evidence seemed to clash with the procedures of a simple miscarriage.

"What happened to me?" she asked. Michael looked down and shuffled the toe of his boot over the pattern in the floor. While he concentrated on keeping his emotions under control, he sensed Emily's impatience.

"Michael?" Emily couldn't recall ever seeing him so hesitant. When he looked up his chin quivered, and she felt a tangible dread descend upon her. "Tell me," she insisted.

"Your heart stopped, Emily." His voice was raspy and unsteady.

Emily took a sharp breath and stared upward while she tried to comprehend it. Was that why the dream she'd just emerged from had seemed so real? Had she come so close to dying that she had seen a glimpse of heaven, however brief? She certainly didn't think she'd had any great vision like ones she'd heard about occasionally, but perhaps the veil had been thin while she had lain unconscious.

Emily turned her attention to Michael, and compassion filled her. He was visibly upset, and now she understood why. "Were you there?" she asked. He nodded hesitantly. "Are you all right?" she added, reaching a hand toward him. Michael shook his head and quickly took the offered comfort. "What happened?" she repeated.

"You just . . . lost so much blood . . . and your heart stopped." Michael leaned over her and buried his face in the pillow next to hers. "I would die if I lost you," he whispered. "I couldn't bear it, Emily. I just couldn't."

Emily fought the tubes in her arms to reach around him and hold him close. The weakness and pain she felt added evidence to what he'd told her, but it was difficult to know what to say.

Michael pulled back to look at her, unashamed of the tears shed on behalf of a love that consumed him. "Emily," he whispered and kissed her hard on the mouth, as if he could somehow feed his strength into her. "You are my life."

Later, while Emily slept, Michael sat near the bed, holding her hand in his. A knock at the door startled him.

"Come in," he called, and Allison peered inside.

"Hi, sweetie." He stood to accept the hug she offered. Then her attention turned to Emily.

"Is Mom all right?" she asked. "Grandma said you'd called earlier—that something went wrong."

Michael explained briefly, proud of himself for his steady voice. When Allison started to cry, Michael had trouble holding his own tears back.

"I couldn't bear losing her," Allison admitted, gently touching her mother's hair while she slept.

"That makes two of us," Michael agreed.

He left to get something to eat at Allison's insistence, though he could hardly choke it down. Returning with a dozen roses, he found

Allison standing outside the door.

"Is something wrong?" The panic in his voice was evident.

"Oh, no," she assured him quickly. "It's just a little crowded in there."

Michael pushed the door open and heard sounds of laughter. His mother was at Emily's side, with Katherine and her husband, Robert, close by. He caught Emily's eyes, and the love they shared jumped out at him with such strength that he felt chills.

"And how are you?" LeNay asked, putting her arms around Michael with a solid hug.

"I'm all right," he lied.

"I don't believe you," she said firmly.

"It's Emily you should be worried about." Michael set the roses on the bedside table.

"Thank you," Emily said weakly and reached a hand toward him. "They're beautiful."

"Emily's health is on the mend," LeNay stated. "But you're the one who watched it happen."

Michael coughed to avoid sobbing. "I'm all right," he attempted to lie again. "Really."

LeNay dropped it then, and the conversation lightened. Soon after the family left, the doctor came in. He declared Emily to be doing well, and added that she could go home in a few days.

"How long should I wait to get pregnant?" Emily asked before he could get away. She felt Michael's hand go tense so abruptly that it surprised her.

The doctor looked at them severely and said in a grave voice, "I'd say after what you just went through, getting pregnant again is not a good idea."

Michael began to chew his thumbnail while Emily turned paler than she already was. "You're over forty, Mrs. Hamilton. You have a nice family. My advice is to quit while you're ahead."

After an uncomfortable silence, the doctor asked, "Is there anything else?"

"Can you tell us why this baby didn't make it?" Michael asked soberly.

"There was no physical evidence that he was—"

"It was a boy?" Emily interrupted.

"Yes," the doctor replied kindly, "a well-formed little boy. There was no evidence that anything was physically wrong. Perhaps the problem was in the placenta. Such things still remain a mystery. It's difficult to say why it happened." Michael nodded his understanding.

"I'll check back in the morning." The doctor shook Michael's hand and set a fatherly hand on Emily's shoulder. Nothing more was said about the baby through the days Emily remained in the hospital.

When the time came, the drive home was silent. For Emily, leaving the hospital without a baby was heartbreaking. For Michael, taking Emily home was a miracle he didn't want to press any further. Mutually, the loss was acute. Neither of them could think of anything to say that wouldn't bring on more pain or confusion. No words were needed to express the depth of their feeling that this baby had been meant to come into their home.

Over the following days, Emily encountered a discouragement she had not experienced in years. Not since Michael had come into her life had she known such depression. Everyone in the family was supportive and loving. They made certain the children were cared for so that she could get the rest she needed, and someone was always close by to keep her distracted. But no one or nothing could take away the emptiness of losing a baby she knew was supposed to be hers, or the ache of realizing that she might be denied the right to have it. Emily tried to have faith and believe that God would work all of this out, but she felt so confused and distraught that it was hard to feel anything but despair.

Michael was gone so little that she began to wonder what he was neglecting in the other facets of his life. They had not yet discussed what had transpired in the hospital. Emily felt a distinct tension between them, but she didn't know where to begin to alleviate it.

One morning, feeling a need to be near him and get on with her life, Emily wrapped Michael's robe around her and walked downstairs to the office where he worked at his writing. A vague hum told her the computer was on before she pushed open the door, but she found him staring thoughtfully at nothing.

"Seeking inspiration?" she asked.

Michael turned and smiled, but it lacked the vibrancy that Emily knew should have been there.

"I think I just found it." He pulled off his glasses and reached a hand toward her. She stepped forward to take it. "Should you be up?" he asked, easing her onto his lap.

"I'm all right," she insisted, resting her head on his shoulder. Emily had a perfect view of the computer screen, but as she read the words there, she couldn't figure how they fit into the story she knew he was working on.

The intensity with which I love her is something I now see I'm only beginning to perceive. How arrogant is man, to believe he has seen the full spectrum of love, and then God steps in with harsh evidence that we know nothing.

Emily leaned up to be certain she'd read that right. At her interest, Michael reached forward and pushed a key to take it off the screen.

"Where does that fit into the book?" she asked.

He hesitated before admitting, "That's my journal."

It took Emily a minute to connect the words she'd just read to herself. It was evident they needed to talk about this, as much as she dreaded it.

"Michael," she said carefully, "you told me what happened when I lost the baby, but you haven't told me how it made you feel."

Michael looked at her with eyes that seemed to say, *How dare you ask me that?* It only convinced Emily more strongly that they needed to talk.

"Perhaps we've already let this go too long." She stood and motioned toward the library door. Michael eyed it hesitantly, but finally followed her in. She settled herself in the corner of an overstuffed leather couch and urged him to sit beside her.

"So, how did it make you feel?" she asked. He didn't answer. "I was under the impression that it's against the law in this house to keep your feelings bottled up, especially when they're hurting you."

"Who told you that?" he responded.

"You did."

"I knew you were going to say that."

"Talk, Michael."

"It was hell." He hesitated, but she waited patiently. "Standing in that room was how I imagine hell must feel—to helplessly observe something that just shreds your heart and soul to pieces."

Emily leaned forward to look at his face. "It was really that bad?"

Michael didn't want to have this conversation, but he knew it had to be done. "Yes, it was." He put his hands behind his head and leaned back against the couch.

"Is that what's been eating at you?"

"You nearly died in there, Emily." He sounded angry.

"But I'm all right now."

Michael sighed. "I know, and you can't imagine how grateful I am." He put his arm around her and kissed her brow.

After a lengthy silence, Emily drew a breath of courage and asked, "Have you thought about the baby?"

Emily felt a tension fill him so abruptly it almost startled her. She leaned back to look at his face. "You were the one who said we were supposed to have that baby, Michael. You haven't told me how you feel about losing it."

"What is there to say?" He swallowed hard. "It's been difficult to accept, but it just has to be. I'm certain it's been harder for you than for me."

Emily wanted to tell him she had found comfort in believing she would still be able to have another child, but she had a difficult time voicing the words. She expected him to be apprehensive, but she never would have believed how much.

"What do you think about what the doctor said?" She attempted to approach through a back door.

"It was pretty hard to take." The subtle terseness in his voice let her know he was only giving surface answers. "I suppose it just isn't meant to be, after all."

Emily was so stunned she gasped. "What are you saying?"

"I'm saying that we have to accept the fact that we will not be having another baby."

"Michael!" she cried, then couldn't find any more words. The one tiny glimmer of hope that had kept her going these days was the thought of having another baby. And there he sat, shattering that hope like a hammer to glass.

"What?" he asked when she only gaped at him.

"We are *supposed* to have another baby."

Michael's voice turned husky. "That pregnancy nearly killed you."

"But it didn't," she insisted, "and it won't."

"That's right, it won't, because you're not going to get pregnant again."

Emily moved away and stood abruptly. "I can't believe I'm hearing this. I can understand this being difficult for you, but we know we're supposed to have another baby. Surely this is just a test of faith."

"Then surely I will fail it," he snapped. "Call me selfish. Call me faithless. But don't think for a moment that I'm fool enough to put your life on the line again. What happened to me in that hospital room is something I will never forget, Emily." His voice was heated, his eyes hard. "I will not risk losing you, and that's final."

Michael rose and left the room so abruptly that Emily was stunned. She wanted to cry, but the numbness was so thick that even tears wouldn't come. How could he deny what he'd once felt so strongly? Emily had heard many stories of women who'd struggled with similar challenges, but managed to have babies and survive. Surely she was worthy of that blessing as well. But it took two consenting adults to make this decision, and one of them wasn't consenting.

A short while later Katherine came to Emily's room, obviously anxious about something. She got right to the point. "What's wrong with Michael?"

"He's just upset about . . ." Emily swallowed hard, "losing the baby." She noted the concern in Katherine's eyes. "Why?"

"I haven't seen him drive out of here like that since you told him you weren't leaving Ryan to marry him."

"Drive like *what?*" Emily couldn't help the sharp tone. She believed she knew her husband well, but this was something she'd never encountered before.

"Oh," Katherine leaned back and folded her arms with an air of disgust, "it's something he started doing when he came home from college the month you married Ryan. He'd get in that Cruiser and take off across the flats, just as fast as he could go. It was common for many years, but I haven't seen him do it since he married you."

"Until now," Emily said thoughtfully, trying to piece this habit of recklessness together with the husband she thought she knew. She couldn't help being concerned, but at the moment she didn't have the fortitude to discuss it with Katherine.

At supper, Michael acted as if nothing had been said. He was considerate and sensitive, but nothing more was mentioned about the baby. His blatantly ignoring the subject made Emily all the more concerned. He was not a man to brush issues aside.

"Are you all right?" she asked later as he sat on the edge of the bed to pull off his boots.

"I'm fine, why?"

There was no tangible reason to believe otherwise, but Emily could feel it. "Katherine said you were out driving . . . rather fast . . . earlier. She told me it's something you used to do when you were upset or angry."

Michael felt somehow cornered, but he reminded himself this was Emily. "It helps me release the . . . tension," he admitted without apology.

"Did it work?" she asked, hoping to get him to open up more about all of this.

"It didn't hurt," was all he said.

"Isn't there something a little . . . safer that could bring about the desired effect?"

"Emily," he stood and took her shoulders, "there is no one or nothing out there to hurt, or get hurt upon."

"Then it's a good thing you live here. You couldn't get away with that in Utah."

"I don't live in Utah."

"What did you do to release the tension in college?"

"I didn't have any." He smiled almost roguishly, and Emily tried to follow his example of letting the tension go—at least for the moment.

Days passed, but she found no peace in trying to make sense of everything. Finally, she approached Michael with a firm question. "Would you give me a blessing?"

His brow furrowed. "Are you ill?"

"Physically, I feel better than I expected. But I'm confused and concerned, and I need to get on with my life."

Michael sighed and looked away. "I'm not certain I'm in the proper frame of mind to give you a blessing."

"You are my husband and my branch president. Perhaps you'd better *get* in the proper frame of mind."

Emily walked away, leaving Michael to wonder what was happening to him. That moment he'd nearly lost her had made something snap in him, and he didn't know how to fix it. He was managing to go through the motions of his calling in the Church, and he was spending the time at home that he knew he should. But his writing was senseless, and somehow his heart wasn't where it should be. At the least-expected moment, the memory of Emily's heart stopping would break into his mind, and the fear of losing her would consume him so fully that he would feel almost physically weak.

He knew it wouldn't be fair to deny Emily the right to a proper blessing as she'd requested. He began to fast, and he prayed fervently that the Spirit would accompany him. The following evening he sought out Robert in the office of the Boys' Home adjoining the house.

"Would you be willing to help me give Emily a blessing?" he asked quietly.

"Is something wrong?" Robert asked with concern.

"She feels she needs some guidance and comfort."

"I'd be happy to. I'm about finished here."

Emily looked up from her painting to see Michael and Robert enter the room. Her heart skipped a beat at the sight of Michael, then it dropped a little at the thought of what lay between them. She felt some hope when he asked in a quiet voice, "Do you still want a blessing?"

Emily nodded firmly, understanding now why he'd brought Robert along. Katherine's husband had joined the Church over five years ago, soon after their daughter Stacy had requested baptism. Though Katherine had supported Robert's choice and their marriage was good, she wanted nothing to do with religion. And their son, Wade, was somewhere in Europe, living what they believed to be a rather colorful life.

Michael took the brush from Emily's hand and set it aside. He urged her to a chair where he and Robert put their hands on her head. Emily felt the Spirit immediately in the warm tears that pressed out, and she was grateful for Michael's willingness to be a spokesman for their Father in Heaven.

In the blessing, she was told that the child she was meant to have would come into her home, though it might take time, and it might not be by expected means. An assurance was given that in spite of the weaknesses of those around her, she would be blessed to know of God's will for her. She was admonished to turn to her patriarchal blessing for guidance, and she was promised that she would live to see her children into adulthood. When the blessing was finished, Robert graciously left them alone.

"Thank you," Emily said to Michael. He gave her a weak smile. "I don't know if that makes you feel any better, but it does me."

"I'm glad to know you'll be around for many years to come, if that's what you mean."

"And it said we would have the chance to have another baby," she added carefully.

Michael was quiet for a moment. "It said that another child would come into our home, but not necessarily in the way we might expect. That could be anything; adoption perhaps. Or maybe that baby was developed enough to be raised in the next life from the point that we lost it. We can't possibly attempt to understand all of this from an earthly perspective, Emily."

Emily swallowed hard. She was trying to keep an open mind, but what Michael said just didn't feel right to her. The dream she'd had during her unconsciousness came back with a degree of comfort. She'd wanted to talk to Michael about it, but the time had never seemed right. Perhaps now it was.

"Michael, I never told you about the dream I had . . . at the hospital."

"About Alexa, you mean?"

"How did you know?"

"You told me you'd seen her, right after you woke up."

Emily wrung her hands. "I'd forgotten. Did I tell you what she said?"

"No," he admitted hesitantly, not certain he wanted to hear it.

"She was holding a baby, a boy, wrapped in a white blanket. She told me she'd take care of him until I was able to. I saw the baby, Michael. He looked like you, but he didn't look exactly like Jess or James. There was no more to it than that. I can only tell you I *know* that baby is supposed to be ours. It may not come right away, but I know it will come."

Michael only stuffed his hands in his pockets and looked at the floor. "Don't you have anything to say?" she asked after an awkward silence.

He looked up at her severely. "It would likely be better if I didn't say anything at all."

"You don't believe me, do you," she stated, wishing her voice hadn't broken. He said nothing. "After the experiences we've had concerning your great-grandmother, you don't believe such a dream would have meaning?"

"Right now, I don't know what to believe."

For a moment anger flew through Emily's mind. This was not like him. It was not characteristic of their relationship to be so distant, so divided. She was nearly ready to question his ability to have been in tune with the Spirit enough to give her that blessing. But the promises in the blessing contradicted his present frame of mind so directly, that it only added to the evidence that God had been speaking through Michael. Emily quickly subdued the anger and tried to feel compassion.

"Michael, I know this is difficult for you. If you want to talk about it, we should talk. Tell me how you feel, and let's deal with this."

"There is nothing more to say that hasn't already been said."

Emily shook her head. "I just can't believe this of you, Michael."

"Actually, I have a hard time believing it myself," he admitted.

"But that's how I feel. It may not be right, but I can't help how I feel. I love you, Emily. I do. I know this must be difficult for you, but I am not willing to risk losing you. I couldn't bear it."

Emily told herself she should be grateful to be loved so deeply. But she felt lost, knowing there was another child yet to come. How could she convince him that everything would be all right?

"Michael, you just told me in that blessing that I would live to see all of my children into adulthood. Isn't that promise enough to know that I would be all right?"

"As long as you don't get pregnant, then we have nothing to worry about."

With the finality in his voice, she expected him to leave the room. Instead he put his arms around her, and she held to him desperately. She loved him so much that she could well understand his fears. If she lost him, she felt certain she couldn't bear it. Their disagreements had been so rare that she didn't know how to handle it. She had told him it was an issue of faith, and now perhaps she needed to remind herself of the same. She needed to have faith that he would come around, that everything would work out.

Later, when Michael was sitting in bed reading, Emily sat beside him and took his hand. "I've been thinking," she said, and he set the book aside. "I was told to turn to my patriarchal blessing for guidance. I know all of this is difficult for you as well, and . . ." She hesitated momentarily when he became visibly tense. "You never had a patriarchal blessing, Michael. Maybe now would be a good time. Perhaps it would help you get through this." The hope Emily had felt in the idea dwindled quickly when she saw his immediate lack of interest in her suggestion.

"I really don't think that's necessary, Emily," he replied. Though it was something he'd occasionally wondered about, at the moment he almost felt afraid of what it might say. A part of him almost believed it would only verify the formless fears smoldering inside him. "I appreciate your concern, but . . ."

When he said nothing more, Emily tried to think of something she could say to help him understand that she believed this was important. Several minutes passed in silence, and she realized there was nothing that would make any difference.

Michael's mood lightened through the following days as the issue was apparently forgotten. Emily kept busy catching up the time she'd spent recovering from her ordeal. Four days after she'd been told to read her patriarchal blessing, she finally found a quiet moment to do it.

A warmth settled into Emily as she read the words: *As you make the sacrifices to pursue your education, great blessings will come to your family.*

For several days she let that thought mull around in her mind, trying to fit it in with the present circumstances. A peace began to fill her at the thought of pursuing her education. It didn't solve the problem concerning the baby, but it gave her something to think about.

Chapter Three

"Michael," Emily said casually at the dinner table after everyone else had eaten and gone their separate ways, "where is the nearest college?"

"Are you speaking for yourself or Allison?" he asked.

"Both, I suppose."

Michael chuckled. "Well, there's no college close enough for you to drop in occasionally for a class or two."

She explained her feelings about pursuing her education, and Michael felt a glimmer of light. If she concentrated on that, perhaps she'd forget about this baby business.

"That would be fine," he said, "but I'm not certain how to work it out. Perhaps we could look into home study or—"

"Perhaps, but . . ." She hesitated admitting her true feelings because they sounded so illogical.

"But?" he questioned when she didn't go on.

"Well, you know since Allison had that accident, she's just not been the same, and . . ."

Emily hesitated when she saw the concern deepen in Michael's eyes. She knew the situation troubled Michael almost as much as it did Allison. The accident itself had been so bizarre—that a rider as skilled and agile as Allison would be hurt so badly while riding. It was something Michael hadn't dealt with well. The weeks Allison spent in the hospital were trying; and then, when she was told that her back could never withstand riding professionally, her dream of being a jockey had been shattered.

Emily cleared her throat and hurried on. "I think it would be good for her to get off to college, but we haven't felt good about sending her alone, and—"

"What are you getting at?" Michael probed impatiently.

"Well, you know how she has been nagging to go to Utah, and—"

"Utah?" Michael interrupted.

Emily just forced it out. "I have this feeling that I should go to BYU and get a degree."

Michael laughed until Emily's expression told him she was serious. "Honestly, Emily. The only way we could possibly do it is to make a major move."

"I know."

"I'm the branch president."

"I know."

"And the children are so young."

"Yes, they are."

"It's just not practical."

"I know, Michael. I'm simply telling you how I feel."

Michael took a minute to absorb her words. He still felt guilty for discrediting her feelings concerning the baby; he'd always trusted them before. And now, despite the apparent ridiculousness of it, he knew he had to at least consider her idea.

"Let's think about it," he said gently, and she smiled. "Perhaps things will work out, if that's what is meant to be."

"Thank you, Michael," she said. Then she began talking about the classes she would like to take, concentrating mostly on art. Michael had to admit it would be wonderful to see her pursue the education that had been interrupted years ago. He had always felt that she would do so one day, but James was not even two yet. And with his position in the Church, it just didn't seem feasible. He could write anywhere, but working with the horses took much of his time. He couldn't just turn his back on all of it now to move halfway around the world. Could he? Perhaps if Emily really thought about it, she'd come to the same conclusions.

But the passing days only made Emily more determined. Twice she showed him the pertinent phrase in her patriarchal blessing and told him how deeply she felt she was supposed to go to

Utah. Michael did his best to reflect her feelings but keep the objective clear. He began to feel like he was either going to have to let her have a baby, or let her go to Utah. But one was almost as difficult to work out as the other was to face. He thought of sending her to Utah without him, but immediately knew that was impossible. He just couldn't do it. They needed each other too much. Finally, not knowing how to handle the situation, he simply tried not to think about it, hoping it might go away.

* * * * *

"Michael," Emily whispered his name softly through the darkness. He grunted in response. "It's been more than a month since—"

"I know," he interrupted before she could say it.

Emily found his hand between the sheets. "You've hardly touched me, Michael." She heard a vague desperation in her voice that reminded her of another time, another husband. She didn't like it. "The doctor said it would be all right. Is there a reason why you . . ." Her sentence slipped into a kiss, but she got little response.

Michael tried to think of the words to tell her his deepest feelings without hurting her. Seeing her come so close to death made her seem so fragile, as if he kissed her too hard, or held her too close, she might break. And then there was the possibility of her getting pregnant. The thought frightened him so badly that he nearly shook. Logically he knew his fears were beyond reason, but that didn't make them go away. He just didn't know how to deal with this.

"Michael, I need you to talk to me," she insisted, turning on the bedside lamp. He squinted up at her, trying to adjust to the light. "Don't shut me out like this and expect me to accept it."

"I'm sorry," he said with sincerity, "I'm just . . . afraid."

"That I'll get pregnant?" she asked cynically.

"That's part of it."

"There are means of protection, Michael. We have used them before for the sake of my well-being."

"I know that, Emily." He sounded insulted. "But there is no guarantee that . . ."

He hesitated and a horrid thought came to Emily. "There is

only one method of birth control that's guaranteed," she said tersely. "Are you possibly hinting that you would consider doing something permanent?"

Michael was surprised at her brashness, but he had to admit she'd hit the nail on the head. "It's crossed my mind."

"You wouldn't," she said with barely concealed anger.

"Not without your approval, no."

"Well, you don't have my approval. We are not finished having children yet, Michael Hamilton. And until we can come to a point where we agree, I trust no drastic measures will be taken."

"Of course not," he insisted. "I admit I'm having trouble with this, but—"

"Yes, that's obvious," she interrupted, not liking the anger she felt. "Enough trouble that you can't even bring yourself to touch me." Emily threw back the covers and got out of bed. "I can't help you deal with this if you won't talk to me, Michael."

"Where are you going?" His voice was edged with panic.

"I'll sleep in the guest room. If I'm going to feel rejected, I might as well be alone to—"

"Rejected?"

"Yes, Michael." She stopped with her hand on the doorknob. "You're not only rejecting my feelings on this, but now you're rejecting me. You can't say I haven't made it perfectly clear that I am in need of some intimacy here. You're letting your fears come between us, Michael. My suggestion is that you'd better deal with them, or you may not like where we end up."

Michael wanted to ask what she meant by that, but she was gone. Part of him knew he should go after her, but he didn't know what to say to her if he did. He started to wonder if Ryan ever felt this way. Did Emily's first husband know he wasn't treating her well, but feel helpless to do anything about it?

At the first hint of dawn, Michael got into the Cruiser and tossed his hat onto the other seat. What little sleep he'd managed to get had been edged with bizarre dreams. They had all muddled together into nonsense, but finally had come to the same conclusion. Emily had died and he was left with nothing.

Michael drove with purpose around the house, through the

thick clusters of trees lining the drive, and beyond the station to the endless stretch of flat land that led to nowhere. He thought about the first time he'd done this. However unintentional, his driving mindlessly had somehow released a part of the rage he'd felt in losing Emily to another man. In the years he'd spent without her, trying to forget her, he had often resorted to the almost numbing sensation of tearing through mile after mile. Some men would drink, others might get stoned, and some might even try to lose themselves with sordid women. But Michael had found only one way to deal with pain and rage and still remain a man of integrity. Even before he'd entered into covenants of righteousness in becoming a Mormon, he had been raised to see the stupidity in substance abuse and immorality. And now, more than ever, he found driving at high speeds over the miles of Australian nothing to be an acceptable outlet. There was no speed limit, no restriction, only a formless thrill to look in the rearview mirror and see the cloud of his homeland trailing behind him.

Michael returned to the house before breakfast, feeling more at ease. He grabbed something quick to eat and went out to work up a sweat before Emily would even be awake. He didn't like this feeling of avoiding the problem, if not her. But at the moment, he could see no alternative that wouldn't bring the tension back all over again.

* * * * *

Emily tried to push away her hurt and anger by delving into old family journals. She spent the entire morning in the library, reading bits and pieces of the lives of Michael's grandmother and great-grandmother. She giggled as she read a particular incident that started some romantic urges stirring. Some people might have found Emma Byrnehouse-Davies a shocking woman in certain respects, but Emily found the love this woman felt for her husband worthy of acknowledging. When Emily realized that the places Emma had described were still nearly the same as they'd been decades ago, she impulsively decided to try it herself.

Looking through her closet, she found a full red skirt and white petticoat set that came mid-calf. She had always liked the old-fashioned feel of it and often wore it to church, or even around the house. It was perfect for her intentions right now. She put them on with a simple white blouse, brushed her hair down around her shoulders, and went out to the stable with bare feet.

Murphy told her that Michael was repairing a fence on the west corral. Emily bridled a horse and mounted bareback. She trotted the animal toward where he was working, feeling a quiver in her stomach at the sight of him in the distance. His well-worn jeans hung loosely over his lean hips and long legs as he bent over to pick something up off the ground. A light-weight, faded denim shirt had darkened with sweat across his back. As Emily approached, he looked up and took off his hat. He wiped sweat from his brow and shaded his eyes from the sun. As if he feared he wasn't seeing clearly, he untangled himself from the fence and stood up straight. She felt his eyes absorb every detail, from her unruly hair to her bare lower legs, showing beneath a flurry of skirt and petticoat.

"Hello, Michael," she said coyly.

"Hello," he replied, unable to disguise the intrigue in his voice.

"Busy?" she asked.

"Nothing that can't wait. Did you need something?"

Emily was tempted to tell him that she needed him, that she needed to know he loved her, that he cared. But she remembered that journal entry and just held out her hand. Michael set the hammer down and stepped toward her to take it. Without a word he swung onto the horse's back behind her and took the reins into his right hand, pushing his left around her waist.

"Where are we going?" he asked.

"Didn't you once take me to a grassy spot in the hills, where there's a stream running near a cluster of trees? I believe your grandmother spoke of it in her journals."

Michael said nothing. He just guided the horse to the right location, as if he'd been there thousands of times. She suspected he had. When he stopped the horse, Emily's heart began to pound. She thought of herself as a conventional woman and wondered momentarily what she was doing here.

"Now what?" he asked, sliding down from the horse. He tethered it to a tree and looked up at her. "Did you want to talk?"

"Perhaps." She smiled and Michael saw her blush. All of this seemed just unusual enough that he felt suspicious, though he couldn't believe she would try to do anything deceptive. It wasn't in her nature.

"Well, you must have a reason for coming here," he observed, hoping to get to a point.

"I do," she replied.

"And what might that be?" he prodded, not certain why he felt a rush of excitement.

"I'm protected," she said softly.

Michael's eyes widened as he grasped the implication. "You mean . . ." he looked around, "*here?*"

Emily smiled. "Your grandparents did." She allowed him a moment to absorb that information, then held out her hand. Michael took it and squeezed. She saw his eyes narrow slightly with skepticism.

"You wouldn't deceive me, would you?" he asked, then immediately regretted it when her eyes showed hurt and disbelief. As long as it was out, he had to reassure himself. "You wouldn't try to get pregnant by . . ." His words faltered with the genuine surprise in her expression.

"Do you trust me so little?"

"I just had to ask."

"I would never do anything to intentionally get pregnant if you didn't approve. That is a decision we must make mutually."

"That's all I needed to hear," he said. A part of him wanted to hesitate for a number of reasons. But his desire for her, coupled with his need to set things right between them, urged him to take her by the waist and help her down. She seemed so tiny as her bare feet touched the ground near his boots. She looked so frail and delicate as she gazed up at him, complete trust and acceptance glowing in her eyes.

"I love you, Michael." She went on her tiptoes to kiss him. "We've made it through so much together. Surely we can make it through this."

"Emily," he murmured, burying his face in the hair billowing around her throat. "I love you so much." He kissed her cheeks, her eyelids, her brow. He found her lips with his and kissed her over and over, wondering why he'd deprived himself of this when it rejuvenated him already. Her love renewed his faith in life and gave him the ability to look at the future with a bright heart.

* * * * *

An hour after Michael had flown out to take care of branch business, Emily answered the phone to hear his voice.

"Hello, beautiful."

"Hello." She blushed at the subtle intimacy in his tone.

"How are you?"

"I'm wonderful. How are you?"

"The same," he replied in a way that made her realize he wasn't alone. "I have a favor to ask."

"I'm listening."

"Is it all right if I bring home guests for dinner . . . and breakfast as well?"

"Who are these guests?"

"Actually, we have some missionaries who are between places to live. They need somewhere to stay tonight. Do you care if I bring them home?"

"I'd be delighted," she said with sincerity. "I'll tell Millie to fix extra, and we'll air out a guest room."

"I knew you'd be a sweetheart about it," his voice smiled. "You always are. We'll be home before supper."

Since Emily had driven Michael to the hangar, she went out to the Cruiser the minute she heard the plane circling and drove into the hangar just as Michael was helping unload suitcases. She smiled at the two young men wearing white shirts and dark ties, then turned to accept Michael's embrace.

"Elders," he said proudly, "meet my wife, Emily Hamilton."

"It's a pleasure." She looked at their name tags as she shook hands. "Elder Mitchell, and Elder Atwood."

"You're American," Elder Mitchell said eagerly.

"The most beautiful American in Australia," Michael added.

"Where are you from, Sister Hamilton?" Elder Atwood asked as Michael turned the Cruiser onto the road.

"Central Idaho originally," she replied. "And then I lived in Utah for many years. How about you?" she asked.

"Elder Mitchell is from Michigan," he replied. "I'm from Arizona."

"How did you end up marrying an American, President?" Elder Mitchell asked.

Michael chuckled. "That's a long story, but I suppose it started with a couple of guys like you. I went to BYU at the suggestion of some missionaries I ran into in Melbourne. I met Emily there."

"That wasn't a very long story," Elder Atwood laughed.

"I left out a few details."

"If you want a long story, read one of his books," Emily said.

"I already have," Elder Atwood replied. "All of them, actually. I couldn't believe it was actually him when we met."

"So, when did you graduate from the Y?" Elder Mitchell asked.

"I'm not going to admit to that," Michael laughed.

"Did you go to the Y?" Emily asked the missionary, her face beaming.

"Just left there four months ago," he replied.

Michael listened patiently and tried to contribute to the ongoing conversation about BYU. Emily's interest was so keen that he began wishing he could take her there. All through dinner he thought about it so hard his head began to hurt. Then, somewhere in the middle of dessert, a voice seemed to say in his head: *Then just go.* Michael ignored it the first time, but when it persisted, his thoughts turned inward. *I can't go. I'm the branch president. Our children would be uprooted. I have a business to take care of.* Again it came. *Just go.*

Michael looked down the table at Emily. The conversation around him slipped further into the distance as he had a clear memory of her bouncing down the bleachers in the BYU stadium.

When the elders had gone to their room for the night, Michael took Jess and James upstairs and helped them get ready for bed. He was reading them a story when Emily peeked in and smiled. As soon as the boys were tucked in, they went across the hall to their own bedroom. While Emily brushed her hair, she began talking again about the education she wanted.

"Michael, do you think I could actually get a degree in art?"

"I think you could get a degree in anything you want."

"Do you think we could afford the tuition?" she teased.

"I could probably scrape it up."

"Michael," she turned in her chair to look at him, "I know it's impossible right now, but can we be thinking about it, and maybe when you're released as branch president, we could possibly—"

"Why don't you start packing?" he asked soberly.

"I know it could be a while, but . . . what did you say?"

"I said you should start packing."

"But . . ."

Michael laughed and shook his head. "I don't know how or why, but I have this incredible feeling that we're actually supposed to go to Utah."

"Oh, Michael." She jumped from her chair and landed on his lap. "Do you really?"

"I really do. It's the most preposterous thing I've ever heard of. It makes absolutely no sense at all, but I think we're supposed to go."

Emily was so happy she didn't know how to act. They sat up late speculating on how to handle the situation, and decided that the only thing holding them back was his church position. With a decision to pray and fast, they decided if it felt right he would ask to be released.

The following day, Michael returned the missionaries to town and came back looking as if he'd seen a ghost.

"What in the world is wrong?" Emily questioned as he sat nearby and stared at the wall. When he didn't answer, she persisted. "Michael, are you all right? Don't tell me someone else died!"

He turned to look at her slowly. "They're going to call a new branch president. I'm going to be released."

Emily gaped in disbelief. It was increasingly evident the Lord wanted them to go to Utah.

At the next family home evening, Michael gathered the children around and announced the news without preamble. "We are moving to Utah."

Allison cheered. Amee grumbled. Alexa decided to act happy about it, apparently so she wouldn't be agreeing with Amee. Jess asked if there would be horses to ride every day. When Michael told him it wasn't likely, he started to cry. James was indifferent. LeNay cried, too.

"That went well," Michael said with sarcasm after the children went up to bed.

"Oh, they're all spoiled," Emily insisted. "It will be good for them to have some changes."

"I think you might be right, Mrs. Hamilton," Michael beamed and they laughed together.

"Should I write and tell Penny?" Emily's eyes lit up at the thought of being with her best friend again.

"Nah," Michael chuckled, "we'll just surprise her." He put on his glasses and looked at the calendar. "If it's all right with you, I think I'll take Allison with me to look for a house while you stay here and get everything under control."

"Thank you, no," she insisted. "I am not flying around the world with those four little maniacs on my own."

Michael chuckled. "I'll come back to get you, I promise. Allison can stay in Utah and get everything ready."

"I think I could live with that," Emily declared. Then she let out a whoop of excitement toward the ceiling.

Michael leaned back and grinned. With any luck, she'd forget all about that baby.

CHAPTER FOUR

Allison chattered almost constantly on the flight from Los Angeles to Salt Lake City. Approaching her eighteenth birthday, she speculated aloud on the changes they might find since she'd left Utah just before her tenth. While Michael listened and made an occasional comment, his own memories filtered in. Some were sweet and warm, others he would rather forget.

With a rented car and a motel room in Provo, they got a good real estate agent and started looking at homes. Days wore on with a tiring search that began to seem futile. Everything was too big, or too small, or too run down, or too gaudy. Michael was adamant that the home they would live in for the next few years must be just right. He wanted enough space to live comfortably, but he also wanted the kind of coziness he'd felt in Emily's home before he'd married her. He was grateful for his inherited wealth that made this entire venture possible. But his intention was to meet his family's needs; nothing more.

"How many times are you going to look at those lists?" Allison asked skeptically as she kicked off her shoes and lay back on one of the two beds in the room.

"Until I find something," he replied. "There's a perfect house out there. We just have to find it."

"Well, I hope you find it soon, because my feet are dying."

"Go soak them," he urged. "Then why don't you order a pizza or something. I think there's a good movie on tonight."

While Allison was in the shower, Michael came across an address that seemed to jump out at him in neon. He told himself he'd go look at it tomorrow. But feeling suddenly impatient, he decided there was enough daylight left to do it now.

When the shower quit running, Michael knocked at the bathroom door and hollered, "I"m going to look at one more house. I'll be back in a while."

"Bye," she hollered back.

Michael drove to the address in Orem, and a wave of nostalgia flooded over him. It was less than a block from the home Emily had lived in before he'd married her. They had loved the people in this ward, and Emily's dearest friend, Penny, lived right around the corner. He laughed out loud and went back to the motel. The next morning he didn't even let Allison have breakfast before he drove her to Orem.

"I think you'll like the location," he insisted, but she looked skeptical.

When he turned down the street she had lived on as a child, he saw the nostalgia come into her eyes.

"Wait," she insisted as they approached her old home. Michael pulled over and watched her emotion. "It looks different. I remembered it being bigger."

"You were smaller." He took her hand and squeezed it.

Allison chuckled. "Do you remember when we raked the leaves that had fallen from that tree?"

Michael noted the crisp, autumn leaves covering the lawn. The maple tree was bigger now, but the memories were clear.

"I'll never forget it," he said with tenderness. "That was the first time we really laughed together."

"I can't imagine life without you," she said.

Michael swallowed hard. It was rare that he even acknowledged to himself that Allison and her sisters were not his daughters, and he was relieved when she changed the subject.

"Is the house you found close by?"

"Right around the corner," he reported and drove her to it. The agent was waiting to show them through, and Michael was pleased to see that Allison liked it as much as he had. She went through each room, deciding who would sleep where and making a verbal list of all they would need to make it home.

"Mom's just gonna have a fit," Allison laughed as they drove away, passing Penny's house.

"Yeah," he chuckled, "I think she will." His thoughts turned to Emily. He missed her dreadfully.

Once the house was purchased, Michael and Allison worked together, cleaning it thoroughly and acquiring the necessities to make it livable. Early one evening they sat together on the kitchen floor to share a pizza, while Michael tried to avoid thinking how badly he wanted to see Emily. He'd never been away from her for more than a day or two since they'd married.

"I'm really getting sick of pizza." Allison interrupted his thoughts. "Once we get settled, are you going to start cooking more?"

"I was kind of hoping to," he admitted. "Millie doesn't let me into the kitchen as much as I'd like."

"You haven't had time to be in the kitchen lately."

He nodded. "True. But with your mother going to school, I might just *have* to cook." Michael looked around, thinking how lonely his surroundings felt. "Do you think it'll feel like home?"

"Once Jess and James take over it will."

Michael chuckled, trying to imagine his boys stomping through the house. Allison became quiet and he nudged her with a gentle elbow. "What's on your mind, sweetie?"

She answered hesitantly. "It just occurred to me that my father is buried here in Orem, isn't he?"

Michael cleared his throat unintentionally and glanced away. "Yes, he is."

He was hoping the subject would end there, but she added almost timidly, "Would you take me there?"

Michael turned to meet her eyes, and what could he say? "If you want to go, I'll take you."

At Allison's request, they stopped to buy flowers. Michael drove to where he believed they'd stopped on their last visit to the cemetery. It had been only a few months after Ryan's death, just before he had taken Emily and the girls to Australia.

"I don't know if I can find it," Allison said with concern. But after a moment's contemplation, she walked directly to her father's gravestone.

Michael stood quietly with his hands in his pockets while Allison arranged the flowers and moved her fingers tentatively over her father's name, carved in granite. She stood beside Michael and leaned her head on his shoulder. He put his arm around her and felt he had to ask, "Do you miss him, Allie?"

"Most of my memories are vague. It seems like a completely different world when I think about it."

She looked up at him and her expression changed. He could almost feel her seeing into his soul. "Is this hard for you?" she asked. Michael glanced down and tried to think of a suitable answer. "I'm sorry," she added before he came up with one. "I didn't intend to—"

"It's okay," he interrupted, wondering if his distress was so obvious. "I must admit that your mother being married to another man for ten years is a bit of a sore point for me." He chuckled tensely when she seemed distressed. "I suppose I've come to think of you and your sisters as my own daughters. It's difficult to comprehend it any other way."

"That's true," she agreed, which made him feel a little better.

They walked quietly back to the car, and nothing more was said about Ryan Hall.

Michael called Emily as he did every evening. They shared the usual conversation of catching up on the day's events, ending with sincere expressions of missing each other. But for some reason the loneliness was more acute than usual as he hung up the phone.

The harder Michael tried to relax and fall asleep, the more his mind trailed into dark thoughts he'd rather avoid. His memory of Emily's heart stopping merged somehow into the day she'd come to tell him she was marrying Ryan Hall. His feelings related to both events were too much alike. He felt certain the only reason he wasn't dealing with the same emptiness now as he had back then, was a miracle too incredible to question. God had spared her life, and Michael was grateful. But his fear of having to live without her again had not subsided in the time since.

Long after midnight, Michael began to wonder if his fear was centered in the prospect of living the remainder of this life without her—or if it was more the reality that she was sealed to another man in the life to come. Of course, Michael knew that following his own death, his family members could have him sealed to Emily, and the simple problem of a necessary ordinance would be solved. He also knew from doing the temple work for his great-grandparents that in the case of a woman having two husbands, she should be sealed to both, so that a choice could be made on the other side. But whose choice was it? If the choice were Emily's, would she choose him over Ryan? A part of him believed she would. But he knew she loved Ryan, because he'd seen first-hand the extent of her grief following his death. Then, too, three of her five children belonged to Ryan. And if the choice were up to God—what did God know and see that Michael could never understand? The resulting turmoil seemed unbearable. The bottom line was simple: The woman he loved was sealed to another man. And her children—all of her children—were sealed under that covenant. Michael was sealed to his ancestors, but that was all. Concerning his marriage and children, he felt alone in the eternal perspective. And nearly losing Emily had brought it home to him all too harshly.

Here in the dark, without Emily beside him, it was easy to allow the memories and the fears to consume him. Michael tossed and turned, contemplating Emily's desire to have another baby, and the threat it posed to her life. He wondered if he could possibly bear living even a year without her. And if he couldn't make it without her now, how could he possibly make it through forever?

Somewhere between two and three in the morning, Michael convinced himself that he had no logical reason to believe that he and Emily wouldn't be together forever. Ryan had not treated Emily well through much of their marriage. And for all of Michael's faults, he instinctively believed that he and Emily were destined to be together. He'd believed it from the moment he first saw her.

But by four in the morning, Michael had to admit that his mind and his heart were not in agreement. What felt right on a logical level simply didn't register with the emotions that seemed to split him apart if he even thought of living without her. Since the first time he'd taken her out in college, she had become the central focus of his life. Just being without her now seemed unbearable. All he wanted was to go back to Australia and feel her in his arms.

Somewhere around five o'clock, Michael resolved to get things under control so he could be with Emily again. Surely everything else would work itself out, if he could only be with her.

* * * * *

The following day, Michael took care of some business while Allison put the finishing touches on the house. When he returned, he was greeted by a wave of cozy warmth. He walked from room to room, appreciating the good taste Allison had learned from her mother. He found her in the master bedroom, putting sheets on the bed he would share with Emily.

"Everything looks great, Allie," he said. "I'm impressed." Allison smiled in appreciation of his compliment.

"Want to see my car?" He gave a conspiratorial grin.

"I thought you were going to get a van for Mom."

"I did. It seats eight. We can pick it up in the morning. But I bought myself a car."

A vague look of envy came into Allison's eyes; it was exactly what Michael had hoped for.

"Come on," he urged, "let's go get something to eat. I might even let you drive it."

Allison squealed when she walked out the door to see a red Geo Storm parked in the driveway.

"I didn't think you were into sporty cars, Dad."

"I'm not usually, but this one was a good price and it gets good mileage. It's not as sporty as it looks, actually."

"Can I drive it?" she pleaded.

Michael feigned reluctance as he handed over the keys. He finally coerced her into taking them to get some tacos, but she insisted they drive through and eat in the car.

The next morning they returned the rented car and picked up the Astro van, which Allison declared to be awesome. When they sat down at the new dining table to eat their first home-cooked meal since they'd arrived in Utah, Michael passed a key ring over to Allison. She picked it up apprehensively, then realized that the little replica of a Utah license plate said "Allison" on it.

"What is this?" she asked with a skeptical look.

"Those are *your* keys to *my* car," he said. "Feel free to use it as much as you need. You buy the gas."

"Oh, Dad!" she squealed and ran around the table to hug him.

Michael laughed and took her hand as she pulled back. "The condition is that you obey the rules, young lady. You've proven many times over that you are responsible and mature, but we're living in a whole different world here, and it could be tough. You do what you're supposed to and help your mom as much as you can, and I'll not begrudge letting you use it all you need. Just remember that it's *my* car."

"I will," she promised. "Oh, thank you."

"You're welcome," he said, then in mock disgust, "I guess we'll have to go buy something else for me to drive. I doubt I'll see much of that one."

The next day they bought a forest-green Blazer for Michael, then made reservations for him to return to Australia.

"I'm a little nervous, Dad," Allison admitted at breakfast the morning he was to leave.

"About being alone, you mean?"

"Yeah."

"We can lock up the house and you can come with me," he offered. "I mean it."

"I know you do. But part of me wants to stay—just to see if I can do it."

"And I think it would be good for you. How about if we tell Penny you're here, and she can be there if you need her?"

"That's a nice thought, but I don't want to ruin Mom's surprise."

"Good point." Michael found himself wishing that Stacy was around to stay with Allison. But ironically his niece had recently returned to Australia, feeling it was better for her to continue her education there.

After breakfast, Michael made a call on the newly-connected phone. He had stayed with Lucinda Swann and her husband during the weeks he'd been waiting for Emily's visa to come through so he could take her to Australia and marry her. But that had been a long time ago, and he wondered if Lucinda would even remember him.

"Sister Swann?" he asked when a feminine voice answered.

"Yes."

"Do you remember a particular foreigner by the name of Michael Hamilton?"

"Do I?" she laughed. "Is this you?"

"It is."

"G'day, mate," she said with a phony Australian accent.

Michael laughed. She'd not changed a bit. "G'day to you, too. Listen, I was thinking I might come to Utah. Would you mind if I drop by?"

"Drop by anytime," she insisted. "We'd love to see you."

"I just might do that."

"It's really you," she laughed. "I can't believe it. You sound as if you're right next door."

Michael chuckled and wrapped up the conversation. Twenty minutes later, he knocked on Lucinda Swann's door. After she got over the astonishment, she laughed and hugged him so tight he could hardly breathe.

"You remember Allison?" He motioned toward her.

"Oh, I do." She took Allison's hands and squeezed them. "But you were just a little girl when you left."

Lucinda invited them in for milk and cookies. Michael explained the situation and swore her to secrecy so they wouldn't spoil Emily's surprise. Lucinda agreed to keep track of Allison, and Allison agreed to call Lucinda each morning to let her know her plans, and each evening to let her know she was home safely.

With everything arranged, Allison took Michael to the airport and sat with him until his flight was announced. She looked up at him with teary eyes and he hugged her tightly.

"I love you, Dad," she said. They exchanged a kiss on the cheek.

"I love you, too, Allie," he answered. "You be a good girl, now. I'll let you know when we're flying in."

"I'll be here."

"It's just an idea, but bring the van. I don't think you'll get all of us in my car."

"Yes, Dad," she grinned, and he boarded the plane. Michael felt hesitant to leave her, but he believed it would be a good experience. She was eighteen now, and a capable young woman. He turned his thoughts to seeing Emily, wishing there weren't so many hours of air time between them.

Thoughts of Emily became so intense that he was grateful to be able to sleep through most of the flight from Los Angeles to Sydney. He called her from the airport, hoping she would be able to meet him when he landed at the station. But she had a visiting teaching appointment and doubted she would be back.

Michael usually enjoyed flying his private plane over the magnificent Australian landscapes between Sydney and his home. But now, his impatience to see Emily only made the flight seem tedious. It was late afternoon and overcast when he finally circled over the house, disappointed that he couldn't see the Cruiser parked there. Emily was likely still gone.

With the plane secured in the hangar, Michael removed his luggage, wondering if Emily had asked someone else to pick him up, since there was no vehicle left waiting for him. He set his luggage outside the door and closed up the hangar, feeling momentarily uneasy, as if he weren't alone. Stopping to listen, he heard nothing but the usual wind rummaging over the flat land surrounding him. He turned slowly to convince himself he was imagining things. His heart quickened before he consciously realized she was standing there.

"Emily," he said breathily, though she was too far away to hear him. For a long moment he just watched her, almost convinced she was only a hallucination. He thought of the hundreds of times he had landed the plane here through his years without her. He'd always longed for someone to be here to meet him, to know that a woman loved him and was there for him. He'd often wondered what it might have been like if Emily had married him instead of Ryan. Through those years he'd never dreamed he would be blessed to have her come back into his life. But there she was, like some angelic apparition, holding a wide-brimmed raffia hat to her head so the wind wouldn't carry it away. That same wind pressed the full, gauzy skirt of a creamy linen dress against her legs.

Her sandaled feet took a step toward him, startling him from a momentary trance. He rushed to meet her and held his breath as she pulled her hat into one hand and wrapped her arms around his neck. He felt her laugh against his face and inhaled the subtle fragrance of whatever she'd washed her hair with this morning. He kissed her face, her mouth, her eyes, her mouth again. He laughed and pressed a hand to her back, lifting her feet off the ground. He laughed again and twirled with her until she wrapped her legs around his waist and arched her head back to catch the wind. He pressed her back against the side of the Cruiser to gain his equilibrium, feeling suddenly like a giddy teenager, but so very grateful to know he was married to this incredible woman. There was nothing to keep him from touching her and holding her to his heart's content.

"I take it you're glad to see me, Michael Hamilton," she said as their eyes met, while their surroundings seemed to keep spinning.

"'Glad' is a wee bit understated," he replied, pressing closer to her, covering her mouth with his. He kissed her until he knew he could bear no more until they were at home, behind closed doors.

Emily insisted on driving back to the house and Michael just watched her, relishing the way she talked nonstop of all that had happened in his absence—details with which she had not wanted to clutter their precious phone time.

"Well, don't you have anything to say?" she finally asked, parking the Cruiser near the side door to the house.

Michael touched her face with the back of his hand. "I would die without you, Emily Hamilton." It came out sounding more severe than he'd intended, and he wondered by the way she glanced down if she had read the meaning between his words. Could he possibly expect her to not notice that something had changed between them? Or rather, something had changed in him. Something deep inside of him longed to just spill it all into her lap—to just give to her all of these fears that had smoldered in him since that moment she'd nearly died. But something deeper and bigger wouldn't allow him to do it, as if keeping it from her could somehow make it less real. He could almost hear her reply forming in the back of his mind. *Yes, Michael, I am sealed to Ryan, and that's just the way it is. Our time together is only temporary, and once I'm gone from this life, that time will be over.*

No, Michael convinced himself, he just couldn't say it. If he never expressed his fear, she could never confirm its validity. Surely the intensity of this love they shared could carry them through even this. He felt certain that, with time, he would get past this and see things more clearly. In the meantime, he would live for now, vowing within to make the most of every moment with her.

"Is something wrong?" he asked lightly when she said nothing for several moments.

"You would not die without me, Michael," she said, and he looked out the window abruptly. "It would be hard, I know. But you're stronger than you think you are."

A casual little laugh erupted from Michael's throat, belying the formidable reaction inside him. "Now you listen to me, Mrs. Hamilton," he said, shaking a finger at her while he pulled her close, "I want you tucking me into bed when I'm ninety, and I'll not settle for anything less."

Emily smiled, apparently willing to brush it under the rug as quickly as he. "I'll certainly do my best," she said and urged him to kiss her. He was just beginning to enjoy it when the doors of the Cruiser flew open and they were assaulted by a horde of giggling children. Michael hugged them all in turn and allowed them to drag him into the house, where his mother and sister were waiting anxiously to see him. He had to admit that life was good, and he was determined to enjoy it.

* * * * *

Emily was the first one through the airport gate, and Allison ran to embrace her mother. Jess jumped up and down impatiently until she bent down to hug him, then Alexa and Amee. Michael carried James off the plane and handed him to Allison while he hugged her tightly.

"You all right?" he asked, touching her chin. Allison smiled and nodded eagerly, but he saw something guarded in her eyes that made him uneasy.

Despite being tired from the long flight, the children chattered constantly about all they were seeing and anticipating. Just past the point of the mountain as they headed into Utah Valley, Emily reached over to take Michael's hand. "It seems strange, doesn't it?"

"Yes," he admitted, "it does. But I think we'll get used to it."

"So much has happened since we last drove this route together."

He chuckled. "But we were going the other direction."

"You promised that when we got to Utah you'd tell me where the house is."

Michael pulled a scrap of paper out of his shirt pocket and handed it to her. Emily read the address and furrowed her brow for a moment. "You're joking," she said.

"No, I'm not."

Emily grinned. "This is in our old ward."

"I know. Right around the corner from Penny."

"I can't believe it," she laughed.

Emily spent the remainder of the drive indulging in memories of her life in Orem, with Penny living next door. Penny had been beside her through the worst of times—some that she'd rather forget. Since Emily's parents had both passed away and her sisters were spread across the country, Penny had been the family Emily didn't have. And Penny had been the one who'd insisted that Emily go to Michael's book signing at the mall. It had brought him back into her life when she'd needed him, even more than she'd realized at the time. Penny and her husband, Bret, had come to Australia for their wedding, and again when Michael received his endowments in the Sydney Temple. They'd stayed close by phone and letters through the years. But the many photographs they'd exchanged by mail could never compensate for the way Emily had missed Penny all this time. The thought of living so close to her again was more than she could have ever hoped for.

"I can't believe it," Emily said again when they drove past the old house, past Penny's house, then around the corner and into the driveway.

Emily kept laughing and hugging Michael and Allison as they looked through the house. "I love it, Michael," she said.

"You can thank Allison for having everything in order. I told you she'd done a great job."

"Oh, you did." Emily hugged Allison again. "It's just incredible."

"I hoped you would like it," Allison beamed.

"Michael, can we go see Penny? I can't stand it."

"I baked some cookies," Allison offered. "Do you want to take her some?"

"That's a good idea," Michael said, "but I think we should handle this right."

Emily walked around the corner with Jess and James and a plate of cookies. Alexa and Amee were too busy to accompany them, as they were fighting over who had the better bedroom. Emily waited in the shadow of a big tree while Jess and James marched up to the door as instructed.

A teenage boy answered and Jess said firmly, "Is your mom here?" Emily smiled at Jess as he turned for approval while the young man went back inside, apparently to get Penny. When she came to the door, Emily had to keep a hand over her mouth to keep from laughing out loud. She was amazed that James stood by his brother so obediently.

"Hi," Jess began his rehearsed speech, "I'm Jess Hamilton, and this is my brother James. We just moved in and my sister made these cookies and my mom told me to give them to you and my dad wants to know if you can come over for dinner tomorrow."

Penny was still gaping at the small boys on her porch when Jess turned around and shouted, "Did I do all right, Mom?"

"Perfect," Emily called as she stepped out of the shadows.

Penny put both hands to her face and started to cry before she flew down the porch steps and into Emily's embrace.

"I can't believe it," she kept saying. "I just can't believe it."

"You'd better believe it," Emily said. "Because it's true. We just moved in around the corner."

Penny laughed again, then wiped at her tears as she saw Michael and Allison coming up the walk.

"Hello, Penny," Michael smiled, and they hugged each other tightly.

"Michael. You haven't changed a bit."

"Just happier," he beamed.

"And look at Allison." Penny touched her face. "She's grown up so beautifully."

"Almost as beautiful as her mother," Michael added, and both mother and daughter glanced down shyly.

"And just look at these boys!" Penny shook her head and repeated, "I can't believe it."

Penny walked around the corner to see the new house, pausing every few minutes to hug Emily and laugh. They sat together in the living room and talked for over an hour, reminiscing and speculating and having a wonderful time, until Michael casually asked, "So, how's Bret?"

Penny's face sobered and tears welled in her eyes immediately.

"What's wrong, Penny?" Emily took her hand and squeezed it. Michael moved to the edge of his seat.

Penny swallowed to gain her composure before she spoke. "I'm sorry," she chuckled humorlessly. "We just found out less than a week ago, and I'm still not quite adjusted to it. I mean . . . I doubt I ever will be, but . . ." Penny bit her lip.

"Penny, what is it?" Emily insisted.

Penny took a deep breath. "Bret has cancer."

"Merciful heaven." Michael leaned back and pushed a hand through his hair.

"I can't believe it," Emily added.

"Neither can I," Penny admitted solemnly. She went on to explain the specifics of a fast-growing tumor in the muscle of Bret's thigh. He was in the hospital about to begin chemotherapy, with the hope of reducing its size before it would be removed. At this point, the prognosis was sketchy. He could possibly lose a significant portion of his leg, or even all of it. If it got out of hand, it could be life-threatening.

"I'm so sorry, Penny," Emily assured her.

"If there is anything—anything at all—we can do to help, Penny," Michael offered firmly, "you can count on us. And I mean that."

"He's right, Penny," Emily agreed. "We owe you a few favors, to say the least. Think where I would be if you hadn't forced me to go to that book signing at the mall."

Penny laughed and cried and leaned her head on Emily's

shoulder. "I'm just so grateful you're here. It's such a miracle."

"Perhaps that's part of the reason we *are* here," Michael said, glancing at Emily. She nodded in agreement, feeling grateful for the guidance of the Spirit that had led them back here, for Penny, if for no other reason.

* * * * *

The warm Utah autumn turned to winter overnight. Jess and James loved the snow. Michael hated it. After shoveling it for three days straight, he walked into the kitchen and announced, "I am buying a snowblower. This is ridiculous." He threw his boots and gloves into the corner of the dining room.

"You're as spoiled as your children," Emily said a little too seriously.

"What's that supposed to mean?" he demanded.

"If you want something, you buy it."

"I'm rich." He grinned. "Be grateful I am, or we wouldn't be here."

"I'm not denying that we are very blessed, Michael, and if you really want a snowblower, fine. But I must admit I'm a little concerned about the children."

"Why? Because *they're* spoiled?" He chuckled and dug through the pantry closet for the hot chocolate mix. "I don't give them everything they want."

"Not quite." Emily took a kettle of hot water off the stove and pointed a finger at him. "But almost. Did you get everything you wanted as a child?"

"It sure doesn't seem like it." Michael sat on a barstool and leaned his elbows on the counter.

"Your attitude about money is good, Michael, but I'm not so sure our children are getting the same picture."

"So, what am I doing wrong, all-seeing, wondrous and powerful wife?"

Emily gave him a sidelong glance of disgust. "Well, like last night for instance."

"What about it?"

"You told Jess that when spring comes you'll probably get him a horse."

"They all miss the horses. I can understand that."

"Michael," she slid a cup and spoon across the counter toward him, "did you have horses when you came here to go to college?"

Michael absorbed it a moment. "No, but—"

"Should they grow up believing their father can provide them with anything they need or want? Shouldn't they learn to be self-sufficient and know how to go without once in a while?"

Michael sipped his hot chocolate and sighed. "So what do you suggest we do, Mrs. Hamilton?"

"Well," she grinned, "since you asked, I've been thinking that we need to get on a budget."

"A budget?"

"We have everything we need. So we figure our living expenses, give ourselves a little flexibility for recreation and extras, then we stay within those guidelines."

"So, what do we do? Lie to our children and tell them the money is gone?"

"I think," Emily came around the bar to sit beside him, "that we can tell them we're on a budget and not lie at all. Tell them that's all the money we have for a month. You don't have to tell them why."

"And I guess I'll have to tell Jess no horse."

"Michael," Emily put a hand over his, "I'm merely telling you what I've observed. You're the head of the family. How far you take this is up to you. I simply feel we should limit their resources a little. I don't think they'll like it, but it's up to us to make sure they grow up with the ability to face life realistically."

Michael touched Emily's chin, and a familiar gaze of adoration filled his eyes. "Why are you always so right about everything?"

"Women's intuition." She smiled and kissed his nose. "And why are you always so agreeable?"

"I learned a long time ago that you have a gift of seeing the big picture."

"The big picture?" she laughed.

"You know, the eternal perspective. And you have a way with those big decisions, too. Like both times you told me you wouldn't marry me."

Emily smiled and met his eyes. She hated to break the mood, but this was a perfect opportunity to bring up what continued to weigh on her. "If you really feel that way, Michael," she said earnestly, "then why won't you believe me when I say we should have another baby?"

Emily wasn't surprised by the hardness that came into his eyes. She knew she'd hit a sore point that hadn't been touched since they'd made the decision to come to Utah. But she couldn't help feeling hurt when he said curtly, "I'm not even going to touch that."

Emily reminded herself that Michael was a good husband and father. Beyond this one difficulty, she could find no reason for complaint. But oh, there were moments when her heart ached for that baby!

Michael finished his hot chocolate and left the room. Emily's dark mood lightened a bit when she got a letter from her sister. Julie had married a Chicago native and had lived there since Emily's junior year in high school. They had kept in touch through letters over the years. And though they had never been close, it was always nice to hear from her.

She was surprised by the nature of the letter, as it contained none of the trivial things that Julie usually wrote to her about. Instead she wrote of a young man named Sean O'Hara, who had joined the Church about a year earlier, following a severe accident. His Irish-Catholic family had turned him out following his baptism, and he had come to Provo with the hope of going to BYU. No one in the area had heard from him since. His name had come up in a welfare meeting, and Julie had mentioned she had a sister attending BYU. The bishop asked if perhaps she could try to find Sean and see how he was coming along. Julie had no more information than that, but her gentle pleading for Emily to follow through on this was something she couldn't ignore.

Emily closed the letter and wondered how she would ever find a particular young man in a heavily populated valley with two colleges and people moving in and out all the time. She opened the phone book and found no listing for a Sean O'Hara. But of course, that would have been too easy. She dialed information and was actually surprised to hear a number repeated back. Emily looked at it for a minute, took a deep breath, and dialed before she had a chance to think about it. Feeling that this *was* too easy, she almost didn't expect an answer. But after two rings she heard an eager, "Hello?"

"Hello," she said, feeling suddenly nervous. "I'm looking for a Sean O'Hara from Chicago."

"This is he," the voice on the other end replied. "May I help you?"

She laughed tensely. "My name is Emily Hamilton. I have a sister who lives in Chicago. Julie Beckstrom. Do you know her?"

There was a long pause, and Emily wondered if she might have the wrong Sean O'Hara. "The name sounds vaguely familiar," he said, "though I can't place it exactly."

"I just got a letter from her. She told me you had joined the Church last year, and attended her ward for only a short time before you moved out here. I've just come here to go to BYU myself, and she asked me to look you up and see how you're doing."

Emily waited through an uncomfortable silence, wondering if he were somehow upset by her call. "So," she finally said, "how are you doing?"

"I'm okay," he stated. There was no denying the emotion in his voice, however subtle. Suddenly Emily felt grateful for making this call. For whatever reason, she had a feeling this man needed something she and Michael had to offer. "What else did she tell you?" His voice became a little more steady, but he sounded somehow concerned.

"Nothing, really," Emily answered, wondering if his hesitance had anything to do with being disowned by his family. She decided not to bring that up.

"I detect a bit of an accent," he said. "Where are you from?"

"Oh," she replied, relaxing a little, "I'm originally from Idaho, but I've been living in Australia the last eight years. I guess it's rubbed off on me." He made a noise of intrigue and she added quickly, "My husband is Australian."

"I see," he said, and she heard a subtle edge of disappointment in his voice. Was this man somehow thinking she was his peer?

After another lengthy silence she asked, "Would you like to come over for dinner on Sunday? My husband is a marvelous cook."

"Well," he seemed more at ease, "I wouldn't turn down a home-cooked meal, but I . . . well, I don't have transportation at the moment. My truck will be fixed next week, and then—"

"We could pick you up," she said easily.

"Okay," he agreed, "I'd love to."

Emily got his address and gave him her phone number. She promised to pick him up Sunday at two.

Emily showed Michael the letter, grateful for the distraction from their last conversation. He was pleased that she had invited Sean over. But Sunday morning, Sean called to tell Emily he had the flu. She asked if there was something she could do, but he insisted he was fine. She promised to call the next day and see how he was doing.

Monday morning, Sean reported that he felt much better. It was just one of those twenty-four hour things. She invited him over for family home evening, and he seemed eager. She told him she'd meet him at a designated spot on campus following his last class.

It was easy to pick out Sean O'Hara. He was the only man who was obviously waiting for someone, an aura of loneliness looking quite at home on him. From a distance he subtly reminded her of Michael twenty years ago, but when she got closer she could see no tangible resemblance beyond height. His hair was dark and stylishly wavy. He wore jeans with hiking shoes, a denim shirt with a tie, and a tweed blazer.

"Sean?" she asked.

He pulled off his dark glasses and smiled. She noticed a significant scar on his left cheek, and another through his left eyebrow. But they in no way detracted from the appeal of his strong features; perhaps they only added to a subtle, rugged quality. "You must be Emily."

"It's a pleasure to meet you," she said and extended a hand. Sean hesitated and looked slightly uncomfortable as he reached out to take it. She noticed that he wore thin leather gloves, and his grip felt somehow unnatural. Only then did she recall Julie mentioning something about an accident. But she just smiled at him as if nothing were out of the ordinary.

"Shall we go?" she asked. "Michael will already have dinner

started."

"You lead the way," he said and motioned with his arm. As they walked side by side he added, "You're really married. That's too bad."

Emily laughed softly at the compliment, then replied, "I'm likely old enough to be your mother, Mr. O'Hara."

"Nah," he drawled skeptically.

Emily chuckled. "I have an eighteen-year-old daughter."

"You're joking." Sean laughed as if he truly couldn't believe it. Emily couldn't help feeling warmed by his sincerity. "I'd like to meet her," he added eagerly.

Emily asked about the classes he was taking as she drove the Blazer toward home. Then, after an uncomfortable lull of silence, she said, "So, you came from Chicago. How do you like Utah?"

Sean stared out his window a long moment, then turned and smiled. "Utah is nice. I love the mountains, and people have been very kind."

"Yes," Emily agreed. "It's nice here."

He asked about Australia, and she told him a little about their home and the things they did. She was relieved when they arrived and he followed her through the front door of the house.

"I'm home!" she called. Jess and James came giggling and met her at the top of the stairs. Michael emerged from the kitchen and greeted her with a kiss before she turned and motioned toward Sean, who was still standing at the door.

"Michael, this is Sean O'Hara. Sean, my husband Michael."

"It's a pleasure to have you here," Michael said, eagerly extending a hand. Again Emily sensed a subtle hesitance from Sean, but Michael acted as if nothing were unusual.

"It's nice to be here," Sean said.

Emily was relieved when Michael and Sean seemed to hit it off. They chatted while Michael cooked, and she was able to get things under control with the children and make certain family home evening was prepared.

They visited as they ate, mostly about Australia and BYU. Sean was majoring in psychology with the hope of becoming a family counselor. His class schedule was heavy, and he was employed part-time at a credit bureau. They seemed to avoid discussing anything personal.

Emily unobtrusively observed Sean and Allison, perhaps hoping they might show an interest in each other. They occasionally exchanged a glance, but she sensed nothing beyond polite acknowledgment.

Sean seemed relaxed, and Emily was grateful for having the opportunity to bring him into their home. It was subtle, but she sensed there were things about his life that were difficult. A guarded, somber aura hovered around him. Had he truly been disowned as Julie had said? And what was this accident she'd mentioned? Was it the reason he kept his gloves on, even when they ate? Emily discreetly noticed he ate slowly and carefully, and she was sure that his hands were difficult to maneuver.

The children ate quickly and went off to do homework or play until home evening. Allison was the first to leave the table. As Michael finished eating and leaned back in his chair to visit, Emily realized that Sean had not touched his steak.

"Are you a vegetarian?" she asked lightly. She was hoping to get past the remaining tension and be able to treat the struggles openly, for his sake if nothing else.

Sean looked momentarily upset, but he chuckled and glanced down. "Actually, no. It looks very good, but I . . . well . . ." Emily exchanged a subtle glance with Michael, then acted on her impulse before she had time to think about it.

"Here," she stood and picked up his plate, "let me heat that up a bit for you. We just get talking, and the food cools off before we have a chance to eat it."

Sean opened his mouth to protest, but she just smiled and he sighed instead. She returned a few minutes later and set the plate in front of him, the steak heated and cut into bite-size pieces. Emily sensed his relief, and perhaps a bit of embarrassment. But she and Michael began talking before he had a chance to say anything. Sean finished his dinner and complimented Michael on the cooking.

Home evening was the usual chaos, but Sean seemed to enjoy it nonetheless. He put in some good comments that made Emily realize his spirit was strong and his testimony deep. Everything went smoothly until Jess asked, "How come your hands don't work very good? And how come you wear those gloves all the time?"

"Jess," Michael scolded gently, "it's not polite to—"

"No," Sean interrupted, "it's okay. It's difficult for me to ignore the problem. I wouldn't expect anyone else to." He smiled easily toward Jess and said, "I was in a car accident, and my hands were cut up real bad. I wear the gloves because they don't look very good."

Jess nodded and accepted the answer. Michael naturally picked up the discussion where they'd left off. They had ice cream sundaes after the lesson, then Sean thanked them profusely and Michael gave him a ride home.

"So," Michael asked, "do you live alone?"

"Yes, I do. It's just a small studio apartment. But under the circumstances, I like it that way."

"Still, it must be lonely."

"Yes, I admit," Sean said, "it's lonely."

"Is your family all in Chicago, then?" Michael asked gently.

"Yes," Sean said casually while he stared out the window.

"Then I assume you'll come over for Sunday dinner."

Sean looked surprised, but his voice was eager. "I'd love to. I should have my truck fixed by then."

"If you need a ride, just ring us up. It's no problem. In fact, if you need to get anywhere in the meantime, we're always coming and going. We'd be glad to help."

"Thank you. I appreciate that. I usually manage with the bus, but it's nice to know there's someone I can call on."

"Is your ward supportive?" Michael asked, hoping he wasn't being too nosy. He liked this young man and sensed a real purpose in their being brought together.

"They've been kind," Sean said, "but there's no one I feel terribly comfortable with. Not enough to ask for help if I needed it."

"Well, you can call us anytime . . . for anything," Michael assured his new young friend as he pulled up in front of the old house where Sean lived upstairs. "And I mean that." Michael extended a hand as Sean opened the door. He shook it eagerly. Sean smiled, thanked him again, and got out. Michael drove home feeling good about the evening. He wondered if Sean O'Hara was part of the reason they'd been prompted to come to Utah.

CHAPTER FIVE

Sean came for Sunday dinner, driving an old Ford truck that Michael quite liked. He told Sean it had character, and the young man agreed. Sean loved the lasagna and stayed until late evening. In spite of his solemnity, he seemed relaxed and it was easy to feel comfortable with him present. Emily couldn't help hoping that he might show some interest in Allison. But it was obvious that nothing clicked between them.

Sean came again for home evening, and tears came to his eyes when they invited him to spend Thanksgiving with them. He ended up staying overnight since it was snowing, and he went to the Christmas parade with the family, helping with the children in a way that he seemed to enjoy.

The following Sunday, the adults were sitting in the living room after dinner. Michael said to Sean, "Do you like us enough yet to unveil those hands?"

Sean looked momentarily surprised, but not uncomfortable. "I doubt you'd want to see them. They're pretty ghastly."

"You've told us more than once that you feel like a part of the family. We want you to feel at home—completely at home." Following a moment of silence that was only a little uncomfortable, Michael added, "Besides, you've eaten here several times and haven't helped with the dishes. You can't wash dishes with those blasted gloves on. You're not a part of the family until you help with the dishes. And with Christmas coming, you might want to consider getting started. I mean if we're going to let Santa know that you'll be here, you might want to start doing your share so you can get that stocking filled."

Sean chuckled and shook his head in apparent disbelief. "I don't understand why you're so good to me."

"Am I?" Michael chuckled. "I thought I was a bit obnoxious."

Emily watched them both closely, wondering how this would turn out. She appreciated Michael's effort to ease the tension, but she wasn't sure if Sean did. They had discussed privately the probability that the events in Sean's life relating to his conversion had been difficult. They enjoyed having him around, but they wondered if he'd ever had the opportunity to share his burden.

When Sean said nothing, Michael persisted gently, "If you're not comfortable with this, then—"

"Oh, no. It's not that," Sean insisted. "You've been good to me, and I appreciate your attitude. I really do, but . . ."

When he faltered, apparently emotional, Emily said quietly, "Do you want to tell us about this accident? You're the one majoring in psychology. Would you like me to tell you it might be good for you to talk about it?"

Again Sean chuckled, seeming a little more at ease. After a tense moment, he finally opened his mouth to speak. Just then the boys started screaming down the hall, apparently fighting over something.

"Excuse me," Emily said, and by the time she returned, Sean didn't seem quite so tense. She sat down and looked him in the eye. He cleared his throat and looked at the floor as he spoke.

"My parents were both born in Ireland. You already knew that. They come from a rigid Irish-Catholic background. I rebelled severely once I was out of high school, and soon hit rock bottom for reasons I'd rather not get into."

Sean took a deep breath and glanced at Michael, then Emily, then to his hands. "I was pretty drunk when I left a bar one night, with a woman who apparently insisted on driving me home. They tell me she hit a truck head on. The driver of the truck didn't get hurt too badly. The woman driving was killed."

Emily discreetly put a hand over her mouth as memories of her first husband's death slipped into her mind.

"Anyway," Sean went on almost mechanically, "I went through the windshield . . . face first."

"Merciful heaven," Michael muttered. "It's a miracle you're alive."

"Yes," Sean almost laughed, "that's what the doctors said, over and over."

Emily swallowed hard. She now understood the scars on his face, but she had to ask, "And your hands were . . ."

"They saved my face, actually," he clarified. "Apparently I put them over my face when I saw the impact coming. The doctors told me to be grateful that I still had a face that wouldn't terrify everyone I met. They said I should be grateful that my eyes were not damaged at all. And I truly am. I thank the Lord every day that my face was spared. While I was struggling just to live through all the surgeries and broken bones, I tried not to think about my hands. When I finally walked out of that hospital, with my name high on their miracle list, I was scheduled to begin reconstructive surgery on my hands. I was told that they looked like hamburger after the accident, and they had come a long way. But as you can see, using them for even the simplest task is a challenge."

Emily glanced warily toward Michael when Sean looked down abruptly and squeezed his eyes shut. "It's okay, Sean," Michael said gently. "You mustn't be embarrassed to show emotion with us. We've had our share of it."

Sean pressed a gloved hand over his eyes and chuckled self-consciously. "I'm sorry," he said through a stifled sob. "I've never really told anyone. It's been over a year, but . . ."

"It's okay," Michael repeated.

They allowed Sean time to compose himself. Emily reached over and took his hand. He smiled sadly at her, and then at Michael. "Before the accident, two Mormon missionaries got me playing basketball with them regularly. They respected my request to not discuss religion. After the accident, a different pair of missionaries came to the hospital every day, once I was out of intensive care. They were there when I took my first steps. They never stopped encouraging me. One day I had to ask myself why they were there for me, and why my life had been saved. It didn't take much for me to realize God wanted me to be a Mormon."

Michael threw Emily a warm smile. She knew he was thinking

of his own conversion. Sean cleared his throat and finished quickly with a statement that left them stunned. "My father told me if I joined the Church, he would have nothing to do with me, and anyone in my family who did would receive the same fate. This included the insurance benefits that would pay for the reconstruction of my hands. I fasted and prayed, and I got a priesthood blessing. I was told that if I made the sacrifice to join the Church, I would be compensated for all I gave up and more. So," he took a deep breath and said with strength, "I was baptized one day, confirmed and ordained the next, then I packed up everything I owned into the back of my truck and headed to Utah with practically nothing. And here I am." He sighed and added, "I truly was blessed. I could tell you a whole string of miracles. My job, my apartment, the money to go to school. It's all been a miracle. But still . . ." His voice faltered with emotion.

In the silence that followed, while Sean struggled to compose himself, Emily turned to Michael and saw her own emotion reflected in his eyes. She knew beyond any doubt why Sean O'Hara had been brought into their lives. And she knew that Michael knew it. She was grateful to be able to open her home to him, and allow him to partake of the family life he'd been forced to leave behind. But there was more, and even if this entire Utah excursion turned out to be a disaster, she was grateful to be here now. If only for Sean O'Hara.

Emily saw Michael nod toward her, and she knew it was a signal of consent to pursue the obvious course. But Emily didn't know where to begin. She was relieved when Michael started it rolling. "If we believe that God brings people together for a reason . . . and we do, of course." Sean looked up, intrigue showing in his eyes as Michael continued. "Then it's obvious why you were meant to become a part of our family."

"I'm afraid you've lost me," Sean said quietly.

"Well, I believe we have much in common. For one thing," he glanced briefly toward Emily, "we've been close to this accident thing before; at least Emily has. It's not an easy thing to go through, in any respect." Michael glanced again at Emily, relieved that she didn't seem upset. "You see, Emily's first husband was killed by a drunk driver."

Sean's eyes widened. "Your first husband."

"Oh, yes," she admitted. "Michael and I have only been married eight years. It's a long story, really."

"And," Michael added, seeming anxious to move on, "I too am a convert. I didn't have to make such incredible sacrifices, but my story has some poignancy that you might appreciate. We'll talk about it one of these days. But most important, Sean, I think we might have something you could use."

Michael and Emily looked at each other and nearly grinned. Sean quickly said, "I don't understand."

"What Michael is trying to say," Emily squeezed Sean's hand and looked him in the eye, "is that we might be able to help you get the necessary work done on your hands."

Sean chuckled in disbelief. "You know a good surgeon?"

"No," Emily smiled, "but I know someone who is so ridiculously rich that he has trouble knowing what to do with all of his money. He's very humble. You'd never realize it to know him, but he's always open to helping with a good cause. I would bet my life that he'd be more than willing to cover your expenses. . . all of them. Whatever it takes."

Sean pressed a hand over his chest, and for a moment Emily wondered if he had stopped breathing. He looked to Michael abruptly, as if he feared Emily was joking. "You're serious," he finally said, his voice husky. "I can't believe it."

"The Lord doesn't make promises that he can't keep," Michael said. "It's only money."

Sean's eyes widened freshly. "What?" He choked out a stilted chuckle. "You?"

Michael laughed. "Guilty." He added to Emily, "I haven't had this much fun admitting I was rich since the day you found out."

"Yes, I remember. We dated for several months before I had a clue."

Michael laughed again and moved from his chair to sit next to Sean on the couch, slapping his thigh lightly. "Welcome to the family, Sean. The only condition is that you keep it quiet about the money. It's something we don't want people to know about; it's got kind of a stigma," he added as if his wealth were something close to leprosy.

"I can't believe it." Sean shook his head slowly and fresh tears filled his eyes. "I just can't believe it." Michael put an arm around Sean's shoulders. Emily moved closer and did the same.

Before classes let out for Christmas, Michael went with Sean to speak with several doctors, getting estimates and some idea of what they would be dealing with. The decision was made to have Sean stay with them whenever necessary, since he would be needing help through the course of this. He already spent enough time with the family that there would be little adjustment. Sean declared daily that it was a miracle, and Michael humbly told him to thank the Lord, not him, and to just keep quiet about the money.

While having Sean in their home brought an added warmth, the underlying tension Emily felt between herself and Michael did not go away. Nothing had been said about having another baby since Sean had come along to distract them from their own problems. But Emily didn't go a day without feeling the ache.

The Sunday following Christmas, Emily sat through sacrament meeting, wondering why she felt down. The Christmas carols lifted her spirits somewhat, but didn't ease the discomfort she was feeling. Even the reality of Christmas was vague. The holidays just didn't seem the same without Michael's mother and sister. But the emptiness was more than that.

Emily observed Sean, sitting between Jess and James, drawing pictures of animals for them. He was such a positive addition to their family that she couldn't help but feel a degree of peace to see him there. Still, she was acutely aware of Penny's absence. Her friend was at this moment sitting at the hospital with Bret, who was temporarily in isolation from everyone but his wife, struggling with the chemotherapy and the possibility of losing his leg. Emily said a prayer in her heart and tried not to worry. She and Michael were trying to keep their spirits up, but there was little to be done. The helplessness was disheartening.

Looking at the ward members surrounding her, Emily acknowledged to herself that there were few families remaining from the ward she'd lived in eight years ago. She knew that it took time to adjust, but she simply didn't feel the warmth she had expected. She felt so disoriented at times that she nearly wanted to cry.

Emily glanced toward Michael and wondered if he felt it, too. She wished they weren't separated by the children sitting between them. Yet even that seemed typical of their relationship these days. In every tangible way, he was sensitive and supportive. She could not even remotely question his being a good man. As a father, he managed a nearly perfect balance of love and discipline. And she admired the way he had taken Sean in. Though Michael was technically old enough to be Sean's father, he treated him much like the brother he'd never had. As a husband, Michael loved and respected her in every way. There was only one problem. Emily's need to have another baby made her heart ache. And how could she possibly feel as close to Michael as she should, when she could not share with him this deep longing and have him understand?

Still, Emily loved him with all her heart. She concentrated on his profile through much of the meeting, until he turned and gave her a faint smile that made her heart skip a beat.

In Relief Society, a young woman cradling her first baby sat next to Emily. "How old is she?" Emily asked quietly.

"Two and a half weeks," the young woman replied.

"She's beautiful," Emily whispered, touching the tiny hand while the baby slept.

The lesson faded somewhere in the distance as Emily watched that baby sleeping in her mother's arms. By the time the meeting ended, Emily was fighting to control her emotions. She hurried to the nursery to get James, hoping no one would stop to talk to her. She turned the corner and nearly bumped into Michael, who already had James in his arms.

"Are you all right?" he asked.

Emily wondered if her distress was so evident. She attempted to muster a lie, but the emotion was so close to the surface that she could only shake her head and turn away with a quickly uttered, "I'll get Jess."

The short drive home was silent with tension. "What's wrong, Emily?" Michael asked once they were alone in the bedroom.

"Nothing I want to talk about," she insisted quietly.

Michael removed his tie and hung it up. "Emily, if something is bothering you, we should talk about it."

Michael's effort was so sweet that Emily felt hopeful when she admitted, "There was this baby at church. She was so—"

Emily stopped when the hardness rose in Michael's eyes.

"Apparently I may talk about anything but that," she observed coolly, unable to help the bitterness in her tone. It was the only way to keep from sobbing.

"I'm sorry, Emily," he said gently. "I'm just . . ." He hesitated and cleared his throat. "I'm just sorry."

Michael walked out of the room. Emily sat down and cried. When she finally appeared in the kitchen to see how dinner was coming along, Michael had everything under control and the children working together cheerfully. With no urging, he put his arms around her and kissed her brow.

"I love you, Emily," he whispered. "You must believe me."

Emily just held him and forced back her emotion. She smiled up at him and touched his face. "I know you do. And I love you, too."

By that evening, as Michael was rounding up the children for scripture study, Emily had come to the conclusion that she was going to have to deal with these feelings one way or another. If she was truly a woman of faith, would she feel so distraught over this? Shouldn't she have the peace of knowing that everything would work out?

"Where's Allison?" Michael interrupted her thoughts.

"I don't think she's come in yet," Sean replied.

"Didn't she say she'd be home at five?" Michael's voice picked up an edge as he glanced at the clock.

"I'm sure she'll be here soon," Emily said. "She's always been dependable."

"Until recently," Michael added, sitting beside Emily and handing over a wiggly James. "She's rarely been on time the last several weeks, or hadn't you noticed?"

"No," Emily admitted, "I suppose I haven't." They heard the car pull into the driveway and Emily added quietly, "We'll have to talk about this later."

Michael nodded and asked Amee if she would begin reading where they had left off. Sean took over handling James, and Emily smiled. He seemed to have a way with handling the little monster. Amee began reading Mosiah chapter twenty-four, but she only got to verse three before Allison came in and hurried downstairs.

"Allison!" Michael called, holding up a hand to indicate that Amee should wait.

"Yeah?" she replied almost sharply.

"I believe you should be up here with us. You're late."

"But I've got to—"

"Allison," Emily interrupted, "please join the family now, and you can do whatever you need to afterward."

Allison slumped into a chair and folded her arms. While she chomped her gum loudly and appeared to be thoroughly bored and disgusted, Amee continued to read. Emily tried to concentrate on the scriptures, but she found Allison's entire attitude a distraction. This was not like Allison. She had always been the attentive, enthusiastic one.

As Amee continued to read the story of Alma's people and the bondage they were suffering, Emily heard something that seemed to cry out to her with an answer to her own dilemma.

"Amee, would you read that last sentence again?" she asked quietly.

Amee cleared her throat and reread the end of verse fifteen. "The Lord did strengthen them that they could bear up their burdens with ease, and they did submit cheerfully and with patience to all the will of the Lord."

Emily tried to hide her tears as Amee continued on. Michael was quick to notice her emotion, as he always was. But she met his eyes, unashamed and full of love. She knew now. She needed to be patient. And when she turned it over to the Lord, submitting cheerfully to this trial, he would ease her burden. She squeezed Michael's hand. He smiled, then asked Alexa to take over reading.

When the children were set loose, Michael reached over and put a hand on Allison's shoulder to keep her there.

"Is something bothering you?" he asked quietly.

"No," she said curtly. "What makes you think something is bothering me?"

Michael exchanged a quick glance with Emily. She was

obviously as baffled as he. Sean graciously stood and sauntered down the hall to where the boys were playing.

"You're making a habit of getting home late these days. Is there a reason why you can't be home when you tell us you will be?"

"I'm eighteen, Dad," she insisted.

"And living under my roof," he said kindly. "You at least owe your mother the respect of not leaving her to worry. I think you owe her an apology."

Allison sighed impatiently. "Sorry, Mom," she muttered without enthusiasm.

"So," Emily said, "exactly who are you spending all this time with when you're not here? You're gone more and more these days."

"Just Ashley," she stated.

"I don't believe we've even seen Ashley since we got back," Michael observed. He knew Ashley had been Allison's best friend as a child, but even then Emily had been concerned about Ashley's influence on Allison. Ashley was from a good family, but her attitudes had often been hurtful to Allison. "Why don't you bring her over for dinner or something? We'd like to see her again."

Allison looked hesitant, and he wondered why.

"You know, Allie," Emily added, "classes will be starting soon. It might be a good idea to start getting to bed earlier so you can handle the hours."

"I will, Mom," she said a little too sharply.

"Your mother merely made a suggestion," Michael stated. "Is there a problem with that?"

"No," she said more quietly.

"Good. We'll expect you in earlier from now on, and feel free to bring Ashley by. We'd like to know who you're out with."

"Okay," she sighed again. "Can I go now?"

"Where are you going?" Emily asked.

"Back to Ashley's house. I'll be home by twelve. Okay?"

"Okay," Emily finally said, "but don't forget that we're having home evening tomorrow. I'll expect you here at six."

Allison hurried down the stairs.

"And bring Ashley," Michael called.

"Something's not right," Emily said when they were alone.

"Boy, you can say that again," he agreed.

They both contemplated in silence for several moments but came to no conclusions.

"You look tired," Michael said, putting an arm around her shoulders. "Do you think you're ready to become a schoolgirl again?"

"I don't know," Emily laughed, leaning her head on Michael's shoulder. "Isn't there something strange about going to college with my own daughter?"

"They won't be able to tell you apart," Michael chuckled, pressing a kiss to her brow.

For the next several days, Michael shoveled snow day and night. "Why don't you get a snowblower?" Emily asked one morning when he came in, wiping sweat off his brow.

"Ah, I need the exercise," he insisted. "Besides," he cast a knowing glance toward Emily, "we can't afford it."

"Oh, get real, Dad," Allison retorted.

"I'm serious." Michael carried some dishes to the table as the children flocked to the kitchen. "The money situation is going to be seeing some changes around here. We have a monthly budget, and once it's gone there's no more until the next month's money comes through."

"You're kidding." Allison especially seemed distressed.

"No," Michael said solemnly, "I'm not kidding."

"What happened?" she demanded. "Did you gamble it all away or something?"

"No," Emily went around the table dishing out hot cereal, "he didn't gamble it all away. And exactly what happened is between your father and me. But you all have to realize that you can't get every little thing you want. We're going to have to tighten things up a bit."

"Does that mean we can't get a horse?" Jess protested. "Dad, you said we could—"

"I know what I said," Michael said gently as he put James into the highchair, "but I'm afraid we're going to have to wait a while for a horse." Jess sighed heavily and Michael continued. "We'll just have to see what happens. But you know, kids, money really isn't everything. We have all we need and we have each other. I don't think we'll even miss it."

"You might not," Allison mumbled in a voice barely audible.

Michael and Emily exchanged a glance that said *we'll try to ignore that one.*

"So," Michael began after the blessing had been said, "today's the first day back to school. Did you have a good Christmas vacation?"

"I don't wanna go back to school," Jess insisted sourly, but Michael wondered if he was just pouting because of the horse.

"Your mom and Allison are going back to school in a few days," Michael added, trying to be positive.

"I hate school." Jess screwed up his face and glared at his Malt-O-Meal.

"Is there a reason you hate school?" Emily asked carefully.

Jess glanced warily at both his parents but said nothing.

"It's 'cause he gets beat up all the time," Alexa interjected.

"What do you mean by that?" Emily demanded.

"The kids at school tease him—real bad," Amee explained.

"They're just nerds," Alexa added.

"Well, you've never said anything about it." Emily looked directly at Jess.

"They don't beat me up." Jess's brow furrowed into a pout. "They just push me around a little."

"A little?" Alexa countered and Jess glared at her.

"Ah, shut up!" Jess growled.

"Jess," Emily scolded gently, "you mustn't speak that way to your sister."

"Jess," Michael put down his spoon and leaned both elbows on the table, "is there a reason you didn't tell us these boys were bothering you?"

"You'll just go tell my teacher or something."

"Jess," Emily explained, "your father and I have no desire to embarrass you, but if you are being mistreated, then perhaps that's the way to solve it. You have the right to go to school and not be bothered."

"They're probably just testing you," Michael said. "Once they know you're not going to put up with it, they'll back off. Things like that happen a lot with the new kid at school."

"It's not 'cause I'm the new kid," Jess said. "It's 'cause I talk funny."

"That's terrible!" Michael snapped.

"Just tell them what your father told me, Jess," Emily said. "Tell them to go to Australia and see how *they* feel. Over there, they'd sound awfully funny."

"I still don't wanna go to school," Jess insisted.

"Sometimes we have to do things that are difficult, Jess," Emily said, "but it will get better. I'm sure of it."

"In the meantime," Michael added, "you just try to stay clear of these . . . *nerds,* and let me know if they bother you too much. Promise?"

"Okay, Dad." Jess managed a smile, and the family proceeded to eat in silence until Michael startled Allison.

"We haven't seen Ashley yet. How is your esteemed friend?"

"She's fine, Dad," Allison said curtly.

"Do we embarrass you?" Michael asked lightly.

"No, Dad, you don't embarrass me."

"I *do* talk funny," Michael added. The other children giggled, but Allison didn't even crack a smile.

Once the children were off to school and Allison had gone back to bed, Emily washed dishes while Michael made a grocery list.

"I'm worried about Allison," Emily admitted. "She's become so . . . distant since we've been here. I hardly feel I know her anymore. It's as if she's keeping secrets from me and doesn't dare get too close, for fear I'll discover them."

Michael stopped and looked up. "I don't think I like that analogy."

"I'm sorry. That's how I feel."

"That's exactly what I mean. If you feel that way, there must be some truth to it."

"Do you really think she's doing something she's not supposed to be, Michael? The thought makes my stomach churn."

"I don't know. But I think we'd better keep a close eye on her. She's certainly keeping Ashley a secret. Maybe doing something about that would be a good place to start."

Later that morning, Michael answered the phone while Emily

sat close by, going over her class schedule.

"No, I'm sorry," he said. "She's still asleep. Do you want me to wake her? I can, really. All right. May I ask who's calling? Ashley!" Michael glanced toward Emily with a conspiratorial grin. "What a pleasure to talk to you. Why, we were just saying this morning that we should have you over for dinner. No, I'm serious. Bring a friend or two along. I'm not such a bad cook. When? How about tonight? Big plans, eh. Well, tomorrow's free here. Great. We'll see you then. Yes, I'll have Allison call you."

When he hung up the phone, Emily was grinning. "Allison is going to be furious."

"I know it." He rubbed his hands together like a mad scientist. "It's the most fun I've had in a long time."

Michael dragged Allison out of bed at noon to have her watch James while he and Emily did some errands. "Oh, by the way," Michael said as he ushered Emily out the door, "Ashley called. Better call her back right away. And oh," he stuck his head back in the door and startled her, "I'll be taking *my* car, as long as you won't be needing it while you're babysitting."

"Good-bye, Dad," she scowled and he closed the door. "And hurry back!" she shouted after him.

Michael opened the car door for Emily, then he got in and turned the key in the ignition. "How about lunch first?"

"Fine by me," she replied. "But, wait . . ." She put a hand on his arm, and he hit the brakes before they even cleared the driveway. "First of all, I need a kiss."

Michael smiled and leaned over to press his mouth over hers. Emily pressed a hand to his face and kissed him again.

"Okay." Emily sat up straight. "We can eat now." They laughed together as Michael drove toward State Street.

The last of their errands was a stop at the hospital to see how Bret was coming along. He'd begun another lengthy chemotherapy treatment, one of many that would go on for several months. They found Penny in the hall outside Bret's room.

"Ah," a grin lit up her wearied countenance, "my favorite visitors." Penny and Emily embraced.

"How's he doing?" Michael glanced toward the room.

"The nurse is helping him now. He's awfully sick. He seems to get more nauseated each time."

"How are you?" Emily asked Penny.

"Oh, I'm holding up," she said with fortitude. "I don't know what we'd do without you. You're so good to us."

"We haven't done anything," Emily replied. "The ward has done so much that there's little left to be done. I can't tend your children because they're old enough to take care of themselves."

"Thank heaven for that." Penny sighed. "We practically live at this hospital. And you're our most faithful visitors. Even when you can't see Bret, you always come to see me. You can't know how much your company is appreciated."

"Maybe we can," Michael said quietly.

"Is there anything you need us to do, Penny?" Emily took her hand and squeezed gently. "Anything at all?"

Penny shook her head. "No, I really can't think of anything, at least since . . ." She stopped and narrowed her eyes on Michael. "That reminds me. I have a word to say to you. Have you got any idea how an immense amount of money ended up in our checking account, Mr. Hamilton?"

Michael's eyes widened. "The Lord works in mysterious ways, Penny."

"You can deny it until you die, Michael. I know it was you." Penny stared at him for a long moment.

"What?" he laughed. "We haven't got any money. Just ask Emily. We're on a budget."

Emily nudged him in the ribs.

"He did it, Emily, didn't he?"

Emily shrugged her shoulders.

"Well," Penny's eyes became moist and she bit her lip, "thank you anyway, even if you won't claim it. I don't know what we'd have done."

"Just pay your tithing, and those blessings fall right out of heaven into your bank account."

Penny nodded firmly, seeming to sense his need to remain anonymous.

The nurse emerged from Bret's room. "You can go in now,

Penny," she said. "I think he's doing a little better."

"Thank you," Penny said.

The nurse motioned toward Michael and Emily and added, "His blood count is better. If you wash up and put on a mask, you can go in."

When they were ready, Penny stuck her head into the room before she motioned Michael and Emily to follow.

"Hello, Bret," Emily said warmly as Penny sat by his side and took his hand.

"Hey," Michael chuckled, "I like the Captain Picard look. It's really quite fashionable."

"Oh, yeah," Bret laughed weakly. "At least I didn't have too much hair to lose on top."

"Are you hanging in there?" Michael asked soberly.

"I'm doing as well as can be expected," Bret admitted. "The tumor is going down in size. So far, so good."

"That's great news," Emily said brightly.

"Hey, when you get past this treatment," Michael said, "I'll barbecue you a burger, just the way you like it."

"Sounds great," Bret grinned. "No one can barbecue like you do, Michael."

"But there's two feet of snow on the ground," Penny insisted.

"Minor inconvenience," Michael retorted.

"When it comes to cooking," Emily interjected, "Michael finds a way."

The conversation flitted through news of ward members and the world, the weather, and teenagers. Penny and Bret had good advice concerning Allison, but at this point there hardly seemed to be a drastic enough problem to do much of anything. When Michael and Emily finally insisted they had to go before James pushed Allison to her wits' end, Bret looked at them intently.

"Thank you," he said. "Your friendship means a great deal to us, now more than ever. I don't know what we'd do without you."

"You have each other," Emily said.

"Yes," Bret agreed, squeezing Penny's hand. "There's nothing like being faced with death to make a man appreciate knowing he's got eternity."

Penny and Emily both smiled sadly at his sentiment, but Michael felt something lurch inside of him. "Take it easy, Bret." Michael patted him on the shoulder and hurried out of the room.

"Is anything wrong?" Emily asked once they were in the car.

"No, why?" Michael managed a smile that seemed to fool her.

"I was just . . . wondering," she said. Then a few moments later, "Are you sure?"

"Yes, Emily," he laughed, "I'm sure."

Emily let it drop, but she sensed something he wasn't admitting to. She hated these feelings of dissonance between them, but at this point she felt helpless to do anything about it. Reminding herself to be patient and have faith, Emily put her concerns away and squeezed his hand.

CHAPTER SIX

Allison was furious when she realized Ashley had been invited to dinner. While she tried fruitlessly to give Michael a good reason for her anger, Michael added one more clue to the mystery. Evidently, Allison's friends were not people her parents would approve of.

When Ashley finally arrived, they were relieved to see that it wasn't as bad as they'd begun to imagine. Her hair was starched into an exaggerated style, she wore too much makeup, and her skirt was something like hot-pants with no inseam. But Ashley seemed pleased with the attention that came with being invited over, and Michael and Emily managed to make even Allison feel comfortable before the meal was finished.

Ashley began coming around more after that, and occasionally another friend or two would slip in and out the door. Michael went discreetly to the family room late one evening to check out the situation. He found an interesting combination of young people sprawled on the floor watching a video. But the movie was relatively decent, and Sean was actually watching it with them. The kids were polite and respectful, and Michael told Emily he'd far rather have Allison at home with her weird friends than somewhere else with them.

The first few weeks of college were a major adjustment for both Michael and Emily. Sean had his first surgery, but since they only worked on one hand at a time, he managed relatively well. A routine was soon established that allowed for all the necessities of family living to be budgeted in, and to help Sean along as well. Emily found true gratification in her opportunity for learning, and a deep peace in observing Michael take over the home and children for the most part.

"You make an adorable mother," she said to him one morning after the kids had finally left for school.

Michael gazed at her in feigned innocence, and Emily smiled. "There's nothing quite like watching J. Michael Hamilton, one of the wealthiest men in Australia, best-selling international author, in my kitchen with a dishtowel tucked into his jeans, making animal pancakes and packing lunches."

"Hey," he pretended to be insulted and gently flicked her with a towel, "don't be ridiculing my *true* talents."

"You're an incredible man, Michael Hamilton." Their eyes met with a familiar electricity and she added, "You're the best thing that ever happened to me."

"It's the other way around, love, I can assure you."

Emily saw Michael's intent gaze gradually fade into a mischievous smile, and she hurried into the living room.

"Where you going, Emily?" he asked through a breathy laugh, following at her heels.

"I know that look," she laughed and dashed toward the hall, but he caught her around the waist and rolled back onto the couch. She ended up on his lap, struggling and giggling while he held her with one arm and tickled behind her knees with the other.

"You fiend!" She tried to sound stern, but her laughter erupted again. "You know I'm too old to be tickled."

"Never," he hissed like a cartoon villain. Then he laughed again as he turned her in his arms and caught her off guard with a lengthy kiss.

Emily pressed a hand into his hair and another beneath his shirt. "I should be studying," she muttered between kisses. "And you should be . . ."

"What?" he asked against her ear when she didn't finish.

"You should be . . ." She laughed when she couldn't think of anything, and he kissed her again.

They both turned in unison when they realized James was watching them. "How long have you been there, sport?" Michael asked, laughing at James' dumbfounded expression.

"You not 'posed t' tikow Mommy," he said firmly.

"I'm not tickling her," Michael replied. "I'm kissing her."

"You was tikowin' her befow," James retorted.

"How about if I tickle *you*?" Michael reached toward James, but he jumped back and giggled.

"I jus' come t' tell ya that ya should clean up th' water in th' bafroom."

"What water?" Emily sat up straight, and James looked hesitantly back and forth between his parents' stern faces.

"I didn't fwush th' apple down da toiwet!" James insisted.

Emily tried hard not to laugh as Michael firmly instructed James on what didn't belong in the toilet. She mopped up the bathroom, then forced herself to go study while Michael removed the toilet to clear the obstruction. She smiled to herself as she listened to his banter with James, who was holding the tools so he could "help" fix the problem.

Emily couldn't deny that she was grateful for the blessing of Michael in her life, in spite of the irony that he was the one holding her back from having the baby she so desperately wanted. But she reminded herself to be patient and have faith, all the while praying in her heart that the Lord would provide a way.

Allison managed to do well through the first several weeks of classes. She kept her curfew and did what she was asked, but Emily couldn't deny the nagging instinct that told her something wasn't right. She made an effort to visit occasionally with Ashley's mother, hoping they could somehow form an alliance to keep tabs on their daughters. But Emily quickly realized that Ashley's mother, like many others, had accepted Ashley's behavior as something out of a parent's control that the child would hopefully grow out of. It was as if she didn't care if her daughter did something wrong. She simply didn't want Ashley to cause any trouble that might result in stress for her parents. Emily discussed her concerns with Michael. Together they prayed for Allison and Ashley, and tried to be keenly sensitive to anything they might do to help the situation.

Michael continued to write at a leisurely pace without deadlines. And he began going to the fitness center every other morning when he realized his body was missing the work he'd done at home— work that actually made him sweat. He spent time regularly with Bret, both in and out of the hospital, and occasionally on one of

Bret's good weeks, Michael would take him to a BYU game. Sean often went too, and the three got along well. As Emily renewed her friendship with Penny, basking once again in the closeness they had shared before, they were both pleased to see their husbands bonding in a way that made it easy to spend time together.

March brought an early warm spell that encouraged many evenings around the barbecue grill during Bret's weeks between treatments. The tumor continued to go down in size, and the outlook was good. After six months in Utah, Emily began to feel more at home in the ward and was pleased with the associations they were developing there. Michael had been called to assist in the deacons quorum, mostly to teach their Sunday lessons in priesthood meeting. He began to like it once he let them know he was bigger than they were. He was also asked to make calls for temple attendance in the ward. At first he was discouraged, seeing the way these people took the temple for granted, when members in his branch back home would save for years just to attend once. Emily encouraged him to share his feelings with others, and after taking the opportunity to bear his testimony on the matter, attendance increased enough that he felt he had made a difference.

On a warm spring Sunday, Emily sat in sacrament meeting and realized that life was good. She could see many reasons for being here, the least of which was her education. Still, she found fulfillment in that. Bret's prognosis, at this point, was good, and Sean's hands had already shown improvement. Emily's heart surged with a deep sense of gratitude to her Father in Heaven for all she was blessed with. And if there was any doubt, she only had to glance toward Michael, who was quietly trying to keep James from crawling under the bench. He finally managed to settle the child on his lap, then he caught Emily's eye with a smile that quickened her heart a little. She truly was blessed.

* * * * *

Emily felt a combination of emotions when she looked at the calendar and realized she was late. It was highly unlikely she could be pregnant; they'd been so careful. If she *was* pregnant, it had to be a miracle. But Michael wouldn't see it that way, and the thought made her heart ache. Not knowing how to feel or what to do, she tried not to think about it, half hoping, half fearing she would start.

When Emily was two weeks late, she couldn't bear the uncertainty any longer. She left early for classes and stopped at the hospital for a pregnancy test. The results came in less than ten minutes, and she stood in the hallway wanting to laugh and cry. The little piece of paper in her hand read: *Positive. Pregnant.*

Idly she walked past the infant nurseries, gazing through the window at the new arrivals. Her arms ached to hold another baby, and joy filled her at the thought of having one. But a little dark cloud crept into her thoughts. Michael would not be happy. She felt certain that as long as she never got pregnant, they would stand undivided. But now she *was* pregnant, and the reality had to be faced.

For several days, Emily told herself that Michael had a right to know. She'd just get up the courage and they'd be interrupted, or she would rationalize that he was in such a good mood and she didn't want to mar it. Then, right on time, the expected nausea began to plague her, and she knew she couldn't keep it to herself much longer.

Emily returned from classes on a warm afternoon to find Michael preparing vegetables for chicken stir-fry. It was one of her favorites, and he knew it; but the smell of wonton soup simmering nearly did her in. She managed to get out of the kitchen without appearing awkward, but she dreaded dinner. After praying hard and willing herself to not be sick, she sat at the table and Amee began serving up the soup. The family was seated, and she was glad Michael didn't ask her to say the blessing. When that was done they all began to eat, except Emily. First she just stared at her soup, wondering why it looked so awful when she usually loved it. Courageously she began to stir it a bit, while she tried to convince herself that it smelled good. She was grateful to have Sean present, as he kept Michael occupied with conversation. She couldn't help noticing how much better his hands looked, and how he was managing to use them with more agility. He still had some work left, but he had come a long way already.

"This is wonderful," Sean commented, then glanced toward Emily. "Michael tells me this is your favorite."

"Oh, it is," she smiled, feeling as if she were lying. "He started cooking for me in college."

Michael gave Emily a grin that made her almost heartsick at the thought of how he would react when he realized the truth. She tried not to think about it and continued to look interested in her food, though she hardly dared smell it.

Again she was grateful for Sean's presence as he declared he had news to share. He had met a woman he was quite taken with. Her name was Melissa James. She was his age, strong in the Church, and majoring in interior design. They'd only gone out once, but Sean declared it was magic. Emily was briefly distracted by warm memories of dating Michael in college, but she was soon brought back to reality by the smell of her soup. Determinedly she lifted a wonton out on her spoon, and a sour taste rose in her mouth.

Michael just had to look up right then. "Are you all right?" he asked. All eyes turned to her. Emily started to nod, then she abruptly shook her head and ran from the table with her hand over her mouth.

Michael was willing to pass it off, until the girls began chattering. "She's probably pregnant," Amee said. "She always does that when she's pregnant."

"Yeah," Alexa giggled, "she about passed out over my scrambled eggs this morning. I thought she was gonna puke right there in the kitchen."

"Alexa," Allison scolded, "not at the dinner table."

Michael slowly set his spoon down. He suddenly felt a little nauseated himself.

"You okay, Dad?" Amee asked.

"I'm fine," he smiled and glanced tensely toward Sean, who looked as if he suddenly didn't want to be there. Pushing his chair back, Michael said, "I'll just go check and see if Mom's all right."

Michael pushed open the bedroom door to see Emily sitting on the edge of the bed, bent over the arm wrapped around her waist, her forehead planted in the other hand.

"You all right?" he asked softly. Her head shot up.

"You scared me," she chuckled, trying not to look at him.

After an unreasonable silence he said, "You didn't answer my question."

"I'm fine." She tried to smile, but still she didn't look at him.

Michael stood beside her and lifted her chin with his finger. "Tell me what's wrong," he insisted. His heart dropped when she bit her quivering lip. "Are you pregnant?" he asked. She squeezed her eyes shut and tears trickled out. "Answer me," he insisted.

"Yes," she choked the word out and looked away.

"Are you sure?" he had to ask.

"I had a test."

"When?"

"A week or so ago."

"And you didn't tell me?" Anger rose in his voice.

Emily looked up at him. "Give me one good reason why I should have been anxious to give you the news."

"Because I have a right to know."

"And it's obvious you're as thrilled about it as I expected you would be." Her sarcasm was biting.

"And how *should* I feel?" he retorted.

"I can't tell you how to feel, Michael, but I can tell you how I feel. Considering the odds of my getting pregnant, this baby is a miracle. I did everything physically possible to prevent this happening, but it happened anyway. I think you're going to have to accept it and live with it."

"I'm not sure I can." His voice turned sour.

"Where is your faith, Michael?"

"It died in a hospital in Australia."

"Well, I've got two choices. I can either have this baby on faith, or I can get an abortion." His eyes shot to her. "You know me well enough to know that only leaves me one choice. Now, you've got two choices. You can either accept this on faith, or you can leave. I didn't make this baby alone, Michael, but I'll have it alone if that's what it takes to get it here."

"I can't believe you'd say that."

"I can't believe you'd expect me to turn my back on one of the spirits that is supposed to come into our home. I want this baby, Michael. I'm not going to pretend that I don't. I'm *glad* that I'm pregnant. We've been told that I would live to see my children grown. I would think you could see some light in that."

Michael stuffed his hands in the pockets of his jeans and looked at the floor. He knew he was being unfair, but these feelings were so difficult to deal with. Still, it was his relationship with Emily that mattered most. He had to overcome his pride for that, if nothing else. The damage was done. There was no way of undoing it now.

"I'm sorry, Emily. I know you didn't try to get pregnant. I guess I'm just going to have to deal with it."

Emily looked up at him, feeling a surge of hope. But a wave of guilt crashed down on her, and she knew she had to admit to the truth or she could never live with herself. "Michael, it's true that I did everything physically possible to prevent the pregnancy, but . . . I'm not going to lie and tell you that I didn't try to get pregnant."

Michael's brow furrowed.

"I've been praying this would happen, Michael. I wanted it, and I—"

"You did *what?*" he interrupted, barely in control. Emily said nothing. "I can't believe it. I . . . I . . . feel like you . . . deceived me, Emily. We agreed that you would not get pregnant unless we mutually made a decision to—"

"No, we agreed that we would use protection until we—"

"Emily! It's like you're asking God to take you back for the sake of this baby."

"It's nothing like that! I prayed for a baby. I could have been told no if it wasn't right. Maybe you ought to start praying to deal with these fears of yours, Michael. Pregnancy is difficult enough without having to deal with this. Go write a book or something and see if you can avoid noticing the symptoms. I can't."

Emily started for the door, but he grabbed her arm and kicked it shut. "Don't walk out on me, Mrs. Hamilton. I'd like you to stop and realize the reason I feel this way."

Emily wrenched her arm from his grasp. "Because you're a stubborn, pig-headed—"

"Because I love you." He took hold of her shoulders and shook her gently. "I don't want to lose you, Emily. I'm sorry I don't see it the way you do, but it scares the hell out of me to think of losing you."

"It's too bad it can't scare some faith into you," she snapped, and her tears turned to sobs.

"Do you hear me, Emily?" he said against her face. "I love you! I couldn't bear losing you!"

"I love you too, Michael," she cried. "That's why I want this baby. It's a part of you."

Michael wanted to tell her that was little comfort when she would be with her children in the next life, but there was no guarantee he'd be with any of them. He ended the conversation with a terse, "Well, I can't do anything about it, but I don't have to like it."

The words bit so deeply that Emily drew her hand back and slapped him before she consciously realized she even wanted to. Michael looked stunned and hurt, but at least she had his attention.

"You're no better than most of the men roaming the earth who have their way and turn their back. Marriage vows don't make your attitude excusable. You fathered this child, Michael Hamilton, and by heaven and earth you are going to accept it. I will not spend every day of my life for the next nine months feeling guilty every time I look at you. Like I said before, you can learn to live with it or you can leave."

Deep inside Michael wanted to cry, but instead he threw anger back as fast as it was being thrown at him. "I'd wager you were never that spunky with Ryan."

Emily couldn't believe he would bring that up—*now*, of all times. She was quick to retort with, "Ryan never turned his back on me because I conceived one of his children."

Michael felt her words strike a nerve—that nerve somewhere deep inside him, as sensitive as a festering sliver. Anger quickly overtook the hurt and fear he couldn't face. He blindly kicked over the dressing table chair. Emily winced and stepped back abruptly. The genuine fear in her eyes reminded Michael to calm down and keep his own ridiculous fears out of this.

Following a long moment of unbearable silence, he finally muttered, "I am not turning my back on you."

"Oh, as long as you see to my physical needs, does that justify the way you're ready to wash your hands of this pregnancy, as if it doesn't exist?"

Michael swallowed his pride and sighed. If he didn't, he knew this could go on all night. "I can't believe we're arguing like this."

"I can't believe it either," she snapped.

"It's obvious I'm going to have to live with it."

"You're damn right you are," she retorted. Michael's eyes widened. In eight and a half years of marriage, he'd never heard her cuss. They stared at each other a long moment, until Emily rushed past him into the hall.

"Where are you going?" he called.

"I need some fresh air," she called back and slammed the door on her way out of the house.

It took Michael a few seconds to remember that he'd left his family—and Sean—at the dinner table. He doubted they would have heard much, if any, of the argument, but there was no hiding the fact that Emily had just stormed out and slammed the door. He took a deep breath to compose himself and returned to find them eating in glum silence. He sat down and cleared his throat, announcing without preamble, "Your mother is pregnant."

No one made a sound except James, who had no perception of what was taking place. Finally Sean said, "Well, that's good, isn't it?"

Michael wondered what to say without sounding like a fool. Amee spoke up to fill the silence. "The last time Mom got pregnant, it killed her."

Sean's eyes widened. Michael looked down and sighed. When no one else said anything, he knew he had to explain. With a voice that almost squeaked he said, "Emily had a miscarriage last year. In the process, her heart stopped."

Sean sighed with enlightenment and seemed suddenly uncomfortable. Michael added with a tense chuckle, "Sorry for the dramatics. I'm just concerned. That's all."

"I can understand why," Sean said. "But surely everything will be all right."

Michael managed a weak smile. "I'm sure it will," he said, but in his heart he didn't believe it.

Emily sobbed to Penny for an hour, grateful for her friendship, but hating the memories of her marriage with Ryan, when Penny had been her only link to sanity. Still, this was different. With Ryan, Penny had had no patience. She would tell Emily to leave him and get on with her life. Yet with Michael, Penny reminded Emily of his goodness and strength, and Emily could only admit she was right.

"He's a saint of a man," Penny insisted, "with a few human flaws. You know from experience that it could be much worse."

Resolved to look at the eternal perspective, Emily returned home to find Michael sitting at the computer, but staring at the wall. She had long ago figured out that he feigned writer's block when he needed time to think. He looked up when he saw her in the doorway and their eyes met with a mutual, silent torment.

"Did Sean go home?" she asked, trying to break the ice.

"I think we scared him away," Michael answered lightly as he took off his glasses. "But I'm sure he'll be back."

"Michael," she said more seriously, "I know we're both angry, and we both feel justified in our anger. Perhaps this is one of those times when we're just going to have to agree that we disagree, and do our best to live with it."

"It would seem we have little choice." His voice was kind, but she didn't miss the aggravation in his eyes.

Emily swallowed the temptation to open it up again. Instead she tried to soothe it. "I'm sorry I got so angry, Michael."

"So am I," he admitted, his eyes softening a bit.

Michael reached out a hand toward her and she didn't hesitate to take it. He urged her onto his lap and hugged her tightly. "I know I'm a fool, Emily," he said in a husky whisper, "but I love you so much." Desperation seeped into his embrace. "I know what it's like to lose you and live without you. I don't think I could face it again."

"Everything will be fine, Michael," she assured him with a warm kiss.

"You just take care of yourself." He pointed a finger. "I mean it."

"I will," she promised and hugged him tightly. She had to agree with Penny. In spite of a few human weaknesses, Michael Hamilton was a saint of a man.

CHAPTER SEVEN

Jess protested adamantly about returning to school at the end of summer vacation. In spite of having an American mother and being in the States nearly a year, he had a definite Australian accent to his voice, and was incessantly teased. Trying to solve the problem through a back door, Michael asked Jess if it would be all right with the teacher to show and tell his own dad. Jess was thrilled, and Michael enjoyed telling the second graders about Australia and all the things that were similar to and different from the United States. He rather enjoyed the opportunity and, seeing the children's interest, felt hopeful that it would make a difference on Jess's behalf.

He returned home to find James asleep and Emily painting at the easel that had become a permanent fixture in the corner of the family room.

"How did it go?" She turned in her chair and smiled.

"It went well," he said. "I think it might make a difference."

"You're a genius," she said, but there was no denying the tension between them when he kissed her before excusing himself to write.

October brought their anniversary of one year in Utah. Emily had several credits successfully behind her, and she was beginning to look pregnant. Michael was supportive, but Emily often felt the tension of his unspoken fears.

Being over forty, pregnant, and going to college left Emily little time for home and family. But they managed to maintain under Michael's direction. Gradually, the tension became less evident; and with other things settling in well, it was easy to almost forget there was a problem.

As they sat together on a blanket, waiting for Jess's soccer game to start, Emily felt peace listening to Michael tally how well the children were doing.

"You know," he said, "Alexa and Amee have actually been getting along. And Amee's doing better with the piano than she ever has. Allison's grades have been good, and Jess really seems to be starting to fit in."

"I think the sports have helped," Emily commented, watching Jess warm up with his team while James played with his own soccer ball close by. "It's hard to tell if he likes the soccer or football better. But he wouldn't have been able to participate in something like this in Australia so easily."

"That's true," Michael agreed.

The game had barely started when Sean came up behind them and startled Emily. "Hello, Mother. You're looking lovely today."

Emily chuckled warmly, and Sean bent to kiss her as if she *were* his mother.

"Where's Melissa?" Michael asked. It was rare these days for Sean to show up without her.

"She had to work late. But I needed to talk to you about something anyway."

They both turned to him curiously, but he said nothing more until halftime.

"You know that I'll soon be finished with the work on my hands—at least as much as they can do." Sean's voice was tinged subtly with emotion.

"Yes," Michael drawled, wondering what he was leading to.

"Well, I've made a decision to do something that might sound a little strange, but . . . well, I guess I should just come out and admit it. I need your help."

After a moment's silence, Michael said, "We can't help you if we don't know what strange thing you intend to do."

"Are you and Melissa getting married?" Emily asked with a sly smile.

Sean chuckled with embarrassment. "No. Not yet, anyway. But give me time. Before I do that, I thought that I should . . . Well," he cleared his throat tensely and drew back his shoulders, "I want to go on a mission."

Emily threw her arms around Sean.

"Is that all?" Michael laughed. "I thought you were going to tell us you wanted to open your own pet store or something."

"I think it's wonderful, Sean," Emily said. "I know you won't regret it."

"Do you really believe I could do it?" he asked earnestly. "I mean, I haven't been in the Church all that long, and I'm older than most of them, but . . ." His eyes glowed with sincerity and enthusiasm. ". . .I really want to. Melissa suggested it. She said she would wait for me. I guess it just never occurred to me before. But when I thought about it, I couldn't help remembering what the missionaries had done for me. The problem is . . ." His expression sobered. "I have no financial backing."

For a moment Michael looked almost hurt. But before he could speak, Sean continued. "I'm planning to sell my truck and anything else I have that's worth selling. But I know it won't even begin to—"

"Sean," Michael put a hand to his shoulder, "there's no need to even ask. You do what you can, and we'll cover the rest. It would be a privilege to support your mission. You shouldn't even have to wonder."

"Oh, thank you!" Sean almost whooped with excitement.

Michael chuckled and put an arm around his shoulders with a fatherly hug. "Maybe they'll send you to Australia."

"Hey, that would be nice," Sean said.

"Oh," Emily added facetiously, "you don't want to go there. Australians are terribly odd."

"You would know," Sean chuckled while Michael pretended to be insulted. Then they turned their attention to the second half of the game while Sean took James to play on the swings.

* * * * *

As Emily passed the time in her pregnancy when she had lost the last baby, she breathed easier and began thinking more about it. This became even easier when Bret finished his final treatment for cancer and was declared sound. The tumor had completely disappeared without any need for surgery, and the doctors believed it would never come back. Michael invited them over for a nice dinner to celebrate, and it was a thrill to see the joy they felt in contrast to the pain and doubt they had been going through a year ago.

That evening, Michael leaned against the headboard to watch Emily brush through her hair. He'd watched her do it at least a thousand times, but he never tired of observing this feminine ritual. A subtle wave of excitement caught him off guard. The stress of children and everyday living had not lessened her effect on him. Even now, with the tension hanging unspoken between them, Michael could not be free of the reality. He loved her more than life. He had no trouble with the concept of laying down his life on her behalf. But he wondered if even that would be enough to make her his forever. He thought of Bret and Penny. They had been confronted with death. But even as hard as that had been for them, Bret had often told him how grateful he was to know they had eternity. If only Michael could know the same.

Like a familiar enemy, the fear crept in, as if it were an entity in itself, attempting to strangle the love between them. Michael wanted to be free of it, but he felt so helpless. Since Emily had come back into his life, he had found they could talk through their struggles. Together they could find a solution to nearly everything, or at least a way to help each other through. But he just couldn't bring himself to talk to Emily about this, as if keeping his fears to himself might somehow make them go away.

Emily had married a man in the temple and was sealed to him for eternity. She had spent more than a decade with Ryan Hall, committed heart and soul to making her marriage work. She had loved Ryan; Michael knew that. Even now, she had not shared as many years with Michael as she had with Ryan. If Michael lost her, if her life were to suddenly end as a result of a difficult childbirth or any other circumstance, would he ever be with her again? Was his only purpose in all of this to raise these children through their earthly existence and then see them back into another man's hands for the rest of eternity? The thought made Michael's stomach churn.

"Are you all right?"

Emily's voice snapped him back to the moment.

"I'm fine," he lied, but he could see in her eyes that she wasn't fooled. Still, she smiled, albeit tensely, and he wondered what secret thoughts might be plaguing *her.* She was far too intelligent to believe that everything was as it should be between them. But she seemed to want to avoid the contention that always resulted when they tried to discuss the fact that she was pregnant, and his unreasonable fears attached to it. At moments like this, Michael could almost see himself from the outside, looking in. He wondered if his fears were ridiculous and just needed to be dealt with. He believed the tension was his doing. But when he tried to find a way to reach back inside himself and solve the problem, his spirit might as well have been weighed down with a ball and chain. He was beginning to believe these fears would accompany him to the grave.

"Michael." Emily sat beside him on the bed and took his hand. Again she startled him from his thoughts. "Are you sure you're all right?"

Michael hesitated. "Yes," he said blandly, "I'm fine."

Their eyes met and somehow he believed she understood—at least to a point. But it had always been that way between them. From the first time they had spoken he'd felt it, as if their very souls had reached toward the other and cried out to be joined as one. He knew such thoughts should give him peace, but they only added to his confusion.

"Is there anything you want to talk about?" she asked, setting a gentle hand to his face.

An unspoken pleading in her eyes made him want to cry. Stoically he shook his head and tried to ignore her disappointment.

"I love you, Michael." Emily touched her lips to his and a familiar magic sparked inside him.

"I love you, too, Emily," he breathed. There was no trouble being sincere about that. "I love you more than you can possibly imagine."

She shook her head and smiled. For a moment her sadness was not apparent. "I think I could probably imagine it." She kissed him again, and while they made love it was easy for Michael to forget that his deepest fear was the prospect of not sharing this with her forever.

Just before Michael drifted to sleep in her arms, he heard Emily whisper near his ear, "Isn't marriage incredible?"

Michael kissed her in agreement, and it seemed only moments later that he saw Emily standing at the edge of a cliff in the distance. She was wearing the gown she had married him in— his great-grandmother's wedding gown. Though the sky above was blue, a fierce wind pressed the dress to her legs, and he saw her waver at the edge of the rocks.

Michael's heart pounded violently with the realization that her life was in danger. He ran toward her, calling her name, begging her not to stand so close to the edge. She paid no attention to him until he came within a few feet of her. Eagerly she smiled and reached her arms toward him. But Michael hesitated, moving slowly and carefully. Her feet were so close to the edge, he feared she might topple over if he even breathed too hard.

Michael sighed with relief as he reached out for her hand. But before he could take hold of her, the force of his effort seemed to push her further away. In an instant she was gone. Michael tried to catch her, but all he caught was an armful of emptiness while her cry of fear echoed across the canyon. And he could see her white-clad figure plummeting toward the bottom of the ravine below.

"No!" Michael cried and sat up with a start. In the surrounding darkness, he felt sweat beading over his face and chest. His fists clenched handfuls of bed sheets, and Emily's hands came against his face.

"What is it?" she pleaded urgently. "Are you all right, Michael?"

"Emily!" He took hold of her as if his heart might stop beating without her.

"You were dreaming," she whispered. "It's all right."

"Emily." He breathed deeply and tried to steady the pace of his heart. Emily held him close and brushed her lips over his brow. Michael tried to convince himself that the fear he felt in his dream wasn't real, but he knew it was.

"Tell me," Emily urged.

Michael shook his head. "I don't want to talk about it."

Emily sighed and held him closer. "Michael," she said, "I know something's eating at you. Why won't you—"

"I said I don't want to talk about it." He lay back down and willed his heart to be calm.

"Why not?" Her voice remained compassionate.

"Maybe if I don't talk about it, it will go away," he said lightly, almost flippantly.

"You don't believe that any more than I do."

"No," he admitted, "but it's the best excuse I can come up with."

"Michael," Emily leaned over his chest in the darkness, wishing she could see his expression, "sometimes I feel like we're strangers. I don't understand it, but I don't want it to be this way. We've been through too much; we've come too far to let something come between us now."

"It has nothing to do with you, Emily. The problem is with me."

"If it has nothing to do with me, then why am I suffering for it?"

Michael turned his head to the side quickly. "I'm sorry, Emily, I just . . ."

"Talk to me, Michael," she pleaded, hating the memories being stirred from these feelings. He said nothing. In the dark she could almost believe it was another time, another husband. How many nights had she begged Ryan to just talk to her, only to be rebuffed again and again?

Emily took a deep breath and reminded herself that this was not Ryan. She reached over and turned on the bedside lamp so she could see Michael's face. Trying to approach this logically, she questioned him with care. "Is it the pregnancy that's bothering you?"

Emily didn't like the way he hesitated, until he answered firmly, "I want this baby, Emily."

"But you're afraid it will kill me," she guessed with a degree of certainty.

He admitted sullenly, "I just can't bear the thought of living without you, Emily. It's as simple as that."

"Then simply plug your brain into some faith and think of what we've been promised. I will live to see my children into adulthood, Michael. Those words came from the Lord, and you know it as well as I do."

"Yes, I know," Michael admitted.

"Then what is it, Michael?"

Michael wanted to tell her. He could feel the words forming in his mouth, but before they could evolve he shook his head and turned away. "Be patient with me, Emily," he finally muttered. "I know I'm not being fair, but don't give up on me."

Emily sighed and tried to bury her frustration. "I could never give up on you, Michael."

She reached over him to turn out the light, then settled her head against his shoulder and tried to sleep. In an effort to be positive, she concentrated on a picture in her mind of holding this baby in her arms and proving to Michael that she had survived it. It was a day she longed for, and in the meantime she would just have to study hard and try to keep her grades up. It seemed there was little else to be done.

Sean's mission call arrived on an extremely cold day. He called to tell Michael it had come, but he wanted everyone to be together when he opened it. With Emily's help, Michael prepared a celebration dinner. Sean and Melissa arrived together, as excited as a couple of children out trick-or-treating. Before dinner the entire family, minus Allison, who was with friends, gathered in the living room to watch Sean open the envelope. Melissa made a noise like a drum roll, and Sean chuckled as he pulled out the letter and unfolded it. He scanned the page quickly, then his face became somber.

"Is something wrong?" Michael asked.

Sean shook his head slowly, his eyes never leaving the page in his hand. He finally looked up, first at Michael and Emily, then at Melissa.

"What is it?" Melissa asked and squeezed his hand with concern.

Sean chuckled tensely and looked back at the letter. "Nothing's wrong. It's just . . . well, it's the last thing I expected."

"What?" Michael asked. "Do we have to choke it out of you?"

Sean looked up to meet Michael's eyes. "I'm going to the Ireland, Dublin mission."

Following the eruption of excitement, they ate dinner and

talked quietly of what this meant. Sean's Irish background was something he'd never thought too deeply about. The fact that his Ireland-born parents had disowned him was certainly a sore point. But he said over and over how much it meant to him to serve his mission in the land of his heritage. They made plans and discussed the things he would need. Melissa's love for Sean glowed in the support and encouragement she gave him. There was no reason to think she wouldn't wait for him. They seemed so right for each other. But Michael couldn't resist teasing her. "So, Melissa, do you really think you can hold off for two years? That's a long time."

"He's worth it." Melissa smiled and Sean hugged her tightly.

"And one day," Sean added, looking into Melissa's eyes, "we'll have a house full of kids and be as happy as Michael and Emily."

Emily met Michael's eyes and had to admit it. In spite of the struggles, she really was happy. Michael pressed a soft kiss to her mouth as if to say that he agreed. They truly were blessed.

CHAPTER EIGHT

Michael turned off the computer and stretched. He glanced at the clock. 12:40 a.m. He must have been doing well to have time pass that quickly. He turned off the light and hurried upstairs, expecting to find it dark and Emily gone to bed. Instead, she was pacing the floor in the living room.

"Allison must be late," Michael said, startling her.

"She said she'd be home by eleven. This is not like her. I've never seen her more than ten or fifteen minutes late, especially when she's got early classes tomorrow."

"I'm sure she's fine," Michael said, putting his arms around her. "But if she's not home soon, I'll go look for her."

Emily sighed and Michael kissed her. "I could take your mind off of it," he smirked and urged her closer. "The best way to bring the children around is to get in the middle of something private, and *poof!* they show up."

Emily chuckled and glanced away. "I appreciate the thought, but I don't think this is the right time. How's the book coming?" she asked to distract herself.

"Rather well, actually. I think you'll like what I did to the hero."

"Tell me," she urged, and they sat close together on the couch while he talked about the points of his latest novel. At ten after one, Emily sat up straight and insisted, "Where could she be? If she does come home, I'm going to strangle her."

"I'll take care of the strangling," Michael said tersely. He walked into the kitchen and took the keys to the Blazer off the rack. He was about to put his coat on when they heard the car pull into the driveway.

"You talk to her," Emily said. "The way I feel right now, I'll slap her silly."

Michael leaned casually against the stair rail where she could see him when she came into the split entry and looked up.

"Oh, hi, Dad," she said, locking the door behind her. "What are you doing up so late?" It was subtle, but Michael noticed she had a little difficulty standing up straight while she took her arms out of her coat.

"You're over two hours late, love."

"Two hours?" She glanced at her watch. "No, I told Mom I'd be home at one."

"It was eleven," Michael insisted. "And you and I both know your mother doesn't have a hearing problem."

"Tell her I'm sorry." She grinned and hurried downstairs, calling softly, "G'night, Dad."

"What is wrong with her?" Emily whispered to Michael from the shadows of the hall. "She acts like she doesn't even care."

"I'll be back in a minute," Michael said and hurried down the stairs. He knocked lightly on Allison's door.

"Who is it?"

"It's me."

"Just a minute," she called. He could tell she was hurrying, rather noisily, to do something. "I'm not dressed." She opened the door fully clothed, including shoes.

"You forgot to give your old dad a hug," he said casually.

Allison turned her face to the side and reached her arms around his neck. "Tell Mom I'm sorry for worrying her," she said almost sincerely, but Michael had sick knots in his stomach.

"Good night," he said and closed the door behind him.

He found Emily sitting on the edge of the bed. "Is she all right?"

"You'd better sit down," he said.

"I am sitting down."

"Just a figure of speech."

"What?" she insisted when he hesitated.

"She's been drinking, Emily."

For a moment Emily couldn't breathe. She gaped at Michael in disbelief as he told her the evidence. "I went down to give her a hug. She tried to turn her face away, but I could smell it on her breath. After spending forty years with a bunch of stable hands, there's no mistaking that distinct aroma."

"What are we going to do?" she asked, then bit her lip to stop its quivering.

"We'd better think about that a little, but to start with, we're getting her up at the usual time, and she's going to classes. Maybe the consequences of a hangover will help a little."

"I just can't believe it, Michael. What would make her do something like that?"

"I don't know." Michael took her hand. "Perhaps she's just been given too much freedom after living such a structured life. But somewhere she's made a bad decision. Heaven only knows why. From what I've observed with others, I'm not sure things like this will ever make sense to parents. We've just got to find a way to help her."

Emily hardly slept at all, plagued with worry for her daughter. She thought of Allison's quiet timidity as a child, and the difficulty she'd experienced losing her father at the age of nine. But she had blossomed following their move to Australia, and Michael had been a good father to her. She'd always seemed so strong and well-adjusted. Emily thought of Allison's riding accident and the way it had affected her. She'd never seemed quite as focused in her goals since then. But she'd always been a good girl. Emily had never entertained the possibility of Allison going astray. But she had. Why? Was there one incident in Allison's life that had eventually spurred this rebellion? Or was it a combination?

Emily thought about it until her head ached, but she came to the conclusion Michael had already stated. It would likely never make sense. They just had to find a way to help her. If only they could.

The following morning, Michael dragged Allison out of bed at 6:30. She moaned about feeling sick and rushed to the bathroom to throw up.

"I think I've got the flu," she insisted, holding her head and her stomach.

"I doubt it's catching," he retorted, but the statement seemed lost on her. "You get to classes, young lady. If you're going to stay out late, you're going to pay the consequences. If you miss your classes without good cause, I will have that car confiscated so quick you won't even see a flash of red when it disappears."

Allison glared at him and went to her room to get dressed.

Emily watched with dismay as Michael urged Allison up the stairs with his hand over her elbow. "You'd better hurry," he said, "or you'll be late. You can rest this afternoon."

Allison looked up at her mother. "Mom, will you tell him I'm sick?"

"Take two aspirin and we'll see you this afternoon," Emily said. Allison huffed out of the house and slammed the door.

"Poor baby," Michael said with sarcasm.

"I'm just grateful you're here to handle this, Michael. I would be lost."

Michael pulled her into his arms and kissed her. "Good morning, Mrs. Hamilton."

"Good morning," she smiled.

"You don't have classes today, do you?"

"No, I don't."

"How long before the kids wake up?" he asked and kissed her again. Emily leaned into him and slid her hands into his hair. James cried in the distance and they reluctantly pulled away from each other.

"Does that answer your question?"

As soon as the other children were off to school and James was set in front of Sesame Street, Michael took Emily by the hand. "Come on," he said, leading her from the family room toward Allison's bedroom.

"What are we doing?"

He pushed open the door and looked with disdain at the slightly messy room. "We're looking for evidence," he stated.

"Michael, we can't just . . . search her things. That's like . . . invading her privacy."

"You can look at it that way if you want," he said. "But the way I see it, if we don't have any evidence, we don't have a case. If we don't have a case, we can't solve the problem."

Emily sighed, seeing his point but wishing she didn't. "Okay, you take the drawers, I'll start under the bed."

Emily pulled out shoes and books and a couple of boxes that she rummaged through carefully. "What are we looking for?" she asked.

"Anything she shouldn't have," he reported, searching carefully through her drawers, doing his best not to leave the contents looking disturbed.

Emily lay on her side to reach under the bed as far as she could. Her hand caught hold of something foreign. She pulled it out, then groaned as she rose to her knees. Michael turned to see three cans of beer held together with the plastic rings that once held a six-pack.

"I don't believe it," Emily said dryly.

"Maybe she uses it to rinse her hair," Michael said lightly, but Emily glared at him. "Just an old joke," he added.

"Yes, I know."

While they continued their search, Emily began praying they'd find nothing more. She didn't want to discover that her daughter was doing things she shouldn't. But she knew Michael was right. If Allison was getting into trouble, they needed to get all the clues they possibly could.

Michael felt almost guilty for rummaging through Allison's underclothes until he pulled them back to see the bottle lying in the bottom of the drawer. "I didn't think it was beer I could smell last night," he said. Emily turned to see him pull out a partially empty bottle of Scotch whiskey.

"Oh, Michael." She sat down hard on the floor and tears welled up. Michael took off the lid and smelled it, then winced. He silently pointed out the mauve-colored lip gloss around the rim of the bottle. Emily sighed and returned to her search of the closet; Michael finished the drawers, then threw back the bedding on the bed.

"What are you doing?" she asked in surprise.

Michael lifted the mattress, expecting to see nothing. He had done it to be funny, since they always did it in the movies. What he saw made his heart sink. He picked up the little plastic bag and dropped the mattress back into place.

"What is it?" Emily asked with a squeaky voice. Then James started to cry. Emily ran to check on him while Michael sat on the edge of the bed, feeling stunned. He opened the bag to smell its contents, and the evidence was undeniable. Emily returned and repeated insistently, "What is it?"

Michael held up the bag by one corner as if it were contaminated. "This, my love, is a hand-rolled joint."

"A what?"

"It's marijuana, Emily."

"No." Emily's eyes became a little more sallow. "Just because it's there, doesn't mean she's using it."

"We can hope," he said, tossing it on the floor with the beer and the whiskey. James started to cry again, and Emily went to see what was wrong while Michael straightened the bed and looked around to see if they'd checked everywhere.

"Did you do the closet shelf?" he called to Emily.

"No," she called back. Michael stood on Allison's desk chair and carefully checked everything there. He was relieved to find nothing out of the ordinary. At this rate, he feared finding a hypodermic needle and cocaine. He checked the pockets of her clothes hanging in the closet, then turned to itemize the room. They'd checked everything but the desk. Michael opened the middle drawer and found the typical office supplies. He opened an envelope and found an odd array of photographs that he stopped to admire. He chuckled from the warm memories they evoked, then prompted himself back to his purpose. He could hear Emily upstairs, putting James in his high-chair. Was it lunchtime already? He had to hurry. Allison could come home any time, especially if she left classes early due to her "illness."

Michael checked the other drawers, relieved to find nothing. He was about to close the last one when he noticed a small box that looked out of place. When he pulled it out, his heart skipped a beat. It was the last thing he'd expected to see. What they'd found already was hard to take, but entertaining thoughts of alcohol and drug rehabilitation had made him feel hope that they could be undone. But this? A knot formed in his stomach that made him want to throw up. He didn't even want to show it to Emily, but she had to know. He sat on the edge of the bed and rested his elbows on his thighs while he turned it over in his hands as if he'd never seen anything like it before. The truth was, he saw things like this all the time, but in *his* drawer, not hers. The thought of his beautiful daughter being—

"Michael." Emily's voice startled him and he looked up. "Did you finish?" He nodded. "You found something else?" He nodded again and held it out for her. Emily hesitantly stepped toward him and grasped the little box. He saw her turn pale and stood up to put his arms around her, fearing she might actually pass out. She clung to him and cried while the box of condoms slipped out of her hand and fell to the floor.

"There are three missing," he reported softly, and she cried harder.

"Michael," she sobbed, "I don't even know what to do. I don't know how to handle this. How could she be so stupid, to be doing these things to herself?"

"I don't know," he muttered and kissed her brow. Trying to be objective, he added, "Maybe they aren't hers. Maybe a friend stashed them there." Emily looked up at him with a vague hope in her eyes, but it seemed futile.

"Now what?" Emily wiped her hands over her face and attempted to gain control.

"We have to ask her."

"I can't do it, Michael. I'll fall apart."

"I'll take care of it," he said reluctantly, "but I want you with me. Just in case I start beating her, you can hit me over the head with Jess's baseball bat."

Emily tried to laugh. "You've never laid a hand on her."

"There's always a first time," he said too soberly.

Michael carried the evidence upstairs and stuffed it under the edge of his bed. He cleaned up the mess James had made of his lunch, then put him down for his nap. Emily sat at her easel, attempting to paint, but she only stared out the window. Michael was just contemplating what comfort he might give her when they heard the car pull in.

"Do we have to do this now?" Emily asked, forlorn.

"It would be better to do it while the others are at school, I think," he said.

"Feeling better?" Michael asked when Allison came through the front door.

"A little," she stated.

"Before you go back to bed," he said, knowing well that she would, "I'd like to talk to you for a few minutes."

Allison gave him a *do I have to?* look, then sulked toward her parents' bedroom, where she knew the serious talks always took place. Michael pointed to the chair by Emily's dressing table, where she sat with a dutiful sigh. Emily appeared in the doorway, where she leaned and folded her arms. Michael sat on the edge of the bed and reached under for the first piece of evidence. Allison's eyes widened subtly, but she said nothing as he dangled the cans of beer in front of her.

"Your mother found these under your bed," he stated.

Allison briefly looked shocked, then Michael was tempted to give her an honorary Academy Award for acting when she turned to Emily with complete innocence. Emily nodded to indicate it was true. Allison's expression turned quickly to self-righteous anger. "Mom? I can't believe you would snoop in my room like that!" Her tone was accusing and belligerent.

"I can't believe it either," Michael agreed calmly, and Allison had to stare at him a moment. "I can't believe your mother would have the nerve to look under your bed."

When his sarcasm became evident, Allison turned back to Emily with a firm, "How dare you invade my privacy by—"

Michael grabbed Allison's arm and forced her to look at him. "How dare *you*," he said through clenched teeth, "bring this kind of crap into my home?"

Allison's face returned to innocence. "I just use it to rinse my hair," she stated as if they might never have heard such a thing before. Michael and Emily exchanged a glance of disgust. "It really works good, Mom. You should try it."

Michael let go of Allison's arm to pull out the next item of discussion. "And do you use this to brush your teeth?"

Allison looked momentarily stunned. "It's not mine," she said bluntly. "One of my friends must have left it in my room or—"

"Who said it was in your room?" Michael interrupted and she

sighed in disgust. "At the bottom of one of your drawers, to be exact. The interesting thing is that it smells a lot like the mouthwash you were using last night." He opened the bottle slowly, then pointed to the lip gloss around the rim. "Isn't that pretty close to your color?"

Allison turned to Emily as if she might rescue her, but she was only confronted with a firm, "I think we'd like the truth, Allie."

"Okay," she said flippantly, "so I tried a little. What's the big deal?"

"What's the big deal?" Emily echoed in a raised pitch.

Michael held up a hand to stop her. "Allison," he said and she reluctantly met his eyes, "first beer, then whiskey. What next?"

"Nothing!"

"This, maybe?" Michael pulled out the joint, and Allison's eyes nearly bulged out of her head. "Boy, when you do a search, you're very thorough," she said indignantly. "I forgot that was even there."

"Where was it?"

"I don't even remember." Her voice turned genuine for the first time since she'd come home. "You've got to believe me, Dad. I've never used that stuff. Somebody gave it to me to try, but I didn't want to. I haven't touched it."

Emily's subtle nod told him she agreed. They knew she was telling the truth. "If you didn't want it, why didn't you get rid of it?"

"I don't know," she said sincerely, "I just—"

"Maybe keep it around in case you get really down," he speculated in a voice like the devil. "Try it with a little booze. See if that helps the effect." His voice returned to normal. "Pretty dangerous little keepsake, don't you think?"

Allison said nothing. Michael tossed the little bag to Emily. "Get rid of that, please."

She left for just a moment, and they could hear the toilet flushing. When she returned, Michael met her eyes, hoping to gain some courage. The worst was yet to come. Wanting to postpone it a little, Michael held out his hand and wiggled his fingers. Allison looked puzzled.

"The keys," he insisted. Her mouth opened to protest, but no words came. "You broke the rules. I get the car back. That was the deal."

"But I won't do it again," she insisted. "I got a little carried away. I'll be more careful, I promise."

"Yes, you will," Michael said. "And you'll also get a ride with me or your mother, or you'll take the bus. Your curfew is ten o'clock on week nights, midnight on weekends, and I want to know where you are and who you're with."

"I'm nineteen years old!" she shouted.

"And obviously not mature enough to keep your own life in line." Michael's voice raised in return. Emily closed the door to keep from waking James. "Now, give me the keys, or we'll see which one of us is stronger."

Allison handed them over, saying snidely, "I can't believe you'd do this to me. One little mistake, and you'd think I committed a felony."

Allison made a groan of frustration and attempted to stand up, but Michael took her arm and urged her back to the chair.

"Now what?" she snapped.

Michael pulled out the little box and held it in front of her face. He was hoping she'd deny it the way she'd denied the joint. He was hoping she'd tell them it was ridiculous to think she'd do anything so stupid. But the guilt welled up in her eyes so fast there was no hiding it. Emily put a hand over her mouth to keep from crying out. Michael swallowed hard in order to keep his voice steady. "There are three missing."

Allison glanced at Emily, then her eyes quickly went to the floor when she saw only anguish. She made no response at all, and Michael wanted to shake some sense into her. When he couldn't stand the silence any more, he took hold of her shoulders and did just that. At the gentle jolt, Allison looked up at him.

"What do you want me to say, Allison? I'm proud of you for taking the responsibility to avoid getting pregnant? Thank you for being conscientious enough to protect yourself from getting AIDS? Should we be pleased about this?"

Michael could see that her mind was working quickly for a defense. He felt certain she couldn't find one, but he underestimated her resourcefulness. "You have no right to say things like that to me," she said. Michael expected a speech about her age and her independence, but she slapped him in the face with a vindictive, "You are *not* my father."

Allison shook free of his grasp and hurried out of the room. Michael was so stunned that it took a full minute before he found the will to even look up at Emily. She saw the torment in his eyes and her heart sank.

"I almost forgot," he muttered breathily. "I had honestly begun to believe she was mine. I wanted to forget that another man fathered her." He pushed his hands through his hair and tugged at it almost brutally. His voice broke with anguish. "But I've only been there for half of her life."

An unreasonable pain rushed up and hit Michael between the eyes, tying every fear in his life together in one convenient knot. His family was everything to him, but in eternity he had to accept the fact that they were not his. Emily was sealed to another man, and all of her children, even this baby he couldn't help begrudging, belonged to a man long dead. Michael tried to swallow the hurt and think of Allison's welfare. He couldn't let his own emotions keep him from dealing with what was obviously a very big problem. If he let her go now, the subject would be dropped as if it meant nothing.

Michael tried to convince himself that his own fear and pain were put on hold as he rushed down the stairs and threw open her bedroom door without knocking. But deep inside, he knew he was kidding himself.

"What?" Allison shrieked.

"Come on, love." He took her arm firmly. "We're going for a little ride."

"But I don't want to."

"It may be the last time you get to sit in this precious car of yours, so you'd best enjoy it."

Emily felt afraid as she watched Michael almost force Allison outside and into the car. He squealed out of the driveway as if the devil were on his tail, then she wondered if perhaps he was.

"Where are we going?" Allison asked, her hands planted firmly on the seat beside her thighs.

"Just a little drive," he said tersely. Michael pulled a cassette out of his jacket pocket and shoved it into the stereo. He turned it up unbearably loud and headed up 800 North toward Provo Canyon. He'd barely rounded the curve into the canyon when he shifted gears and pushed the accelerator to the floor.

"Michael!" Allison shrieked, but he pretended not to hear her. How dare she call him that now? After nearly a decade of being her father, he was suddenly Michael again.

"You're going to kill us," she screamed as he swerved around one sharp turn after another. "If you want to commit suicide, fine, but leave me out of it!"

Michael continued to ignore her while he drove just as fast as he could possibly manage. A lack of traffic made it easy to fly through the canyon, and he found a degree of satisfaction in Allison's fear. Maybe it would scare the hell out of her.

"Dad!" she screamed without thinking. "You're doing almost ninety. Get real!" Still he ignored her, liking the way the speed and the loud music muffled his own pain.

When they were nearly out of the canyon, Michael pulled onto a gravel turnout and slammed on the brakes. The car spun 180 degrees before it stopped.

"Are you *crazy*?" Allison snapped.

Michael turned off the ignition and the music stopped. "Maybe I am," he said coolly. "But what do you care? I'm just out to have a good time. I just wanted to see if I could do it. Look how awesome I am. I just survived a canyon at eighty-seven miles an hour, and you were here to share the thrill."

"I wasn't thrilled," she insisted skeptically.

"Well, I wasn't thrilled to see you drunk last night."

Allison turned to look out the window. "I wasn't drunk."

"Excuse me. You were only slightly tipsy. While you're out there playing with life at a hundred miles an hour, the people who love you are terrified that you're going to crash and burn. And don't you dare try to tell me you're not hurting anyone but yourself. If you could have seen your mother today when she realized what you've been doing . . . *you* should have been the one holding her while she cried, Allison. But you weren't, so I had to see it. I had to feel it, and I'm not even *your* father. Excuse me for invading your sweet life, Allison. I tried not to mold you into a spoiled little rich brat, but maybe I failed. Perhaps you would have preferred that I'd left you and your mother and sisters to live the life *your* father left to you. Now you've got an ultimatum, young lady. Either you straighten your life out, or you may live elsewhere. I will not tolerate or condone what you are doing."

"Maybe I should move out," she said harshly. "It's obvious we're not seeing eye to eye on this. Mom obviously loves you, but maybe it's time I moved on."

"You're nineteen, and so blasted independent. I guess that's up to you, but know this. You walk out of my door, and don't expect any help from me."

Allison turned with shock in her expression.

"Oh," he chuckled cynically, "I'm not *your* father, but if I take away the money, you sure as hell notice."

"I don't know why you're being so cruel to me," she snapped.

"You started this cruelty bit, babe, so don't throw your guilt onto me. Maybe you should leave, Allison. Get a job, find an apartment. Just try life in the fast lane and see if you can steer any better than I just did. But remember this, I can drive that fast because I've been driving for nearly thirty years. I've seen a lot of this world, and I'm not impressed. You stake out on your own, and I can guarantee you're not going to like it. Just remember, you get nothing from me as long as you're determined to live this way. If you were making every effort to do what's right and seek out a good life, I'd do all I could to help. But it'll be a cold day in the outback before I support your bad habits."

Allison said nothing, and Michael didn't know what else to say. He'd probably already said too much. He turned the car on and Allison took hold of her seat fearfully. But he drove the speed limit and they arrived safely home. Allison went to open the door, but he grabbed her arm. "If you stop drinking and keep your curfew, you can have the car back. And if you love this . . . guy you're sleeping with, then bring him over for dinner and let's do this right."

Allison jerked her arm out of his grasp and ran inside.

"Are you all right?" Emily asked when she walked in the kitchen.

"Barely," she growled, burying her head in the fridge. "Your husband just tried to kill me."

Emily looked dubious until Michael walked in the kitchen. "I was just trying to show her what it's like to drive recklessly through life."

"He drove ninety up the canyon," Allison tattled like a child.

"Michael!" Emily gasped.

"It was eighty-seven."

"He scared me to death," Allison persisted, attempting to get her mother's sympathy. Michael could see she was trying to come between them, and it made him angry. It was the last thing he and Emily needed.

"That makes us even," he said to Allison and walked out of the room.

Emily found Michael writing, wearing headphones. She pulled them off his ears and put them briefly on her own. The volume made her wince. "You know, Michael, even *Icehouse* could make you go deaf if you have it too loud."

"What was that, I can't hear you," he said. Emily looked at him in disgust and he laughed flippantly. He returned to his writing vigorously, as if it might avoid any confrontation.

"Michael," she said, but he kept typing. She put her hands over his and he stopped. "I think we need to talk."

"About what?" he turned in his chair to face her, feigning innocence.

"Don't you think you could have made your point a little less . . . dangerously?"

"No," he answered, pulling off his glasses and nibbling on the earpiece.

"This is not Australia. You can't drive your frustrations out like that and get away with it." When he said nothing, Emily narrowed her eyes and tried futilely to figure where he was coming from. "I just do not understand you these days, Michael."

"That makes two of us," he said without looking at her.

"Well, I have something to say that I have to say."

"So get it over with." He looked up at her like a defiant child.

"I can't believe you would purposely do something so foolish. You could have been killed. And where would that have left me?

Don't you dare think you can go out and do things like that with the possibility of leaving me alone to raise these children and live with your memory."

Michael absorbed it. "Are you finished?"

"Yes."

"Good, because I have something to say that I have to say." He paused and she nodded hesitantly, indicating that he should go on. But she wasn't prepared for the intense bitterness in his voice. "I can't believe you would knowingly pray to get pregnant—something you knew would risk your life, with the possibility of leaving me alone to raise these children and live with your memory."

CHAPTER NINE

Emily was so hurt she couldn't respond. She couldn't even find the will to walk away. Several minutes after Michael turned around to continue writing, she finally managed to go upstairs. She found Allison sprawled on her bed, looking dismayed.

"Did you want to talk about something?" Emily asked, trying to distract herself from her own pain.

"Not really," Allison said, but it was the first time in weeks she'd come into Emily's room this way.

"Do you mind if I ask you some questions?" Emily said, thinking she might not get another chance.

"Go ahead, but I might not answer them."

Emily cleared her throat. "Are you in love, Allison?"

Allison looked up at her mother and answered honestly. "Not really."

Emily squeezed her eyes shut. "Are you sleeping with someone, then?"

"Yes."

"Has there been more than one guy?"

"No."

"Why, Allison?" Emily pleaded, trying not to get emotional.

"I don't know," she said as if she'd been insulted. "But honestly, I just don't think it's as big a deal as you make it out to be. Ashley's been doing it for years."

"Allison! Is that what started all of this?"

"I have my own brain, Mom. Ashley didn't tell me what to do with my life. You can't blame her."

"Do her parents know?" Emily asked, sitting on the bed beside her daughter.

"I don't think they have a clue," Allison said as if it were sad. "And she even had a miscarriage last year."

Emily grimaced. "Allison, I don't want you to get defensive. I appreciate you being honest with me, but I have to ask you: Do you realize what you're toying with? Do you have any comprehension of the kind of misery that will come into your life from living this way?"

"I've gone to church all my life, Mom. I've listened to what they have to say. Now don't go and cry on me, but I'm not so sure I believe all of that. I mean . . . look at you. I've seen you go through one rotten thing after another for the sake of living . . . *religion*. I'm just not sure it's worth it."

"My life hasn't been easy, Allison, but I have a great deal of peace within me."

"Well, that's okay for you, but not for me."

Emily had to consciously will the tears not to surface, knowing they would only make the situation worse.

"I told Michael that maybe I should move out."

"What did he say?" Emily asked in panic.

"He said that would be fine, but he wouldn't give me any money. I suppose you'll stand by him on that."

"I'm not sure what his reasons are, but I don't think it would be right to support you if you're going to live in a way that we feel is self-destructive."

"That's basically what he said," she muttered in dismay.

"Are you going to leave?" Emily asked, unable to conceal the anguish in her voice.

"I don't know, maybe. I'm a woman now. I ought to be able to make my own decisions. But it's obvious I can't do that as long as I'm living here."

Emily thought frantically of something to say as she felt her daughter slipping irretrievably away. "Allison, I want you to stop and think about the future. Look years ahead and see if this is what you want for yourself. Don't you want to find someone to love and live a good life with—"

"Oh, come on, Mom. There's no such thing as happily ever

after. Your first marriage stunk, and it's easy to see that you and Michael are not happy."

Emily wished she could explain that things were not as they appeared. The tension between her and Michael did not take away the fact that they loved each other very much. Despite their opposing views on this one issue, Emily felt warmth in realizing how his love for her was made evident by so many other things. She realized she should stop more often and remind herself of that. With fresh confidence, she turned to Allison and said, "You're wrong. And maybe one day, when you discover whatever it is you're looking for, you'll realize what real love is all about."

"You really love him, don't you?" Allison asked, as if it was impossible to believe.

"I really do. He has blessed our lives more than you will ever realize."

"Well, he hasn't blessed my life today." Allison stood up and moved toward the door. She hesitated long enough to say, "I'm sorry if I'm a disappointment to you, Mom. I've just got to be me."

Once alone, Emily collapsed on the bed, letting the full anguish of the situation take hold. She cried helplessly into her pillow until a warm hand on her shoulder startled her.

"Michael," she cried as his arms came around her. She held to him desperately and felt strength from his embrace. It was true. He *did* love her. And she loved him. In an effort to forget the present, she urged his lips to hers and let his kiss carry her from the pain and the fears to a higher sphere of life. The world fell away at his touch, and she lost herself in a passion as familiar to her as the sun rising in the east. Even the struggles between them gained a fresh perspective. Though it might take time, Emily knew in her heart that, somehow, everything between them would be all right. If only she could believe the same about Allison.

* * * * *

That night Michael had the same dream. Four times now it had invaded his sleep. His effort to save Emily from falling always pushed her over the cliff, and he'd wake up sweating from the fear. A part of him wanted to share it with Emily. She'd always had a gift for analyzing dreams. But the truth was, he didn't want to know what it meant, and he didn't want to talk about it. So, he did his best to shove it down deeper with the rest of his fear and forget about it.

Through the next several days, Allison grumbled about not being able to take the car, but she came home on time and purposely breathed in Michael's face to prove that she hadn't been drinking. Though she made a point of calling him Michael rather than Dad, he and Emily were both hopeful that the problem had been nipped in the bud and everything would be all right.

The following Sunday, Emily was sustained as second counselor in the Primary, and Michael realized he'd be going to Sunday School alone. He took James to the nursery and ambled into the Gospel Doctrine class with little enthusiasm, especially when he realized it was a substitute teacher. As the lesson commenced, he could see that the teacher was well rehearsed in the scriptures and basic doctrine. But he was practically a newlywed, almost fresh off his mission, and it was evident he had little experience in real life. There was a lack of spiritual maturity, perhaps, and his concepts were a bit too idealistic for Michael.

Michael quietly listened to the discussion, accepting that this man was giving a good lesson, and as a person he would eventually reach his own spiritual potential. The concept went awry when the teacher announced, "Now I'd like to move on to the second portion of this lesson, which is temple sealings."

Michael literally slid down in his chair and folded his arms. His mind retorted with a sarcastic, *Go ahead. Make my day.*

While the teacher prompted the reading of scriptures and quotes concerning the importance of families being sealed, Michael's mind echoed with Allison's firm declaration: "You are *not* my father." When he managed to force that out of his head, he could hear the branch president who had married him and Emily, saying with finality, *for the period of your mortal lives.* He thought of kneeling at temple altars with Emily to do countless sealings, none of them his. The fact was hard. She was sealed to Ryan Hall, and all of her children had been born under that covenant. His own children, his own flesh and blood, were sealed to a man who Michael was beginning to resent more and more. When he'd married Emily, he'd had the faith that everything would work out. But these days, such faith was hard to come by. Nearly losing Emily hadn't helped any. The thought of spending any portion of his life without her was unbearable. To think of not being with her on the other side was worse. He simply couldn't deal with it.

Michael's mind became more tuned to the lesson as it started to make him uncomfortable. This man, for all his good intentions, was telling these people that if they were faithful, they would find opportunity in this life to be sealed to their loved ones. He admonished them to take care of it and see that it was done. Michael realized he was mostly speaking to those who might be procrastinating going to the temple when they should, and that was fine. But he was giving a definite impression that everything should be neatly summed up here and now, in this life. He even told the story of a woman who had married in the temple, then the marriage ran into trouble. She had been concerned about the sealing, but it was canceled after a divorce and she was able to be sealed to a man she met later in life. He said firmly that if it was not bound on earth, it would not be bound in heaven. And he said it as if there were no exceptions.

Michael's heart started to pound in a way he recognized from experience. It was the Spirit prompting him to speak. But he didn't want to speak. He didn't want to embarrass this guy, which he knew he would if he said what he was thinking. He didn't want to turn the class into a debate session, and he certainly didn't want to verbalize what caused him so much anguish. On the other hand, it wasn't right for these people to believe it was so black and white. Maybe someone in the room needed to hear what Michael had to say.

While he was contemplating this, the teacher said, "Let's talk for a minute about the blessings of the temple. Brother Hamilton," he said and Michael's head shot up, "you have a beautiful family, and I know you attend the temple regularly with your wife. Could you tell us your feelings on the blessings that come from the opportunities you've had there?"

If Michael acted on his impulses, he'd have hit the guy. Instead, he straightened in his chair and cleared his throat. "I'd like to say that

I don't think the issue we're discussing is as cut and dried as it seems to be."

The teacher chuckled uncomfortably. "Maybe you should clarify that, Brother Hamilton."

"Isn't it possible that on the terms of faith, what is not bound on earth *will* have a chance to be bound in heaven?"

"It says in the scriptures, which we have already quoted, that—"

"I know what the scriptures say, and I don't mean to be impertinent here or detract from the lesson, but I'm having a problem with this."

"I don't understand," the teacher replied, obviously attempting to conceal his frustration.

"Then perhaps I should explain." Michael glanced at the clock, relieved that they still had some time left. He hesitated, trying to be rid of his ill feelings so he wouldn't speak out of line. The words came to him and he felt grateful. "We often hear that there is the letter of the law, and the spirit of the law. I've always been more of a spirit of the law kind of person. While I served as branch president in Australia, I saw many circumstances that taught me this gospel is not always black and white. There is often an exception to a rule. Those exceptions are the true test of faith in this life."

"But surely if—" the teacher began, but Michael held up a hand to stop him.

"Before you feel you have to defend yourself, I would like to tell you a little a story to illustrate my point." The teacher nodded, and the class remained in hushed silence. Michael bet they couldn't wait to get out of here and spread the news about how Brother Hamilton disrupted the class and shed his own light on the gospel today. He glanced around, relieved that he didn't recognize anyone in this room who would have known Emily when she was married to Ryan.

"I knew a girl at BYU who fell in love with a nonmember. They planned to get married, but circumstances led her to marry a member instead. She followed the guidance of the Spirit and knew she was doing what the Lord wanted her to do. She married in the temple and her marriage turned bad, but she was faithful and diligent and she helped get him on the right path. After ten years of marriage, he was killed and left behind three children. Then this college sweetheart came back into her life. He hadn't married and he still hadn't joined the Church, but at that time he came to his senses and was baptized. They were married and had two more children. Now tell me, Brother Morgan, who is that man sealed to?"

There was no response but a blank look.

"He might have been a little stubborn, but the facts are that he never drank, he never smoked, he never committed immoral acts. He was raised on the Bible and tried to live its teachings. He joined the Church and has been a faithful member. But the fact remains, his wife is sealed to her first husband, who was not necessarily a good husband, but then he wasn't awful either. Perhaps he's proving himself on the other side and waiting for her to come back to him and continue what was bound on earth. This woman's children, including the two from her second marriage, are sealed to her and her first husband. So where does the black and white of what you're telling me fit in with that? You just said that if a person was faithful, everything would work out, and what is bound on earth will be bound in heaven. No exceptions."

After a lengthy pause the teacher said, without sounding dismayed, "I stand corrected. Perhaps you could enlighten us all. Obviously you've given this situation some thought. What do you think will happen?"

"I think that if God is God and he's as just and fair as he claims, he would not let this man's diligence be for naught. Surely he will be with the ones he loves in the next life." Michael heard those words come back to him and felt strangely comforted, though the feeling remained somehow distant. He finished with a firm, "But then, I don't know. It's a confusing position to be in."

The teacher's brow went up and Michael felt heads turning more obviously in his direction before he realized he'd just personal-ized the story. "Yes," he admitted softly, "like you say, I have a beau-tiful family, and my wife and I enjoy the blessings of the temple. But the truth is that my three older children are not my children at all, and my two little boys are sealed to a man I didn't even like. I try to have faith, but it's not always easy, especially when things happen like . . ." Michael realized what he was about to say and hesitated; but the Spirit urged him on, and he had to believe that someone needed to hear this. "Like last year, when Emily's heart stopped after she lost a baby." His voice cracked and he hesitated again. "The worst part of nearly losing her was knowing that we are not sealed to each other and there is no guarantee that I would ever have her again."

Michael heard sniffles in the room and suddenly felt uncomfortable. He came to his feet. "I apologize for monopolizing the lesson. If you'll excuse me, I should see if my son is beating anybody up in the nursery."

A chuckle of comic relief filtered through the room before Michael left. He went into a stall in the men's room and leaned his head against the door. He'd never acted on a prompting and come out feeling like such a fool.

Michael's thoughts remained grudgingly fixed on what had happened in Sunday School while he supervised the girls making Sunday dinner. Amee cut lettuce. Alexa shredded cheese. Michael stirred the simmering meat for tacos and stewed over reality.

"Can I help, Dad?" Jess asked, and he looked down to see the mirror image of his childhood.

"Why don't you set the table?" he said absently. "Amee, hand Jess some plates so he can set the table."

"Okay, Dad. Just a minute."

Emily came in wearing one of his sweatshirts, which quaintly accentuated her pregnancy. She went on her toes to kiss Michael, then started mixing some punch. "It's always such a relief to get out of those pantyhose."

"And Amee can't wait to get into them," Michael added.

"Dad!" Amee said with disgust and he chuckled. "I'm almost twelve."

"You're still eleven," he corrected.

A knock came at the door. Alexa and Jess both shouted, "I'll get it!" and ran.

"Quiet," Emily scolded. "James just barely went to sleep."

"It's for you, Dad," Alexa shouted. Jess started to whine because he hadn't gotten to the door first.

"Cool it, kids," Michael called, wiping his hands on a towel as he headed for the door. He stopped on the stairs when he saw the Gospel Doctrine teacher and his pretty young wife standing in the entry. "Hello," Michael said, then grabbed Jess gently by the shoulder to interrupt his whining. "Did you finish setting the table?" Jess shook his head. "Please do it, and you can answer the door next time."

Jess surprisingly did as he was told, and Michael turned back to his visitors. "I suppose I owe you an apology," Michael said.

"Actually it's the other way around," Brother Morgan said, holding out a loaf of homemade wheat bread. "My wife baked this just yesterday. I'd have baked it myself, but you wouldn't consider it a peace offering if I had."

Michael chuckled and glanced down as he took it. "Thank you. That's very thoughtful. But don't think that you have to do this because—"

"Brother Hamilton," he interrupted gently, "I'm here because I need to say something for my sake as well as yours. My wife is here because I can't face my mistakes without her holding my hand." His wife smiled up at him. "This is my wife, Diane, by the way."

"It's a pleasure to meet you, Sister Morgan," Michael nodded. "The bread looks delicious. I'll have to hide it from the mob if I want any to myself."

Brother Morgan smiled tensely and opened his mouth to speak, but Michael realized this was extremely awkward. "Would you like to sit down or—"

"No, that's all right. I can tell you're about to have dinner and—"

"No, please." Michael started up the stairs and they had little choice but to follow. Michael paused by the kitchen and Emily smiled at the unexpected visitors. "This is my wife, Emily," Michael said. "Emily, Brother and Sister Morgan."

"Hello," Emily nodded, then to Michael, "Diane and I have met."

Michael handed her the bread. "You'd better hide that, darlin'. We'll have bread and jam after the kids go to bed."

Emily chuckled then said to Sister Morgan, "It looks delicious. Thank you."

Michael continued the introductions. "These are my daughters, Amee and Alexa." He pointed purposely to the wrong ones.

"Dad!" they said in unison and he chuckled.

"Actually," Michael corrected, "that's Amee and that's Alexa. I just like to infuriate them. That's Jess setting the table; you already met him. James is asleep, and Allison is . . .where's Allison?" he asked Emily.

"Still asleep, I believe," Emily called.

"That figures," Michael said under his breath. "Sit down," he added, moving into the living room.

"Thank you," Brother Morgan said, but he remained at the edge of his seat. Michael sat across from them on the other couch. "I just want to say to you, Brother Hamilton, that my father always told me I was a know-it-all, and one day I was really going to offend somebody if I wasn't careful. What you said today was very humbling, and I appreciate the courage you had to say it. I apologize for being so narrow-minded, and I'm calling myself to repentance."

"There's no need for that," Michael chuckled tensely.

"Please, accept my apology and my empathy. I had no idea."

"All right, if it'll make you feel better."

Brother Morgan stood and his wife followed. Michael rose to shake his hand and felt warmed by this man's humble offering.

"Will you stay for dinner?" Michael asked impulsively.

"Oh, we didn't come to impose or—"

"We'd be delighted, honest," Michael insisted. "Please stay."

The Morgans graciously accepted, and they were soon all seated around the table, building tacos.

"You really have a lovely family," Sister Morgan commented.

"Thank you," Michael said proudly and took Emily's hand across the table. "We're expecting another."

Emily barely managed to hold back the tears as Michael's eyes glowed with acceptance. Oh, how she loved him!

After the Morgans left, Emily asked him quietly, "What was that all about?"

"Oh," he said lightly, "nothing really. He was just talking about the temple, and I offered an objective point of view."

Emily prodded him to expound, but he deftly changed the subject by teasing her about how fat she was getting. They ended up laughing and she tried to forget about it. But in her heart she knew something was eating at him. She only prayed they could deal with it before it caused any *real* problems.

Time passing lessened the nausea, and Emily managed to get through her classes and studying more easily. Michael said nothing one way or the other about the pregnancy, but he was supportive and sensitive to her needs. The doctor advised her to take every precaution considering her age and having recently miscarried, and Michael was often scolding her for lifting or reaching for insignificant things. He was always there to make certain James was taken care of so she needn't lift him, and either he or Allison lugged the laundry up and down the stairs.

Through the holidays, Emily began to feel peace concerning this baby. Everything seemed to be going fine, and she felt confident that this was the little boy she had seen in her dream.

Sean left for his mission the week after Christmas, and it was a memorable experience for the whole family. Melissa spent a great deal of time with Michael and Emily, which made them all miss him a little less. But even in his absence, Sean's testimony and willingness to serve a mission seemed to bless their home with a special spirit.

Tension descended again, however, when Allison started coming home late occasionally, and more than once it was evident that she'd been drinking. Michael wanted to take away some privilege to threaten her into being good, but she'd already lost the car, and since she'd taken a part-time job, she didn't depend on him for the money he'd long since cut off. They prayed for her and tried to talk, but it seemed they had to accept the fact that the problem was in Allison's hands, and they could not alter her free agency.

On a day when Emily finished with classes early, she fixed herself a sandwich while Michael took laundry to the basement. James was sitting at the bar eating lunch, since he'd recently declared he was too big for a highchair. Emily was looking for something in the fridge when she heard him say, "I high bigger on de bar, Mom."

She turned around to see him kneeling on the edge of the bar. "Get down from there," she insisted and walked toward him with the intent of holding him there until Michael could lift him down. Before she got there, James attempted to scoot back onto the barstool, and it fell out from under him. Emily caught him before he hit the floor, but she didn't like the sharp pain she felt in her middle as thirty-one pounds of toddler fell against her.

James started to cry, frightened from the near fall, and Michael took the stairs three at a time. "Is he all right?" Michael came around the corner to see Emily sitting on the floor with James in her arms.

"Just scared," she said. "He nearly fell off the bar, but I caught him."

"You *caught* him?" Michael asked dubiously.

"I'm all right," she lied, wishing she could ignore the pain and the way her belly felt unnaturally tight and hard. But there was no ignoring the fear in Michael's expression as he helped her to the bedroom.

"I don't like this at all," he said with a harsh edge.

"I'm sure I'll be fine," she insisted. "Just let me rest."

He had barely left her alone when she felt something wet and hurried to the bathroom. If the pain wasn't already enough to frighten her, she nearly fell apart to see that she was bleeding significantly. She sat in the bathroom and cried until she realized they had to get to the hospital. If she hemorrhaged again, she could likely . . .

Michael was trying not to worry about Emily while he made a grocery list with suggestions from Allison.

"Chocolate cupcakes," she said. "And barbecue chips, and frozen pizza—the good kind."

"In your dreams, girl," Michael said while he jotted down frozen vegetables and toilet paper. "We're on a budget, and—"

"Michael!" Emily's panicked cry from the other room sent him into a frenzy. He tossed the pad and pencil and raced down the hall, Allison at his heels. He turned the corner into the bedroom to find her leaning against the bathroom door, gripping the knob as if it could save her. Her other hand was pressed against her lower abdomen. Her eyes blatantly announced she'd been crying.

"What?" Michael practically shrieked.

"Something's wrong," was all she said before he scooped her into his arms and carried her the few steps to the bed.

Michael tried to ignore the fear pounding in his chest. "What?" he demanded gently. "Are you in pain? Are you—"

"I'm bleeding," she murmured. At the same moment, he looked down to see a bright red bloodstain on his shirt sleeve where he'd held her.

"Dear God, no!" he cried. Fear knotted inside him so tightly that he could hardly think what to do.

Allison exclaimed from behind him, "I'm calling 911!"

Michael sighed a degree of relief. He knew they could be here in three minutes, and it would take at least ten to drive her to the hospital himself.

"Hurry!" Emily urged.

Michael went to his knees beside her, pressing his hands to her face. "Don't you die on me, Emily Hamilton! Do you hear me?" The inevitable tears pressed painfully into his eyes. "I won't stay here alone without you," he practically shouted. "Do you understand? I won't!"

"It's okay," Emily whispered, and actually smiled. "I was promised . . ." Her words disappeared in the whine of a siren that stopped just outside.

"Don't you *dare* die on me!" Michael pressed his face to hers. He could almost imagine her bleeding to death right here in his arms. Memories and fears assaulted him brutally as he forced himself back to make room for the paramedics. They worked quickly and soon had her en route to the hospital. The second she was gone, Michael grabbed his keys from the rack.

"You keep everything under control, Allison. I'll call you later."

Allison looked afraid, but numbly agreed.

Michael was amazed at how calmly he managed to drive to the hospital, when in his mind he wondered if he'd ever see his sweet Emily alive again. He hurried through the doors of the emergency room and was reminded of the night he'd carried nine-year-old Allison in here with an inflamed appendix. He was told that Emily was in good hands and he would have to wait. But he wondered how he was supposed to sit here in a room with several other people and not make a scene. His mind wandered back to a hospital room in Australia and the reality of those moments when Emily's heart had stopped beating. If she died now, would he *ever* be with her again?

Michael tried to distract himself by staring at an odd variety of fish swimming in a large aquarium. He noticed the woman across from him grimacing slightly when she saw the bloodstain on his shirt. But he didn't care. He only wanted to be with Emily; to hold her, to somehow keep her from dying.

Michael held his breath when a doctor he'd never seen before appeared and called quietly, "Mr. Hamilton?"

"Right here." Michael shot to his feet.

"Your wife is going to be fine," he said with a smile. Michael wished he could just collapse into the doctor's arms and bawl like a baby.

"Thank God," he muttered, then added more coherently, "Can I see her?"

"You should be able to go in shortly," he answered, then guided Michael to a chair and sat beside him. The doctor gently explained that the placenta had pulled away from the uterus wall, which had caused the severe bleeding. And of course, the baby was no longer alive. He suspected the strain of Emily catching James had not caused the problem, but perhaps just hurried it along. He felt the baby would not have made it much longer anyway, under the circumstances. He told Michael that everything had been cleared out of the uterus and Emily would be fine. With a friendly pat on the shoulder, he left Michael, saying, "I'll check on her soon."

Michael timidly entered Emily's room to find her staring at the ceiling, tears creeping into her hairline. He couldn't help crying himself at the joy of seeing her alive and well. He held her hand and touched her face, laughing and crying, but not knowing what to say.

Emily's pain became amplified in her compassion for Michael. Reluctantly she met his eyes. "I'm so sorry, Michael. I really never believed this would happen again."

Michael cleared his throat. "There's no need to apologize."

"But I . . ."

Michael put his fingers over her lips to quiet her. "Your heart is still beating, Emily. That's all I ask."

Emily nodded helplessly, then the doctor came in to make certain everything was stable. Michael observed Emily as she was checked. She actually looked pretty good. The doctor told them it was good that she'd gotten to the hospital as quickly as she had. But now that it was over, Michael didn't feel the threat against her life that he'd felt the last time. The difference was that he saw the baby.

The doctor actually encouraged them to see it. Emily kept her eyes shut, but Michael couldn't help being curious. He simply assumed it was a boy until the doctor said warmly, "She would have been a beauty."

Emily's eyes shot open. "What?"

"It's a girl," Michael answered when he saw the evidence for himself.

A wave of confusion rushed over Emily that only emboldened the pain. It was all so mind-boggling that she couldn't even begin to think about it.

Chapter Ten

"Are you sure you don't want to see it?" Michael asked Emily.

Apprehension gave way to the realization that if she didn't see the baby, she might not believe it. It wasn't as difficult as she expected it to be; in truth, it gave her an abstract kind of peace. But that peace was short-lived as she was taken to a room for recovery, and the reality descended.

Michael felt a concern for her that far exceeded his own guilt over what had just happened. The way she stared at the wall with glazed eyes was something he didn't know how to approach. He wondered if the Lord was trying to tell him something, but he felt hesitant to ask. It had just been proven to him that Emily had made it through the ordeal without any life-threatening episodes. So why couldn't he let go of this fear?

Glancing at the clock, he was reminded to check on his family.

"Penny," he said when she answered the phone, "where's Allison?"

"She asked if I'd come over a couple of hours ago. She left with Ashley but wouldn't tell me anything."

"Great," Michael said sarcastically. "Is everything else all right?"

"Fine. What about Emily?" she asked impatiently.

"She lost the baby," Michael said quietly, "but she's doing fine."

"I'm so sorry, Michael," Penny said.

"So am I," he admitted, and realized that he meant it. "Do you mind staying a while longer, Penny? I'd like to be with her until—"

"Stay as long as you can get away with. Everything's fine."

"Thank you, Penny. You're a blessing."

"Give Emily our love," she added before hanging up.

Michael expected some reaction from Emily concerning the phone call. But she just stared at the wall.

"Emily," he took her hand and squeezed it, "are you all right?"

"I'm fine," she said, but he knew she was lying.

"I don't believe you," he insisted gently.

"I don't want to talk about it, Michael." Her voice was edged with weariness.

"Perhaps you should anyway."

As Emily slowly turned to look at him, her eyes pierced him deeply. "Michael, forgive me if I find it difficult to discuss this with you. But I'm not sure if I can deal with losing this baby, and you didn't want it to begin with."

Michael wanted to somehow protest or defend himself, but a tight knot of guilt caught in his throat. He knew she was right.

"I can't remember the last time you opened up and talked to me, Michael, so don't expect me to pour my heart out to you." Emily turned back to the wall and silent tears seeped out of her eyes. "I just want to be alone."

Michael sat in the chair by the bed, unable to leave, unable to comfort her. He wanted to cry, but even his emotions seemed to be wrapped up in a tight wad. When he finally remembered that he had children at home, he pressed a kiss to her brow and squeezed her hand. "I love you, Emily," he said, but she made no response. He slipped quietly out of the room, wondering what had gone wrong with their lives.

Trying not to think about the pain, Michael returned home to find Bret and Penny watching T.V. in the family room. He sighed and sat down across from them. Penny clicked it off with the remote.

"You okay?" Bret asked.

Michael gave a phony smile. "I'll be all right, but Emily's taking it pretty hard."

"Is there anything we can do?" Penny asked warmly.

Michael gave an uncomfortable chuckle. "I'm not sure there's anything to be done, Penny. You've got enough troubles of your own."

"We're here to help each other," Bret insisted.

"I know," Michael tried to smile but it faded quickly, "and we're grateful for that, but . . ." He chuckled humorlessly. "You've got a doctor's appointment tomorrow, eh? I'm sure you're looking forward to that."

"Oh, it's always a thrill," Bret said with light sarcasm. "But it's nice to know it's just a follow-up. The worst is behind us."

"It's late," Michael added. "Thank you for staying with the kids, but . . . well, you should get some sleep."

"If you need to talk . . ." Bret offered.

"Nah," Michael shook his head, "I'm fine, really." He glanced around. "Did the kids give you any trouble?"

"They were fine," Penny insisted as she stood and helped Bret along.

"Allison didn't say anything about her plans?"

"Not a word," Penny replied.

"I ought to spank her," Michael scowled, not totally serious.

"I doubt it would do any good," Bret offered.

"You're probably right," Michael agreed. "Thank you for being here."

"Glad we could help," Penny said on their way out.

In the silence that followed, Michael replayed the ordeal, ending with Emily's blatant refusal to talk to him. The last hurt more than the rest combined. He wanted to be angry, but the truth was harsh. He had earned it. He deserved it. But by heaven and earth, he didn't know what to do about it. He felt completely overwhelmed by a confused helplessness that seemed so powerful at times he believed it might drown him.

Michael lost track of the time as he stared helplessly at the wall, thinking about Emily doing the same. He eventually drifted to sleep on the couch, torn between worrying about Emily and being anxious about Allison. A car door outside startled him awake. He glanced at the clock and tried to focus. 3:56 a.m. He had no trouble becoming coherent before Allison walked through the door.

"Where have you been?" he demanded.

"What difference does it make?" she snapped.

"I asked you a question and I expect it to be answered, young lady. You were left in charge of the children, and you had no business expecting Penny to come over here when she has plenty of stress in her own life."

"Penny likes to be with the kids."

"That's not the point, Allison. Now, where were you?"

"I was . . . with some friends . . . and I fell asleep."

Michael wanted to accuse her of lying. He knew she was. But what proof did he have? What could he possibly say to make her realize what she was doing to her life? Besides, he felt too much pain of his own to push this any further. When he only gazed at her in silence, she moved past him and started down the stairs.

"Allison," he said, and she turned back defiantly. "Aren't you even a bit concerned about what happened to your mother?"

A degree of guilt rose in Allison's eyes that redeemed her slightly. "I'm sorry," she admitted. "How is she?"

"She lost the baby. Physically, she will be fine. Emotionally, she's not doing well at all. The last thing she needs is to start worrying about you again. We'll keep this little episode between us, but so help me, girl, if you do anything to upset her while she's trying to deal with this, you're going to have to deal with me."

"Are you finished?"

Michael swallowed hard and reminded himself to not take his frustration out on Allison. "Yes," he said quietly. "I'm sorry, Allie. I don't want to come down on you, but . . . I'm just worried." He pushed his hands through his hair. "It's been a long day."

Allison watched him a moment and said, "I'm sorry about the baby, Michael."

Michael looked up, surprised to see sincerity in her eyes. "Yes," he admitted, "so am I."

When Allison hesitated he impulsively asked her, "Do you ever wish your father were here instead of me?"

"Nah," she shook her head easily. "He was a bigger jerk than you are."

A hint of a smile touched her expression before she hurried on to her room, but Michael didn't find it funny at all.

Michael checked on the other children and pressed a kiss to each of their faces while they slept. Then he shuffled to his own bed, but found sleep impossible as he vividly recalled Emily's ordeal. As he thought it through again and again, something that should have been obvious occurred to him. A painful tightness crept over his chest. Abruptly he sat up in bed and pressed a hand there, as if he could ease it. But the reality couldn't be denied. There had been many moments when he'd been grateful they'd made the decision to come to Utah. Many good things had come from being here already. But as Michael recalled the doctor saying it was a good thing Emily had been taken to the hospital so quickly, he thought back to their long drive the last time she'd lost a baby. And Michael *knew* that if they had been living in Australia today, Emily would not have made it there alive. He recalled those words in Emily's patriarchal blessing that had prompted their move; that great blessings would come to their family as she pursued her education. There was no greater blessing to him, or these children, than to have Emily still with them.

Michael pressed his head into his hands and muttered aloud, "Thank you, God." He lay back down and tried to relax, but he was so absorbed with gratitude that all he could do was watch the light of day gradually brighten his surroundings.

At eight o'clock, Michael knocked at Allison's door, then opened it slightly when he heard her groan an indiscernible response. "Sorry to wake you, love, but I've got to get your mother at the hospital. I need you to watch the kids."

Allison groaned again but swung her legs over the edge of the bed. "Okay, I'm coming. Just give me a minute."

"Thank you," Michael said, then ran upstairs to serve breakfast and make sure the house was in reasonable order. When Allison shuffled into the kitchen, he grabbed the keys and kissed each of the children good-bye.

"I'll see you all later," he said. "Have a good day at school."

"Will Mom be home when we get back?" Alexa asked.

"Yes, she will, love."

"Is she sick?" Jess asked.

"I guess you could say that," Michael answered dryly.

"Penny told us she had another miscarriage," Amee said.

Michael had to stop a minute and realize that he hadn't taken the time to explain all of this to the children. As all five of them looked to him expectantly, he felt a fresh awakening of his fatherhood. And with Emily absent, a startling chill told him it would always be this way if he lost her. Trying not to think about that, he took a moment to sit down and explain enough to alleviate any fears.

"Yes, Amee, she had another miscarriage."

Jess's face screwed up in a puzzled grimace.

"The baby inside her died, Jess," Michael stated.

"Will she have another one?" Alexa asked.

"I don't know," Michael said, "but the important thing right now is that your mother is going to be just fine. She is very sad about losing the baby, and she is going to need a lot of rest. But she'll be back to normal before we know it."

Michael wanted to believe that, but as Emily barely acknowledged him when he entered her room, he knew there were wounds from this loss that ran deep.

It didn't take Emily long to immerse herself in the old routine. She studied and attended her classes faithfully. She was ambitious around the house and made an effort to spend quality time with the children. Letters passed back and forth between them and Sean regularly, and Melissa continued to visit as she prepared to go on her own mission. Penny spent time with Emily nearly every day, attempting to keep her spirits up. Allison was surprisingly helpful and cooperative. But weeks passing didn't erase the emptiness in Emily's eyes, and the distance between her and Michael seemed to grow steadily wider.

Michael knew he should try and talk to her, but the very thought of approaching the subject made him feel like a hypocrite. When time didn't alleviate the tension, Michael had to face up to a simple fact. This problem had started with him, and if he didn't do something to get Emily to talk, the pain would never stop.

He prayed, and even fasted, for guidance in approaching her. But as he sat beside her on the couch one evening and took her hand, fear nearly made him back down. He would have never believed that talking to Emily could be so difficult. He tried to tell himself it could wait, but the children were all in bed and she didn't have to get up early tomorrow. It was the ideal moment.

"Can we talk?" he asked. She said nothing. "You know," he began after a long moment's contemplation, "I've been praying, Emily, and . . . well, I want you to know that I . . . Emily, I'm so sorry for the way I've been about all of this. I know how much you wanted that baby, and . . ."

He hesitated when she squeezed her eyes shut and tears seeped out.

"Emily, please talk to me. I know I haven't been fair, but you must understand that my intention was never to hurt you. *Please* . . ." The desperation in his voice caught her attention and she turned to look at him. "Please," he repeated in a whisper, "tell me how you feel. Tell me what I can do to mend what's come between us. I can't live like this."

Hope flooded over Michael when she reached her arms around his neck and pressed her face to his shoulder. He felt a sob erupt from her chest, and he held her while she cried. It was as if she had only needed him to open the door. She was more than willing to pass through it.

"I love you, Emily," Michael whispered as he held her. Emily took his shirt into her fists and pressed her face to his chest, allowing all the hurt and sorrow to rush out in torrents.

As the pressure began to ease, Emily reminded herself that it was not Michael's fault she had lost these two babies. And, in spite of their struggles, he was the stabilizing force in her life. Beyond her testimony of the gospel, her love for Michael was a constancy she could depend on. It proved itself now in the way he held her. Just when she had believed she could not endure this trial any longer, he was there, saying what she needed to hear, holding her close, ushering her sorrows into the open air where they didn't seem so overwhelming.

When her emotion was spent, Emily relaxed against him, praying inwardly that they would finally be able to get beyond what stood between them. She lifted her head to look into his eyes and a subtle, warming peace washed over her. It was reflected by the intensity of his eyes and the faint smile at the corners of his mouth. With her fingers she touched his stubbled face, and idly pressed her thumb over his lips. She thought it funny that at this moment she would recall how she'd felt the first time their eyes met. Her feelings now were somehow the same as they'd been that day in college, more than twenty years ago. It was as if their spirits had connected with that first glance; and after that, nothing had ever been the same. Even now, in spite of change and hardship, the commitment was there—a commitment that she believed had begun long before they were ever born into this life. And it would go on forever.

Slowly, gently, Emily touched her lips to his. She felt Michael's breath quicken against her face. She drew back to study his eyes, holding them tight with hers while her fingers moved meekly down his throat to the hint of dark hair showing above the top button of his shirt. She felt his heartbeat as she pressed her hand beneath the fabric that covered his chest. For a long moment they watched each other, the air thick with anticipation. Emily felt the excitement of a new bride as she wondered what his reaction might be. Could he see in her eyes the desire to be touched and held? Did he know she was already tingling inside, knowing what he was capable of doing to her senses? Did he believe, as she did, that this intimacy they shared in their marriage could help them cross the barriers that stood between them?

Emily caught her breath as Michael shifted in his seat and set a hand against her back. In one hardly noticeable movement, she was closer to him, keenly aware of his need for her. There was no tangible change in his expression, but she knew he'd taken hold of her thoughts. She felt his hand wander into her hair until he held the back of her head in a grip so tender she hardly felt it, yet it surged with unspoken power as he guided her within his reach. It took no words for Emily to *know* he loved her, and he would love her forever.

In the midst of a time-stopping kiss, everything changed. They were no longer a man and a woman, co-existing in a world of struggles and constant change. They were lovers. Nothing mattered but the mutual fulfillment of a God-given gift, and the covenants that tied them together.

Michael's touch became intimate, his kiss full of passion. Emily found herself beneath him on the couch, submitting herself freely and eagerly to his will. And loving every moment of it. Then, with no warning, Michael shot to his feet. He looked down at her with expressionless eyes, and she wondered if something was wrong. Were the problems between them so great that he would stop now and . . .

Before she fully caught the teasing smile in his eyes, he had lifted her into his arms. He carried her down the hall and into the bedroom with an anxious stride, kicking the door closed and deftly locking it as he allowed her feet to slide to the floor. Emily eased her fingers through the buttons on his shirt, while he lifted her skirt into his hands.

"You're mine, Emily," he murmured ardently against her face. "Only mine."

Emily smiled in agreement and kissed him hard, missing the significance of what he'd just said.

Long after the passion had subsided, Michael held Emily close in peaceable silence. He traced his fingers over her back and occasionally pressed a kiss to her bare shoulder. He felt completely loved and completely in love. He felt cleansed and secure and confident in their commitment. There was no better moment to approach what he knew had to be faced.

"Emily," he said warmly, and she stirred as if waking from a dream. A smile teased around her eyes as she rolled over to look at him. "Talk to me," he insisted softly. Her brow furrowed as she oriented herself to the conversation they'd barely begun before the emotion had carried them into this blissful interlude. "Tell me," he urged gently. "We can't solve it if you don't talk."

Emily sat up abruptly and pulled the sheet around her. Michael feared the mood had been shattered, but her voice was benign when she spoke. "Michael, how many times have I said those same words to you and—"

"I know. I know," he admitted. "I sound like a hypocrite. I *feel* like a hypocrite. But I'm begging you to talk to me. Just tell me how you feel."

Emily couldn't help her apprehension. In her heart she knew his stand had not changed. In spite of all that was good between them, she feared this would only end in another stale argument. But she could not do what she had criticized Michael for doing. He had opened the door, and she had to pass through it.

"I'm just . . . confused," she admitted.

"Confused about what?"

"I *know* I am supposed to have a baby. It was a boy I saw in my dream, Michael. So, where does this little girl fit in?"

"Maybe she will be yours in the next life, Emily. Perhaps that was all the life she needed to live. Or maybe it's something we simply can't understand from our perspective. Perhaps you need to have the faith that everything will work out as it should and not worry so much about it."

Emily looked at him severely. The intensity in her eyes brought those words back to him, and he turned away. Now he really felt like a hypocrite.

"I don't understand, Michael. How can you say things like that to me when you are so unwilling to let me have another child?"

"I don't know," he admitted without looking at her.

"I assume your stand remains firm." He said nothing so she clarified, "You would rather I didn't get pregnant again."

"I'm not . . . comfortable with it."

"Could you be a little more specific?"

"I don't want you to get pregnant again," he stated, trying not to sound upset.

"Why?" she pleaded.

The severity in his voice deepened. "Because I could not bear to live without you. It's as simple as that."

"But, Michael," she took his hand, "I was promised that I would live to—"

"I know that," he retorted. "In my head, I know that, Emily. But in my heart . . ." He pressed a hand to his chest and looked away. Emily waited for him to go on. "I can't really explain it. It's just . . . hard for me."

"How can you sit there and beg me to talk to you, and yet you won't even—"

"All right. All right." He drew back and lifted his hands in resignation. "You win, Emily. I'm a fool and a hypocrite. Does that make you feel any better?"

Michael pulled on his jeans and moved to the window. He opened it and leaned his hands on the sill, inhaling the gush of fresh air. "I'm sorry, Emily," he admitted, hating the way reality crashed back down around them any time this came up. "I'm just having trouble with this. These problems are my fault. I admit it. Doesn't that count for anything?"

"Not if you don't do something about it."

"And what would you have me do?" he shouted, turning abruptly toward her.

Emily's eyes hardened on him and her voice picked up a husky quality. "I remember so clearly, Michael, how you sat across a table from me and told me exactly what you thought of my relationship with Ryan."

Just hearing the name, Michael winced inwardly.

"You told me that you would not allow your wife to hurt for any reason, intentionally or otherwise. You said that if someone who loved you told you that you had a problem, you would do something about it."

Michael felt as if he had turned to stone. He knew that no amount of anger or pride could change the truth of what she'd just said. The bottom line was simple. In a roundabout way, Emily had stated the premise of the entire problem. Michael summed it up with a starchy, "So, once again, I am put on a scale opposite Ryan Hall."

"It's not like that and you know it."

"From my point of view, Emily, you have no idea what it's like."

"How can I when you won't tell me?"

"There are some things that are just . . ." Michael hesitated and swallowed his emotion. "That are just too difficult to talk about."

It wasn't his words as much as the look in his eyes that made Emily realize she was only seeing the tip of a very big iceberg. Something was eating him alive inside—something she didn't understand and couldn't get him to talk about. She felt chilled from the inside out as it became obvious the bridge between them would never be rebuilt until this problem was solved. Emily's heart filled with compassion as she tried to comprehend his inner struggles, whatever they may be. But one thing was very clear. "I love you, Michael," she said with strength. He looked down and stuffed his hands in his pockets.

Michael had expected her to come back with more evidence of his hypocrisy. Heaven knew he deserved it. But her genuine expression of love touched him in a way that made him almost believe he could get past this. He didn't know how, but he knew he wanted to—for Emily, if not for himself.

"Michael," she said gently, "maybe . . ." she hesitated and he met her eyes, "maybe we should get some help. Perhaps a little counseling would . . ." Emily stopped when his expression became hard and unreadable. She remembered all too well the many times she had approached Ryan about this, only to be rebuffed.

Michael almost wanted to laugh. He didn't know why, but the relief was so immense. "Counseling?" he questioned soberly. Emily nodded. Michael shook his head, and the disappointment he'd hoped for was evident. "I'm sorry, Emily, but I don't think we can afford it." Her eyes widened in disbelief for an instant before he added, "We're on a tight budget."

Emily narrowed her eyes, trying to look past his sober facade. She smiled when she caught the subtle sparkle of humor. When he smiled back, she started to laugh. He laughed with her as the tension evaporated once again.

"I love you, Michael," she finally managed to say.

"Yes, I know," he said in a tone that brought the seriousness back to her eyes, "and that's why I will do whatever it takes to make this right, Emily. If it dries up my entire family fortune to save this marriage, so be it."

"I don't think counseling is *that* expensive. If it were, I think we'd—"

The phone's ringing startled them both. Emily glanced at the clock. "It's past midnight. Who on earth could it be?"

Michael reached for the phone while they silently feared bad news about Allison, who should have been home by now. Michael answered, then he sighed and covered the mouthpiece to whisper, "It's my mother."

Emily breathed easier as she relaxed to listen to his side of the conversation, but he didn't say enough to give her any idea why LeNay had called so late. For twenty minutes, Emily listened to Michael listen to his mother. Then he finally hung up the receiver and drew a deep breath.

"Wow."

"Wow, what?" she probed.

Michael rubbed a hand over his face as if it would help him think more clearly.

"What?" she prodded impatiently.

"I don't know, Emily, but I think this could be the answer."

"The answer to what?" She was beginning to feel infuriated.

"Emily," he said eagerly, "an infant was brought to the boys' home just a couple of hours ago. A boy."

Emily held her breath and leaned back as she grasped the implication. "How old?"

"The doctor said he's not more than three days old." Michael paused. "He was found abandoned in an alley in Brisbane."

"Oh, no!" Emily put a hand to her mouth. Tears surfaced as her intense desire for a child made such abandonment incomprehensible.

"Is he . . . all right?"

"Mother said that it appears he hasn't suffered any ill effects from the ordeal. He's presently content and eating well, but . . ."

"But?"

"He has Down's Syndrome, Emily. Perhaps that is why he was abandoned. Of course it could take time, but . . ." His eyes penetrated hers. "Emily, do you think we could handle it?"

"If it's what the Lord wants us to do, I think we can do anything. But don't think that this will take away the need for my having another baby."

Michael stared at her hard, willing himself not to start another argument. "All I ask is that you keep an open mind. Maybe you're so set on having a baby that you're not being objective."

Emily wanted to argue his point, but she couldn't. She truly believed she was supposed to give birth to a son. But she agreed to think about it, and for the next three days she thought of little else. She didn't know for certain if adopting this special spirit would take away her longing for a baby of her own, but she felt it was right to do it nevertheless. She came home early the following afternoon to eagerly tell Michael, "I think we should take that baby."

"So do I," he admitted.

"It will be difficult, I know, but I believe it would be worth it."

Emily began to feel joy in the prospect of getting this child, and waited eagerly for Michael to call his mother. She felt impatient when he couldn't get her, and reluctantly went to buy groceries. When she returned he was sitting on the couch, looking abnormally glum.

"What?" she asked, setting her bags absently aside.

"The baby has been claimed, Emily."

She sat down.

"The grandparents discovered their daughter had given birth and the child had disappeared. They will be taking him. They're good people."

"I see," was all Emily said before she went quietly to the bedroom and cried. The ache was so deep for a baby that she began to wonder if she could bear it. But in spite of the pain and the tension, Michael was always there. She couldn't deny that she had much to be grateful for as she poured her heart out in prayer and managed to make it through the following days. She sensed a softening in Michael that became tangible when he made an appointment with a marriage counselor affiliated with BYU. The first two sessions felt unproductive, but there was little tension between them. They agreed it would take time to acquaint the counselor with the situation before they could get to the heart of the problem.

Through all of the stress and concern, Emily was vaguely aware that Allison had become more distant. She had stuck to her curfew for the most part, and accomplished her assigned chores. But Emily was worried for her in a way she couldn't define. It was as if the problem went far deeper than she could possibly imagine, but there was nothing tangible to grasp.

Emily's helplessness with Allison only seemed to deepen her helplessness over wanting a child that she was beginning to believe she would never have. The counseling sessions became more intense, and Emily started to dread them. After their fifth attempt, her frustration was evident.

"Is something bothering you?" Michael asked as he turned the Blazer out of the parking lot and toward home.

"I was just wondering how much we've paid this guy to tell us what we already know."

"And what is that?" Michael asked warily.

"He's told us we have a good relationship, and we are able to communicate rather well. We are committed and we love each other. There only seems to be one thing standing between us, which you seem hesitant to talk about—something that seems to be festering inside of you that you don't want to have touched. I knew all of that before we started."

Michael said nothing for three miles. "I'm sorry, Emily. I suppose these things take time."

Emily leaned her head back and turned to look at him. "I guess we have forever, don't we?"

Michael knew the comment was intended to comfort him, but he couldn't bring himself to acknowledge it. He'd long ago stopped believing they had forever; at the very least he had to wonder.

"Michael," she said cautiously, wondering why she felt hesitant, "perhaps we should go to the temple together. It's been a few months since—"

"I'm sorry, Emily." The terseness of his voice was more biting than he'd intended it to be. But the thought of being in the temple with Emily seemed little more than alcohol to sting his wounds.

"What do you mean by that?" she asked, her voice barely steady as she recalled the hurt she'd felt when Ryan had quit going to the temple. Inactivity in the Church had followed, and their marriage had gone from bad to worse.

"I just can't go right now," he stated, his eyes fixed acutely on the road.

"Why not?" she asked, her voice quivering.

Michael glanced toward her, not surprised at the anguish in her eyes. He didn't expect her to understand, but he couldn't bring himself to explain. He blinked several times and turned his eyes back to the road. "I'm truly sorry, Emily. You deserve someone better."

Emily couldn't believe this. She was stunned beyond reason. "There *is* no one better," she cried. "But I need you to tell me what's wrong here. This is no small thing, Michael."

"I know," he said, then he said nothing more.

Michael went to bed early that evening, having said very little at all. At twenty past one, Emily crawled wearily into bed.

"Are you asleep?" she whispered.

"No," he said right away.

"Allison's not home yet."

"I know." He rolled onto his back and sighed. "I wish I knew what to do with her, Emily. How can you love someone so much and be so infuriated?"

"I think the two go together well," she admitted in a tone of wisdom. She took a deep breath. "Did you know the car is gone?"

Michael leaned up on his elbows. "No, I didn't," he said tersely.

"Your keys are missing from the desk drawer."

Michael sighed and rubbed his eyes as if it might make him see Allison's motives. "It would seem this is getting worse rather than better."

"I'm afraid so," Emily replied in an emotionless voice that was becoming common. "Sometimes I wonder where we went wrong, or what we could have done differently to—"

"There's no good in that, Emily," he said gently. "We're not perfect parents, but we've loved her and we've tried to teach her well. We have to remember that she is a free agent. "If only she would—"

Michael's sentence was cut short by a loud crash outside. He leaped out of bed and ran toward the door while he pulled on a big T-shirt that hung over the top of his pajama pants. Emily grabbed her robe and followed on his heels.

Emily gasped as she stepped through the open door and saw Michael running across the lawn. The red Geo was smashed against the tree in the yard. Horrid images of the past rushed over Emily as she hesitated, waiting for Michael to deal with this.

Adrenalin pumped as Michael found Allison with her head against the steering wheel. He tried the door but it was jarred, so he ran around the car and opened the passenger side. He nudged her gently and her head came up groggily.

"Are you all right?" he demanded.

"I think so," she said, seeming disoriented.

After making certain nothing was broken, Michael dragged her from the car and laid her on the lawn. Emily ran over to kneel beside her. While Michael checked her more closely for injury, Allison looked up at her mother.

"Oh, hi," she said lightly. "I think I missed the driveway."

Emily wanted to slap her, but it was evident that Michael had enough anger for both of them.

"Is she all right?" Emily asked, almost hoping for a few broken bones that might keep her home and humble for a while.

"Just a little bruised, as far as I can see." He scooped her into his arms and carried her inside. Emily followed, surprised that he took her into the bathroom and put her in the tub, fully clothed.

"What are you doing?" she questioned.

Michael turned on a cold spray and aimed the shower head for Allison's face. "I want to talk to her *now*," he answered grimly. Allison choked and gasped until she was trying to stand up and get out of the tub.

"Are you crazy?" she snapped groggily, and would have fallen over the edge if Michael hadn't caught her.

"I was about to ask you the same," Michael growled. He sat her on the closed toilet and threw a towel at her. "You'd best sober up, girl, because I want you to remember this conversation in the morning."

As always, Emily was grateful that Michael was handling the problem, but she wondered what approach he might take. When he began, she appreciated his directness but didn't like the feelings it stirred in her. "Do you have a clue what you just did?" Michael demanded. Allison said nothing. Michael took her by the shoulders and shook her slightly, forcing her to look at him. "Answer me!" he shouted at the risk of waking the other children. Still she said nothing. "I want you to tell me what you just did!"

"I ran into a tree," she hissed.

"And you're lucky it was just a tree, young lady. It could have been somebody's child, or somebody's *father*," he emphasized. Emily felt it coming now and bit into her knuckle. Michael took Allison's chin into his hand and spoke directly into her face. "Your father was killed by a drunk driver, Allison. A seventeen-year-old girl ran a red light doing sixty and smashed your father into a corpse. Do you hear what I'm saying? If she had survived, she would likely have served time for manslaughter."

Allison's eyes showed enough emotion that he knew she was getting the point. "Kind of puts a different perspective on being an irresponsible little brat, doesn't it?" He released her so abruptly that she barely kept her balance. "Now put on some dry clothes and go to bed before I'm tempted to give you a few more bruises. A good, hard spanking would probably do you some good."

Allison stumbled out of the room, and Michael leaned his forehead against the wall with a groan of self-punishment. "I'm sorry, Emily. I didn't intend to be so graphic."

"I think your point was well taken," she said and hurried back to the bedroom.

The next morning, Michael called a tow truck and the insurance company. He took a loss on the car and decided it was better if they didn't even have it around. After breakfast, he and Emily went down to check on Allison. She was awake, staring at the wall in a way that reminded Michael of Emily.

"Are you all right?" Emily asked.

"A little sore," she admitted.

"Do you remember anything?" Michael asked skeptically.

"Every word," she retorted, then her voice softened. "I had forgotten."

"Forgotten what?" Emily asked gently.

"That Dad was killed by a drunk driver. I'm sure you told me, but I guess it didn't register."

"Does it make a difference?" Michael asked.

"I'm not going to drink and drive anymore, if that's what you mean."

"That's not exactly what I had in mind," Michael grumbled.

"I'm sorry about the car, Michael," she said almost sincerely.

"You're sorry?" he chuckled without humor. "I don't care about the stupid car, Allison. It's gone and I hope I never see it again. But you took it when you had no right or permission, and you're darn lucky you weren't hurt . . . or killed. And you're even luckier no one else was a victim of your carelessness."

"I know," she admitted. Michael and Emily exchanged a questioning glance. This was not like Allison to be so agreeable.

"Is something else wrong?" Emily asked.

"What do you mean?" Allison replied, slightly tense.

"What she means is, was there a particular reason you were so intent on destroying yourself last night, or did you just do it for the thrill?"

Emily almost wished they hadn't asked when she said bluntly, "I think I'm pregnant."

Emily sat down. Michael turned away and distractedly pushed a hand through his hair.

"How do you know?" Emily asked, proud of herself for the calm tone of her voice.

"I'm just . . ." she glanced toward Michael then whispered, ". . . late. I've never been this late."

Emily had hoped this wasn't going on any more, but it was obvious she'd been wrong. "I don't know what to say, Allison." She shook her head in disbelief. "I'm glad you're being honest with us, but I just never thought anything like this would happen. I can't even think straight."

Michael took over. "Do you love this . . . guy?" he insisted.

"Not enough to spend the rest of my life with him, if that's what you mean."

"Then marriage is out of the question."

"You'd better believe it," Allison added strongly.

"Does he know?" Emily asked.

"Wait a minute," Michael interrupted. "Could we know this guy's name? His ghost lingers around here like a bad dream, and we don't even know the jerk's name."

"He is not a jerk," Allison protested.

"He's sleeping with my daughter!" Michael shouted.

"Your *step*daughter," Allison corrected.

"Well, he's sleeping with my daughter," Emily snapped, sick of the point in protest.

"His name is Jack," Allison said more softly.

"Fine," Michael quieted down as well. "Does *Jack* know?"

Allison hesitated. "He thinks I should have an abortion."

Emily groaned and buried her face in her hands. "After what I have been through trying to keep a baby," she said without looking at Allison, "I can't believe you would even consider it."

"I'm not considering it," Allison said and Emily looked up. "I just told you what he thought. I don't think I could ever go through with something like that."

"Well, that's comforting at least," Michael observed.

"But don't think I'm ready for a baby." Allison sat up in bed and hugged her pillow. "Not yet, I mean. I'm just not ready."

"I'll give you some credit for realizing that," Michael said sincerely.

"Then there's only one option," Emily said. "If you—"

Michael interrupted with no hesitation. "Your mother and I will adopt the baby and raise it as our own." Emily looked up at him, eyes wide. "When we go back to Australia, no one will ever know the difference."

"I wouldn't count on that," Allison said. They looked at her in question and she clarified, "Jack is African-American."

"He's black?" Emily squeaked.

"Does that bother you?" Allison asked, as if daring them to show symptoms of prejudice.

"I wouldn't care what color he is, if he was decent enough to marry you before he slept with you." Michael folded his arms and added, "We'll adopt it anyway."

Little more was said until Emily crawled into bed that night and Michael pulled her close. "Is it possible that this could be that baby?" he whispered.

Emily wanted to tell him she hadn't thought about it, but the truth was she'd thought of nothing else all day. "Perhaps," she admitted. For the next several days, Emily stewed over the possibilities and realized it was the best solution. It would be far easier to raise Allison's child as her own than to see it go to someone else, though she understood that perhaps it was meant to go to loving parents elsewhere. She filed the idea away as a comforting probability, knowing that she had plenty of time.

The next morning Allison announced jubilantly, "False alarm, Mom. I'm not pregnant after all. Just stress, I suppose."

Emily went discreetly to her room and cried. She had to be grateful that Allison would be spared the trauma of an unwed pregnancy, but she couldn't deny the disappointment.

Allison merged into a happy-go-lucky mood that made her next move all the more shocking. When she hadn't come home at two in the morning, Emily was so full of nerves she thought she'd die. Michael urged her to pray with him, then he suggested that maybe they look in her room. "Perhaps we can find an address book or something that might give us a clue."

The first shock on entering her room was that it was immaculate. Allison was not known to be a slob, but her bed was rarely made and there was always something cluttering the floor. But everything was in its place and clean. There was an envelope on her dresser, with *Mom* written on the front.

Emily's hand trembled as she picked it up. She began to shake as she tried to break the seal and handed it to Michael. "You read it," she insisted, "I can't."

Michael took out the handwritten letter and cleared his throat. "Dear Mom, I don't expect you to understand why I have to do this, but I don't want you to worry." Michael paused as Emily broke into tears and pressed her face against the front of his shoulder. "I'm not certain where I'm going or when I'll be back. But one of these days we'll see each other again."

Emily pulled Michael's shirt into her fists and sobbed as he finished the letter. "I'm sorry for the hurt I've caused you. I want you to know that it's not your fault. You've been a good mother and I love you." Michael's voice broke. "Love, Allison."

"I can't believe it," Emily cried, feeling like a broken record. She was always saying that about Allison.

"There's a P.S.," Michael added and read aloud, "I took some money from Michael's drawer. Tell him I'll pay him back."

Michael tossed the letter on the desk and held Emily close. "How did she know where you kept cash?" Emily asked once she had calmed slightly.

"That's what I was wondering. But whatever was in there won't be enough to take her very far."

* * * * *

At their next counseling session, little was said. The counselor encouraged them to discuss what was troubling them. They finally got to the loss they felt from Allison's running away. But the counselor observed it was not something that appeared to be coming between them or affecting their relationship. They appeared to be united in their concerns for the children.

Through an unbearable silence, Michael watched Emily and felt suddenly aware of the hurt he'd caused her by his unwillingness to talk. As a fiction writer, he'd studied human nature enough to know that his reluctance to deal with this might be normal, but it wasn't healthy.

"Perhaps," the counselor finally said, "we have reached a point where I am unable to help you any further."

Emily sighed and Michael felt the guilt of her frustration on his shoulders. But he felt helpless to do anything about it. He listened absently as the counselor summed up the good things he had seen in their relationship. He reminded them to stay committed and communicate, and he rambled a few minutes about the theory of mid-life crisis. It was common, he told them, for a person to reach a point of emotional struggle for any number of reasons during the middle years of life. Often it came down to questions concerning what had been accomplished in life to that point, and what would become of the remainder of that life. It often resulted in uncharacteristic behavior, and strain in relationships usually occurred. He assured them of his confidence in them to have the intelligence to work many things out on their own, then summed up their work, encouraging them to contact him again if he could help.

For several minutes, Michael and Emily sat silently in the Blazer. Again he sensed her emotions and wondered what he could say to get beyond this impasse. He put the key in the ignition but didn't find the will to turn it. The silence continued and his heart began to pound.

While Emily felt something close to despair, she prayed with everything inside her that she could find some hope. If Allison's running away, with no word in weeks, wasn't bad enough, this tension between herself and Michael just seemed to steadily deepen with no explanation. She knew she had much to be grateful for, and reminded herself of that. But how could she go on living with this inner turmoil? Inside she prayed harder, while she began to wonder if she was just going to have to accept all of this and learn to live with it.

"Uh," Michael nearly croaked, "I think we need to talk."

She looked up abruptly, and her sigh was unintentionally loud. The last time they had *talked*, it had ended in one more conclusion that this problem was unsolvable.

"I don't blame you for being skeptical, but give me a chance to . . ." Emily's eyes filled with a hope that gave him some momentum. Now that he'd opened this up, Michael sought quickly for the words to explain his feelings and somehow avoid the deepest hurt that he dared not voice. Not yet at least. *One step at a time*, he reminded himself.

He turned slowly to meet Emily's eyes. "I've done a lot of thinking lately about my life," he began. "I don't know." He chuckled tensely. "Maybe this is my mid-life crisis." He pushed a hand through his hair and continued. "There have been six moments in my life, Emily, that have affected me so deeply that I can hardly comprehend it. Do you know what they are?"

Emily felt the evidence of her prayer being answered by the genuine softness in his eyes. She shook her head, then admitted, "I could probably guess if I thought about it long enough."

"The first is when my father died," he said, and she nodded. She knew it had been hard on him, as young as he was.

When he said nothing more, she speculated aloud. "Could one of them be the witness of the Spirit that made you decide to join the Church?"

"Very good." He smiled, feeling some relief in the evidence that she knew him so well. Following more silence, he finally admitted, "And one is the moment you told me Ryan was dead."

Their eyes met, and it was difficult for Emily to comprehend the poignancy she had shared with Michael when she had been torn between her love for him and her commitment to Ryan. The intensity of his expression made her wonder over the deeper thoughts between his confessions.

"That's three," she said when it became evident that he wasn't going to say anything more without coaxing. "We're halfway there."

"The other three are similar to each other," he said quietly while she looked out the window. "They are the moments when I realized you had left me."

Emily's eyes shot to his, demanding clarification. At the very least, he knew she wanted to know how these things related to the unspoken problem between them. He was surprised at how prepared he was to tell her.

"You see," he began, "to this day, I have trouble finding words to describe the agony I went through when you told me you were going to marry Ryan. Those years without you were hell, Emily." She turned away, feeling somehow guilty for what he'd gone through, even now. "And then," he went on, "there was the moment when I looked into your eyes and knew you would never leave him. In some ways, I believe I was so accustomed to being alone and hurting that it wasn't difficult to feel comfortable with it. In another way, I think it hurt more deeply the second time. But . . ." He took a deep breath. "That hurt forced me to look at all of this in a different light, and I ended up joining the Church. How can I begrudge it?"

"Does appreciating what it did for you make the hurt go away?" she asked, beginning to see where this was headed.

Michael shook his head subtly and looked away. "Maybe that's why the moment your heart stopped catapulted me into this formless dread." He looked at her deeply. The torment in his eyes took her back to those other moments he'd just reminded her of. "Don't you see, Emily?" He leaned toward her and his voice lowered. "Since the moment we met, my life has been good as long as you were in it. How can you expect me to even consider living without you at all? And if you were to die as the result of a pregnancy, how could I live with myself, knowing I was the one responsible for—"

"But Michael," she interrupted gently, "I was promised that I would live to—"

"I know that, Emily." The tension in his voice let her know they were getting back to the sore point that had shut the conversation down the last time this came up. She touched his face tenderly, hoping to urge him on. "On a logical level, I can think it through, and I know that's true. And there are times when I can believe it on a spiritual level. But . . ."

His words faded into the first emotion she'd seen since his confessions had begun. She guessed with a degree of confidence, "But emotionally you can't accept it, because there is too much hurt related to it."

"I guess that about covers it," he said a little too vehemently. The finality in his voice almost made her feel despair. He'd admitted to some strong feelings, but she knew he'd still not told her the whole truth.

And one fact still remained. "Well," she said after another lengthy silence, "my heart, my mind, and my spirit are all in complete agreement. I am supposed to have another baby."

Emily waited for a response, then realized she wasn't going to get one. Michael turned the key in the ignition and drove toward home. She kept her tears silent and her head turned away, reminding herself to have faith and be patient. She had become pregnant before in spite of their efforts to prevent it. Surely it could happen again. She cautioned herself to have compassion for the hurt Michael had admitted to, and not lose perspective on her love for him. But deep down inside, Emily felt just plain weary.

CHAPTER ELEVEN

Emily sat in the doctor's office waiting room, glancing over the lists in her planner. It helped distract her from the reason she was here. But as she stared at the date, a deeper pain set in. Allison had been gone two years this week. She would be twenty-one now, a woman in every respect. But Emily didn't even know if her daughter was still living. There had been no contact at all, and at moments the heartache and worry brought on tangible pain.

So much had happened since Allison's departure. James was in kindergarten and starting to read. Jess had learned to love school, and was so involved in sports that they could hardly keep up with him. Amee and Alexa had gone into the Young Women's program, and they were beginning to behave so grown-up at times. There had been dance reviews and piano recitals, awards and achievements. And struggles. But for the most part, they were the same old struggles, and Allison would not be surprised by them.

Still, there were moments when Emily wished she could simply write Allison a long letter and tell her of all the trivial things of life she was missing. Emily was approaching the final stretch on her way to earning a master's degree, and talk of the future was turning toward their return to Australia once her education was finished. Penny had become a real estate agent and was managing rather well. Bret had been made the bishop and was expected to live a long life, with no prospect of his cancer returning. Sean had returned from a successful mission and was doing well. He had a good job, a better apartment, and he'd bought an old car that he managed to keep running. Melissa had left for a mission to South America while Sean was in Ireland. She had also returned, and Emily felt certain they would soon announce their plans to marry. The two went so well together, it was difficult to comprehend them apart.

Emily thought of her friends and family and knew she had much to be grateful for. But, oh, how her heart ached for Allison. If only she knew! And when Emily thought of her purpose for being where she was at the moment, she ached for other reasons as well.

The nurse called Emily's name and she slammed the planner closed, trying not to think about the reality. In her heart she knew what was wrong with her, but she wasn't willing to face it until she heard it from a professional. She was embarrassed by the tears she shed when the doctor told her. But by the time she got home, her emotion had turned into a numb hopelessness.

At the dinner table, Michael didn't miss the shadow in Emily's eyes or the fact that she barely touched her food. "Are you all right?" he asked after the children had rushed off to play.

Their eyes met and Emily's heartache deepened. There was no tangible reason to feel that their marriage wasn't good. He adored her and she knew it. Still, she knew he was hurting, though she had yet to understand why. And there was no denying the hurt she felt. On this one issue they stood divided, but he had won. It was too late.

"Emily," he startled her, "are you all right?"

Searching for a distraction, she glanced at the can of Coke in his hand. It was the perfect excuse to throw back some of this pain. "You really shouldn't drink so much of that stuff. You've told me yourself you don't feel as good when you drink too much caffeine."

Michael furrowed his brow and rubbed a thumb through the beard he'd grown, trying to figure where she was coming from. He took a long swallow of his drink but said nothing.

"You're addicted to the caffeine, Michael. Admit it. You've always got a Coke in your hand."

"I admit it," he said, not wanting an argument.

"It's not good for you, Michael. You know I'm right."

"Yes," he said, "you're right."

"Then why do you keep drinking it?"

"Better caffeine than Scotch whiskey," he stated, trying to be funny. But Emily didn't smile.

"If you really want the whiskey, Michael, you could probably get it easy enough."

"Emily," he said, leaning his forearms on the table, "I grew up in an environment where liquor was readily available. I was never tempted. I am not tempted now."

"That's something of a relief," she said facetiously.

"Emily," his voice became stern, "something is bothering you, and I seriously doubt it's my addiction to caffeine."

Emily glanced down and fidgeted with her napkin. "I went to the doctor today."

Michael's heart raced for a moment as he wondered if something was wrong. He saw the hesitance rise into her eyes, and his first assumption seemed logical under the circumstances. "You're pregnant," he guessed, almost wishing that she was. If nothing else, perhaps it would ease some of his guilt and give him a chance to make right his bad attitude the last time.

The irony tore at Emily as she watched her husband. If what Michael said wasn't bad enough, he just had to smile when he said it—as if her being pregnant now would have been all right. The emotion suddenly rushed forward. It was more than she could bear.

Emily stood from the table so fast her chair tipped over. She ran down the hall as if the pain might catch up and smother her. Michael caught her around the waist as she reached the bedroom door. She tried to push him away, but he took hold of her wrists and forced her to face him.

"What?" he demanded, his pulse racing with fear.

Emily only hung her head and sobbed.

"What?" He clenched his teeth and shook her gently.

Still she didn't answer.

"Merciful heaven, Emily, don't tell me that you're going to die or—"

"I'm not going to die!" she snarled. Then she nearly collapsed against him, pulling his shirt into her fists. "But I almost wish I could."

Michael took her face into his hands. "Tell me!" he demanded.

"I *can't* get pregnant any more, Michael," she sobbed, her voice edged with bitterness. "I am forty-four years old," she shouted in his face, "and my child-bearing years are *over!*"

Michael let go of her and took a step back. He was so stunned he could neither move nor speak. Emily cried and paced as she ranted through every detail of her symptoms and what the doctor had told her. When she finally ran down, she slumped onto the edge of the bed and stared at the wall.

"I'm so sorry, Emily," he said quietly.

She turned to look at him with hard eyes. He wished he hadn't said it when the many times he'd said it before came back to him in silent, empty reverberations.

"You're *sorry?*" she echoed. The bitterness in her voice was justified, but it twisted the knife in Michael's heart. He pressed a hand to his chest as if it could somehow ease the pain, then he turned to leave, unable to face her another moment.

"Don't you dare walk out on me!" she shouted and grabbed his arm. His height advantage of ten inches seemed insignificant as she pushed him against the wall, her anger overpowering the pain that left him weak.

"Enough silence," she said in a husky voice. "You'd better talk, Mr. Hamilton, or you might as well go back to Australia right now. I'm hurting, Michael, and I'm not going to hurt alone."

"Emily." His chin quivered and his voice broke. "I . . . I know I wasn't fair . . . about the baby . . . but . . . I always believed I'd have a chance . . . to make it . . . right."

"When?" her voice rumbled. "We're not college kids with our whole lives ahead of us, Michael. It's been three and a half years since I lost that baby and nearly died. And you still haven't dealt with it." She stepped back, as if being close to him was suddenly distasteful. "And now it's too late. I hope you can live with that, Michael, because I'm not sure I can."

She walked away, and Michael turned to press his head against the wall. He groaned and tears burned into his eyes. He hit the wall with his fist and slid to his knees. How many times in his life had he gone through the agony of wondering how it might have been if he'd just done something different? He thought he would have figured it out by now. But in his heart Michael believed he was a proud, arrogant fool. And not even Ryan Hall, with all his chauvinism and insensitivity, had ever hurt Emily as much as Michael had. How could he spend the rest of his life, let alone eternity, facing up to the consequences of this? He felt sure that Emily was sealed to the man who deserved her, and he wouldn't blame her if she never forgave him.

Michael hit the wall again and cried in agony, "Dear God above, what have I done? What have I done?" He groaned and wrapped his arms over his head. "Can you ever forgive me?" he cried. "Ever?"

Emily heard Michael hit the wall and stepped back into the hallway. Instantaneously she felt all of her hurt and anger melt into compassion. She had told him she would not hurt alone. It was evident that she wasn't. Since the day they had met, Emily realized they had never suffered alone. Even through a decade, separated by an ocean, they had suffered the same ache. And now, the genuine power behind his remorse stirred her. The warmth of the Spirit made it clear to her that God understood Michael's innermost fears, even if Emily didn't. As she watched the evidence of Michael's pain, it was easy to reaffirm what she had always known. The atonement of Jesus Christ covered all suffering, compensated for all pain—even this. There was no such thing as *too late*. It was easy to shift the burden to her Savior's shoulders, because she had done it so many times before. As she literally felt it lifted, the bitterness and anger melted away. And though she knew it would not be easy, she knew she would be able to face it. As long as she and Michael had each other, she knew they could face anything.

She finally found the voice to speak. "Michael."

He glanced up, startled and embarrassed—and uncertain.

Emily knelt beside him and wiped away his tears. She couldn't find the words to tell him all she felt. But she took his face in her hands and kissed him in a way that expressed all of her love and acceptance. And forgiveness.

Michael took hold of her as if he were drowning and she were his air to breathe. He scattered kisses over her face and throat, then pressed a hand through her hair, marveling at her beauty, her strength, her love.

"Emily," he moaned, "I love you. You must believe me."

"I know you do, Michael. I do."

"Can you ever forgive me, Emily?"

"I already have," she whispered, and he pressed his face to her shoulder and cried. Emily just held him.

They sat together on the floor in the hall until James came running in to find them. "Daddy, Daddy," he said, his voice full of joy and enthusiasm. "Come see. Come see." He tugged at Michael's hand.

"All right," he chuckled, "I'm coming."

As Michael rose to his feet, he paused to touch Emily's face and kiss her once more. She was too good to be true, he decided.

"Come on, Daddy," James insisted.

"Can Mom come, too?" Michael asked.

"Of course," James said in a perfectly adult tone. He led them outside and around the corner of the house, where he stopped and pointed to an overgrown rose bush that looked pretty pathetic to Michael. He thought that he should have pruned it weeks ago.

"Can you see it?" James asked vibrantly.

"See what, honey?" Emily asked.

"The rose. See, it's coming back. It died when it got cold, and now it's warm and it's coming back. Isn't it beautiful?"

Together Michael and Emily bent down to see the single, tiny bud beginning to open, with hints of the white rose petals peering through.

"It certainly is beautiful," Emily said, hugging James tightly. Her eyes caught Michael's and she knew that he felt it, too. They had a beautiful family, and evidence all around them that life always had the chance to start again. Emily prayed that perhaps, if nothing else, this might move Michael to find the inner peace she knew he lacked. And with time, she believed they could find happiness unlike anything they had ever known.

* * * * *

Michael lay staring at the ceiling. He couldn't deny his gratitude for Emily's love and forgiveness. It certainly made life easier. But neither could he deny the reality of what he was responsible for. Earlier she had asked him if he could live with it. He wasn't sure he could. By his own fears and stubbornness, he had denied Emily the right to have a baby that he had once *known* was to come to their home. From another perspective, was there a spirit on the other side, waiting to come to earth, that would be sent elsewhere? For the rest of mortality, Michael would wonder where that child had gone. Would it be raised in a home with love and strength, or born into a life of misery? Nothing but a miracle could fix this problem, but he wasn't sure if he was a man worthy of miracles. The very fact that Emily was a part of his life at all seemed a miracle to Michael. Perhaps he'd already had more than his share.

Michael finally drifted to sleep, merging reality into the same old nightmare. He couldn't count the times he had dreamt of Emily falling over that cliff, and the helplessness he felt in watching her fall. Gradually the dreams had lengthened, and in his sleep it seemed he was endlessly climbing down into the ravine to find her. He could see his booted feet descending at a sharp angle, rocks and gravel falling beneath every step as his body was nearly parallel to the mountain.

But tonight the dream changed. He was suddenly climbing upward. Michael looked down to see his feet struggling to find a hold amongst the jagged rocks. He looked up to see his hands groping for something to hold onto to lift himself up another step. When he finally reached the top, exhausted and uncertain of where he was, he woke up, sweating, heart beating wildly. He found Emily sleeping beside him and wondered what it all meant. Were his dreams simply a release of subconscious fears and mental garbage, or were they trying to teach him something? He didn't deny that the Spirit was capable of working through dreams, but to him it made no sense. He seemed to be endlessly struggling and groping to reach something, all the while terrified and feeling alone, as if Emily was gone forever and it was somehow his fault.

Three and a half years since he'd nearly lost Emily, and still he was struggling. But as he lay staring again at the darkness above him, almost feeling it tangibly surround and take hold of him, Michael finally did what he had been hesitant to do before now. With purpose, he closed his eyes and prayed.

Through all of this, Michael had never stopped going to church. But he had stopped going to the temple. He had never stopped living the basic commandments. But he had stopped reading his scriptures. He had never broken his temple covenants. But he had allowed fear to take hold of him and make him subject to the confusion and despair that Satan would have him fall victim to. He had lived the Word of Wisdom. But he knew his addiction to Coca-Cola was some kind of subconscious rebellion. Every time he looked in the mirror, he could see the evidence. The beard and longer hair, however well-groomed, were just futile attempts to hide the pain in his eyes. He had never stopped praying. But his prayers had become mechanical and often meaningless.

Tonight, however, Michael prayed with his heart and soul. He prayed that God would forgive him for the things he'd done that had hurt Emily. And he prayed for help to overcome this fear once and for all and get on with his life. He told God that he wanted to understand why Emily would be with Ryan in the next life. And if it had to be that way, he prayed that he could learn to live with it and appreciate what he had here and now.

Michael fell asleep without ever reaching an *amen*. But he woke up feeling a little less down and oppressed. It was just a glimmer of hope, but it was enough to believe that God had heard his prayer and life would get better. It was only later that day when he remembered that it often gets darkest before the light. And sometimes it just has to get worse in order to get better. If Michael had known how much worse it would get, he might have left the house then and there to find a bottle of Scotch whiskey.

The doorbell rang while Michael was molding meatballs. "Will somebody get that?" he hollered. But when it rang again, apparently no one heard. He grabbed a paper towel and cleaned his hands on his way to the door.

The woman on the porch was unpleasantly thin and in her late sixties, Michael guessed, dressed in a lavender polyester pantsuit. Before a word was exchanged, she looked him over with a glare that made him wonder if she had thoughts of doing him damage with the oversized purse she clutched at her middle.

Michael's eyes moved to a tall, dark-haired man, near his own age, standing down a couple of steps, looking passively bored. He looked somehow familiar in a way that rubbed Michael wrong, though he couldn't pinpoint it.

"May I help you?" Michael finally asked.

"You must be Mr. Hamilton," the woman snipped, as if his accent had given him away.

"Yes," Michael drawled skeptically.

"I'm here to see my grandchildren."

"I'm sorry?" Michael leaned forward and narrowed his eyes. He was sure he'd missed something. If she hadn't called him by name, he'd have told her she had the wrong house.

Just as the reality started to take hold in Michael's mind, she clarified tersely, "I am Joan Hall, and your wife is the mother of three of my grandchildren."

Michael tried to give a congenial smile, but nothing about this woman made him want to. The last thing he needed right now was a visit from Ryan Hall's mother.

"Come in," he said dryly. Mrs. Hall entered and the silent man followed. Michael knew now this had to be Ryan's brother. The resemblance was striking, and he hated this turn of events already.

"Go on up the stairs and sit down," he said. "I'll just . . . go and see if I can find the girls."

While Mrs. Hall perched herself at the edge of the couch and studied her surroundings with a wrinkled nose, Ryan's brother slouched into the rocking chair and reached for a newspaper. Michael went to find Emily.

"What?" She pulled off her headphones and looked up from her painting, immediately noticing his distress.

"Your mother-in-law is here," he reported.

Emily clicked off the stereo and set her brush aside. "From Australia? She didn't call or—"

"Your *other* mother-in-law," he clarified, unable to help the cynical tone. Even without the reminder of Ryan Hall's part in this family, he simply didn't like these people.

Emily's eyes widened. "Ryan's mother?" she whispered, astonished.

"As charming as ever," he added, motioning Emily toward the

hall. "I think I'll let you handle this."

Michael reluctantly followed her back to the living room. Allison had kept in touch with her grandmother over the years through letters and phone calls, and occasionally there was some trifling contact with Alexa and Amee. But the younger ones didn't remember their father's mother, so cared little for the occasional card or letter. And Allison had long since stopped caring about anything.

"What a surprise," Emily said, proud of herself for the enthusiasm in her tone, however stilted.

Mrs. Hall nodded and almost smiled. "Hello, Emily. It's good to see you again." Her words were clipped.

Michael observed the exchange and wondered how Emily was feeling. He couldn't help but remember the trouble Ryan's mother had given her soon after his death. Their relationship had been strained at the very least.

"I assume you met my husband, Michael." Emily reached out a hand for him, suddenly needing him near for reasons she didn't understand.

"We met," she said, throwing a condescending smile in Michael's direction. "You remember David," she added, motioning toward the man slouched in the chair.

David tipped the corner of the paper down and nodded toward Michael and Emily. "Hi," he said and resumed his reading.

Emily was reminded so much of her first husband that he might as well have scraped his fingernails down a chalkboard.

"So," Emily tried to smile at Mrs. Hall, "what brings you here?"

"Well," Mrs. Hall answered, clearing her throat, "I hadn't gotten a letter from Allison for quite some time, and I was a bit concerned. David has just been home to help me take care of some little details, and I'm going back to Arizona with him. I'll be staying there indefinitely."

"Hot place, Arizona," Michael said. Mrs. Hall lifted a skeptical eyebrow.

"It will be an adjustment." She spoke to Emily, who tried to smile politely but hated the memories assaulting her.

Ryan's mother had never liked or respected her daughter-in-law, and David's very presence reminded Emily of Ryan as he had often been in their marriage, silently arrogant in his own world. She tried to recall that Ryan had changed a great deal before his death. They had been on the road to a better relationship. But still, she couldn't help being reminded of the pain she had endured, being shut out and put down for ten years.

"Anyhow," Mrs. Hall rambled on, "I just thought I should stop and see how my girls are coming along. Of course Allison had informed me you'd moved back to Utah, and I had the address from her letters. How is Allison?"

Michael and Emily exchanged concerned glances. Emily sat down next to Mrs. Hall.

"Uh . . ." Emily cleared her throat and glanced to Michael for support. "The reason you haven't gotten a letter from her is that . . . well, she isn't here right now. She's . . ."

"She ran away from home," Michael stated matter-of-factly. Emily had wanted some help, but she would have preferred something a little more tactful.

"Oh, no!" Mrs. Hall gasped. "What on earth have you done to make her want to get away like that?"

"I don't think her home environment could have been any better," Emily began to justify. "Michael and I—"

"Actually," Michael interrupted, a subtle anger brewing in his eyes, "I beat her every morning and stood over her with a whip while she did a minimum of ten hours' hard labor each day."

Emily stared at her husband in disbelief. Mrs. Hall gasped in astonishment and clutched her purse more tightly. David peered over his newspaper.

"Well," Mrs. Hall huffed, "I've never heard of such a—"

"I think he's kidding, Mother," David stated in a demeaning tone. "Don't be such a dolt."

"Michael has an interesting sense of humor," Emily interjected, giving him a sidelong glance. Mrs. Hall glared at Michael dubiously.

"I can assure you," Emily continued, "that Michael is a wonderful father to *all* of the children."

Michael's lips tightened further at Emily's apparent need to justify. "If you'll excuse me, I've got meatballs in process."

Michael hurried into the kitchen, wishing he couldn't hear bits and pieces of the conversation. Emily's attempt to explain Allison's departure, and the events leading up to it, went far beyond what Michael believed necessary. Mrs. Hall's questions and responses were subtly stern, even unkind. "Well, Allison is twenty-one," Emily said vehemently. "We're terribly concerned about her, but after all, she is old enough to be on her own."

"Emily," Michael called in a congenial voice, "could I get you to help me here for just a minute?"

"Excuse me," Emily said and hurried to the kitchen. "What do you need?" she asked.

"Could you please turn on the stove and stir that sauce," he said in a normal voice. "My hands are a mess, and . . ." he added in a whisper as she was doing it, "could you please remember who and what you are and stop apologizing to that woman!"

Emily looked up at him, astonished. "Michael," she whispered sharply, "I am merely trying to make her understand that—"

"I'm sorry, Emily, but that's not what I'm hearing."

"Is that all you need?" she asked in a normal voice.

"Yes, thank you," he replied kindly while his eyes hardened on her.

Emily returned to the living room and sat down, trying not to show her discomfort. She wanted to believe there was nothing to Michael's observance, but she had to wonder. Was it possible, after all these years, that just being with these people put her back into the slot where she had once been?

"So," Mrs. Hall said, "how are the other girls?"

"Oh," Emily brightened, "Amee and Alexa are doing well. They're out delivering papers right now. They are both in the Young Women's program; Amee especially loves it. Alexa is totally involved with sports. She's on a soccer team and—"

"Soccer?" Mrs. Hall repeated. She might as well have said mud wrestling.

"Well, yes," Emily replied. "A lot of girls do it these days. She quite enjoys it. There is no reason to . . ." Emily stopped when she heard that apologetic tone seep into her own voice. She looked up to see Michael leaning in the doorway, wiping his hands on a dish towel.

"Alexa is an excellent soccer player," Emily added with confidence. "She is one of the best on her team."

"She especially enjoys being the goalie," Michael added with a spark of pleasure in his eyes. "You should see her block that ball after a rainstorm. She *loves* the mud."

While Mrs. Hall sat there gaping and David continued to peruse the newspaper, Emily was relieved to hear the girls come in.

"Here they are," Michael said histrionically, "pretty and prettier, though it's hard to decide which is which."

The girls smirked at Michael and hurried into the kitchen, not caring to notice the company seated in the living room.

"What's for dinner, Dad?" Amee called. "It smells disgusting."

"I think it smells good," Alexa retorted. "Oh, awesome! It's those porcupine meatball things. I love these, Dad," she called louder. Emily didn't miss Mrs. Hall's obvious distress at the girls calling Michael *Dad.*

"I'm glad somebody does," he said, then motioned them toward the living room. "We have company. Come in and be polite, if you think that's possible."

The girls hovered in the doorway with Michael until Emily said, "Come in, girls. This is your Grandmother Hall, and Uncle David."

"Grandma Hall?" Amee questioned, moving a few steps into the room. "Oh, hi," she said without expression.

"Hello, Amelia," Mrs. Hall said. Amee winced visibly. Michael snickered quietly. "You're so grown up. The last time I saw you, you were barely two."

"I don't remember that," Amee admitted politely.

"Alexa," Emily urged, "say hello to your grandmother."

"Hi," Alexa said quietly.

"Hello, Alexandra," Mrs. Hall smiled almost warmly. "You're both lovely girls. Aren't they lovely girls, David?"

David folded the paper and finally set it aside. "What was that?"

"I said, aren't the girls lovely?"

"Ah, yes." David showed a human expression at last. "Lovely girls."

Glancing back and forth, Michael was unnerved by the physical resemblance the girls, especially Amee, shared with their uncle.

"This is your Uncle David," Emily said again when the girls looked at him in question.

"Are you my father's brother?" Amee asked.

"That's right," Mrs. Hall answered for him.

Michael wanted to slither back into the kitchen, but his curiosity kept him there.

"You look like my father," Amee said tonelessly.

David lifted a brow as if this pleased him. Mrs. Hall virtually grinned. "Do you remember your father?" she asked, holding out a hand toward Amee.

Amee looked hesitantly at the outstretched hand and stepped forward to take it, if only to be polite. "No, I don't," she admitted, "but we have lots of pictures."

"Your father was a very handsome man," Mrs. Hall said dreamily as she pulled Amee down next to her on the couch and reached out a hand toward Alexa. Alexa sat down dutifully and screwed up her face as Mrs. Hall put an arm around her.

When there was a length of silence, Amee piped in with, "Dad's a great cook. I was just teasing about the meatballs being disgusting. Can you stay and eat with us?"

Michael and Emily exchanged a subtle, wary glance. But they could hardly scold Amee when they had emphatically taught their children to be gracious and generous. Michael had never once had someone in his home with dinner cooking and not invited them to stay.

"Is it all right, Dad?" Alexa asked.

"Of course it is, love," Michael said warmly, if only for the pride he felt in his daughters. The thought caught him off guard. They were not *his* daughters. Never had he been so aware of it as now. He didn't quite like the way they were calling him *Dad*, while talking about their *father*, a man long dead.

"We certainly don't want to be a burden," Mrs. Hall said, and almost seemed to mean it.

"It's no trouble," Michael said with sincerity. "I always cook too much."

"Yeah," Amee piped in, "that's why we're always having leftovers."

"Do you cook often?" Mrs. Hall asked, looking at Michael directly for the first time since she'd sat down.

"Oh, he does nearly all of the cooking while I'm in school," Emily explained. "But he enjoys it," she added warmly. "It's always been that way, ever since college."

"Yes, that's right." Mrs. Hall seemed to have caught a mouse to play with. "The two of you dated in college, didn't you?"

"Yes we did," Emily stated firmly. Michael's presence reminded her not to apologize or justify. "I went to Australia with Michael the summer before Ryan and I were married."

This seemed to somehow distress Mrs. Hall, which made Michael smile.

"Isn't that a coincidence—that the two of you would get back together so soon after Ryan passed on," she commented snidely.

"I think dinner is ready," Michael said before she had a chance to elaborate. The memories assaulting him were getting worse by the minute.

"Where are the boys?" Emily asked as Amee and Alexa set the table and she helped put the food into serving dishes.

"They were still in front of that new video last I checked," Michael reported, and she went downstairs to get them. Michael sent Amee to invite their guests to the table while Emily herded the boys to get washed up.

"Ah," Mrs. Hall said as they were seated, "these must be your boys. Allison told me some about them in her letters." Emily introduced Jess and James, but they paid little attention.

The meal proceeded without conversation, but not in silence. James said he hated meatballs, and Jess knocked over his milk while trying to tease his brother. The girls kept giggling as if they could read each other's humorous thoughts, and Michael got up three times to get something from the kitchen that had been forgotten.

Just before dessert Mrs. Hall commented, "This meal is very good, Mr. Hamilton. Where did you learn to cook?"

"I just always did it," he replied, "and I took a few classes here and there. As a teenager, I often cooked for the stable hands."

"Stable hands?" she questioned as if it were in a foreign

language.

Michael leaned his forearms on the table and spoke to her as he might to a child. It was the only way he could carry on a conversation and not be rude. "Yes, Mrs. Hall, stable hands. My family owns and operates what we call a station. I believe you would call it a ranch. We have far too many horses to keep track of on our own. We breed them and train them for many purposes. I grew up with the stable hands. I worked with them. I often cooked for them. Now they are my employees. Do you want to know anything else?"

He was hoping she'd say *no*, but she responded with an eager, "Is it a profitable business?"

"Most of the time, yes," he stated. He could almost hear it coming, and wasn't surprised when she took it a step further.

"You are rather well off, I hear."

Emily nearly winced from the statement. She knew Michael's humble attitude about the money. In all the years she'd known him, she had never heard him say anything about his wealth to draw attention to it. Until now.

"Actually, yes, I am rather well off, Mrs. Hall. My great-grandfather inherited an enormous fortune, and through the generations it has been invested and used wisely."

This caught David's interest. "How much land do you own?"

"Well, David," Michael said condescendingly, "if you must know, I've never bothered to actually count the acreage. I'm sure somebody must know. I only know it takes several minutes to fly over it."

"Fly?" Mrs. Hall echoed.

"Yes," he turned to her to clarify, "I own three private planes, and I fly them myself."

"My goodness," Mrs. Hall shook her head, "you *are* well off, Mr. Hamilton."

"Yes." He leaned back and gave a phony smile, giving Emily the urge to slap him. "Before I married Emily, I was listed as one of the wealthiest bachelors in Australia."

"You were?" Emily's surprise softened her anger for the moment.

"Yes, love," he nodded toward her, "I was."

Emily tried to divert the conversation. "Being able to fly came in handy when he was branch president. He had to cover a lot of territory."

"You were branch president?" Mrs. Hall seemed to like him more by the minute. "Why, that's equivalent to a bishop, isn't it?"

"Yes, it is," Michael stated, more like his humble self.

"Funny, Allison never mentioned that."

"There were a lot of things Allison likely never mentioned," Michael said curtly.

Emily was relieved when no one questioned him on that, and he didn't seem eager to explain. Following a lull in the conversation, Michael picked up his barely-touched meal and carried it to the kitchen where he began to wash dishes. When everyone else was finished, Emily told the girls to get some photo albums out and show them to their grandmother. She returned Jess and James to their video, then cleared the table.

"How long do you suppose they're going to stay?" Michael asked while she helped him load the dishwasher.

"I don't know, Michael," she said quietly, then she caught his hand in hers and made him stop. "This must be very difficult for you. I assume that's why you were in there bragging."

Michael let out a guilty sigh. "I'm sorry about that. I just—"

"Don't tell me." She wrapped her arms around him. "Let me guess. She seemed so eager to be impressed, you couldn't resist impressing her."

"I guess that about covers it."

"It's all right, Michael. I understand."

Michael looked into her eyes and reminded himself that this was also difficult for her. "Are you all right?" he asked.

"I'm sure I'll manage," she said, and Michael bent to kiss her. Just when he was beginning to really enjoy it, Mrs. Hall cleared her throat loudly in the kitchen doorway.

"I'm so sorry," she said when they both glanced in her direction, "I was just needing a glass of water."

While Emily got the water, Michael felt Mrs. Hall surveying him freshly, as if she couldn't imagine him and Emily having an intimate relationship that might warrant such a kiss in the kitchen. He wanted to ask her if she had any idea where Jess and James had come from.

"Thank you, Emily," she said when the water was provided. Mrs. Hall went back to the living room. Michael and Emily finished the dishes in silence. Emily suggested the girls each play a piano piece for their grandmother, which helped ease the discomfort a bit.

Long after the children went to bed, Mrs. Hall was still looking through old photo albums, commenting to Emily about Ryan doing this, and Ryan doing that. Emily politely endured the conversation while Michael looked on, bored and tense. David sat at one end of the couch, snoring softly.

When Michael couldn't take it any longer, he rose with a loud yawn. "It's past our bedtime. It doesn't look like the two of you will make it to Arizona tonight. Do you have a room yet, or—"

"We hadn't really thought about it," Mrs. Hall said, suddenly gasping at the time on her watch. She noticed David snoring then and nudged him awake.

Emily threw Michael a cautioning glance before she said kindly, "You're welcome to spend the night, of course."

"Oh, we wouldn't want to be a burden," Mrs. Hall said once again. Michael wondered if this visit was little more than an alternative to paying for a motel room. The timing was unbelievable. He wondered if God had sent them to teach him something. Or had Satan prompted them to come and taunt him in his misery? Perhaps a little of both.

"Why don't you take Allison's room," Emily said as she stood. "I'll show you where it is. There's a bathroom next to it."

"Oh, that's sweet of you, dear," Mrs. Hall said, actually sounding genuine.

"You can take the couch, David," Michael said. "That way you won't have to move."

"Are we staying?" David asked his mother through a yawn.

"It looks as if we are. I hope we don't outdo our welcome."

"No chance of that," Michael said on his way to the bedroom, his sarcasm too subtle for anyone but Emily to recognize.

When the guests were settled in, Emily found Michael sitting up in bed with a notebook and pencil idle on his lap.

"No inspiration tonight?" she questioned as she began to dress for bed.

"Not hardly."

"Michael, it's not as bad as all that. I mean, one night in ten years. I think we can live with it."

"I don't like them, Emily."

"I don't like them, either. But face it, we're related."

"*You're* related. I'm not."

"I'm not either, if you want to get technical," Emily interjected. "But our daughters are."

"They're not *my* daughters, Emily," he said sadly.

Emily looked at him in surprise. "You're the only father they've ever known, Michael. You're my husband, and that makes you their father. I thought this issue was settled years ago."

"Well, it seems to be unsettling at the moment."

"I don't think we should talk about this right now," Emily said on her way into the bathroom. "I think we should just get some sleep, endure them a little longer, and talk about it next week when we're not in the middle of it."

Emily came back a few minutes later to find Michael unmoved, staring at the wall.

"Are you all right?" she asked, sitting beside him.

"I have a question, Emily."

"Go ahead."

"I just met Ryan once. I know only what you told me about him. David resembles him a great deal, from what I remember."

"Yes, he does. They were often mistaken for each other by those who didn't know them well."

"But . . . did Ryan . . . *act* like that?"

"Like what?" Emily asked, suddenly finding it necessary to fidget with the edge of a blanket.

"Well, let's see. He totally excluded himself from the conversation, as if he were too good to be a part of it; at least that's the way I saw it. He was patronizingly silent to the children. He spoke to his mother with little or no respect. Am I getting an accurate picture?"

"Ryan was a different man before he died, Michael."

It was tempting to tell Emily exactly how much that very fact was eating away at him. "I'm talking about before that. Before he changed, Emily."

Michael was not prepared for the tears he saw in Emily's eyes when she looked up at him. "Yes, Michael," she said, "he was very much like that. Just watching David tonight brought the memories back so vividly I wanted to scream. I spent ten years living with a man like that, Michael. And until this evening, when you told me that I didn't need to justify and apologize, I had forgotten how much I really had changed. Ryan changed when I made it clear that I wouldn't put up with it." Emily took his hand and squeezed it. "You did that for me, Michael. You taught me how to respect myself and believe in myself." She touched his face. "It's one of so many things that make me love you."

Michael pulled her into his arms and just held her. He wished he could tell her how much that meant to him, but the words just wouldn't come. He loved Emily more than life, and the only thing about the love he shared with her that bothered him was the fact that Ryan Hall still had something that Michael didn't. If what was bound on earth would be bound in heaven, Michael was nothing more than a solitary soul on a brief earthly mission. The thought of turning his wife and these children over to another man in the next life was more than he could bear, more than he could even consider talking about.

Instead, he concentrated on the moment. If he could forget about eternity and just love her now, perhaps the rest would go away. He turned on soft music and lit the tall candles on the dresser. When the candle wax had dripped down to practically nothing, he had almost forgotten that Ryan's mother and brother were sleeping in his home. He thought how shocked and disgusted Mrs. Hall would be if she knew what was taking place under the same roof. Emily kissed him and he didn't care.

Michael drifted to sleep in her arms and immediately felt himself climbing that inevitable rock wall. Endlessly he groped for handholds, striving to reach higher. His muscles ached and his mind felt weary. When he finally reached the top, he expected to wake up, as if his subconscious accepted this as a dream. It had happened so many times before. But this time, as he collapsed onto the plateau, he looked up and saw Emily standing above him, wearing her wedding gown, reaching a hand toward him.

"Emily," he said and almost heard himself speak it aloud. He felt immense relief as her hand slipped into his and she helped him to his feet. She wasn't dead, after all. She was alive and real and here. He pulled her into his arms and held her tightly. But her embrace felt somehow restrained, unnatural. She pulled back to look at his face and smiled warmly.

"I'm so glad you've come," she said. "We've been waiting for you."

With his hand firmly in hers, Michael followed Emily across the plateau, until he realized they were inside a home, though he couldn't remember entering it. The dwelling was spacious and beautiful, unlike anything he'd ever seen before. Peace and tranquility filled him to the core as he looked around a large dining table to see each of the children. They were all dressed in white, looking as they always had at dinner. Allison was there too, a peaceful glow about her. Emily motioned Michael to a chair between Jess and James. As he moved toward it to be seated, his view of the table broadened. And there, at its head, was Ryan Hall, looking just as Michael remembered him the one time they'd met, only a few months before his death. Ryan came to his feet and smiled at Michael with acceptance. Emily went to Ryan's side, and Ryan put a fatherly hand on Jess's shoulder. The numbness Michael felt erupted into a volatile fury and he lunged toward the table, crying from the depths of him, "No!"

Emily heard Michael's cry and turned over to find him sitting up, breathing sharply, the sheets clenched in his fists.

"You were dreaming again," she said softly.

Michael could only nod as a tangible sickness began to smolder inside him.

"Same dream?" she asked. He had yet to tell her about it, but she was beginning to hate the way these dreams wouldn't end.

Michael shook his head, suddenly afraid that speaking would relinquish what little control he had over his churning stomach.

"Michael," she whispered intensely, "please tell me about it. Maybe if you—"

She stopped when he ran to the bathroom and slammed the door. He was obviously quite ill, but she doubted it had anything to do with a virus.

Michael thought the dry heaves would never end. Just when he thought he had it under control, the memory of his dream would assault him again and bring that sick, churning feeling back. Finally he willed himself to not think about it, fearing he'd pass out if he didn't get some control. He sat on the bathroom floor with a wet towel against his face, wondering what was wrong with him. How could a nightmare make a grown man physically ill?

A soft knock at the door startled him. "Are you all right, Michael?" Emily asked.

"I'm fine," he said. "I'll be out in a minute."

Michael splashed cool water on his face and blotted it dry. He brushed his teeth and gargled twice, as if it could somehow wash away that sick sensation of seeing Emily—and his children—with another man.

"Are you sick?" Emily asked when he finally emerged from the bathroom, looking pale and drawn. He wanted to lie to her and tell her he had the flu or something. But before he had a chance, her discernment picked up on the truth. "Are your dreams so bad?"

He glanced at her warily, and she saw the truth in his eyes.

"Do you want to tell me about it?" she asked gently.

Michael wanted to tell her. With all his heart, he wanted to just cry it all out to her and hear her tell him it was ridiculous and they would be together forever. But in his mind, he could hear her response. *"Yes, Michael,"* he imagined her whispering, *"I am sealed to him. There is nothing to be done about it. You're going to have to learn to live with it."*

"Michael," Emily urged, "please tell me."

"I can't." The words choked out, and he curled up weakly on his side of the bed.

Emily's heart ached with helplessness and concern as she turned off the light and snuggled close to his back, wishing she could just make it go away—whatever it was.

CHAPTER TWELVE

Michael's state of mind put him on edge more than usual as Mrs. Hall and David were preparing to leave. Emily had suggested that he hide away and write until they were gone, but he felt a need to be there. Instinctively he wanted to know what they might say or do, as if they were somehow the enemy and he needed to spy to know what he was up against.

Michael blessed and cursed those instincts when Mrs. Hall drew Alexa and Amee close to her on the couch to tell them good-bye. "You know," she said, "it's a wonderful thing for you girls to be Latter-day Saints and to have been born in the covenant."

"What does that mean?" Alexa questioned.

Emily felt a sharp chill rush through her. Her glance darted to Michael, but she saw no change of expression.

"Your father and mother were sealed in the temple when they were married," Mrs. Hall went on in a voice of apparent wisdom, "and even though your father died at a young age, and you girls do not remember him, you can always know that one day you will all be together in heaven. You girls, and Allison, too, were born into that eternal marriage, and that means your family will be together forever, even after death."

Amee and Alexa seemed to contemplate this for a moment. Emily tried to rub the chill from her arms, wondering why Mrs. Hall's words made her so uncomfortable. She glanced at Michael as he rubbed a hand over his mouth. His eyes were hard, almost glazed.

"But Grandma," Alexa asked intently, "what about Jess and James? Won't we be with them in heaven, too?"

"Why, Alexandra," Mrs. Hall's voice picked up an edge of astonishment, as if the child's ignorance was appalling, "Jess and James are not your father's children. They are only your *half-*brothers."

She said the last words as if describing some kind of plague. Emily watched Michael, wanting to rush to him and tell him not to listen. Knowing his emotions were vulnerable anyway, she couldn't comprehend the hurt and frustration he must be feeling. Still, she wasn't prepared for the way he shot out of his chair and took a long stride toward Mrs. Hall. All eyes turned to him, and Emily prayed he would not say or do anything to make the situation worse.

"Mrs. Hall," Michael said with barely concealed anger, "in my home, we do not attach the word *half* or *step* to any relationship of a family member. We are a family of brothers and sisters and parents. I am truly sorry for your son's untimely death, and the pain it has undoubtedly brought into your life. But I will not regret the opportunity I have had to be a father to these girls, and a husband to Emily. We are a family, Mrs. Hall, now and forever. And *no one*," he pushed a hand sharply through the air and pressed his teeth together, "is going to come into my home and tell me otherwise."

Mrs. Hall came to her feet, apparently not intimidated by Michael's authority, not to mention his height. "Mr. Hamilton," she snapped, "my son is a father to these girls, and he will be for time and all eternity. I was there when those vows were exchanged, and they *will* be bound in heaven."

"Those vows are on the condition of righteousness, Mrs. Hall. Were you also there when your son degraded and belittled his wife until her self-esteem amounted to *nothing*? Were you there when your son spent time and money on another woman, then came home and ignored his wife and children? Did you see the way he—"

"I'll have no more of these lies!" Mrs. Hall shouted. She turned to Emily. "How can you tolerate this attitude toward your first husband, when—"

"He's telling you the truth," Emily interrupted in a quiet, firm voice that caught Mrs. Hall's attention. "I loved Ryan very much, and he made some positive changes before he died. But I will not pretend our marriage was something it was not. Temple marriage is a wonderful thing, Mrs. Hall, but it's only a beginning, not an end. The way two people buoy each other up through life, the respect they give to one another—*that* is what makes an eternal marriage. The sealing is only a technicality. The achievement of that sealing is done in the home. I can't tell you how it will be in the next life, Mrs. Hall, but I know that God is just and fair, and we will receive what we have earned. I have the faith to know that I will be with those I love forever."

Michael watched Emily, so many emotions churning inside him that he couldn't decide whether to run away or scream. Knowing he could do neither, he just stood there, appreciating some of Emily's points, and feeling a bizarre kind of anguish from others. When the room hung in tense silence, Michael suddenly felt like a fool for having made such an issue of this. Mrs. Hall was leaving, and they would likely not see her again for another ten years—maybe never. Perhaps she was a little misguided, but he knew it was not his place to judge her or her motives. And in spite of the things Ryan had done to hurt Emily, it was not Michael's place to confront his mother with those facts.

Looking around at the troubled expressions of his wife and daughters, Michael reminded himself of who and what he was. He pushed the pain down a little deeper and stepped back. "I'm sorry," he said to Mrs. Hall. "Please forgive me for getting so angry."

With that Michael left the room, hoping Emily could smooth it over. He turned on the computer to write, but he could only stare at a blank screen. His mind wandered back to that moment when Emily's heart had stopped, and he'd believed he would never see her again. At moments it seemed like only yesterday, and even now the thought made his fists clench by their own will. It seemed he was often so absorbed in his effort to bury all the fear and confusion, that time had lost its essence.

He thought of the news Emily had recently given him, that their opportunity to have children was over. A shiver of cold dread rushed through him, as if to tell him that time had run out. He couldn't bury it any longer. At this moment, Michael felt so keenly in touch with his emotions that he feared the pain would somehow devour him.

"Are you all right?" Emily's voice startled him and he turned in his chair to look at her.

He couldn't answer. "Did she leave angry?"

"She didn't seem terribly happy, but I think she'll get over it."

"I'm sorry I said what I did, Emily. She didn't need to know that Ryan had—"

"Maybe she did." Emily walked behind Michael and pushed her hand beneath his shirt to rub the back of his neck. "You're tense. Do you want to tell me why?"

"No."

"What she said was unfair, Michael. You mustn't let it upset you. These are your children; *all* of them."

"Are they?" he asked, his tone cynical.

Emily stopped a moment and pondered the severity of that question. A deep dread seized her. Could this possibly be a clue to what was eating at Michael? Hoping to console him, she answered firmly, "Yes, they are."

"Perhaps now," he countered, "but what about—"

Emily winced when the phone rang. She wanted to ignore it, but Michael was quick to grab the receiver, as if it had saved him from saying something he didn't want to.

"No, she's not busy," Michael said and handed the phone to Emily. He turned off the computer and left the room, while Emily tried to concentrate on matters of primary business.

Michael poured himself a glass of Coke, wishing he had something stronger, though he doubted he could bring himself to drink it. He was stupid, but not that stupid.

He sat on the couch and tried to relax, tried to think of the good points in his life, the things he had to be grateful for. But all he could envision was the prospect of spending eternity alone. He knew in his heart that hell was not fire and brimstone and eternal burning. Hell was dedicating your whole life to something you love, and then having to let it go forever. While a part of him believed that God would not be so unfair, the rest of him was so consumed by fear that he couldn't imagine any other possibility.

Michael squeezed his eyes shut, wanting to be free of his thoughts, but all he could see were the images from his nightmares.

All he could feel was the torment of losing Emily to a man he didn't even like, let alone respect. And yet Ryan wasn't so bad. He had changed before he died. How could Michael put himself on the opposite end of the scale and not see his own faults? As much as he loved Emily, Michael knew he had hurt her—badly. And even if Michael could bring himself to believe that he treated Emily better than Ryan had, he knew that Ryan had something Michael didn't. Mrs. Hall had unkindly reminded him of that—as if he needed reminding.

Michael heard a subtle groan escape his throat as he thought of Emily kneeling at a temple altar with Ryan Hall, exchanging eternal vows. Perhaps if he had not been so proud and unyielding, he would have joined the Church ten years earlier, and Emily would have married him the first time around. How different it all could have been! Oh, the peace he would feel to just *know* that he would be with Emily and these children forever! But all he had was now. And even that was being blown to hell because of these wretched fears.

The pain became so intense that Michael wondered why God had abandoned him to this agony. He no sooner thought it than he had to ask himself what he had done to put distance between himself and God. He told himself to get up right now and go pray, or at least open the scriptures. But the very thought was rebuffed by confusion and guilt. Why hadn't he dealt with this sooner? Why had he let it get so out of hand? He thought of Emily and just wanted to hold her in his arms and cry his heart out to her. But it was as if the fear of losing her held him back, as if he could somehow ease some of the pain by not letting himself get too close. He had hurt her in a way that seemed irreparable to him. As always, she was quick to forgive. But Michael wasn't sure he could forgive himself for denying her the right to have that baby.

As the pain rushed closer to the surface, Michael realized he couldn't push it down any longer. He had to face it or die. At the moment, dying seemed easier. All he wanted was peace. But the very idea seemed to mock him, as if a voice whispered in his head that he was not worthy of peace.

Needing to somehow release the pressure in his head, Michael began to pace. At first he circled the room slowly, methodically. Then his pacing gained momentum, until he felt like a caged animal, and the devil himself held the key. "Please, God," he muttered, "let me be free of this. Please . . ."

A tiny glimmer of hope surfaced as he caught sight of the family pictures, set out in various sizes of frames across the top of the piano. Michael set his drink down and fondly touched the glass-covered faces of his sons, and the daughters he had raised and nurtured. He picked up the most recent family portrait, trying to comprehend the part he played in all of this. As he set the picture down, Michael's eye caught the little glass temple on the shelf above the piano. He knew well where it had come from. Emily told him it had adorned the top of the wedding cake when she and Ryan were married. Allison had found it in Emily's cedar chest and requested that they put it out. At the time, Michael had hardly given it a second thought. But now. . .

Feeling something hard and painful ooze from the very core of him, Michael held the little temple close to his eyes, examining the intricacy of the blown glass, noting how the sunlight filtered through it, reflecting a rainbow of colors at certain angles. In a flash, the last twenty-two years passed before his eyes. He felt sure that all of this was somehow his fault. If he had done something differently, somewhere along the way, Emily would have been his forever, not someone else's. The thought stung an already festering wound. All logic and sensibility fled. Michael could bear the pain no longer.

With no premeditation, Michael hurled the glass temple across the room, where it hit the wall and shattered into a million pieces over the carpet. Emily heard the crash and took the stairs two at a time.

"Michael!" she called. "What happened?" She stopped at the top of the stairs. Their eyes met, then his shifted guiltily to the glass on the floor. Emily's eyes followed and widened. The scene sent her heart pounding into her throat as she tried to comprehend what kind of feelings would make him do such a thing. She was still wondering what to say when he rushed past her and grabbed his keys from the rack. Emily's stomach churned as she recalled his long-time habit of dispelling anger.

"Where are you going?" she asked, her voice edged with panic.

He said nothing.

"Michael," she pleaded, following him down the stairs, "please don't leave like this. Let's talk. I know something is terribly wrong. *Please* . . ."

Michael rushed out the door, leaving it open. Emily tried to pray and think and feel her instincts all at once. She knew she had to stop him . . . if she could.

"Amee," she called, "watch the children. Dad's upset. I don't know how long we'll be."

Amee nodded, seeming to sense the alarm Emily felt.

"Michael!" Emily rushed across the lawn as he opened the door of the Blazer. "Please wait. Let's talk."

Michael hesitated a moment and glanced over the window in her direction. She felt some hope, but it was dashed when he got in and slammed the door. The engine started, and Emily ran around to get in the other side. She had barely hurled herself into the seat when he squealed out of the driveway and headed toward 1600 North.

For several minutes, Emily just watched him. She didn't know what to say, where to begin. The hardness in his eyes was etched with pain. The way he completely ignored her made his irrationality all the more frightening. She had seen him go through many emotions, and the last few years had been hard. But only now did she begin to see that the turmoil in him was far worse than she had ever imagined. Uttering a silent prayer for their safety, Emily fastened her seat belt and reached across Michael to fasten his. He paid no attention.

"Talk to me, Michael," she said softly as he turned onto the freeway and headed north. He said nothing. "Where are we going?"

After a ridiculous silence he stated, "I'm just going for a drive. I didn't invite you to come along."

"You're not yourself, Michael. Let's stop and talk about this. Michael, do you really think that . . ." She was startled by the way he shifted gears and pressed the pedal to the floor. "Michael, how fast are you going? For heaven's sake, slow down!" He ignored her. "Michael, this is not Australia. You can't drive a hundred miles an hour to relieve your frustrations. Are you listening to me?" she shouted. But he was like a horse wearing blinders, his eyes fixed to the road, his knuckles turning white with one hand at the steering wheel, the other at the gearshift. "Michael," she said more softly, "stop this madness and think about what you're doing. You're not yourself."

"I agree with you on that," was all he said, but she felt some relief when he slowed down to exit at Lehi. He kept to the speed limit through town, but Emily's heart raced again as he headed west on a long stretch of highway, as if nothing could hold him back.

Emily gripped the seat next to her thighs as if it might save her. "Michael," she repeated, "this is not Australia. Will you remember which side of the car the steering wheel is on? If you don't get a ticket for speeding, you could kill us both."

Michael only put more pressure on the gas pedal, and Emily saw the speedometer reach toward ninety miles an hour. "I didn't invite you to come along," he repeated.

"Well, I did!" she shouted. "If you're trying to kill yourself, you're going to have to take me with you!"

"I am not trying to kill myself," he argued, but at least he was talking.

"Then exactly what *are* you trying to do?"

"I just need to drive."

"Why?"

He said nothing.

"Is it what Ryan's mother said?"

Michael glanced at her but said nothing.

"It is, isn't it? She's an old bat, Michael. Why would her opinions upset you so much? I don't understand."

"I don't understand, either."

"Then let's talk about it," she insisted, but he fell silent again.

Desperately, frantically, Emily prayed. She tried to recall where their conversation had been going earlier when the phone call had interrupted. It was about the children. She had told him the children were his, but he had begun to argue when that call seemed to save him.

"Michael," she said gently, trying to ignore the speed, trying to imagine guardian angels clearing a path for them, "is it what she said about the children?" She added in response to his silence, "Michael, they are *your* children. *All* of them."

Michael shot hard eyes toward her so fast that she knew she'd hit a nerve. "No, Emily, they are not."

"You are more of a father to those girls than Ryan ever dreamed of being. You've been there for them through all their ups and downs. How can you say that's not fatherhood?"

"That might work now, Emily," he said soberly, "but only for now."

The intensity of his words pierced her deeply. "What are you saying?" she managed in a whisper. She could hardly believe the implication. "Is that what all of this has been about?" she asked. "Is that what's been bothering you all this time?"

Michael's expression only hardened, but a warm quiver inside told her she had found the truth. Knowing the difficulties had begun when she'd nearly died, Emily began to see the light.

The Blazer slowed down and Emily held her breath. Michael looked at the dashboard, then slammed a fist against the steering wheel.

"What?" she questioned intently.

"We're out of gas," he snarled.

Emily closed her eyes and mumbled an audible prayer of gratitude as the Blazer slowly came to a stop and choked into silence. Michael got out and slammed the door, then he kicked the tire. He paced back and forth with impatient strides and pushed his hands through his hair. Emily left her door open and went to him, taking his arms into her hands. She was relieved when he stopped and looked down at her, apparently willing to listen. "Michael," she said gently, "listen to me. We can talk about this."

Michael wanted to just take her in his arms and cry it all out. The words were on his tongue, but he couldn't say them. She'd already come so close to the truth, but a part of him seemed to believe that if he didn't tell her, she wouldn't be able to tell him that he was right—that they couldn't be together forever. It was as simple as that.

"Talk to me!" she shouted in his face.

Emily saw a brief softening in his eyes and nearly expected him to break down and get to the heart of this problem. But the glimmer of hope shattered when he pulled free of her grasp and stated coldly, "I need to get some gas." He pointed a harsh finger at her. "You stay here!"

Emily numbly watched him walk away, unable to stop him, unable to follow. It wasn't until he was out of sight that she wondered if she should have gone with him. She paced frantically, prayed zealously, thought fiercely, then prayed more. She thought of the children and hoped they were all right. She remembered the shattered glass on the floor and feared they would get hurt. Would Amee have the sense to vacuum it up? Emily prayed she would. "Please, dear Father," she muttered, "watch over my home and children. And please," tears welled up and she looked skyward, "please let us make it through this alive."

A car pulled up beside the Blazer. For a moment her heart pounded with fear, until Michael got out with a gas can. Michael thanked the driver in a kind voice, and the car pulled away. She watched him pour the gas in. He said nothing, didn't even look at her.

"Why won't you talk to me?" she asked. When he didn't even acknowledge her, Emily became angry. "You're beginning to remind me of someone else." He looked up at her sharply, pausing in his effort to screw the gas cap on. He obviously wanted an explanation, so Emily gave him one. "There are moments when you remind me all too much of what it was like to be married to a man who wouldn't talk to me. At times I could almost believe you're no better than Ryan."

Michael looked at her severely. He wanted to scream. He wanted to run. Instead he simply asked her, "Where are the keys?"

"Why, so you can try to kill us again?" Emily fondled the keys in her pocket, feeling a degree of control from having them.

"Give me the keys, Emily. Let's go home."

"I'll drive," she stated.

"Give me the keys!" he shouted.

Emily only glared at him.

While his eyes seemed to plead for help, his expression remained hard, his lips pressed together tightly.

"There is nothing we can't overcome together, Michael. I love you. You love me. What else matters?"

Michael pushed his hand brutally through his hair and tugged at it. "You just don't get it, do you?"

"How can I when you won't tell me?" she shouted. "We have to talk!"

"Well, I can't!" he snarled. "It hurts like hell to even think about it. How can I possibly. . ." Michael heard his voice crack and felt a pounding between his eyes. Emily waited. "How can I . . ."

"It's the sealing, isn't it?" she guessed with a degree of confidence. His eyes confirmed it against his will. The pain she saw there broke her heart, and she wondered why she hadn't seen it before. Had she just assumed all these years that he believed as she did? She felt her anger melt into compassion. "Michael, we will be together forever. We *will*."

"I used to believe that." The hardness returned to his voice. "But not anymore."

Emily's brow furrowed. Tears welled into her eyes. "Why?"

Michael lifted his chin in a gesture of fortitude. Now that she had opened the door, the words spilled out with a calloused edge that didn't allow him to feel the pain. "You are sealed to another man. My daughters are not mine at all. And my sons . . . *my* sons, Emily, are sealed to you—not to me—and you are sealed to another man." Michael clenched his fists in front of him. "A man I didn't even like, Emily." His voice picked up a trace of the pain. "*I can't live with that!*" he added through clenched teeth.

Emily stared at him, dazed and afraid. What could she possibly say? The only consolation she could think of sounded utterly trite, but it was the best she could come up with. "The sealing was a technicality, Michael. Ryan didn't live up to those covenants."

"He changed before he died, Emily."

"Not enough to make me want to be with him forever."

"How can you say that?" he shouted "Do you think I didn't see the way his death affected you? Do you think I don't know how much you loved him?"

"Yes," she said, trying to remain calm in spite of the fury in his eyes, "I loved him. A part of me still does. But I had nothing to compare to. He never would have changed completely, Michael. I know that."

Michael shook his head in frustration. It was all so gray and confusing.

"Michael," she said gently, "we can be sealed. After we die, our children can do it for us. It can be—"

"That's no guarantee, Emily."

"Sealings are not meant to be a guarantee, Michael. It's a necessary ordinance. It takes a lot of work and commitment to carry it through. There is no reason why we can't be together forever."

"I could come up with a lot of reasons," he growled.

Emily swallowed hard and reminded herself to stay calm. "You are a better man than he, Michael. I will always—"

"Oh, no," he stopped her. The rage that filled his eyes chilled Emily to the marrow. He pointed a harsh finger at her. "You just told me that I was no better than Ryan."

Emily squeezed her eyes shut in a self-punishing grimace.

"No amount of gentle words will change facts, Emily. *I am no better than Ryan Hall.* Did *he* deny you the right to have a child you knew you were supposed to have? Some things are unforgivable, Emily. And *he* is the one you're sealed to."

For a moment of stunned silence, Emily stared at him, wondering what to say to make a difference. The man before her was not the Michael Hamilton she knew. What had made him so hard and bitter? How could she possibly reach through that cold exterior and find a way to touch his spirit without deepening his doubts?

As Michael realized he had exposed his deepest fears, the pain rushed up to hit him between the eyes. His effort to remain emotionless was waning quickly. He couldn't stand there and face her another minute.

When Michael reached out his hand, Emily felt some hope until he wiggled his fingers impatiently. "Give me the keys."

"No. I'll drive."

"Give me the keys, Emily!" He felt desperate, as if his emotion might explode if he didn't do something. He had to find a way to release it, and at the moment, having his foot against the gas pedal seemed the only painless possibility.

Emily shook her head firmly. His attitude had transformed her hurt into anger.

Michael heard the faint jingle in her pocket and reached his hand in to try and get the keys. Emily pulled them into her fist and moved away, but he caught her arm. She kept her fingers tightly around them, feeling a harsh desperation. Michael pressed a hand around her wrist and squeezed until it hurt.

"Stop it!" she demanded, but he pulled her arm behind her back so abruptly that the keys fell to the ground. He picked them up and threw the gas can into the back while Emily rubbed her tender wrist.

"You're a fool, Michael Hamilton," she cried as he got in and started the engine. "If you think you can solve anything by acting this way, you're nothing more than a fool."

"Are you coming or not?" he asked and put the Blazer into gear.

Emily got in and barely had the door closed when he peeled into a U-turn and headed back toward Lehi. Frantically she fastened her seat belt and did the same to Michael's, ignoring the glare he gave her. "Why are you treating me this way?" she demanded as the speedometer rose to sixty, seventy, eighty.

"Because I'm a fool," he stated. "I'm no better than Ryan."

"You don't really believe that."

"Yes," he said firmly, "I do."

"Michael, we can work this out. Satan is doing this to you, Michael. He's using your fears against you. Can't you feel that?"

He said nothing, but Emily sensed she was on the right track. The change in his expression was subtle, but she knew him well enough to see it. "Why are you so afraid?" she asked.

"Do you really want to know?" he asked, glancing at her as a deep pleading seeped through the anger.

"Yes," she put a hand on his leg, "I do."

Michael swallowed hard and began to chew his thumbnail. Emily noticed a slight quivering of his bottom lip and prayed they had finally reached the edge. But the silence dragged on.

"Michael," she said gently, "if you're afraid of something, it will destroy you. You can't let that happen. If you don't talk about it, I can't help you."

He said nothing, but she sensed him softening.

"Please, Michael," she whispered, "I love you. I'm here for you."

Emily prayed inwardly for the right thing to say. She was

surprised at how quickly she thought of Job. Only last week they had discussed the Biblical story in her Institute class. For the first time in her life, she felt she understood it. Perhaps if Michael understood it, then . . .

"Michael," she said anxiously, feeling somehow desperate for time, "please don't be like Job."

"What about him?" he snapped.

"He lost everything, because he—"

"I always hated that story," Michael interrupted. "I always wondered how God could allow such things to happen to a man who was so good and tried so hard."

"I always felt the same way, Michael, but . . ." She tried to quickly form the words in her mind, feeling a formless desperation. If she didn't say it right the first time, she wondered if she'd ever get another chance. "Michael, we talked about it in Institute. Job had one problem. He was afraid."

At this, Michael snapped his head toward her until he remembered he was driving.

"It's right there, Michael. Job himself said that the things he had feared had come upon him. Michael, don't you understand? Job was afraid he would lose everything—and he did. Faith and fear cannot exist together, Michael. Your fears are eating you alive. Please, Michael, don't throw away what we have because of your fears. Please," she sobbed, "think about what you're doing. Let me drive, and we'll talk about it. When Job realized he had brought the sorrows upon himself, when he repented and overcame them, the Lord blessed him with all that had been taken away and more. Please, Michael, you must talk to me. We can be together . . . now *and* forever. We can. I know it with all my heart."

Emily felt the first ray of real hope when he turned to her, tears brimming in his eyes. For a moment, all of the anguish and confusion fell away. Their spirits seemed to reach out to each other. Emily could almost read his fears, and prayed that he could grasp her faith enough to get them through this. She forgot that he was driving over ninety miles an hour. She forgot about the danger until his eyes shot back to the road, then widened in horror.

Emily turned to see a heavily-loaded farm truck crossing the road ahead. Her hands gripped the seat at her sides. She knew they weren't going to be able to stop in time. Somewhere in the distance she heard Michael express what she couldn't find the voice to say. "Dear God, we're going to die!"

"No!" Emily screamed, raising her arms in front of her face as if they could stop the inevitable collision. She could feel more than hear the screech of tires beneath them as Michael pulled the wheel sharply to the left. The Blazer spun and slid. Emily was barely aware of the power pole that stopped them as it became a part of the vehicle behind her seat.

* * * * *

Michael didn't know how long he lay with his head against the steering wheel, drifting in and out of consciousness. A bizarre montage of memories assaulted him, ending with Emily telling him about Job and his fears. Then his mind seemed to merge into the nightmares that had plagued him for so long. He reached out for Emily, but she inevitably fell over the cliff and he heard her cries as she plummeted to her death. *Emily!*

"No," Michael heard himself say on the edge of coherency. "Emily. No." His head came up abruptly, and he groaned from the pain. Well, at least he wasn't dead. Would the Lord be merciful enough to give him another chance in this life to make it right, to prove that he could overcome these fears and be worthy of Emily?

"Emily!" He turned abruptly to where she had been sitting before the impact. "Please, God, no!" he cried. Her face was turned away. She lay motionless, leaning against the back of the seat that had shifted several inches to the left from the impact to the right side of the Blazer. Michael attempted to reach her face, but fierce pain shot through his left leg and he groaned. He tried to twist toward her without moving his leg, but his entire left side throbbed at the slightest movement. Suppressing the pain, he unfastened his seat belt and leaned carefully toward her. With a trembling hand he touched her chin and turned her face to his view.

"Merciful heaven," he cried as her head lolled toward him,

blood trailing over the right side of her face, "what have I done?" Michael ignored the pain and leaned toward her, carefully shifting her head to his shoulder. He cried like a baby, holding his face to hers, feeling frantically at her throat for a pulse.

"Please, dear Father," he cried. "Please don't take her from me now. You nearly took her once and let her come back. Please!" He looked upward and squeezed his eyes shut. "Please let her come back to me. I know I've been a fool." He pressed his fingers harder where he knew the artery was, groping for any sign of life. Was it a faint pulsing of blood he felt, or simply his imagination? "Give me another chance, dear Lord, please. Please!" he howled, holding her tighter.

In that moment, he was struck with the conscious realization that she wasn't breathing. Keeping one hand against that artery, Michael tilted her head back and pinched her nose with the other. Instinctively he covered her mouth with his, blowing air into her lungs with purpose. Once, twice, three times. Nothing happened. Again he pressed his mouth to hers, much like he might have kissed her, consumed with passion. But his only passion now was a desire to have her live. With fury he tried to force his life into her, holding her closer as his desperation mounted. "Please, God," he cried and gave her another breath, but something inside told him his efforts were futile.

He became vaguely aware of sirens in the distance. The reality began to seep in, and Michael hung his head in despair. "Dear Lord, what have I done?" He thought of Emily's faith and wondered why he hadn't been man enough to follow her example and believe that they were meant to be together. And now it was too late. He wanted to die. He just wanted to die.

Then, somewhere in his memory, he heard Emily whisper to him, "Remember, Michael, I was promised I would live to see my children into adulthood. Have faith, Michael."

Michael took a deep breath and squeezed his eyes shut. He tried with all he had to block out everything but his desire to have her live, to be with her forever.

"Dear Father in Heaven," he stated firmly, "by the power of the Holy Melchizedek Priesthood, I pray that she might live, as she has been promised, to raise her children, to do all the good she can do in this world."

Michael kept praying, kept his fingers pressed to her throat. The sirens were getting closer now, and while he needed their help, he nearly feared their intrusion. In that moment he believed that only God could save her, and only he could exert the necessary faith to make it happen.

In desperation Michael finally spoke the amen, unwilling to face what seemed inevitable. She felt as lifeless as a rag doll. "Oh, Emily," he cried, burying his face in her hair, "my sweet Emily. Can you ever forgive me? If you would only forgive me, I'd do anything to have you back, to . . ."

Michael hesitated. He held his breath. Had he felt something beneath his fingers? He pressed them tighter to her throat, then sobbed a triumphant laugh when he felt a definite pulse.

"Merciful heaven," he cried, "you're alive." His tiny glimmer of faith blossomed with this tangible hope, and he prayed with every fiber of his being. Eagerly he pressed his mouth to hers again and blew the breath of life into her lungs. He'd barely begun when she coughed and gasped, and he felt her chest rise and fall as she took a deep breath.

"Oh, thank you, God!" Michael sobbed and pressed his face to hers, relishing the feel of her labored breathing against his skin. *"Thank you."*

CHAPTER THIRTEEN

Michael insisted they get Emily out first, but they had to move Michael to get to her. He passed out from the pain and woke up in a moving ambulance. When he realized the full impact of what had just happened, he became consumed with a heart-sickness that he believed he'd never be free of. In the midst of the pain, he was vaguely aware of his surroundings as he was wheeled into a hospital. *Was this where Ryan died?* he wondered briefly, and then he could only think of Emily. He had felt the evidence of life in her, but he wondered if it would hold out. He knew she was hurt badly, and he knew it was his fault. How could he ever live with the reality of the reason that accident occurred? It was as if a madman had been driving. What had possessed him? Why had he been so *stupid?*

They did X-rays and tests and calmly soothed his questions about his wife. It seemed forever that he lay staring upward, waiting for the conclusions, and then he was told they were taking him into surgery. There were apparently no internal injuries, but his left leg was badly broken. A rod would be put in his lower leg that would help the bones heal properly. Just before they put him under the anesthetic, Michael demanded, "My wife. Please, tell me everything. Is she—"

"She's going to be fine, Mr. Hamilton." A nurse took his hand. He squeezed his eyes shut and tears trickled into his hairline. "She's in serious condition." His eyes came back open, full of question and fear. "Her right kidney is bruised. She has some broken ribs and a punctured lung on the same side." Michael groaned in self-punishment. "Beyond that, she's just bruised up and needed a few stitches. I believe she'll be all right."

"Tell her I love her," he said.

"Right now, she's unconscious, but—"

"Tell her anyway, please."

"In no time you can tell her yourself."

Michael nodded and allowed the anesthetic to take hold. He woke up with more physical pain than he had ever endured in his life. He begged for something to ease it, then waited for what seemed like eternity before it took effect. As the physical pain let up, the reality descended freshly, and he wanted to tear his way out of this room and find Emily. Each time he closed his eyes he could feel the collision over and over, ending with Emily lying limp in his arms. He wondered how he could ever face the children, knowing what his foolishness had done to their mother when . . .

"The children!"

Michael tried to sit up and groaned from the pain. He pressed a button for the nurse and she came quickly. "I need to make a phone call," he insisted. "Will you help me? I—" He stopped when the nurse motioned someone else into the room.

"You have a visitor," she said. "Perhaps he can help you."

Michael tried to focus his eyes, then he nearly collapsed from relief. "Bret! Thank heaven for small miracles."

"I've been thanking heaven for some big ones. Your being alive, for instance."

"Where are the children, Bret? I can't believe we left them alone when—"

"It's all right, Michael." Bret put a soothing hand to Michael's shoulder. "Amee called us soon after you left. Penny's with them now."

Michael sighed and closed his eyes as Bret went on. "She said you left angry and Emily went after you. She found some broken glass and was scared."

"I guess she had good reason to be," Michael said glumly.

Bret pulled a chair close to the bed and set a hand on Michael's arm. "Do you want to tell me what happened?"

"Not especially."

"Michael," Bret urged, "I'm the closest thing you've got to a best friend in this country . . . and I'm your bishop. Maybe we ought to talk." When Michael shook his head slightly, Bret added, "Are you in pain?"

"Not much."

"You look dazed. Is the medication getting to you?"

Michael nodded, then said, "I nearly killed her, Bret." Tears leaked out of his eyes. "She's the only woman I have ever loved. She is *everything* to me, and I nearly killed her."

Bret's voice was calm and firm. "She's fine, Michael. I just saw her. They're watching her closely, but she's stable."

Michael lifted a hand and curled it into a tight fist. The intensity in his eyes apparently caught Bret's attention. "I was driving like a maniac, Bret. It was my fault that accident happened."

After a long moment Bret asked, "What were you angry about when you left?"

Michael squeezed his eyes shut.

"Do you want me to let you rest?" Bret asked.

Michael looked up at him and realized the medication was doing him in. But more than that, he needed time to think this through. "Can we talk later?" he asked and Bret nodded.

"I'll come back."

"You'll see that the children are—"

"The children are fine."

"Will you tell Emily that I love her?"

"She's unconscious, Michael."

"Tell her anyway."

Bret hesitated, then he nodded. "I'll tell her."

Michael drifted in and out of pain and consciousness with no idea of the time passing. His thoughts were tormented with regret, his heart ached. When he woke feeling as if he'd passed the worst of it, he asked the nurse how long he'd been there. The middle-aged woman with a name-tag that read *Marge*, told him it was Monday morning and he had come in Saturday.

"I need to see my wife," he requested.

Marge looked determined to tell him it was impossible, but her words were gentle. "You really shouldn't be up and about just yet."

Michael leaned forward. "If I have to get up out of this bed and crawl to see her, I will."

"That might be rather difficult, Mr. Hamilton, if not embarrassing." Her voice was firm, but he caught a sparkle in her eye.

"Then why don't you help me?"

Marge walked out and returned seconds later with a wheelchair. "This is going to hurt," she said, throwing the sheet off him.

"I suspected it would." Michael carefully eased his leg over the edge of the bed and grimaced.

"I don't get the impression you care," Marge said while she offered experienced support to help him into the wheelchair.

"Not at the moment." Michael's voice betrayed the strain as he settled himself carefully.

"You're bruised up pretty bad, Mr. Hamilton." Marge kindly helped situate his legs and covered them with a folded blanket. "We wouldn't want you to be immodest, now."

Michael chuckled. "I doubt my wife would care, even if she were conscious."

"It's not your wife I'm worried about," she said and wheeled him into the hall.

"Good point." Michael appreciated her lighthearted distraction.

"Do you have children?" Marge asked.

"Five."

"Wow," she chuckled. "And who are they with now?"

"The four younger ones are with friends. The oldest doesn't live at home anymore."

"Why, you don't look old enough to have a child all grown up."

"Neither does my wife. But Allison is twenty-one. Actually, mother and daughter could pass for sisters, except that we haven't seen Allison for two years. She ran away."

"Oh, I'm sorry to hear that," Marge said with genuine compassion as she leaned against the wall in the elevator. "I know myself what a heartache children can be."

Michael wondered what Allison would think if she could see them now. He would certainly be eating some words.

"How far do we have to go?" he asked impatiently.

"Almost there," Marge said, then she paused and peered around a corner as if they were on some secret mission. "It looks clear."

"Where are we going?" he asked warily.

"Intensive Care, of course," she stated. "They're just keeping an eye on her."

Michael's heart began to pound before they entered the room, but he wasn't prepared for the rush of emotion when he saw her. Marge wheeled him close to the bed and put a gentle hand on his shoulder.

"She *is* very pretty," Marge said quietly.

"Yes," Michael barely managed to say, "she is." In spite of the stitches across her forehead, the bluish tint to parts of her swollen face, and her matted hair, she was still the most beautiful woman on earth.

"I'll leave you alone for a few minutes, but don't plan on staying too long. We could both get in trouble."

"Thank you," Michael said as she slipped from the room.

For several moments he just gazed at her face, pale enough to be dead. He glanced around at the medical paraphernalia attached to her: oxygen, blood, drainage tubes, I.V.s, monitors. It was like reliving a bad dream, but this time he was to blame. He wondered if he could ever live with himself.

With hesitance Michael took her hand, fondling the wedding band she wore. He was wondering what to say to her if she were conscious, when she opened her eyes and looked at him. Michael heard pulse beats in his ears and felt himself sweat. He could almost feel the words forming in her mouth, and he was prepared to take them like a man. *You idiot*, he could hear her say in his head, *you nearly killed us both. How could you be such a fool?*

"I want . . ." Her words came with difficulty. She was weak and her mouth was dry. Michael glanced around, expecting her to do the same, to indicate what she wanted. Water? Something for the pain? But her eyes were fixed on him.

"I want to . . ." she began again.

"What?" he leaned closer, his brow furrowed. "Tell me what you want, Emily. Anything."

"I want to be with you . . . forever . . . Michael."

Tears leaked out of her eyes, and Michael couldn't bear the emotion any longer. With quiet desperation he tried to move closer, fighting the bed rail, the tubes, the pain, just to be able to touch her. With a hand against her face, Michael buried his head in the blankets at her side and cried like a child. Emily pushed her fingers into his hair, toying with it gently as if they were snuggling on the couch at home.

"Michael," she said and he lifted his face toward her. She pressed her fingers to his lips and wiped his tear-stained cheeks. "Everything's going to be all right."

Fresh tears welled into Michael's eyes. As always, he marveled at her faith, her willingness to forgive, her love for him.

"They told me you were in surgery."

"Have you been conscious since then?" he asked.

"In and out," she smiled faintly, almost apologetically. "Are you all right?"

"I'm fine," he insisted, "but what about you?"

"I'll be all right," she managed to say, seeming distracted.

Michael watched her closely. She was struggling to breathe, and he wondered if he should get someone to help her.

"I should go and—"

"Wait." She stopped him with a hand on his arm. "I have to . . . tell you something. I've been . . . lying here . . . just wanting to . . ." Her breathing became more labored and Michael began to panic, but he sensed her need to say this and forced himself to hold off. ". . . to tell you . . . I love you, Michael . . . I love you."

Michael fought to keep his emotion under control, if only for the sake of her condition. "I love you, too, Emily . . . more than life."

"I know." She smiled again, and Michael relaxed as a nurse came in to check on her. "That's why I'm still here."

Her last words caught Michael off guard. He wanted to question her, but she was already distracted by the increasing difficulty in breathing and she turned to the nurse. Marge came in a moment later to take him back to his room.

"How's she doing?" Marge asked.

"It's hard to say," he answered tonelessly.

"How long have you been married?" the nurse added lightly, and Michael sensed her attempt to distract him.

"Eleven years," he stated.

"Now, wait a minute," she chuckled. "You just told me you have a twenty-one-year-old daughter."

"We do. I mean, well, Allison is Emily's daughter, but . . ." His voice softened with the heartache. "But I love her like my own."

"Isn't that the way it goes," Marge went on. "Why, these days, families are so mixed up, if we couldn't take on others' children and love them, where would our children be?"

Michael expected the conversation to discourage him, but what Marge said lifted him a bit. It was true that he wasn't the only man in this type of situation. He had much to be grateful for, and he reminded himself to keep that in mind.

Marge helped Michael back into bed, and he realized he was exhausted. Why was he so weak from a stupid broken leg? Marge brought him something for the pain, and he slept soundly in spite of the bizarre images of his dreams. He awoke to find Sean sitting by the bed, looking especially somber.

"Hello, Michael," he said.

"Hello," Michael replied, catching something in Sean's demeanor that made him uneasy. "How long have you been here?"

Sean hesitated. "Since they called me."

"Since *who* called?" Michael asked intently.

"Michael," Sean leaned forward, "the hospital called Bret, and Bret called and asked me to meet him here, and—"

"It's Emily, isn't it?" Michael tried to sit up and groaned. "Dear Lord, what's happened to her now? I've got to see her, Sean. Please help me get up and—"

"Calm down, Michael. You can't go see her right now."

Michael didn't realize how frantic he was until Sean gently urged his shoulders back to the bed. "What happened?" he asked more slowly.

"She's got some blood clots in her lung."

Michael squeezed his eyes shut.

"They told me it could go either way. It's serious."

Michael put a hand over his mouth to keep from crying out.

"Bret and I gave her a blessing. She asked for it in a more coherent moment."

"Thank you," Michael uttered hoarsely.

"I believe she'll be all right," Sean added with a crack in his voice. "I really do."

"She just *has* to be." Michael's voice was strained, his eyes grew distant. "She just has to be."

"What happened, Michael?" Sean asked firmly.

Michael attempted to deflect the question. "How did you find out?"

"I went to the house Saturday evening. Penny was with the kids. The hospital had just called. The girls were practically hysterical. They said you were very upset when you left."

Michael glared at him, then turned to stare at the wall.

"Michael," Sean said when he got no response, "your children are understandably having a hard time with this. I'm including myself in that, because you're the only family I've got. Now, I think we have a right to know what's going on here."

Michael squeezed his eyes shut. "I really don't want to talk about it."

Sean leaned back in his chair with a frustrated sigh. After an extended silence he said, "It's no secret that you and Emily have been dealing with some struggles."

Michael looked at him then, silently questioning how he knew *that*.

"Do you think I'm stupid?" Sean snapped. "I have no doubt that the two of you love each other very much. But I've spent enough time in your home to know that everything isn't as it should be. Do you want me to pretend I hadn't noticed? Do you want me to tell you how much you changed during the two years I was on my mission? Do you want me to pretend that I don't know you left the house angry and you were driving like a maniac when the accident happened? If I did that, do you think it would all just go away?"

Sean stood, grasped the bed rail, and leaned over Michael. "Listen to me, Michael. You've been like a father and brother all rolled into one. You've had more influence on my life than I could ever measure. I know it's no coincidence that I was blessed to come into your home, and I could never repay what you've done for me. But I have something to say that I know you need to hear. Maybe that's why I came into *your* life. So listen, and listen good. I've spent a lot of hours studying human behavior, Michael. I'm well on my way to becoming a counselor. Do I have to tell you that you're not going to solve any of this by burying it? Or should I tell you that if Emily dies and you haven't dealt with it, life could get pretty tough?"

Michael responded with anger. "You just told me you believed she would make it, that—"

"I'd like to think she will, Michael," he interrupted. "And so would you. But it's not in our hands. In any case, whether she lives or dies, you're not doing yourself, or her, any good by pretending there isn't a problem."

"Counselor or not, Sean, you have no idea what I'm dealing with here, so—"

"Maybe I don't," Sean interrupted in a quiet voice that caught Michael off guard, "but I'll tell you what I do know. I woke up in a hospital once, Michael. I had seventeen broken bones at the top of my list of injuries. My hands were like raw hamburger. I was *drunk* when that accident happened. And a woman died in that car with me. I laid in that bed for weeks, tearing myself to pieces over it. I'd been an utter fool, and the consequences were hard to swallow. I had to face up to the *real* reason I'd been drinking that night, and I had to deal with it. So, feel sorry for yourself if you think it will help, Michael. But one of these days you're going to have to face up to the simple facts. And the sooner you do it, the better for you—and for Emily."

Sean straightened himself and took a deep breath. "If you want to talk about it, just let me know. If you don't want to talk to me, talk to *somebody*. But don't hurt yourself, or her, any more by hoping it will go away."

Michael contemplated Sean's remarks through several minutes of silence, then he met his young friend's eyes and couldn't deny the truth in what he'd said. He reached out a hand and Sean took it in a firm grip. "I'll work on it, okay?"

"Okay," Sean said, his voice trembling. He leaned over the bed to embrace Michael, whispering close to his ear. "I couldn't bear to lose either one of you. You're the only family I've got left. I could never tell you how much you mean to me."

Michael chuckled as Sean stepped back from the bed. "It's the other way around, kid. But don't forget . . . you've got Melissa."

"Yes, well." Sean stuffed his hands in his pockets and looked at the floor. "It's not the same."

"Is something wrong?" Michael asked.

"No, not really," Sean answered, but he seemed tense.

"Did you ask her to marry you?"

"Yes," he stated dryly.

"And?"

"She told me she had to think about it." He chuckled humorlessly and added, "I just didn't expect it. I thought she was as sure as I am. But all I can do is wait."

"I'm sure everything will turn out," Michael said. "You've had too many miracles in your life to think that the Lord would let you down now."

Sean smiled. "That's true." He added soberly, "And the same for you, Michael. Don't forget that."

The words echoed through Michael's head long after Sean had left. He contemplated them deeply, if only to distract himself from his helplessness concerning Emily. He was still deep in thought when Bret came to check on him, reporting that Emily was still critical. They talked casually for a while until Bret got down to business.

"I think we need to talk, Michael. I'm here as your friend. If you need to talk to your bishop, just let me know."

Michael nodded, feeling hesitant but knowing this had to be faced. If anyone needed a friend right now, it was him.

Bret got right to the point. "Do you want to tell me what you were angry about when you left the house?"

Michael thought about it. "No." Then he recalled what Sean had said. "But I suppose I ought to. Maybe I should talk to you as my bishop. You can help me repent of my sins, can't you?"

"That depends on what kind of sins you're talking about. You've been in my position before. You know what I can and can't do."

"I'm sorry, Bret, but I never had anybody come to me and tell me they nearly killed their wife because they were acting like a complete fool."

"It was an accident." Bret attempted to console Michael, but it only made him angry.

"Let me make this clear to you, Bret." Michael leaned toward him, his eyes on fire. "I was driving over ninety miles an hour when I saw that truck pull out. Emily *begged* me to slow down, to talk to her, to see reason. But I wouldn't listen to her."

Michael expected Bret to be appalled or upset. "Why wouldn't you listen?" was all he said.

"I don't know," Michael groaned. "I felt like a madman. I was just so *angry*, and *scared*, and . . ."

"Which brings us back to my original question," Bret said when Michael's words drifted off. "What were you angry about when you left? Were you angry with Emily?"

"No," he said emphatically.

"Then Emily had nothing to do with it."

"Oh, Emily has *everything* to do with it, but I was not angry with her. I was just *angry*."

"So, tell me about it. I'm not in any hurry, and it doesn't look like you're going anywhere."

Michael sighed and wondered where to begin. "Before I married Emily, I had some trouble dealing with the fact that we could not be sealed. But I . . ."

Bret's eyes widened and Michael paused to ask, "What?"

"I'm sorry. It's just that I . . . well, I'd almost forgotten that it wasn't always this way with the two of you."

"Well," Michael grumbled, "I almost managed to forget myself, but . . ." The emotion began to grab Michael and he swallowed hard. "Before we came back to Utah, Emily lost a baby and . . ."

"Yes, I knew that," he said to urge him on.

"Did you know her heart stopped?"

"Yes, Penny told me about it. I believe Emily called her soon after."

"Something happened to me in that hospital room, Bret. The thought of losing her was more than I could bear, but when I realized we were not sealed, and the children . . . the children . . . *my* children . . . are sealed to Ryan Hall . . . I just . . . I don't know. I just couldn't deal with it. I was terrified to let Emily get pregnant again. I was terrified of losing her. And I just couldn't bring myself to talk to her about it, to face it, as if I could ignore it and make it go away."

Michael looked at Bret solemnly. The emotion was evident. "I love her *so much*," he said with strength. "And those kids." Michael shook his head in disbelief. "How can I live with the reality that they will not be mine? I love those girls as much as I love my own sons."

"And this has been bothering you all this time?"

Michael nodded slowly. A shiver of emotion caught him.

"And that's what you were angry about when you left the house?"

Michael nodded again. "Ryan's mother and brother came by the night before."

"You're kidding." Bret almost chuckled.

"I couldn't believe the way she walked into my house and made me feel like some kind of an outsider. She had Emily trying to apologize right and left, while Ryan's brother sat there like a clone of some ghost come back to haunt us. Maybe if I hadn't let my fears get so out of hand, it wouldn't have bothered me so much. But I really started to lose it Saturday morning when she told Amee and Alexa they would be with their father in the next life."

"I see," Bret said when Michael was apparently finished. "I can't say I understand how you feel, but I can see why it would be hard to take. Does Emily know how you feel?"

Michael groaned. "She does now. She finally managed to break through these wretched walls and get the truth out, just before . . . the accident."

"And what does Emily say?"

"She told me that I was letting my fears destroy what we have together. She believes we can be together forever . . . if we want it, and believe in it. She believes that God will make it right."

"I agree with her."

Michael's brow furrowed. "How can it be that simple? We're Mormons, Bret. We believe in temple marriage."

"In cases like yours, it's a matter of faith that it will all work out as it should."

"But I don't have that kind of faith, Bret. I have not been the kind of man who will be worthy of that kind of blessing."

"I hear Satan talking, Michael."

"Is that a big surprise?" He chuckled humorlessly. "I opened the door and let him in."

"How's that?"

"By . . ." Michael stammered in frustration, "by . . . letting my fears get hold of me, and then I stopped going to the temple. My prayers became almost meaningless."

"Did you start drinking or something?"

"Just Coke."

"Did you cheat on your wife?"

"No!"

"Did you stop paying your tithing or going to church?"

"No. Is this a temple recommend interview?"

"Not at the moment. This is your friend talking. Did you ever stop taking care of your family and serving others and living the basic commandments?"

Michael sighed as the point began to sink in. "No."

"Then what's the problem? Where is this man who is so unworthy of spending eternity with the family he loves and cares for?"

Michael looked hard at Bret. "He's on the opposite side of a scale from Ryan Hall. It's always been that way. For twenty-two years I have felt somehow measured and compared to that man. And Ryan's got one thing I haven't got. *He is sealed to my wife and children!*"

"It's only a technicality that can be taken care of."

"Yes, I know. After I'm dead, it can be taken care of . . . but . . . it can't be that easy."

"Why? Because you've tortured yourself over it for so long that you can't believe the solution would actually be simple?" Bret paused and shifted in his chair. "It's not easy, Michael. It takes a lot of hard work to remain righteous and take care of a family in this life. It takes patience and tolerance and enduring to the end. It does take faith. It's not easy, Michael, but it is simple. If you can push through the clouds of darkness and confusion that Satan surrounds us with, it truly is simple."

"Maybe I've already blown it," Michael felt the need to protest. "Maybe it's already too late."

"Michael, if there is one thing I've learned, being a member of this church all these years, it's that God never—never—gives up on us. It's *never* too late."

A warm chill confirmed the truth of Bret's words to Michael, and emotion overwhelmed him. While the peace and hope were evident, he couldn't get past the consequences of his anger.

"What else is bothering you?" Bret asked carefully.

"I'm just such a *fool*!" He slammed his fists into the bed at his sides. "When I think of how I hurt her, how I let my fear come between us . . . she wanted another baby, Bret. Deep in my heart, I knew we were supposed to have one. But I let my fears hold me back. And now it's too late."

"Too late?" Bret raised an eyebrow.

"Menopause," Michael said quietly, and Bret nodded.

"And then, as if that weren't enough, I nearly killed her, for heaven's sake." He looked at Bret and curled his hand into a fist. "How can she possibly want to spend eternity with me after what I've done to her?"

"I don't know. Why don't you ask her?"

Michael thought of his visit to Emily's room that morning and the things she had said to him. He wanted to believe it, but memories always intruded.

"What are you thinking?" Bret pressed.

"She told me this morning she wanted to be with me forever."

"There you have it."

"But she told me Saturday I was no better than Ryan. How can I be sure that she isn't just patronizing me? She loved him, you know. She really did."

"Yes, I know." Bret sighed, resisting the urge to literally shake Michael. Instead, he felt prompted to illustrate what he felt was an important point. "Michael, maybe your memories have become distorted over the years. I'm not here to judge you *or* Ryan, but I would like to share with you a simple observation. I've seen the way you treat Emily and the kids. I know how much you love her. Just how well did you know Ryan?"

"I met him once. It was not a pleasant occasion."

"I know Emily has told you about their relationship, at least to a point."

"Yes," Michael agreed, not liking where this was headed.

"Penny and I spent a lot of time with Ryan and Emily, you know."

Michael cringed to hear their names put together that way.

"We were neighbors, and with Penny and Emily being close, we barbecued, played cards, helped each other in the yard. I was always a little amazed at the way they interacted. I had a hard time believing a man could treat a woman like that."

Michael lifted a brow as the story began to take a different course than he'd expected.

"It was often subtle, and I would remind myself not to get involved. I know Emily tried countless times to get Ryan to see what was obvious to others, but he'd have nothing to do with anything that might have made their relationship better. They were little more than newlyweds when they moved into that house, but even then, the problem existed. One of my clearest memories of Ryan is a little . . . disturbing."

"Go on," Michael urged when he hesitated.

"A few days after Alexa was born, Penny and I went over to see how they were doing. Emily had only stayed in the hospital for twelve hours because the insurance wouldn't cover any more unless there was a medical problem. We found Emily nearly in tears. Alexa was a fussy baby and allowed her very little sleep. Amee had an ear infection and had been crying all day and the night before. She was fourteen months old, practically a baby herself. I asked Emily if she wanted a blessing. It was apparent the birth had been difficult, and she was struggling. She told me she had asked Ryan if he could call someone to give her a blessing. He'd told her she would be fine and he didn't think it was necessary."

Michael turned his gaze toward the wall as he listened, trying not to betray the turmoil rising in him. How well he remembered the anger he'd felt when he found out how unhappy Emily had been, while he had been alone, longing for her.

"I asked Emily where Ryan was, and she told me he'd gone to get groceries and a prescription. Penny asked if they had eaten yet, and Emily said they hadn't. The Relief Society had offered to bring some meals in, but Ryan told them they didn't need it. She laughed it off and told us Ryan had gone to the store to get some soup or something he could heat up. When Ryan came home I was already angry, but I was telling myself not to judge. He came in grumbling about having to go to the store and the cost of food and medicine. Emily was trying hard not to cry. When she asked what he had gotten for dinner, he said it was on the counter. She and Penny went into the kitchen. Emily could barely walk. Do you know what was in there, Michael?"

Michael turned to look at him, surprised by Bret's evident anger.

"He had brought home chicken, and clearly expected her to cook it. I honestly believe if Penny hadn't gotten upset, Emily would have done her best to make dinner. Now what kind of attitude was Emily living with that made her believe she had to do something like that in order to be a good wife to him?"

Michael couldn't answer.

"He was abusing her, Michael. He didn't hit her, but I believe what he did was just as bad."

In spite of the difficult images, Michael appreciated the point. Still, he had a counter point that he felt was important. "But he changed before he died, Bret."

"Yes," Bret admitted, "he began to change when *you* confronted him with the prospect of losing his wife. Emily gave him many opportunities to change. She loved and nurtured him. Only when he was faced with losing her did he come around."

"Didn't I do the same thing? I hurt her. I shut her out. And I wasn't willing to face my own fears until I was confronted with losing her."

"You made some mistakes, Michael, but I still don't think it evens out the odds. I didn't tell you all of that to encourage you to compare yourself to Ryan. You shouldn't do that. If he had been a paragon of spirituality who had treated Emily like a queen, God would still find a way to work it out so that both of you could be at peace in eternity. I don't know how, but I know he could do it, because he is God. And we can't possibly comprehend what it will really be like. The only thing that matters here is your faith, Michael, and the desires of your heart. You're a good man, and you have every right to be with the woman you love forever."

"Even though I nearly killed her?"

"You're being awfully stubborn," Bret observed, a hint of frustration in his voice.

"Yes, I suppose I am."

"I would imagine the position you're in now is likely very humbling."

"You can say that again," Michael chuckled tensely.

"But you can deal with it, Michael. Life goes on, and we always have another chance. Even if Emily had died in that accident, I believe it all would have worked out in the next life. It will probably take some time, but I believe you can come to learn for yourself why the Lord allowed these things to happen as they did. You're a good man, and I believe you're a lot stronger than you think you are."

Several minutes of silence allowed Michael to absorb his friend's remarks.

"Thank you, Bret," he said when there was no other point of argument he could possibly come up with. "I'll work on it. I appreciate you, I really do." He drew a long sigh. "Did I ever tell you how much I appreciated your being with us when I went through the temple the first time?"

Bret chuckled. "Oh, it was quite a sacrifice," he said with light sarcasm. "Having to fly to Australia at your expense to go through the temple, and then go on . . . what did you call it?"

"Walkabout," Michael smiled.

"It seemed like sight-seeing to me." Bret shook his head and chuckled again. "It was pretty hard to take."

"Well, I'm glad you enjoyed it," Michael said, "but . . ." The mood sobered as Michael's emotion became evident. "I just wanted you to know how grateful I was to have you there. It was one of the most memorable days of my life."

"It was my pleasure."

Bret reached out a hand and Michael grasped it firmly. Their eyes met with an unspoken bond of friendship, and Michael's voice broke as he asked, "Do you think Emily will make it through this?"

"You tell me."

Michael leaned back and sighed, trying to focus on the promise

Emily had been given that she would live for many years yet. Perhaps that was a good place to start exercising a little faith.

CHAPTER FOURTEEN

After Bret left, Michael's dinner was brought in, but he hardly touched it. He pleaded with the nurse to help him go see his wife, but she was not as understanding as Marge had been. When he asked about Emily's condition, he was simply told it was still critical. It could go either way. Michael felt as if he'd go mad, staring at the ceiling, fighting the drowsiness of pain medication when he wasn't fighting the pain. He was sitting up in bed, flipping through T.V. channels with the remote, when Penny stuck her head in. "Are you decent?" she asked.

"No, but I'm covered."

"I brought you some visitors. I hope you don't mind." Michael lifted a brow in question. "Your daughters have been begging to come since yesterday morning," she explained as Amee and Alexa moved timidly into the room.

Michael laughed from the pure joy of seeing them. He opened his arms and they hurried to either side of the bed while Penny slipped quietly back into the hall. Michael kissed them and held them close, until he realized they were both crying.

"Whatever's the matter?" he asked as they drew back slightly and he touched their chins in a familiar gesture of affection.

"We were so scared," Amee admitted, wiping at her face. "We thought you and Mom were going to die—and all because of what that old lady said and—"

"Now, wait a minute, love," Michael interrupted, "that old lady is your grandmother."

"I don't like her," Alexa insisted.

"And why not?" Michael asked, wanting to agree but knowing it wouldn't be appropriate.

"Because of what she said about you," Amee answered. "She said you were a liar. You're not a liar, are you, Dad?"

"Well, I've made some mistakes and I'm far from perfect, sweetie, but I don't think lying is one of my problems."

"She said that Jess and James would not be with us in heaven, and . . ." Amee broke into a bout of sobs and Michael pulled her to his shoulder.

"It's okay, darlin'," he soothed.

"Is that why you were mad when you left?" Alexa asked while Amee cried.

"What she said upset me, yes," he answered. "But there was a lot more to it than that. When I get home from the hospital, we'll have a little meeting and talk about it. In the meantime, I'm going to tell you what your mother told me. She believes we can all be together forever, as long as we have the faith to make it happen."

"Do you believe that?" Amee asked with an innocence that pierced him.

Michael hesitated. "I want more than anything for us to be together forever. Nothing means more to me than that."

"You said," Alexa interjected, "that we would be a family—now and forever."

"Did I say that?" Michael asked with the same innocence. Both girls nodded firmly, and he pulled them close to him again. "Then I must have meant it."

The girls smiled and Alexa commented, "You shaved off your beard. How come?"

"Actually, one of the nurses helped me," he admitted. "What do you think?" He rubbed his face thoughtfully.

"I like you either way," Amee said with enthusiasm.

Michael urged them to sit on the edges of the bed where they leaned their heads against his shoulders, much like they did to watch T.V. at home. He asked them about church, and school, and friends, and what Penny had fed them since he'd been gone. They chattered and giggled and distracted Michael from his fear for Emily's life, and his regret that this had happened at all. Then, with no warning, Alexa asked, "Dad, did you get in the accident because you were mad?"

Michael swallowed the knot in his throat and reminded himself that he had taught them to be straightforward and communicate their feelings. "Yes, Alexa, the accident was my fault. I was angry and upset, and I was driving too fast."

Tears accompanied his admission, but the girls wiped at either side of his face. "Why are you crying, Dad?" Amee asked.

"I guess I'm just feeling bad about what I did. I shouldn't have let my anger get control of me like that. Your mother is hurt very badly, and I know it's my fault."

Four young arms wrapped around him with perfect acceptance. "It's okay, Dad," Amee said, looking into his face. "We all make mistakes, but we have to put it behind us and look ahead."

"Who told you that?" he chuckled.

"You did," she smiled. "Lots of times."

"I'm just glad you're okay, Dad," Alexa said, "and I'm glad we can be together forever. You're still the best father in the whole world."

Michael had to use great willpower to keep from crying again. Instead, he uttered a silent prayer of gratitude for the blessing of these two beautiful daughters.

They chatted on about trivial girl things while Michael listened with pure pleasure. They asked him questions about the accident that he managed to answer without getting upset. They asked about his surgery and closely examined his leg.

Penny peered in with a smile. "I hate to break this up, but you girls need to get to bed, and I bet your dad is worn out."

"I'm okay," he smiled, "but Penny's right. You've got school tomorrow. You be good now. I need to talk to Penny a minute. She'll be right out."

The girls kissed him and left reluctantly. Penny set a bag by the bed. "Bret said you asked for some things. The girls packed it."

"Thank you."

"Are you all right?"

"I'll be fine," he stated. "How are you faring? Have the Hamilton monsters destroyed your well-being yet?"

"They're just fine," Penny laughed, "and so am I. Bret has kept them busy much of the time."

"I can't thank you enough, Penny. You've always given so much to us." She looked down humbly and he added, "Thank you for bringing the girls. I needed that."

"I thought it couldn't hurt. Bret told me everything. I hope you don't mind."

"We've never had secrets before. Why should we now?"

Penny smiled and shrugged, then her expression sobered. "I just saw Emily. They weren't going to let me in, but I persisted." Michael's eyes told her he wanted to know everything. "She's not doing well, Michael." Penny's eyes filled with moisture, and her voice caught.

Michael sighed, then he hit a fist into the bed. "I feel so blasted helpless. I should be with her."

"They told me you could get on crutches in the morning. Maybe by then she'll be doing better." Penny nodded toward the bag and managed a smile. "We brought you something modest to hobble around in."

"Thank you," he said again. She nodded and started out the door, but he stopped her. "Penny, I'm sorry."

"Sorry? For what?"

"I know how much you love Emily. I'm . . . I'm sorry for putting her through this . . . and you."

"Michael, I have had the utmost respect for you since the day we met. One little mistake isn't going to change that."

"Even if Emily dies?" he had to ask.

"She's not going to die, Michael. But even if she did, I know that losing her would be hardest for you. I know how much you love her. Don't be so hard on yourself, Michael. In the eternal perspective, this is not nearly as bad as it seems."

Michael wanted to respond, but a knot was stuck in his throat. He nodded and she left him alone.

Michael spent a restless night, pondering the circumstances and trying to mesh them with his feelings and all that Bret had said to him earlier. He thought of Emily, and cried and prayed. When dawn's first light was filtering into the room, Marge came in to check his vitals.

"Boy, am I glad to see you," he said with jubilance. "These other women don't treat me as well as you do."

Marge chuckled and almost blushed. "How are you feeling today?"

"Exhausted and frustrated. You *are* going to get me some crutches so I can go sit with my wife, aren't you?"

Marge smiled conspiratorially as she checked his blood pressure. "I'll see what I can do. If you eat your breakfast all gone like a good boy, it might work in your favor."

"I'll eat every bite," he promised.

By late morning, he finally made it to Emily's room. Marge wheeled him to the door. In spite of his protests, she was right when she said he'd be too weak to make it that far on his own. Michael moved carefully to Emily's bedside and nearly collapsed in the chair. He had thought the last time he'd seen her that she could look no worse, but she did. There were so many tubes and monitors attached to her, he couldn't begin to fathom what they all were. He thought of the scars that would remain from this ordeal, always there to remind him of his foolishness. He prayed that the hidden scars would not be so severe.

Michael sat by her side much of the day, and Marge even brought his lunch to him there. By late afternoon, his body felt the strain. He knew he should go back to his room, but he dreaded the separation. Even as she drifted in and out of consciousness, barely aware that he was there, he felt better being with her.

He contemplated going back to his room, but wondered how he'd get there. The nursing shift had obviously changed, and he wondered if someone would come looking for him. He entertained the thought of just lying down next to Emily and drifting off, but he knew it was impossible.

He had about made up his mind to just grit his teeth and make his way back on the crutches, when peace and strength personified walked into the room.

"Mother?" He couldn't believe it. "Am I hallucinating?"

"Not even close." LeNay crossed the room and put her arms around him with a firm yet careful embrace. Michael laughed and hugged her again. "How are you?" she asked, setting a motherly hand to his face.

"Better now," he smiled.

LeNay looked him over, then her eyes saddened as they took in Emily and all the machinery surrounding her. "I wish *I* were hallucinating."

"That would make two of us," he said wearily, pressing Emily's limp hand to his lips.

"Oh, my dear, sweet Emily." LeNay moved to the other side of the bed and pressed her face to Emily's. She pulled back with tears in her eyes. She looked at Michael and asked the question he dreaded most. "How did it happen, Michael?"

He diverted it briefly. "How did you get here?"

"On a plane, son. Did you think I walked?"

"If you wanted to get somewhere badly enough, I wouldn't put it past you."

She gave him an affectionate glare.

"Let me reword that, Mother. How did you know?"

"Penny called me right off. I got the first flight available. Someone's got to take care of my grandchildren while you're lounging around here."

"I must say I'm glad to see you," Michael said, attempting to ignore the pain in his leg. He wondered how long it had been since he'd taken anything for it.

"You don't look very comfortable," LeNay said and Michael felt embarrassed, as if his mind had been read.

"Actually, I'm not," he had to admit. He glanced at Emily. "I don't want to leave her, but I really should be getting back to my room. I think I'm overdue on something for the pain."

"What can I do?" LeNay was quick to take over.

"If you can find me a wheelchair and help me into it, we'll be set."

LeNay found one just outside the door and rolled it close to Michael as he was struggling to get up with his crutches.

"Are you all right?" she asked.

"No," he managed a chuckle as he slid into the wheelchair, "but I'll get over it if—

"Mother?" Emily's faint voice stopped them.

LeNay quickly moved to Emily's side and took her hand. "Yes, it's me, love." She smiled down at Emily as if nothing in the world were wrong.

"I thought I heard someone," Emily managed to say. "Have you . . . seen Michael?"

LeNay glanced unobtrusively toward Michael.

"She hasn't been that coherent all day," he whispered.

At the sound of his voice, Emily turned carefully.

"Michael." She reached a hand toward him and he wheeled the chair as close as possible. "I was dreaming about you."

"What did you dream?" he asked, his heart pounding just to see her move, hear her speak.

Emily glanced at LeNay, then an almost mischievous smile touched her lips. "Come closer," she said in a near whisper. Michael ignored the pain and eased onto his good leg to lean over her, putting his ear near her lips. He managed to blink back the tears as Emily whispered intimate thoughts that made him long for life to be as it had been. He raised himself up slightly to look at her as she almost giggled. He was tempted to kiss her until a grimace overtook her.

"Oh, Michael, I'm hurting . . . please . . . tell them to . . ." She didn't finish, but LeNay nodded toward Michael and hurried out to find a nurse.

While LeNay was gone, a nurse Michael hadn't seen before came in and put a hand on his shoulder.

"Mr. Hamilton?" she asked.

"Yes."

She smiled kindly. "I'm not accustomed to having to hunt down my patients. I'll wager you're needing something for the pain by now, and it's about time for your supper. Can I take you back to your room?"

Michael thanked her and told her his mother would wheel him back in a few minutes. She offered to take the crutches with her and said she would be waiting for him.

"Emily," Michael said, wanting to take advantage of their moment alone. She turned weakly toward him and he felt a rising tide of desperation. "You've got to hold on. Do you understand?" She answered with a barely detectable nod. "I want you to reach inside yourself and find every grain of faith you've ever had, and use it to get up out of this bed and walk away from here. Do you understand?"

For a moment, all evidence of pain fled from her expression. Her eyes glowed with that same faith she had always possessed. "Remember, Michael," she said in a voice that pierced him, "I was promised I would live to see my children grown."

He wanted so badly to talk to her about that, about so many things. But the pain returned to mar her countenance, and the nurse appeared with something to ease it that would send her back into unconsciousness.

"I've got to go to my room, love," he said, squeezing her hand gently. "I'll come to see you again first chance I get."

Emily nodded, and LeNay wheeled Michael into the hall.

"You're having a hard time with this," she stated in the elevator.

"You could say that," he answered, then said nothing more. He was relieved when his mother didn't press it. She left him in his room while his needs were taken care of, and returned after he'd eaten.

"Feeling better?" she asked, sitting close to the bed.

"Much better, thank you."

LeNay took his hand, speaking with all the perception and wisdom of a good mother. "Except for that pain in your eyes; those pills can't get rid of that."

Michael pressed a hand over his eyes as if he could hide the truth of what she'd said. He tried to blink back the emotion, but he knew she couldn't miss the tears brimming in his eyes when she pulled his hand away and held it tightly.

"It's okay," LeNay said with affection. "There is nothing that expresses the balance of life so much as a true man having the courage to cry when it hurts, instead of hiding behind the facade of masculinity to save his pride."

Michael shook his head slowly, awed at his mother's wisdom. "Where do you come up with these profound adages of life?"

"I just live with an open mind," she said humbly. Then her eyes penetrated him. "Why don't you tell me what happened, Michael." It was not a question.

Michael knew better than to skirt around the issues with his mother. He swallowed the knot in his throat and cleared it. "I was acting like a fool, driving ninety miles an hour, because I was angry."

LeNay covered her shock quickly. She said nothing.

"Emily begged me to be rational. I didn't listen, and I nearly killed her."

It was subtle, but Michael saw his mother tremble with . . . what was it? Anger? Hurt?

"Why were you driving like that with Emily in the car?"

"She knew I was angry, and she got in to try and stop me from doing something stupid."

For minutes of unbearable silence, LeNay stared into Michael's eyes, as if she could read the deeper motives. When he couldn't bear it any longer, he insisted almost sharply, "You must have something to say."

"What do you want me to say, Michael?"

"Something; anything! For crying out loud, I just did the stupidest thing I've ever done in my life. Can't you tell me I ought to be ashamed of myself, or something? Nearly everyone I've talked to is so blasted forgiving and understanding, I can't take it."

"What's your point, Michael?" she asked quietly, but he could see a controlled fury building in her eyes.

"Why isn't anybody angry with me? *Everyone* should be angry with me."

"Perhaps the people who love you realize that you will punish yourself sufficiently without their help."

"It's a nice theory, but I'm not sure I can live with it."

"You're going to have to live with it, Michael. You should be grateful she's going to survive this, and that she won't be permanently crippled."

"Oh, that makes me feel better," he said with sarcasm.

LeNay shot out of her chair and put her hands firmly on Michael's shoulders in one agile movement. "I don't want you to feel better, Michael. You *should* be ashamed of yourself. You're a grown man, and you should have known better."

Michael bit his lip and turned shamefully away, but LeNay touched his chin and made him face her. "Even if you had been alone, Michael," she went on in quiet fury, "you still had no business driving like that. You could have killed someone. You could have killed *yourself!*" She shook him slightly. "You're a husband and father; a man of many responsibilities. You had no business putting yourself at risk and taking no thought of what the consequences might be to those who love you.

"So, you go ahead and suffer, my boy, because you've got no business feeling better just yet—not until you can grasp the full spectrum of what you've done and face up to your Father in Heaven with a broken heart and a contrite spirit."

Tears rose into LeNay's eyes. She looked at him long and hard, then she pulled him close and cried against his shoulder. Michael held his mother and cried with her, feeling somehow better, whether she wanted him to or not. How grateful he was that she had joined the Church and understood the things he needed to hear.

LeNay stayed another hour or so, urging Michael to talk through all of the anger that had led up to the accident. She gave him a slightly different angle on the same concepts Bret had discussed with him, and left him with a mother's perfect faith that everything would be all right.

The next morning, Michael was released from the hospital with specific instructions and some prescriptions. He called home and was assured that his mother had everything under control, then he called Sean and told him he wouldn't be needing a ride until later.

Michael sat next to Emily's bed and played it all through in his mind over and over. It all came down to one conclusion. If he could be forgiven, and forgive himself, he had to rededicate himself to living worthy of the life he wanted in eternity—and having the faith to know he could achieve it. As he prayed more than he had in months, Michael came to know that it would be a long, hard path to find peace within himself. But he knew it was not impossible. Still, he had only to turn and look at Emily and feel a weight come back upon his shoulders. He wondered why God was so merciful and compassionate toward him when he had been such a fool. And he wondered why the events of his life had led up to this moment, in this way. He wondered until his head ached, then he reminded himself to concentrate on the faith, not the questions.

He was lost in his inner turmoil when Emily's raspy voice startled him. "Where are you, my love?"

Though it was subtle, he could hear an increase of strength that gave him hope.

"I'm right here with you." He smiled and took her hand.

"How's the leg?" She nodded toward it, propped on a chair with a pillow beneath it.

"As good as could be expected, I suppose, for an old man like me."

"Be careful what you say, my love. You're not much older than I am, and it's an insult to criticize a woman's age."

"Sorry," he said with a crooked smile, grateful to see her sense of humor shining through.

"How's the rest of you?" she asked more seriously.

"I'm a little bruised up and tender, but I'll live."

"And how are you in here?" she asked, touching her fingers to his chest.

Michael couldn't find any words to say that wouldn't either be dishonest or make him cry.

"Am I to assume you're not ready to talk about that yet?"

Michael nodded, relieved by her perception. "Let's just work on getting you out of here first."

"Okay," she said, her voice weakening slightly, "but when I come home, we *will* talk about it."

"Yes," he said firmly, "we will . . . I promise."

She smiled faintly. "Michael, will you kiss me?"

Their eyes met with tangible, unspoken longings that were too familiar in their relationship to deny. Michael carefully stood on his good leg and leaned over the bed, meekly touching his lips to hers. He opened his eyes slowly to find her watching him. She fought against the tubes in her arm to lift her hand to the back of his neck.

"That's not good enough," she whispered and urged him closer.

Michael held his breath and pressed his mouth over hers, reminded of those moments when he had tried to save her life. In spite of Emily's weakness, her response was vigorous, even passionate—perhaps tainted with the same desperation he felt within himself. For a brief, inviolable moment, the fear and regret evaporated, and Michael believed he could pull all of her pain into himself and hold it for her. Longing for more, Michael carefully persuaded a hand beneath her head to accommodate his reach. She moaned from her throat and he kissed her harder, eased her closer. He ached to lie beside her, to love her fully. But he knew it was impossible, so he just kissed her on and on, trying to convince himself, if not her, that a kiss could compensate for all they were unable to share. He thought of their intimacy the night before the accident, as always in awe of what making love to Emily could do for him. In their years of marriage, it had always been the constancy that bound them together through the trials of everyday living. And Michael believed now that just holding her, sharing with her that most sacred part of marriage, could heal so many of the wounds inside him. But it would be a long time before her bruised and broken body could tolerate any more than a kiss. And so he kissed her again, promising her with no words spoken that one day they would share the fullness of life, once again, together.

CHAPTER FIFTEEN

Going home was both wonderful and difficult for Michael. It was great to see the children, and to watch his mother enjoy being a part of their lives again. LeNay had taken over efficiently, and left Michael plenty of time to recuperate. But being home without Emily only added to the torrent of anguish he felt.

Bret was good to drive Michael to the hospital each morning. And Sean always stopped by after classes to drive him home again in the evening, so he could spend his days with Emily. Michael watched the slow but steady progress of her healing, always with a prayer of gratitude in his heart that she was past danger and would live to help him get beyond this anguish. He kept her updated on the children's activities, and felt true joy when she was finally stable enough to see them.

Michael and Emily spent their days talking of many things, but neither of them had yet reopened the conversation they were having when the accident occurred. Michael knew it had to be done, but as he'd told her, he felt it was better to get a little further with the physical healing first. He often sensed that Emily wanted to talk about it but didn't quite dare. Still, he wasn't surprised when she took his hand one rainy afternoon and said in a somber voice, "Michael, I don't remember anything about the accident. Were you . . . conscious?"

Michael nodded slightly and pushed a hand through his hair. He found the courage to look at her and she smiled. "It's okay, Michael. My prayers were answered." He lifted a brow in question and she added, "I've been praying for years that I would be able to understand what was hurting you. And . . . I prayed that we would both make it through alive."

The emotion of the accident and all that had led up to it came rushing back. Michael moved quickly to take Emily in his arms.

"I thought you were dead," he cried, his cheek against hers. "I couldn't find a pulse right off. And you weren't breathing. I held you and I prayed, and . . . and I gave you a blessing . . . and then you started breathing. Oh, Emily," he sobbed, pressing his lips to her brow, her eyes, her cheeks. "I nearly killed you, Emily. I was a fool, and . . . I wouldn't listen to you . . . and I nearly killed you."

Michael held her and cried. With all the tears he'd spent, the real anguish had waited until now. He sobbed himself into exhaustion, then he sat on the edge of her bed and held her against his shoulder. "Can you ever forgive me, Emily?" he asked to break the silence.

"There is nothing to forgive, Michael."

"Oh, no," he lifted her face to look at him, "don't give me that. I would far prefer that you yell at me, that you hit me or something. My mother yelled at me. I deserved it. I deserve it from you, too. If you don't yell at me I'll—"

"Michael," she touched her fingers to his lips, "I've had a lot of time to think. I can't tell you why things have happened this way, but one thing stands out very clearly to me. In all the years I've known you, I have never seen you get angry for selfish reasons." Michael's brow furrowed in question.

"Do you remember right after Ryan died, the way you got so angry with me for being too proud to ask for help with the money? And for being too hard on myself for my guilt and regrets? I have never seen you get angry with me—or the children—unless you were concerned for our welfare. When I realized why you were so angry, Michael, I stopped to think about it, and . . . well, I wondered how many women are so blessed. I'm married to a man who loves me so much that he became blinded with anger at the fear of losing me." Emily's voice broke, and she pressed a fist to her heart. "Do you have any idea what that means to me?"

"I appreciate your sentiments, love," he said, "but the fact still remains that I was driving too fast, and I nearly killed you."

"It was your faith that got me through, Michael. I'm here now, and that is all that matters."

Michael tried to smile. He reminded himself that it would take time to get past all of this. He should have known Emily would be pure about this, as she had been all of her life. He was glad that she felt peace, but it was going to take more than that for Michael to feel the same.

Three weeks after the accident, Emily was ready to be released. The children chattered excitedly over breakfast about their mother coming home. Michael asked Bret and Penny to go with him to the hospital, since he still had trouble getting around. He'd mastered driving the week before, but he doubted he could help Emily if she needed it.

The three of them stopped outside the door to Emily's room when a nurse rushed in and a different one rushed out. Michael stopped her. "What's wrong?"

"I'm sorry, Michael, but Emily won't be going home just yet."

"What happened?" he demanded.

"I'm sure it's nothing serious, but she's been vomiting, which was very painful as you can imagine. And she's having some trouble breathing since it happened. The doctor doubts it's anything to worry about, but he won't release her until it's under control. Even the flu can be pretty traumatic after what she's been through."

Michael nodded his understanding and threw a glance of disappointment toward Bret and Penny.

"Can I see her?" Michael asked.

"Go on in. They're just checking her vitals now."

Michael turned to Bret and Penny.

"Listen," Bret said, "why don't you stay with her for a while? We'll come back for you this afternoon."

"Thanks." Michael shook Bret's hand and Penny gave him a quick hug. "Will you tell Mom and the kids that—"

"Maybe we'll take the kids up to Salt Lake to the zoo or something," Penny said. "They could probably use some time out. They'll be disappointed."

"Good idea," Michael agreed. "You're wonderful."

"We're not *that* wonderful," Penny said, holding her hand out and wiggling her fingers. "*You* buy the tickets and lunch. We're broke."

Michael grinned and reached for his wallet. "I'm glad to see you've grown beyond your pride, Penny. There's hope for you yet." Michael handed her a hundred-dollar bill.

"I don't think we'll need that much," she protested.

"After you come and get me later, why don't you take your husband out to dinner."

"Thanks, Michael." Bret shook his hand again. "You take care, now. Be patient. It won't be much longer."

Michael entered the room to immediately see his disappointment mirrored in Emily's eyes. But he also saw the evidence of strain. She was weaker and more pale than the day before. When the nurse left them alone, Emily said apologetically, "I guess I have to stay."

"I know. They told me."

"The doctor thinks it's probably the flu, but he asked for some tests just to be sure. He doesn't want to take any chances."

"I'd rather have you stay a little longer and know you're all right."

He kissed her forehead and squeezed her hand. "How are you feeling right now?"

"Better, but I really hurt. I thought my right side was going to burst."

As always, Michael felt regret with each mention of her pain. But he tried not to think about it.

The following morning Michael went to church with his family, then he drove himself to the hospital. He found Emily sitting in a chair by the window, dressed in a hospital gown with a blanket over her legs. It was good to see her out of bed, but when she looked up at him, he could see evidence that she had been crying.

"What's wrong?" he asked, sitting on the edge of the bed.

"I can go home tomorrow," she said tensely, fidgeting with the edge of the blanket.

Michael leaned his forearms onto his thighs and looked at her severely. "What's wrong, Emily?"

"They did some tests and found out why I've been sick."

When she said nothing more he became impatient. "Okay, so

what is it?" His nerves were on edge. Were there more complications? Did they find some disease? Cancer?

"Michael," she said, tears spilling, "I'm pregnant."

Michael leaned back slowly and reminded himself to breathe. "But I thought that . . ."

"So did I, but apparently I should have researched menopause a little more thoroughly. The doctor told me in some cases it's possible for a woman to get pregnant up to two years after the symptoms begin."

Michael closed his eyes briefly as a sigh consumed him. He had been given a chance to redeem himself. He had prayed for a miracle that might give them the opportunity to have this baby. But . . . the timing! He could already feel the fear on her behalf creeping into him. When he looked at Emily, it was evident that she shared his anguish.

"I thought you would be happy about this," he stated.

"I am," she insisted. "I mean . . . you know I want this baby, but . . . Michael, I don't know if I can do it." She pressed a trembling hand over her face. "I feel so sick already, and I hurt so badly." While she cried, Michael managed to kneel on his good knee and tuck the other leg between the bed and the chair. He urged her head to his shoulder and held her, giving him just enough time to think this through.

"It's all right, Emily. I'll be with you every minute. I will."

She looked at him dubiously. He couldn't blame her after the way he'd reacted the last time she got pregnant.

"You're pleased about this." She seemed in a state of shock.

"I don't want to see you suffer, Emily, but . . ." He tried to remember how she had put it to him once. "I prayed for this baby, Emily. This baby is a miracle."

Emily was so touched that she almost forgot the difficulties that lay ahead. She laughed and held him tightly, until Michael realized there was something more bothering her.

"What?" he insisted gently.

Emily swallowed hard. "Michael," she said, her eyes full of torment, "it's worse."

"What's worse?" he demanded, his heart suddenly pounding.

"The doctor is concerned because . . . with all the . . . the . . . medication . . . and the . . . X-rays . . . and . . . Oh, Michael. There is a good chance . . . that this baby . . . will have problems."

Emily mumbled on and on about not being able to do it. Michael knew this was a good place to start making things right. "Emily." He took her shoulders and looked into her eyes. "Calm down and listen to me." He took a deep breath. "It is my fault that you are in the condition you're in now, both the accident *and* the pregnancy. I am prepared to take full responsibility for both. I am going to spend every minute for the next nine months holding your hand, if that's what it takes to get you through this. It's obvious that this baby is meant to come, and we have to exercise the faith to see that it makes it here alive and well."

The hope that rose in Emily's eyes made Michael realize how much his attitude had affected her in the past. How ironic marriage was; when one's faith seemed to run dry, the other could actually come up with enough to get them through.

"But what if . . . the baby . . . has something wrong . . . and . . ."

"Emily." He took her face in his hands and said with a conviction that surprised even him, "This baby has a strong spirit. It will be fine." Seeing the doubt in her eyes, he knew they had to accept the possibility of problems, but he had no question about his stand on that. "And if it's not," he added quietly, "we will love it just the same."

"Oh, Michael," she pulled him close, crying softly, "I love you so much. You are such a strength to me."

"It's the other way around, love."

"I can do anything if I have you with me. *Anything!*"

"I'll be there, Emily, always."

"Forever," she said.

Without too much conviction, but a degree of hope, he echoed it. "Forever."

* * * * *

Emily came home to a banner strung across the front of the house, and more hugs than she knew what to do with. But even

James had been trained in the art of careful hugging so he wouldn't hurt Mom. When the commotion settled down, Michael found Emily propped up on the bed with pillows, reading to James. He leaned in the doorway to watch her, loving the way she laughed and occasionally pressed a kiss to James's head.

"Why don't you run along and play," Michael said when he noticed Emily looking drained.

After much urging, James left the room and Michael sat on the edge of the bed. "How are you?" He kissed her lightly.

"I'm exhausted," she admitted, then she smiled. "But I'm so happy to be home."

"Not as happy as I am to see you here," he insisted.

Emily leaned back and sighed. "Do you know what I want?"

"A root beer float?" he guessed.

Emily shook her head. "It sounds good, but that's not what I *really* want."

"Chinese food?"

Emily grimaced and held her stomach. "Thank you, no."

Michael chuckled. "You're just going to have to tell me."

"I want sugar cookies with gobs of frosting."

"Gobs?" Michael laughed. "We could probably come up with that if you give us a little time."

"Do you know what else I want?"

"I'm not even going to guess."

"I want a long soak in the bathtub."

"Now, that we can take care of at a moment's notice."

"How about right now?" she asked.

"You're not too tired?"

"Not for that. I've been dreaming for three weeks of soaking in a real tub. But I might need some help."

"You won't embarrass me," he said, and hobbled into the bathroom to start running the water. "You want bubbles?" he called to her.

"Just a few."

When he nearly had it ready, Michael turned to find her leaning against the basin, sweat beading over her face, her breathing labored.

"What have you been doing?" he insisted.

He didn't miss the distress in her voice. "I just walked all the way from the bed," she croaked. "I can't believe how weak I feel."

"Considering how weak I felt after surgery for a broken leg, I can well imagine how weak *you* must feel. Just take it easy, and I'll take care of you."

"How can you take care of me?" she asked lightly. "You're practically a cripple yourself."

"Well, between me and Mother and the kids, I think we'll manage."

"Yes," she smiled and pulled him gingerly into her arms, "I think we will."

Michael had helped Emily in and out of the bathtub many times in their years of marriage, but he wasn't prepared for the shock of seeing her now. He had spent countless hours in her hospital room, and had been present during many medical procedures relating to the accident. But only now did he see the full sweep of just how bad it was. After so many weeks, he would have assumed the effect might have lessened, yet Emily's body, predominantly the right side, was a mass of hideous bruises and scabs. He did his best to remain unemotional and remember that time would heal *all* wounds.

Weeks passing allowed the healing to take place. Michael managed to get around pretty well with a leg brace. Emily gained strength and felt the pain less and less. Nausea from the pregnancy, combined with the complications of the accident, kept her confined to bed much of the time. But Michael did as he had promised, staying close to her through every moment of pain and sickness. He almost believed that proving his devotion to her in this way could somehow help him toward compensating for all the pain he'd caused her.

Beyond answering the children's questions, the cause for Michael's anger and the resulting accident were never discussed. Michael rededicated himself to prayer and scripture study, and gradually he felt more comfortable with himself and his relationship with God. But still he wondered and worried over a few critical aspects of his life.

A day didn't pass without speculation over Allison's whereabouts. Just as with other areas of his life, Michael tried to have the faith that she would be all right and come back to them. He was able to encourage Emily through the darkest moments, which in turn seemed to strengthen his own faith. But still, he wondered.

On a warm afternoon, LeNay took the kids to the park. They'd not been gone long when Melissa came by—alone. They hadn't seen her without Sean since they'd both returned from their missions.

"Can I talk to you?" she asked Emily, before they had a chance to question the reason. "Alone?" she added carefully.

"Sure." Emily motioned toward the bedroom, and Michael graciously went to the kitchen with a mind to bake something chocolate.

"Is something wrong?" Emily sat on the edge of the bed and motioned for Melissa to sit beside her. Melissa squeezed her eyes shut and took a deep breath. Emily had sensed a subtle tension between Sean and Melissa recently. Michael suspected it was because Sean wanted to get married and Melissa wasn't sure. Emily only had to wonder for a moment if that was her reason for being here.

"Emily," she finally said, "how do you know . . . I mean *really* know, if you should marry someone?"

Emily was taken momentarily off guard as she realized the question hit something tender in her. When she didn't speak right away, Melissa went on.

"Sean told me a little about the situation with Michael and your first husband. I hope you don't mind. Obviously you made the right choices at the right times, Emily, and I need some help here. I love Sean." She started to cry. "I really love him, Emily. He's a wonderful man . . . but something just doesn't feel right. I can't explain it. There's no logical reason for it. I just feel . . . confused."

Melissa took a deep breath. "Did I tell you I got a job offer in California?"

"No," Emily admitted, surprised.

"Well, you know I've had my degree for a while now. I sent a resume to this place several weeks ago. It's a great job, Emily. It's what I've always wanted. But I wonder if I'm just wanting to take it so badly that I'm not seeing this reasonably."

"If you're truly meant to be with someone, is it necessary to choose between a job and a marriage? I'm sure if it's right, you would be able to work it out."

"I'm so confused," Melissa repeated. "Is it because I'm just too . . . cautious, or is there more? How can I know, Emily? I don't want to hurt him, but . . ." She paused and pushed her hair back with a trembling hand. "I just don't know what to do."

"Oh, Melissa." Emily put an arm around her and let her cry. "There's only one thing you *can* do." Melissa looked up, her eyes narrow with interest. "It's impossible to know the long-range effect of our decisions. We have to trust in the Lord. You have to study it out in your mind, and then you have to fast and pray and ask the Lord specifically if your decision is right. When you feel that undeniable peace, you'll know you've made the right choice. It may take a long time to know *why*, but if you put your life in the Lord's hands, you can't go wrong."

Melissa absorbed Emily's words, then sighed deeply. "And what if the Lord tells me not to marry Sean? How can I tell him . . . what can I say?"

Emily realized it was a difficult question to answer. Sean was so much a part of the family, and she knew how much he loved Melissa. To lose her would break his heart. But that didn't change the truth of what she was telling Melissa. "If you know in your heart that you're doing the right thing, you'll have the Spirit to help you. It wouldn't be easy, but . . . you'll know it's right."

They talked for nearly an hour, and Melissa left with a commitment to fast and pray. But Emily knew already what the answer would be. Melissa's confusion was evidence that marrying Sean was likely not meant to be. Emily talked to Michael about it, and together they prayed that Melissa would be guided to make the correct decision. And that Sean would be able to accept it, either way.

Michael had trouble going to sleep that night. He lay awake for hours, reliving in his mind the weeks following Emily's decision not to marry him. It was one of the most difficult things he'd ever faced. He hoped that Sean would have the strength to make it through better than he had. This situation was just one more thing that made Michael feel as if he and Sean were some kind of soul mates. Already Michael's heart ached with empathy, and Melissa hadn't even made her decision yet.

CHAPTER SIXTEEN

"What's wrong?" Michael asked Emily as soon as she walked through the door with his mother. LeNay graciously went off to find the children.

"I'll tell you what's wrong." Emily pressed her dress over her belly. "Look at me."

"You look pregnant," he said.

"Michael, I look six or seven months pregnant. I'm less than halfway. The doctor said it might be gestational diabetes; he told me it can cause babies to grow too big. I have to go in tomorrow to have some tests taken."

Michael put his arms around her, doing his best to ignore the fear that always crept in. "I'm certain everything will be fine."

"Michael," she cried, "what if something is wrong? What if—"

"Now, hold on." He touched her chin. "We promised each other we would have faith."

"I know," she whimpered, "but sometimes I . . . I'm just so scared."

Michael pulled her close. "I know well how you feel, love. But we can't be scared, Emily, we just *can't*."

"Be strong for me, Michael. Sometimes I just don't think I have anything left to give."

"You're doing beautifully, Emily." He drew back to look at her. "What else did the doctor say?"

"He said that the pain I'm still feeling from the accident is normal; that I appear to have healed well and everything looks fine otherwise."

Michael smiled. "Now, there's some good news." He hugged her again. "We have much to be grateful for, Emily."

Michael sat with Emily through the tests. Diabetes was eliminated as a possibility, and the doctor ordered an ultrasound. Michael held Emily's hand while they prepped her. Without a word, they shared the fear that a problem might be detected. The doctor who performed the procedure talked casually while he moved the instrument over Emily's belly and watched the monitor.

"There's the little heart pumping," he said, and they looked eagerly to see what he pointed out. He showed them a foot, a hand, a well-formed head, internal organs that appeared to be functioning normally. The thrill was indescribable. The doctor then became silent as he apparently looked for something. The grayish images blurred to the untrained eye while he made contemplative noises.

"Is something wrong?" Michael asked.

"Not that I can see," he replied, then continued looking and contemplating. When he apparently came to a conclusion, he looked at Michael and Emily. "I want to show you something." He moved the sound waves over one side of Emily's belly. "You see the head here."

"Yes," Emily said, though it was difficult for her to distinguish.

"And moving up from the head, because the baby is upside down, you can see the shoulders, arms, spine, and legs. If you look closely right there, you can see that this baby is a girl."

Emily said nothing, but she couldn't help feeling disappointed. The baby Alexa held in her dream was a boy, and she knew it.

"I'll take your word for it," Michael chuckled, unable to see the distinction.

"Now," the doctor said, "look over here." He moved the instrument to the opposite side of her abdomen, just below her ribs. "Can you see this, Mrs. Hamilton?"

Emily concentrated. "It looks like what you just said was a head on the other side."

"Exactly," the doctor chuckled. Emily's heartbeat quickened. "And this is a spine, arms, legs." Now that he had the present position down, he quickly moved the instrument to make his point clear. "See this hand? You can make out the fingers. And here is a hand.

And here. And here."

"There's four hands," Michael said. "Good heavens," he sighed breathlessly. "There are *two babies* in there."

Emily laughed out loud, and one of the babies on the screen rolled over.

"Congratulations," the doctor said while he continued to look.

"There aren't three, are there?" Michael asked.

"No," the doctor chuckled, "I was just going to see if they're both girls."

"The other one is a boy," Emily said with confidence.

"I think you're right," the doctor replied. "There it is, plain as day."

"Now *that* I recognize," Emily said. "It *is* a boy. Michael, it's a boy."

He hugged her and they laughed together. In the car on the way home, Michael kept laughing intermittently. "I don't believe it. Twins."

"I don't think there are any twins on my side of the family," Emily said. "I wonder where it came from."

"My grandmother was a twin," Michael said.

"Emma?"

"I thought you knew."

"I must have forgotten."

"Emma and Tyson were twins. They were the only children Jess and Alexa had except for Lacey, whom they adopted."

Emily pressed a loving hand over her middle. "Emma and Tyson. What do you think?"

"I think that's a good idea," he grinned.

The joy of having twins soon descended into reality when Emily's obstetrician told her the facts. The pregnancy would be difficult. Twins alone would be a strain, but adding to that her age and the stress of the accident, the prospect of the coming months was grim. She would be extremely restricted, possibly even bedridden for the last several weeks. Knowing they were in for some difficult months ahead, they decided the family had to know. Michael called them together and made the announcement. "We found out a few days ago that your mother is going to have a baby girl." The children squealed with delight and he added, "She's also going to have a baby boy."

Speculative glances shot back and forth across the room as everyone wondered if he was teasing.

"Twins!" LeNay finally shrieked.

"That's right," Michael said proudly. "One of each."

LeNay laughed. "Just like Tyson and Emma."

"That's what their names are," Michael said proudly.

"You've already named them?" Amee asked.

"Not officially, but—"

"Well, this is wonderful, Michael," LeNay beamed.

"Not completely wonderful," Michael's tone softened. "We're going to continue to need your help, Mother. And you children have got to help the way you did when Mom came home from the hospital. She's going to have to stay down much of the time, and we're going to have to work together to get through this."

"Well, it's certainly a good thing I'm here," LeNay said with pleasure.

"Yes, it is," Emily agreed. "It just never seemed right without you."

Sooner than expected, complications set in. Emily spent some time in the hospital, then was released with strict instructions to stay down flat, for her own health and safety as well as the babies'. They made arrangements for some home study courses to keep her occupied and working toward her degree. Another ultrasound at six months revealed what appeared to be a heart problem with the little boy. There were many speculations and concerns, but through much prayer and fasting, they knew that all they could do was wait and have faith that God would work all of this out according to his plan. Emily suggested that they not consider the problem at all, but instead think of Tyson as a normal, healthy child. If he was born with a problem, they would take it on the best they could.

Through the course of all this, Sean was rarely around. He and Melissa were still dating, but there was obviously tension in the relationship. The job Melissa wanted had fallen through, but the same company had an opening coming up. While Melissa believed it was right for her, Sean felt he should stay at BYU to finish his degree. Just as with their own circumstances, Michael and Emily could only pray that everything would work out as it was meant to.

As Emily's confinement became more cumbersome, she was easily discouraged and often spoke of Allison, wondering and worrying. Michael did his best to have faith and remain positive, but there were moments when the doubt and confusion crept in and tried to smother him. He kept close to the scriptures and filled his heart with prayer, sharing both with Emily night and day.

On a dark day in October, Emily took hold of his hand and said with a strained voice, "If only I could go to the temple, Michael." She touched his face and he felt it coming. "You could go, Michael. Go for me, please. Pray for Allison, and just sit in the celestial room for me."

Michael felt the need to tell her what she already knew. "I don't have a recommend, Emily."

"Then you'd better get one," she said.

Michael hesitated, then he nodded in agreement. The next evening he was sitting in Bret's office at the church. They talked of trivial things, and it felt no different than sitting on the back lawn or at a ball game. Then Michael's friend slipped into his role as bishop. "So, you're ready to go back to the temple."

"I believe I've missed it," Michael said, then began to chew his thumbnail.

"Is that the only reason you've chosen now to take this step?"

Michael cleared his throat tensely. "Well, Emily can't go, and . . . maybe one of us ought to be there. We could use the blessings, I think."

"That's a good enough reason." Bret smiled and leaned back. "But I get the feeling you're nervous."

Michael tucked his hand under his arm as if it might keep him from chewing on his thumbnail. "I suppose I am. I've had some pretty mixed feelings about the temple in the past. I don't want to take those feelings with me, Bret. I want to go there and find peace, but sometimes I wonder if—"

"I hear those doubts coming through, Michael. If you seek peace, there is no reason why you won't find it."

Michael said nothing. He wanted to believe that, and he prayed inwardly that he would. Bret proceeded to ask the recommend questions without reading them. Michael thought each word before Bret spoke it. They were easier to answer than Michael had expected, and he wondered what part Satan had played in making him believe he was less worthy than he actually was. He'd even conquered his addiction to Coca-Cola. But that last question caught him and he hesitated.

"Michael," Bret said when the silence grew too long, "is there a reason that *you* don't feel worthy to attend the temple?"

Michael swallowed hard. "I'm still having trouble with this, Bret. Every hour of every day I am so keenly aware of Emily's suffering, and I know in my heart it would not be this way if I hadn't been so proud and stubborn and—"

"You've got to forgive yourself, Michael. The atonement is there for you. Christ has cleared the path for you to be free of this, but you have to reach out and take it."

Michael leaned his elbows on his thighs and pressed his head into his hands. "I know," he said through a lengthy sigh. "I've been praying for forgiveness; I have. I have felt the Spirit come back into my life and I am grateful, but still . . . I wonder why it had to be this way. Why couldn't I have learned my lesson without hurting her?"

"That's something only the Lord can help you understand. But I believe that with some time, it will happen."

Michael stood in the foyer of the church for several minutes, just looking at the little piece of paper in his hand. He thought of all the temple represented and felt a surge of hope. He returned home to find Emily propped up in bed, watching a video of *Casablanca* for the fifth time this week.

Michael leaned in the doorway and glanced toward the television that had been added to the bedroom to ease her confinement. In a poor attempt to imitate Bogart, he said, "Play it again, Emily. You might have missed something the first time."

Emily laughed ridiculously. "I don't think Humphrey Bogart would have made it with an Australian accent, my love."

Michael feigned a hurt expression and sprawled himself onto the bed at her side, leaning his chin in his hand. She turned off the television with the remote control and bent briefly to kiss him. "How did it go?" she asked.

Michael reached into his shirt pocket and pulled out the temple recommend. Emily smiled and touched his face.

"I have an appointment with the stake president the day after tomorrow, and I'll plan on going to the temple the following day."

Emily motioned him closer and put her arms around him. Michael relaxed his head against her shoulder and pressed a hand over her belly. "You looked about this size when you were ready to deliver James," he said.

"I feel pregnant from the chin down." She laughed it off, but Michael knew from closely observing her that she was constantly uncomfortable, and often hurting.

"Is there anything I can get for you?" he asked, idly rubbing his hand over the babies, as if he could somehow make contact with them.

"Not at the moment, but—"

They were both startled by the hefty kick that seemed to respond to Michael's hand.

"I believe Tyson likes you," Emily giggled.

"How do you know it isn't Emma?" he asked, prodding gently with the hope of getting another response.

"I just know," Emily said, not certain herself how she did.

The baby kicked again and Michael laughed. He kissed Emily's belly then pressed his ear to it. "Yo, Tyson, are you in there? Are you being good to your sister?"

At the sound of his voice, Emily's middle came to life. They both laughed until Emily suddenly went tense and groaned.

"What?" Michael asked.

Emily let out a slow breath and tried to relax. "Sometimes it feels like those ribs on the right side are going to burn a hole right through me. While you're down there, tell your children to have a little mercy on their mother."

Instead, Michael took her hand and pressed it to his lips. "It shouldn't have been this way, Emily."

"What's that supposed to mean?"

"If it weren't for the accident and—"

"Michael." She put her fingers over his mouth. "We are alive, and we are together, and we are going to make it through this."

Michael held her close, marveling at her goodness, wondering why it had to be this way. He wished he could somehow take the pain from her and endure it himself. He felt sure it would be appropriate.

Michael tore himself away to see that the children were all getting ready for bed. As always, they gathered around Emily's bed for family prayer before James was tucked in and the others went to their rooms. Michael made certain Emily had everything she needed before he went downstairs to write for a while before turning in. She picked up a book from the bedside table and had barely begun to read when she heard the front door open, then slam shut. Heavy footsteps bounded up the stairs. She might have thought it was Michael if she hadn't known he was writing.

"Emily?" Sean's voice boomed from the hall. He sounded angry.

"I'm here—of course," she called. He appeared in the bedroom doorway, looking as upset as he'd sounded. Hoping to lighten the mood, she added, "Where else would I be?"

Emily almost felt afraid as he moved toward her. "What did you say to her?" he demanded.

Emily was so stunned she could only gape at him, wondering what had happened.

"Hey," Michael said from the doorway, startling them both, "that's my wife you're talking to."

"I'm sorry," Sean said, then he repeated more gently, "Emily, what did you say to Melissa?"

"It would help if I knew what you're talking about," Emily said quietly, while she feared this was the moment they had been dreading. "Did something happen?"

"She left me!" Sean choked the words out. "She took that job in California, and she's gone. And she told me she'd taken *your* advice. Now, what did you tell her?"

As Sean leaned toward Emily, Michael stepped toward them, concerned. Emily lifted a finger to stop Michael, then she pressed her hand to Sean's face.

"She asked me how I had known it was right to marry who I married. I told her the only thing I *could* tell her, Sean. The Spirit let me know who to marry and when. I told her to fast and pray, and she would know whether or not it was right."

Sean's countenance softened as he apparently realized he had no cause for anger. He hung his head and his expression filled with grief. Emily wrapped her arms around him. Michael sat next to Sean on the edge of the bed and put a soothing hand to his shoulder as he slumped wearily into Emily's arms.

It was late before Sean finally went home. Michael tried to offer empathy without dwelling on the pain he'd felt when Emily had left him. But there was some gratification when Sean seemed to gain strength from Michael's story. He left with the assurance that it was impossible to know how it would all turn out, but he had to have faith that his life was in the Lord's hands. Michael and Emily knew it would be difficult for Sean, but at least he had found a family; and they were glad to be there for him.

As always, the night was restless for Emily. She tried to stay as quiet and still as possible, not wanting to disturb Michael. But he seemed to have a sixth sense about her discomfort and was always there. As he lay holding her, drifting in and out of sleep, she wished, as she often did, that she could reach inside him and pull out his deepest thoughts. She didn't sense the fear and hardness she had seen in the past, but there was still a part of him that seemed somehow obscure. She longed to talk to him, but he had been so sensitive about anything relating to the accident that she feared bringing up the conversation they had been sharing when it happened. In her mind she thought of a dozen different ways to approach it, but the only thing she could bring herself to say was simply, "I love you, Michael."

"I can't hear you," he said, "I'm asleep."

Emily giggled and kissed his brow.

"I love you, too, Emily Hamilton."

"I know," she said and drifted off to sleep.

The phone rang shrilly through the darkness. Emily awoke, heart pounding, and reached for it while she glanced at the clock. 2:33 a.m. "Hello," she said groggily, hoping it wasn't someone from Australia, calling to see how they were doing.

"Mom?" Allison's voice squeaked from the other end.

"Allison?" She grabbed Michael's arm and he reached frantically for the light. "Where are you? Are you all right?"

"I'm okay. Mom," she hesitated and Emily could tell she was crying, "I'm in Las Vegas, and . . ."

"Las Vegas?" Emily repeated for Michael's benefit. He sighed and closed his eyes.

"I want to come home, Mom, if you'll have me."

"You don't have to wonder about that, sweetie."

"I bought a bus ticket, but I only had enough money to get to St. George." There was a pause. "Could you meet me there?"

Emily bit her lip to keep her voice steady. "I would be more than happy to, Allie, but I can't right now. I'm pregnant, and I can't get out of bed. But I'm sure that—"

"Do you think Dad could come?" she interrupted.

Emily looked at Michael, her eyes glowing through the tears. "I'm sure that Dad would be happy to come." Moisture filled Michael's eyes as well. "When will you be there?"

Allison told Emily the time, then added, "Mom, I'm sorry."

"It's all right, sweetie. We'll talk when you get home."

Emily hung up the phone and Michael pulled her into his arms. They cried and held each other for several minutes before Michael could ask, "What did she say?"

"She said she wants to come home, but she only had enough money to get a ticket to St. George. I told her you'd meet her there. It's a six-hour drive. You'd better leave soon."

Michael laughed and jumped out of bed. "I'll have her home for dinner."

Through the long drive, Michael realized he was nervous. What would he say to her? Should he be casual so he wouldn't frighten her off? Or was it better to let her know how he really felt? He stopped only once for gas and a quick meal, and arrived in St. George twenty minutes before the bus was due.

He nervously paced the parking lot in the hot sun, watching the road regularly. When the bus finally appeared, his heart pounded and his stomach turned to knots. He couldn't believe how much he loved her.

Michael watched people file off the bus, fearing he might not recognize her. When she finally stepped down, he recognized her all right, but he felt sick at the sight of her. He stood where he was, uncertain and afraid, until he realized that she was, too. In a gesture of acceptance, Michael pulled his hands from his pockets and opened his arms. She took a few hesitant steps, then ran and threw her arms around him. Michael held her tight and cried with her. He smoothed her matted hair and whispered words of reassurance. "It's all right, Allie. You're as good as home. Everything's going to be fine."

Allison looked up at him, shame and fear showing in her eyes. Michael's brow furrowed as he took her chin and tilted her face in the light. One eye was blackened, and her face was discolored with fading bruises. He wanted to ask her what had happened, but he knew there would be plenty of time for that. Instead he asked, "Are you hungry?"

"I haven't eaten since yesterday morning," she admitted.

Michael tried not to feel upset. "Do you have any luggage?"

"No," she stated.

"How about if we get a motel room? You can get cleaned up a little while I go get us something to eat." Allison nodded, and he guided her toward the Blazer. She hesitated as he opened the door.

"It's blue. I thought it was green." Allison stepped back and squinted. "Or did I remember wrong?"

A sick knot tightened in Michael's stomach. "You remembered correctly. This is a different Blazer."

She looked up at him in question while he held the door for her. "I'll tell you about that later. Let's get you something to eat."

Allison climbed in and leaned back wearily against the seat as he got in and turned the ignition. The silence was almost palpable as he drove to a motel and parked near the office. "I'll be right back," he said and she nodded.

Michael had seen better motel rooms, but Allison looked as if she were in the lap of luxury when she walked through the door.

"Well, it's clean at least," he said. He tossed a bag onto the bed. "On a hunch, your mother had me get some of your things. Looks like it's good I did." Allison nodded gratefully and Michael cleared his throat. "Why don't you clean up, and I'll get us something to eat. What sounds good?"

"Anything, really," she said. He remembered that she hadn't eaten since yesterday morning and decided to move on.

"I'll hurry," he said, locking the door behind him.

Michael ordered some food, then went to find a phone booth while he waited.

"Hello?" Emily answered eagerly.

"Yes, it's me," he said.

"Was she there?" Her voice bordered on panic.

"Yes, she was there. I got a motel room so she could clean up. I'm waiting for a pizza."

"You sound . . . upset."

"Your hunch to send some things was on the mark. She had nothing. She looks like she hasn't combed her hair in a month. But as far as I can tell, she's all right. She's got some bruises on her face."

"Bruises? What from?"

"I don't know. We haven't had much to say yet."

"Are you all right?" Emily asked.

"I'm . . . concerned," he said. "I just wanted to let you know I've got her. We'll start home in an hour or so. I didn't want you to be shocked when you see her."

"Thank you for calling," she said. "And don't speed."

Emily wished she hadn't said that when the ensuing silence grew far too long.

"Don't worry, Emily." His voice was barely steady. "I will never go past the speed limit again as long as I live."

"I'm sorry, Michael, I didn't mean to—"

"It's okay. Just take care of yourself."

"Tell her I love her."

"Yes, ma'am," he said like an American cowboy and she chuckled, grateful for the comic relief.

Michael returned with pizza, salads, and root beer. Allison was sitting on the edge of the bed, trying to comb through her wet, tangled hair. She looked better clean, and she certainly smelled better, but the bruises on her face stood out more prominently without the smudges of dirt. The clothes he'd brought looked baggy on her. Had she lost weight?

"It smells wonderful," she said as he set the food on the table and motioned for her to join him.

"Let's bless it and we can eat," he offered. Allison sat and bowed her head. Michael said a quick, sincere blessing on the food, and offered gratitude for Allison's safe return. When she looked up after the amen, there were tears in her eyes.

"Something wrong?" he asked, pulling the foil off her salad and passing it across the table.

"I can't remember the last time I heard a blessing on the food," she said.

"You want to talk about it?" he asked gently.

"Right now, I want to eat." She smiled sweetly and dug into her salad. At first she ate slowly, seeming to relish every bite, then she gained zeal and it was evident she was starving. He wondered what she had eaten yesterday morning. A piece of bread, perhaps?

"Don't overdo," he cautioned. "You'll make yourself sick. We'll take it with us, and you can have more when that settles."

"Good idea," she said with her mouth full. The meal passed in silence as Michael hardly knew what to say. When she'd apparently had her fill, she cleared off the table and threw away what they were finished with. Michael closed the pizza box and set the drinks on top of it to take with them.

"Have you got what you need?" he asked.

Allison picked up the bag he'd brought. "I left the old clothes in the bathroom. If it's okay with you, I'd rather not keep them."

"Good idea," he said, and led the way out to the Blazer.

Michael stopped for gas and asked her if she wanted anything. She picked out a magazine and eyed the candy bars like a child in a toy factory.

"Get a couple for the road," he said and she smiled.

For the first fifty miles, she looked at her magazine and said nothing. She finally got tired of it and set it aside.

"Your mother sends her love," Michael said, hoping to begin a conversation. "She was so happy she could hardly speak."

Allison managed a weak smile but said nothing. She looked blankly out the window for another forty miles, then said out of nowhere, "Mom said she's pregnant again. Is she going to make it through this time?"

"It looks that way. She still has several weeks to go, but the doctor ordered her to stay in bed. It's kind of a unique situation."

"How is that?" She leaned her head back on the seat where she could see him.

"She's going to have twins," he said proudly.

"Twins?" Allison laughed.

"A boy and a girl. We're going to name them after my grandmother and her twin brother. Emma and Tyson."

Allison wrinkled her nose slightly. "I suppose we can get used to that."

"I suppose," Michael smiled.

"Twins. Wow. That's awesome."

"That's what I thought."

"You're happy about this, aren't you?"

"Yes, Allison, I am. I finally came to my senses." Though Allison had never been told directly of the problems between him and Emily, he felt sure she knew much of the cause for tension.

"Well, I'm happy for both of you," she said with genuine affection.

"We're happy you came back," he said, hoping to get to the subject.

"Are you really?" she asked.

"More than you can imagine," he said fervently.

Allison's voice broke. "You don't know how much that means to me."

"Maybe we ought to talk about what happened before we get home," he suggested gently.

"I guess we should." She looked down at her hands, fidgeting nervously in her lap. "I don't know why I left, really. I was just frustrated with life and believed that getting away would solve it. Jack dumped me; I guess that had something to do with it. A guy I knew was going to Vegas to get a job, so I went with him. He helped me find an apartment with some other girls. Well, actually it wasn't really an apartment. It was more like a room with a sink and a stove and some dirty mattresses on the floor."

Michael rubbed his face with one hand as he drove, trying not to show too much emotion. He didn't want to thwart her flow of conversation before he got the whole story.

"I got a job at this greasy hamburger joint, and I made enough to pay my share of the rent and eat—barely. I started looking for a better job, and I got one working in a nursing home."

"Really?" He couldn't help being surprised.

"Yeah," she smiled. "They said that it was hard to keep good help because it wasn't a very enjoyable job, but I actually liked it. I just helped take care of the older people who couldn't take care of themselves anymore. Some of it was disgusting, but I'd feed them and bathe them and just talk to them. Some of those people were so wonderful, Dad. I started to really love them. I was saving money and looking for a better place to live, then I . . ."

Her chin quivered and she looked out the window. Michael knew this was the part he'd been dreading—whatever had happened to send her crawling home.

"There was this guy," she said tonelessly. "He was dating one of my roommates, and when they broke it off he asked me out. He was all right, but I didn't really get too excited about him. After a couple of dates, I tried to tell him this just wasn't going to work. He left really mad, and . . . the next night he . . ."

Michael's heart pumped painfully as he feared she was going to tell him the worst. He reached over and took her hand. She met his glance and continued in a teary voice. "He came in to where I worked and started beating on me. He dragged me outside, and I thought he was going to kill me, but somebody called the police and they got there just in time. I was fired because of the incident, then I found out that one of my roommates had left town and taken my money with her."

Michael reached up to wipe away a tear and press his hand to her face, as if he could take away the pain.

"My rent was due and when I couldn't pay it, they kicked me out then and there. I had a bag with most of my things, but it was stolen while I . . ." She hesitated. "Well, I fell asleep behind a warehouse. When I woke up, it was gone. I tried to get a job, but no one would even look at me in this condition. I had enough money in my pocket to get to St. George. I remembered your calling card number and used it to make the call."

"You should have used it a long time ago."

"I know," she whimpered. "I wanted to come home, but I know I hurt Mom so badly, and you. I'm sorry, Dad." She sobbed into her hands. "You were always so good to us. I guess I just didn't want to admit how much you'd given me. But I want you to know how grateful I am that you came into our lives."

Michael turned to Allison, not ashamed of the tears. "I love you, Allie. I couldn't possibly love my own flesh and blood more."

"I know that. And I feel the same about you." She wiped her face with a napkin and blew her nose. "I always knew you were a good father, but until I moved out I didn't realize how much. One of the girls I was living with . . . she told me how her stepfather had done unspeakable things to her. And there she was, basically surviving as a prostitute. Another girl's mother was a drug addict. You can't imagine, Dad, what kinds of things those people have been through. You told me once that the world out there didn't impress you. I was stubborn, and I had to see it for myself. In a way I'm glad I did, but I don't ever want to live that kind of life again. I've been to hell and back, and now I'm staying out."

"That's my girl," Michael grinned. He concentrated on the road while he told Allison everything that was going on at home. She was excited to know that LeNay was staying with them, and said several times that she couldn't wait to see her mother and the kids. He told her what was going on with Sean and Melissa, and it crossed his mind that perhaps Allison's return could make a difference to Sean now.

Michael watched Allison relax as the conversation became easier. He caught himself staring at her for as long as driving would permit.

"What?" she said, self-consciously pushing her hair back from her face.

"Nothing," he chuckled. "You just . . . remind me so much of your mother when I met her in college."

Allison glanced down timidly. "Mom was beautiful."

"Sweetie, your mother gets more beautiful every year."

"You really love her, don't you?"

Michael hated the way memories of that accident flooded his

mind at the least expected moment. He felt somehow hypocritical as he said, "Yes, Allison, I really do love her."

CHAPTER SEVENTEEN

After a considerable silence, Allison asked a question that Michael was totally unprepared for. "Did you ever meet my father?"

Michael shifted in his seat. "Once."

"Was it at the house?" she asked with a purpose to her voice that made Michael uneasy.

"Yes, it was. Why?"

Allison looked out the window. "It doesn't really matter. It's just that I've always wondered, but . . ."

"Yes?" he prodded when she hesitated.

"It was you," she said with certainty.

"I'm afraid you've lost me, sweetie."

Allison cleared her throat tensely. "I remember . . . one night . . . lying in bed. I could hear them arguing about . . ."

"About what?" he urged, though he wasn't sure if he wanted to hear it.

"Well, they weren't really *arguing*; not like they had before that. But he was upset. He said something about how it had made him feel to come home and find another man in his house, threatening to take away his wife and children."

Michael kept his eyes fixed on the road. He could feel his hands sweating around the steering wheel.

"The first time I saw you was a few months after my father died, but I remembered that and wondered if it was you."

"It was me," he admitted. "But I didn't exactly *threaten* to do anything." He glanced at Allison and saw a need for explanation. "I respected your mother's marriage, Allison, even though it broke my heart and tore me to pieces. I never got over losing her. When she came to my book signing, I insisted that she and I get together and talk. She didn't want to, but I insisted and she did. I asked her if she was happy. I believed I could get on with my life if I knew for certain that she was."

Michael shifted his grip on the steering wheel and sighed. "She tried to lie to me, Allison. She didn't want me to know the truth. When I realized how unhappy she was, I asked her to leave him. She fasted and prayed about it and made the decision to stay with your father. When I met him, she had already made that decision. I told your father why I was there, because I believed he needed to know. I had hoped it would make him treat her better."

"He did, you know," Allison said with full acceptance, when Michael was expecting to be somehow ridiculed for intruding upon her family.

"Yes," he admitted, "I know. Your mother did the right thing. She is a woman of incredible faith. Of course, neither of us knew at the time that he would be killed. It was a very bittersweet time in our lives." He glanced at Allison. "But I've often wondered if it was most difficult for you."

Allison shook her head slightly, seeming frustrated. "I guess what I'm trying to tell you is . . . well . . ." She looked at him with mist rising in her eyes. "My father was a hard man to love. Many of my memories are indifferent, some are not good at all. I remember arguments being common, and I hated the way he treated her. There were times when I think I almost blamed myself for his death, because I'd often wished he would go away. Maybe that's one of the reasons I've struggled these last few years. I've talked to Mom some about my feelings toward my father, and she's told me that I need to forgive him and be grateful for the life we have."

Allison gazed out the window and Michael sensed her emotion. "What I'm trying to tell you is that . . . well . . . if nothing else, being away from home has made me forgive my father. I know he never intended to hurt Mom . . . or me. But more than that, I want you to know how grateful I am for everything you've done for us." Allison's tears got the better of her, and she had difficulty speaking. "I said some awful things to you, and I want you to know that I'm sorry."

Michael took her hand and squeezed it.

"I hope my father will forgive *me* for this," she went on, "but I have to tell you that *you* are the only real father I've ever known, and I wouldn't want it to be any other way."

Michael reached over to quickly wipe the tears from Allison's face. "I can't tell you how much that means to me, Allie. You and your sisters mean the world to me. I hope you know that."

"I know," she nodded. "It's always been that way." She chuckled and dried her eyes. "I used to try and imagine how it might have been if you *had* taken us away. I believe it all worked out the way it was meant to, but it was nice to know that Mom had someone who loved her— someone else who wanted to see her rescued."

Michael felt suddenly more emotional than he could handle if he tried to speak. He drove several miles before he found a steady voice. He realized there were some things Allison needed to know before they got home. The miles were passing quickly, and he felt an urgency to suppress his emotions and get it over with.

"Allison," he said gently, "I have to tell you a couple of things." She looked over at him with interest. "First of all, your Grandmother Hall came by last spring."

He was surprised at how quickly she picked up on what he considered most difficult. "Oh, that must have been a *great* time for you." Her sarcasm somehow made him feel like she understood.

"It was one of the worst days of my life, if you must know. Actually, it was two days. They stayed overnight."

"They?"

"Your Uncle David came, too. He looks a lot like your father, you know."

Allison seemed somehow troubled, but Michael saw the evidence of how she had matured when she said, "It's very sad, the lack of love and respect they have in their family. I suppose that's why my father was the way he was."

"Yes, it is sad," Michael agreed. "I didn't mean to speak badly of them or—"

"It's all right, Dad. I understand. She can be a difficult woman. I can just bet what she had to say."

The combination of her empathy and calling him *Dad* just

about did Michael in. She apparently picked up on his emotion when she put her hand over his. "What *did* she say?"

Michael gave an embarrassed chuckle as tears leaked out of his eyes. He tried to clear his vision, and Allison handed him a napkin. "She . . . uh . . ." He chuckled again, but it came out sounding more like a sob. "Well, the hardest thing was that she told Amee and Alexa they were sealed to their father and they would be together forever. When the girls asked her about . . ." Michael paused to gain some control of his emotions. "When they asked her if they would be with Jess and James in heaven, she . . ."

Michael shook his head, and it was a full minute before he managed to speak. "I'm sorry, Allie. I didn't think it would be this hard for me after all these months, but . . . I just . . ."

He was relieved when Allison spoke and he could quit stammering. "I'm assuming she said something to imply that Jess and James were not a part of the same family."

"That about covers it," Michael said.

"But you know that's not true."

"I should, I suppose."

Allison seemed surprised at his emotion, but not without empathy. "Have you talked to Mom about the way you feel?"

Michael glanced at her almost sharply as she hit a very big nail on the head. He fixed his eyes on the road and swallowed hard. "Not like I should have. For some reason it's difficult."

The full spectrum of all that had happened in the past four years came rushing back to Michael, and he suddenly found it difficult to drive. As memories of the accident assaulted him, he pulled off to the side of the road and tried to get some control of his emotion, grateful for Allison's apparent understanding.

"Are you all right, Dad?" she asked.

"I'll be fine." He tried to laugh.

"This is more than just Grandma's visit," she guessed.

"Much, much more," he stated.

"Do you want to talk about it?"

Michael turned to look at Allison. She was very much like the little girl he had taken into his heart when he'd first married Emily, and yet she had gained so much maturity since he'd last seen her.

Could this opportunity possibly be the answer to his prayers, that he might come to terms with all of this? Allison knew better than anyone the life Emily had lived, with and without Michael. Still, he couldn't talk to her without first broaching something she had to know, but he dreaded telling her.

"The day your grandmother left, something happened that . . . well . . ." Michael told himself to just say it and get it over with before he had a chance to think about it. "Allison, do you remember the day I drove up the canyon like a maniac and scared you to death?"

She almost giggled. "I remember."

"Well," Michael swallowed hard, "after your grandmother left, I was hurt and angry . . . and it wasn't just the things she had said. There was more to it than that—things I couldn't bring myself to talk to your mother about, and . . . well, I was driving like that. Your mother was with me."

He saw Allison's eyes widen as she seemed to anticipate what was coming.

"I saw a truck crossing the road, but I couldn't stop in time. I . . . I tried to turn, but . . . there was a terrible accident. I nearly killed her, Allison."

She put a hand over her mouth and squeezed her eyes shut. Michael wanted to die.

"She had broken ribs and a punctured lung, among other things. Blood clots developed in her lung, and we nearly lost her more than once."

Allison started to cry, and Michael wanted to just find a hole and crawl in it. But he would prefer facing her wrath—justified as it was—here in privacy, rather than in front of the family when she heard the bad news elsewhere.

"I'm sorry, Allison," he said. "I don't blame you for being angry with me or—"

"Oh, no," she shook her head vehemently, "it's not that at all."

She wrapped her arms around him and held him tightly while she cried. Michael was reminded of the child she had once been as she clung to him. He thought of all she had been through and found his own hurts and fears falling into perspective. Even the way he found it difficult to let go of his own regrets seemed somehow petty and insignificant.

When Allison finally gained some control of her emotion, she drew back and smiled up at him. "It might sound silly, but . . . you can't imagine how nice it is to know I'm not the only one in this family who has made mistakes and done something stupid."

The chuckle that erupted from Michael surprised even himself. Before he knew it he was laughing. Allison laughed with him, sharing an unspoken kinship that meant more to Michael than he could tell her. They had both felt anguish over Emily's unhappiness in her first marriage, both resented Ryan's attitude and the hurt it caused. And they had both made some big mistakes and paid some big prices.

As their long drive continued, Michael found it easy to tell her about his fear of losing Emily and the way it had gotten out of hand and come between them. He didn't feel their age difference. Allison was a woman now, and they were able to talk in a delicate balance of father and daughter, adult to adult. Before they reached Utah Valley, Michael felt himself coming one step closer to finding that inner peace Bret had talked about.

Michael grinned when they pulled into the driveway to see a huge banner across the front of the house that read, "We love you, Allison." Yellow ribbons were tied all over the yard.

Allison got teary when she saw it. Michael squeezed her hand and they got out of the Blazer. The children came running out of the house, throwing themselves around their sister. Michael carried her bag into the house and they all followed him in, chattering away all at once. LeNay met them in the entry with a tearful embrace.

"You'd best hurry up to see your mother," Michael said. "She can't get out of bed."

Everyone trailed Allison down the hall and gathered in the doorway as she moved quietly into the room.

"Allie?" Emily cried and held out her arms. They held each other and wept. Emily touched her face and hair, laughing and crying in disbelief. When the greetings were finished, the family gathered around Emily's bed and listened as Allison told her story again. Tears were shed while a warm spirit hovered around them. Michael finally herded the children off and took his mother to the kitchen to prepare dinner, leaving Emily and Allison with some time together.

"You look so uncomfortable," Allison commented. "Is there anything I can do to—"

"Oh, I'm always uncomfortable." Emily smiled. "There's little to be done."

"Is that because it's twins," she asked, "or because of the accident?"

Emily's expression sobered. "Michael told you."

"He cried more than I did on the way home," Allison said quietly.

Emily felt somehow upset to think that Michael had opened up to Allison when she could hardly get him to talk about it at all. But perhaps Allison's being a part of this could help it come out in the open.

"Maybe it's none of my business," Allison said, "but I think you need to talk to him."

"I've tried, Allison. Something's been eating at him since I lost that baby and my heart stopped. Just before the accident, I finally realized it had something to do with the children being sealed to your father, but . . . well, he just doesn't seem to want to talk about it."

"Mother," Allison took Emily's hand and looked at her intently, "he believes that his part in this family is only temporary—that in eternity he will be on the outside."

"He said that?"

"Not in so many words, but yes."

Emily felt suddenly so emotional she couldn't speak. Allison seemed to understand by the way she kissed her mother on the cheek and said, "Maybe you should talk to him." Then she left Emily alone. Emily used the time to pray for a way to let Michael know exactly how she felt about this issue that was causing him so much grief. She was surprised at how quickly the answer came.

After dinner, Allison spent time with her brothers and sisters until they went to bed, then she pleaded exhaustion and embraced Michael, Emily, and LeNay before going down to her room.

"I can't believe she's back," Emily said to Michael as he sat on the edge of the bed to pull off his boots.

"It's been quite a day. She's like a different person. Well, no," he corrected, "she's more like the real Allison, but more mature."

"Well said."

Emily hesitated before saying, "Is that why you found it so easy to talk to her, when you find it so difficult to talk to me?"

Michael turned slowly to look at her, feeling somehow guilty. "I'm sorry." He glanced away tensely. "It just kind of . . . happened."

"It's okay, Michael. Really, it is. But one of these days, I'd really like you to tell me what's going on inside of you. I know this has been difficult for you, and I have some clues, but I'd like to know all of it—when you're ready." She paused and added, "How about now?"

Michael thought about it a moment then shook his head. "I need a little more time, Emily. I'm . . . well, I'm hoping that when I go to the temple, I'll be able to put it into perspective a little better. I've been praying for that. And I'm going too fast." He met her eyes. "Just give me a little more time."

Emily nodded. "Okay. Why don't you tell me a bedtime story?"

She was glad when he gave her the expected response, "I don't have any that you haven't already heard."

"What? The great J. Michael Hamilton has no story for his wife?"

"Sorry." He chuckled humbly.

"Well, then, I'll have to tell you one."

Michael looked intrigued. She motioned to the chair by the bed and he sat there, leaning his forearms on his thighs.

"A long, long time ago, in a place far, far away," she began.

"Is this *Star Wars?*" he asked with a little laugh.

"No," she sounded insulted, "it is not *Star Wars.*"

"That's a relief. I've seen the movie at least ten times."

"This is a story you haven't heard before," she said. "It's an Emily original; except that . . . well, someone did tell it to me once, in a roundabout way."

"Okay. I'm listening."

"In this faraway place, a world was being planned, and all of the spirit children of a great Father were brought together to help bring this wonderful event to pass. There was a man—a prince among men. He was a valiant, noble spirit, and he worked closely with his

Father in many things. He fought valiantly in the war between good and evil, where the free agency of these spirits was challenged by the Prince of Darkness.

"As this great world was being brought together and plans were set into motion to send the spirits down, each in their own time, the Father brought this man to his side and asked his heart's desire. 'There is a woman,' he told the Father. 'I love her with all my heart and soul, and I wish to be with her forever, whatever the cost may be.' The Father was pleased with the valiant one's wish, and asked for this woman to be brought to his side also. He placed her hand in his and promised them eternity if they would take the roundabout course that would bless the lives of others through their earthly existence.

"He talked to them of the pain and difficulty they might endure, and the way their promises to each other might appear to be for naught. He told them of their potential, of the children they would have, and he told this young man of the mission he was foreordained to accomplish. For he would go forth in a time and place where there was much to be done, and into circumstances that would allow him the means to do it. But he would be deceived, and born into a situation that would make it difficult to find the road he must travel. Still, the Father promised him divine guidance, and an instinctive ability to find his way, provided he lived worthy of it."

Emily's eyes became distant as she continued. "And there was another man, one who struggled with his faith, who had not been so firm in his convictions through the fight for free agency. He had chosen to follow the Prince of Peace, but his heart was often unsure. The Father saw potential in this man and believed that his earthly existence would better prepare him for a mission he would fulfill when he returned to the Father. But this man needed some extra help, and it was requested of the valiant one that he and this woman he loved, for a brief time on earth, sacrifice some of their time together to give this man the chance he needed. Of course they agreed, and the Father promised them incomparable joy in return for this sacrifice."

Michael found her story fascinating, and assumed it was something she'd come up with through her restless hours with nothing to do. But when he saw tears pool in her eyes, he began to grasp that it had deeper meaning. He felt somehow dazed as she went on, keenly aware of the warm chills rushing up his back and down again.

"The valiant one left for earth before the other two, giving them a few minutes to get acquainted before they followed. The valiant one was born halfway around the world from the others, but as promised, he was blessed with the instincts he needed to seek out a path that would bring them together."

Only then did Michael grasp the personal implications of Emily's story. Was she so bored that she had come up with these heavenly fairy tales, implying a perspective of their lives that was too incredible to comprehend? While a burning inside urged him to believe it was true, something formless tempted him to discredit it as nonsense.

Emily sensed a rising distress in Michael and took his hand as she continued. She was surprised to find it trembling. "The valiant one struggled much through his years of searching for the path the Father had planned for him. He often became confused and afraid, for the Prince of Darkness worked especially hard on him, drawing on his weaknesses and blowing them into enormous stumbling blocks. At times he even came to believe that he was not the valiant one at all, and—"

Emily stopped when Michael shot out of his chair, turned his back, and pushed both hands into his hair.

"Don't you like my story?" she asked with perfect innocence.

Questions riveted back and forth in Michael's mind, the most prominent being: *If what she says is nonsense, then why am I reacting this way?* Through Michael's eyes, he had seen himself as a man who had grown up wanting for nothing, and had fallen apart when he was denied the only thing he'd ever really wanted: Emily. He had been blessed enough to end up with her in the long run, but felt unworthy of her because of his many faults and imperfections. He had believed he was meant to join the Church, and his testimony of the gospel was strong. But he'd always figured he was stubborn and prideful for not joining sooner, for not being able to accept that Emily belonged to another man, for not being able to forgive himself for the hurt he'd brought into her life. How could he possibly be this valiant, noble spirit she spoke of? And yet everything inside of him seemed to be crying out for him to accept this concept and take hold of it. He didn't discredit Emily for having the eternal insight to come up with such a thing, but still, it had to be fiction. It just couldn't possibly be a—

"Michael, do you want to tell me why you're so upset?"

He willed himself to take a deep breath and sit down. "I'm sorry. I just . . ." He couldn't finish. "Emily, where did you come up with this *story?*"

"I was hoping you'd ask me that," she said, and he nearly wished he hadn't. "Do you remember, just before we were married, how difficult it was for both of us to accept that we couldn't be sealed?"

Michael nodded stoically.

"Do you remember how we fasted and prayed, and when we talked about it, we agreed that it felt right, and we knew everything would be okay?"

Michael nodded again.

"I just assumed at the time that you had felt the same peace about it that I had. I had no idea that you were struggling with those feelings all this time."

Michael looked at the floor, embarrassed and somehow ashamed.

"Michael," she took his hand, "at that time—before we were married—I had a dream."

His head shot up to look at her.

"I remember telling you I'd had a dream, but at the time it didn't seem appropriate to go into details. I should have taken the opportunity long before now to share it with you. Perhaps it would have saved us much heartache. I just assumed that you felt the same way I did."

Emily hesitated, wondering where his mind was. His eyes were expectant, and she reminded herself to continue. "I remember it as clearly as if it were yesterday. I saw you and me together with our Father in Heaven as a plan was laid out for us. It was evident that Ryan's part in it was for a different purpose; that you and I were meant to be together from the start, and we had been promised eternity if we were faithful."

Emily felt the warmth all over again, marveling at having been given such a beautiful vision. But she felt unbearably frustrated with Michael as he said, almost callously, "And what if I'm not faithful enough, Emily?"

She bit back a sharp retort and tried to remind herself of the perspective. She answered with a calm voice, "Michael, you told me you were going to fast and go to the temple, and then we could talk about it. Perhaps that would be best."

Michael was both relieved and disappointed as the conversation came to a sudden halt. He hardly slept that night as memories, fears, and dreams merged together into a muddle of confusion. He began a fast following lunch and kept mostly to himself, allowing Allison and Emily time together, and himself the opportunity to ponder on all that had happened.

That evening, as he sat in the stake president's office to complete his temple recommend process, he felt suddenly unsure, but hesitant to open it up. They talked casually for several minutes as Michael was asked questions about his background and his family. The interview went smoothly and without any reason for Michael to feel uncomfortable. He watched this good man sign his name across the bottom of that little white paper and slide it across the desk. Their eyes met as the recommend passed hands, and Michael saw something come into the president's expression just before he said, "I feel impressed to give you a blessing, Brother Hamilton. Do you feel that would be appropriate?"

"I wouldn't protest," he tried to say lightly, hoping to cover his emotion.

"Is there a reason you think I should feel such a prompting?"

Michael pushed an unsteady hand through his hair. "It's been a long time since I've been to the temple, President. I've been having some personal struggles, but I'm doing my best to understand and come to terms with them."

Michael didn't want to say anything more, and was relieved when he wasn't questioned further.

"Perhaps we should pray together first," the president suggested, then he asked Michael to offer the prayer. Michael tried to feel the

Spirit, but still felt somehow uncertain.

When that was done, the stake president placed his hands on Michael's head. He was prepared for, and fully expected, an outpouring of peace and guidance. But the words that came forth somewhere in the middle of the blessing left Michael stunned and trembling as tears streamed down his face.

"You are one of our Father's chosen spirits, of true nobility. You fought valiantly in the war for free agency before this world came into being, and you were blessed with the promise of your heart's desire as you came to earth, knowing you would be hurled into many struggles that would lure you into Satan's power of confusion, fear, and guilt. As you forgive others, you will find your own mistakes melt away as if they had never occurred. As you live the gospel and strive to keep the commandments, the desire of your heart will be granted as you were once promised in a former life—the desire to be with those you love most forever."

When the blessing was finished, Michael felt embarrassed by his emotion. But the stake president's eyes also showed signs of moisture as he took a seat next to Michael and leaned forward. Following a long silence, thick with the warmth of the Spirit, the president cleared his throat and said quietly, "You mentioned that you joined the Church in your thirties."

"That's right," Michael said, wondering where this was leading.

"Did you ever get a patriarchal blessing, Brother Hamilton?"

Michael swallowed hard, beginning to grasp the significance of the question. "No, I didn't. It just never . . . seemed right."

Their eyes met again, and there was no need for Michael to be told that the blessing he'd just been given had great significance. He wondered then if getting a patriarchal blessing earlier might have saved him much agony.

"Perhaps that's something you should consider doing," the president finally said. "You're never too old to learn more about yourself."

"I just might do that," Michael replied. They talked briefly, then Michael walked home, so full of emotion he could neither laugh nor cry. He stopped more than once to just gaze at the star-lit sky and marvel at the perspective of life and the mercy of God.

It was late before he finally wandered into the house, somehow fearing the intrusion of real life upon these feelings that were just beginning to jell as something he could possibly accept. When he walked into the bedroom, Emily looked up in concern. She said nothing, as if she sensed the spell he was under, and feared breaking it. He felt drawn to her side, where he slid to his knees and buried his face in the folds of her nightgown, against the mound where the twins were thriving just out of sight. She gently stroked his hair while he just held her. No words were spoken, but he knew that she understood.

Michael slept little through the night, but he used the time to pray and ponder. He knew he had drifted off when something startled him awake. He listened a moment, wondering what it might have been, then he realized Emily was crying.

"What's wrong?" He turned over and reached for her in the darkness.

"It just hurts," she whimpered.

Michael eased her face to his chest and tried to soothe her.

"I'm so tired of hurting, Michael. I just want it to be over."

"I know," he whispered. "I wish I could take the pain, my love. I wish I could endure it all. I would do it, you know. In an instant."

"Yes, I know." She held him closer. "But you can't, and sometimes I . . . Oh, Michael, sometimes I don't know if I can do it."

"You can do anything, Emily; *anything!*"

"You keep telling me that, Michael, because I'm not so sure. I need you," she cried.

"I'm here," he cooed, "always here."

"I'm so sick of just lying here, day in and day out. It just feels like it will never end."

"Think of your other pregnancies, Emily. You said the same thing. They ended. Life goes on."

"But it was never like this," she cried. "Oh, listen to me. All I do is complain."

"Personally, I think you should complain a whole lot more, love. You do a lot of smiling and gritting your teeth, if you ask me."

"Why are you so good to me, Michael?"

"I could never be good enough to you," he whispered and continued to hold her until she cried herself to sleep.

Michael rose before dawn and kissed Emily warmly before leaving for the temple. Driving through deserted streets, he continued to analyze all that had happened, all that had been said. As he turned a corner and the temple appeared above him on the hill, the first rays of the sun peering over the mountain behind it, Michael felt a window into heaven open up before him, its light shining through. He pulled into a parking place and sat in the car for several minutes, just absorbing it. There was something he had missed, something so essential that he had overlooked; and as the stake president's words came back to him, it all fell into perfect place. *As you forgive others, you will find your own mistakes melt away as if they had never occurred.*

That was it, he thought with certainty. He had never been able to let go of his fear of losing Emily to Ryan, because he had never forgiven Ryan for the way he had treated her. Allison had forgiven him. Emily had forgiven him. Even Bret and Penny had forgiven him. They could all see the perspective. And now he could, too.

The temple experience was more incredible than Michael had remembered. He felt the Spirit close to him, and wished Emily were there. Pondering the experiences of his life and the things he had learned, Michael knew he had a ways to go. But he'd come one step closer to finding that inner peace.

Michael stepped into the celestial room and gazed up into the chandelier, attempting to comprehend the beauty of heaven. He had a feeling he was being watched, and quickly glanced around the room, surprised to see Sean sitting casually as if he'd been waiting for quite some time.

Michael sat down beside him and spoke in a hushed whisper. "Is this a coincidence?"

"Actually," he answered with the same quiet reverence, "Emily told me last night you were planning to go to the temple early. I felt the need to talk to you, and thought this was a good place. I got in the first session and figured you'd end up here sooner or later."

Michael smiled and leaned back, gazing again at the domed ceiling.

"You okay?" Sean asked quietly.

Michael nodded serenely. "I'm doing better, I think." He gave

Sean a penetrating gaze. "How about you?"

"I'm doing better, I think."

Michael smiled and patted his shoulder. "So, what did you want to talk about?"

"Well, first of all, I wanted to thank you . . . for sharing your experiences with me. When I look at you and Emily now, and think of all you've gone through, it gives me the hope that God has something in mind for me that will make me forget all about missing Melissa."

"I'm sure you're right," Michael agreed, grateful to know that he'd made a difference in Sean's struggles. "Is that the only reason you've been waiting here for me?"

He wasn't surprised when Sean said, "No. Actually, I wanted to talk about you." Michael lifted a brow in surprise as Sean continued. "I've been praying for you a lot lately, Michael. I know it's been tough . . . since the accident . . . and before."

Michael glanced down and pressed a tense hand down his white pant-leg. By the feelings inside, he was reminded that he did have some things to deal with yet.

"Maybe I'm off, Michael," Sean continued quietly, "but I got thinking about everything you've told me about your experiences with Emily, and how it all tied in to your experiences with coming into the Church. It reminded me of some things that came up on my mission, and I wanted to share it with you."

Michael looked into Sean's eyes, more intrigued now than tense. "I'm listening."

"You know, it's common for new members to let their testimony lean a little too much on something besides their own, personal belief in Jesus Christ. Some lean on the missionaries. Some are drawn in by the social life of the Church. Whatever it is, they are the ones who eventually become inactive, or struggle with their beliefs. It's not uncommon for someone to marry in the temple, then when the marriage goes bad, they allow all the other temple covenants to be neglected. If our beliefs depend too heavily on another human being, we'll always be disappointed. We all lean on others at one time or another, but in the long run, we have only our own testimony to carry us through." He paused and looked severely at Michael. "Are you with me so far?"

"I'm with you." Michael nodded.

"You told me, Michael, that instinct led you to BYU, but it was Emily that first took you to Church. When she left, you stopped going. When she came back into your life, you started again. I know, because you made it clear, that your decision to join the Church had nothing to do with her. You believed she would spend the rest of her life with Ryan. But what happened to that new and fragile testimony when Emily came back into your life so quickly?"

When Sean said nothing more, Michael admitted, "You've lost me somewhere."

Sean put a hand on Michael's knee and leaned toward him. Michael wasn't certain where this was headed, but he knew beyond any doubt that Sean's purpose for coming into their lives was not solely for Sean's benefit. Instinctively he knew this was significant.

"I know you have a testimony, Michael. I've seen it. I've felt it. But it just occurred to me yesterday that perhaps. . . well, how do I say it? Is it possible that your testimony is too integrated with your love for Emily? Are you accustomed to leaning on her light, instead of learning to believe in and love yourself as a son of God? When you look for the answers, do you look to the Savior and trust in Him? Or do your emotions draw you elsewhere?"

Michael inhaled sharply and held his breath. He looked away and put a hand over his mouth, allowing his breath to escape slowly through his fingers. Was it true? Somewhere along the way, had he unconsciously done as Sean suggested? He turned to look at Sean and felt the truth of it. But he needed time to allow it to settle in with everything else he'd learned.

"I just thought I should tell you that," Sean said after a lengthy silence. "You think about it, and if you need to talk. . ."

Michael nodded in appreciation. "Thank you, Sean. I think you might have something there." Sean smiled serenely. Michael put a hand on his shoulder and added, "Do you think your parents have any idea what kind of man you've become?"

The emotion rose so quickly in Sean's eyes that Michael nearly regretted saying it. But Sean said easily, "I don't know, but I think that maybe someday they'll have the chance to find out. Perhaps the

Lord will make it possible to mend those bridges eventually."

"I'm sure you're right," Michael said. They exchanged a firm embrace and reluctantly left the peace of the celestial room. Sean hurried to get to a class. And while Michael wanted to share these things with Emily, he felt more of a need to sort them through more thoroughly. He drove up Provo Canyon and parked the Blazer. Wandering along the bank of the Provo River, he felt a little closer to understanding what he believed the Lord was trying to tell him. He lost track of the time as he prayed and pondered, and was reminded of the prophet Enos.

Michael feared Emily would be worried when he got back in the Blazer and realized it was late afternoon. He stopped at a phone booth and called her, telling her he was going to make a quick stop before coming home. She told him Sean had called after his first class. He'd suspected Michael might need some time alone. As always, Emily was understanding.

Michael's errand went quickly and he hurried home, going straight to the bedroom. He gently laid a dozen red roses on the bed, and the paper around them crinkled as he knelt over Emily and kissed her warmly.

"Feeling better?" She smiled as he drew back and touched her face.

"Yes, actually, I think I am."

"Want to talk?"

"Maybe later," he said. "Right now, I just want to be right here." He settled his head onto her shoulder and snuggled close to her side.

Emily picked up the roses and inhaled their fragrance. "They're beautiful," she said. "What's the occasion?"

"They're forgiveness roses," he replied, urging her a littler closer. Emily pressed her lips into his hair, and he knew that she understood.

CHAPTER EIGHTEEN

Long after Emily fell asleep, Michael lay close to her, wondering why he wasn't exhausted. He felt somehow drained, yet full of vitality.

Feeling a gentle nudge against him, he realized it was a baby's kick. He marveled at the way Emily slept while the babies moved freely within her. He lost track of the time as he played with them, pushing and prodding gently in response to their nudges. At moments he could almost feel the distinct outline of a little foot.

The babies both settled together, as if they were of one mind. The moonlight cast an almost eerie glow over the room, and Michael watched Emily sleeping, marveling at the life he shared with her. Just to be with her each and every day, to sleep by her side, to be a part of everything she did; it all seemed a miracle to him. He thought about the babies and tried to imagine what it might be like when they arrived. Like Emily, he longed to have it over with, to know it was behind them. Five weeks remained until the due date, and even though they'd been told that twins usually come early, it still seemed like such a long time to wait.

Michael drifted to sleep and dreamt of holding his new babies, one in each arm. Then, in a sudden flash of horror, it was like that moment when Emily's heart had stopped. The room spun as he tried to get someone to help him hold the babies so he could get to her and keep her from dying. He awakened with a gasp and found the room dark since the moon had moved on.

"Michael!" Emily's voice came with a hint of urgency. "Are you awake?"

"Yes. What's wrong?"

"I feel . . . wet," she cried. "I think I'm bleeding, Michael. I'm afraid to look."

"Merciful heaven," he muttered and reached for the lamp on the bedside table. He held his breath while she peered beneath the sheet then leaned back, her eyes wide.

"Oh," she gasped, "there it goes again."

"What?" he demanded.

"I'm not bleeding," she announced. Michael's sigh of relief caught in his throat when she added, "My water just broke."

"Merciful heaven!" he repeated. "It's too soon, isn't it? I mean . . ."

He stopped when she grimaced. "I don't think there's time to speculate and analyze, Michael. I think you'd better get me to the hospital—*now!*"

Michael frantically pulled on his Levis and boots. "Tell me what you need. We didn't even get a bag packed or—"

"I'm sure they'll have what I need for the moment, Michael. I'm not worried about packing a bag. You'd better wake your mother . . . and Allison," she added as an afterthought.

"Allison?" He hesitated just after he pulled a sweatshirt over his head.

"I want her to come."

Michael nodded and hurried down the hall. Allison was as surprised as he at Emily's request, but eagerly complied. LeNay calmly assured Michael that everything would be fine as she followed him toward the bedroom, only to find Emily walking down the hall, a long coat over her nightgown, nothing on her feet.

"What are you doing?" Michael growled.

"I can walk to the car, for crying out loud. I don't think I need to worry about staying down to keep them from coming too early."

LeNay shot Michael a cautioning glance and he patiently let Emily make her way down the stairs to the door. Allison was waiting in the entry, dressed and alert.

"Are you all right, Mom?"

"For the moment," she said unsteadily.

"We'll be praying for you," LeNay said. "Let us know."

Emily smiled up at her. Michael noticed Emily waver a little and tossed Allison the keys.

"You drive," he insisted and lifted Emily into his arms without her permission. He groaned and she chuckled. "You've gained weight, my love."

"Nonsense," she said, "you're just getting old." Emily grimaced then as a contraction took strong hold.

Allison held the door and Michael gently eased Emily into the back seat of the Blazer. He went around and got in next to her.

"Drive the speed limit," Michael said as Allison backed out of the driveway.

"No, hurry," Emily insisted with an edge to her voice that tempted Michael to panic. She leaned back against him and clamped her hands onto his thighs with a grip that made him realize the pain was coming hard and fast.

"Give me a blessing, Michael," she insisted.

"Now?" He felt too panicked to try and feel in tune at the moment.

"I need the power of the priesthood to make it through this, Michael. Something tells me this is going to be—" Her sentence merged into a groan. "Please . . ." she implored.

Michael willed himself to calm down and think clearly. He took a deep breath and put his hands on her head. While Allison sped carefully through the empty streets, Michael blessed Emily with the strength she needed to make it through this and live to see her children and grandchildren raised. She was blessed with the assurance that everything would be all right, according to the will of the Lord, in spite of how things might appear. When Michael said the *amen* he was amazed, but not surprised, by the source of those words. He felt the power flowing through him, and found that it eased his own fears.

Allison pulled into the hospital parking lot and jumped out to get a wheelchair.

"How you doing, love?" Michael asked, keenly aware of the signs of increasing pain.

"I can't do this, Michael," she insisted. "I can't. Don't make me do this."

"I don't have the power to take the pain away, love. You'd better talk to the Lord about that."

Emily bit her lip to keep from crying out when Michael moved her to the wheelchair. She was barely out of the elevator when she was lifted onto a bed, since Allison had gone ahead to tell them she was coming. Michael leaned over Emily with her hand in his as the bed was rolled down a long hall and into a delivery room.

Somewhere on the edge of the pain, Emily was vaguely aware of Michael's soothing voice, telling her over and over that it was almost over, it would be all right. But her only conscious awareness was the pain. She'd given birth before and had certainly not enjoyed it, but never had she felt such pain. The remnants of her accident injuries throbbed until she thought they alone would kill her. The contractions soon ceased coming and going; instead she felt a constant, unyielding pain that made her writhe and groan.

Michael tried to tell himself to stay calm. He had watched Emily give birth before, and it was not a pleasant experience. But she had always maintained a certain composure, even through the worst of it. But this; this was a nightmare. He caught Allison's frightened expression and wondered if she should be with them. Inwardly he prayed for the strength and guidance he needed to get Emily through this. Once she was settled into the stirrups, Michael leaned over her and put his hands on either side of her head. With his face only inches from hers, he spoke to her in a gentle command. "Emily, are you listening to me? Look at me."

Emily only squirmed back and forth, ignoring him, saying over and over that she couldn't do it.

Michael took her face into his hands. "Look at me," he said slowly, ignoring what the medical staff was doing around them, but aware of a nurse hovering close by to prompt him.

"Emily, look at me."

She finally focused on him, albeit her eyes were glazed and strained. "I can't do it, Michael. I can't."

"Listen to me," he said gently. "You can do anything; even this. I am here. Allison is here. We're going to help you."

"I can't. I can't," she murmured. Then she began breathing so sharply he feared she'd hyperventilate.

"She's got to slow down," the nurse said quietly.

"Emily, breathe," Michael said. She ignored him. "Breathe!" he shouted in her face. How old was James? How long had it been since they'd done this?

As if the nurse had read his mind she said, "In through your nose. Blow it out through your mouth."

Michael repeated it. "In through your nose, Emily." He did it. "Blow it out through your mouth." Michael kept doing it, breathing in her face, over and over, until she tried to do it with him. She took hold of his upper arms and squeezed so hard it almost eased some of his guilt for not being able to take the pain. He was just about convinced she was going to calm down and take this reasonably, when her head shot back and she cried out in anguish.

"Something's wrong," he said instinctively to the nurse. "She's never done this before."

"It's all right," he was informed. "In another minute she can start pushing."

Michael realized then that it wasn't just instinct. He repeated again what the voice in his head had told him. "Something's wrong," he insisted.

He was ignored, but when the doctor told him she could push, he hoped they could just get this over with.

"Okay, Emily," he said. "Take a deep breath. I'll do it with you."

Emily tried to concentrate, but the pain was only worsening.

"Okay, love, push," Michael told her at the nurse's prompting. Emily took a deep breath and bore down, then cried out again.

"Whoa!" the doctor said behind Michael. "Something's wrong. Fetal heart tones are down."

Michael sighed and panicked at the same time. At least maybe they'd listen to *him*.

Emily cried out again and wished she could die. She looked into Michael's face and saw fear in his eyes as he spoke. "You hold on. Do you hear me? You're going to make it through this. Do you understand me?"

She wanted to tell him she couldn't do it, but she hurt so badly the words wouldn't even form. Like a glimmer of light she remembered Michael's blessing, and his own words when he'd told her that he couldn't take away the pain, but she could talk to the Lord about it. Emily squeezed her eyes shut tightly. With her thoughts she concentrated on reaching upward to communicate with her Father in Heaven. *I can't do this any more,* she told him. *I'm putting it in your hands.* A moment later the pain came on stronger than ever and she cried out toward the ceiling, "Please, God! Take this pain from me!"

Emily relaxed so suddenly that Michael's heart pounded with fear. He looked down at her and held his breath. She lay motionless, staring with glazed eyes, unblinking. "What happened?" he demanded, certain she was dead. Just when he was ready to shake her, she blinked and looked at him.

"It would seem that God heard her," the nurse said quietly in response to Michael's question.

Michael looked into Emily's eyes and caught his breath when he saw the evidence. There was no logical explanation for her pain to cease. Yet, the tranquility in her face was evident.

"Prep her for a C-section," the doctor ordered. "We've got to get those babies out of there."

Michael turned to question him until he felt Emily's hand on his arm. "It's okay, Michael. There's no need to do that."

"There's no need for that," Michael said to the doctor.

"Mr. Hamilton, I know this is difficult, but if we want these babies to live, we've got to move fast and—"

"Doctor, I know you're a spiritual man. If she says we don't need to do that, then maybe we ought to try once more."

The doctor leaned back and sighed. Emily bore down again, seeming uncomfortable, but not in pain. Emma was born less than a minute later, head first and perfect. They laughed and cried as the baby was wrapped up and handed to Michael. He was glad now that Allison had come as their eyes met and he handed Emma over to her.

"You have a daughter now," she said to him.

He knew she meant this was his first blood daughter, but it was easy to say, "I have four daughters now, Allie."

While Allison was admiring the baby, Michael and Emily admired each other, basking in the awe of this partnership they shared in creating life. He saw the distress come over her face and knew the other baby was coming. A degree of her pain returned as she bore down to bring Tyson into the world, but it was little compared to what she had felt before.

"Oh, Michael, he's beautiful," Emily declared as he was laid in the crook of her arm. Tears came as she added, "He looks just like I saw him . . . in my dream."

Michael could almost reach out and touch that baby's spirit as his little eyes opened and seemed to take in everything with great zeal. He reached over the baby to kiss Emily and wipe away her tears, but the moment was intruded upon by a nurse who gently eased Tyson away.

"You'll be able to see him later," she smiled gently, but with a look in her eyes that made them panic. "His color's not good. We need to see that everything's all right."

"It's his heart," Emily said, trying not to be upset. She met Michael's eyes, and with no words spoken they both understood that it was in God's hands. Trying to be positive, Emily turned her attention to her newest daughter, content and safe in the arms of her oldest daughter.

"Oh, Mom, she's incredible. I can't believe how little she is."

"She is a tiny one," the doctor commented. "But she appears to be doing well."

Emma too was taken to be examined, and the nurse invited Allison to come along and observe. Michael held Emily's hand as the placenta was delivered and everything was put in order. When it was done Emily's pain returned, and Michael was reminded of when he'd come out of surgery. They gave her something for it as soon as she was taken to a room to recover, but she still had difficulty relaxing. Michael sat on the edge of the bed at her request, and leaned back next to her, holding her close.

"What happened in there, Emily?" he asked quietly.

Emily knew what he was referring to, but she had trouble finding words to describe it. "I don't know, Michael," she finally said. "I can only tell you that, even though I was aware of the pain, I was somehow distanced from it, as if a wall were brought down between my consciousness and the pain."

Michael recalled having heard once that a woman giving birth was in close partnership with God. He knew he had just witnessed that first hand, and he was in awe of the gift of life itself.

"How did you know they didn't need to do the C-section?" he asked.

"I just knew everything was all right." She nuzzled close to him, acutely aware of the ache in her lower body but not caring. The peace she felt within could not be marred by anything. Not even the news they received an hour later.

"Your little boy's heart is severely malformed," the doctor informed them gently. "He will only live a few days at the very most. His heart could stop at any time."

He went on to explain the technical details, but Emily barely heard them. With that same kind of distance she had felt in the delivery room, she was drawn away from the doctor's gentle explanation to the memory of a dream. When she had first miscarried a boy, Alexa had come to her and told her she would take care of the baby until Emily was able to. That dream had kept Emily believing she was to have this child, but only now did she understand it. She would not be able to raise this child here and now, but Alexa would take care of him until they could be together again. In the same moment, Emily understood the purpose of this little girl. She could almost hear a voice in her head telling her that Emma was a gift, a child that had been denied the right to come down elsewhere. Emma was being given to them to help compensate for the pain of not having Tyson with them here on earth.

As soon as the doctor left, Michael turned to Emily, the emotion evident in his eyes. "Michael, you have to call Bret—and Sean."

Michael shook his head, too numb to think what she could mean.

"That baby has to be named, and we need to do it now."

Michael nodded in agreement. He didn't like it, but he was grateful she had the sense to make an important decision. Michael called his mother, then Bret and Penny. LeNay said she would call Sean. A few minutes later, Tyson was brought to Emily's room. The nurse said nothing, but they knew the doctor had told her the baby should spend what little time he had with his parents.

Michael and Emily sat close together, talking to each other and the baby. Looking closely, they could see that something wasn't right. But still, he was a beautiful little boy that Emily declared looked much like Michael. Emily told Michael about her dream and how she could see now what it meant. Together they cried and prayed together. Emily declared that she was grateful to at least know this was not the end of their time with this child. Though Michael didn't feel the assault on his nerves that the topic of eternity had once provoked in him, he wished that he could *know* in his own heart, as Emily did, that they would be together forever.

Bret and Penny arrived with the family, who had found Allison near the nursery admiring Emma. Sean eased into the little room and they all hovered close together while Michael told them that Tyson would not be staying long. He announced that they would be giving him a name and a blessing now, then he turned to Emily and asked, "What's his middle name?"

"I don't know. You decide."

"I don't know either," he echoed.

"It'll come to you," she said, then motioned for him to go on. Emily expected to feel upset by all of this, as Michael was joined by Bret and Sean to name her baby. But as he began the blessing in a firm, steady voice, she found that she felt nothing but peace.

When Michael got to that part of the blessing where the name should be spoken, he hesitated. A name appeared in his mind so naturally that he almost laughed. Instead, he simply stated without qualm, "Tyson Ryan Hamilton."

Tyson was still living late that evening. Michael found he was so exhausted that he had no choice but to go home and try to sleep. Emily had been resting peacefully for quite some time, but Michael had difficulty tearing himself away.

When he finally crawled into bed, exhaustion took hold of him immediately and he slept with no trouble. He woke up feeling startled and realized the room was bright with daylight. Knowing he had been dreaming, he tried hard to recall the dream to mind. When he remembered, his heart began to pound. He had just seen his great-grandmother, Alexa, holding Tyson in a white blanket. She told him that she would take care of him until he and Emily were able to.

Michael was at the hospital in a matter of minutes. Emily was not in her room. He found her seated in a rocking chair in the nursery, holding Tyson and crying. The baby died a few minutes later.

The day after Emily and Emma came home from the hospital, the family drove to Idaho for a graveside service. Tyson would be buried next to Emily's parents. The drive was hard on Emily, her fragile physical condition compounded by her loss. Sean went along, and as always, he was good to help with the children. He was quiet and thoughtful, but he seemed at peace.

As the miles passed, Emily's mind wandered over the years she had struggled to have this baby. And now he was gone. In her mind she understood. She knew she would be with her little son again. She knew that life was eternal. But in her heart, she missed him. Little in her life had been so hard as the realization that her infant son was being buried in the cold, dark earth. She thought of the pioneers and wondered how they had coped with the deaths of loved ones along the way. But just when she got the lowest, Michael was there beside her, reminding her with a simple glance and a kiss that love didn't end with death, and she had much to be grateful for.

Upon their return, Emily spent much of the next few days in bed. Michael was close by, helping her with Emma and coaching the other children through their interest in the baby and her care. Little was said about the absence of her twin brother, but Michael and Emily knew they shared the ache.

Sean continued to hover around the house, showing a distant interest in the baby. "Do you want to hold her?" Emily asked on a particularly gray afternoon.

"Oh, I don't think that—"

Sean's protest was interrupted as Emily lowered the bundled Emma into his arms. After a minute he relaxed a little and began to rock her gently back and forth, smiling serenely at the tiny dark eyes peering up at him. "She's beautiful," he finally said, but Emily was not prepared for the emotion in his voice.

"Your day will come," Michael said, patting Sean on the shoulder. Sean looked up with tears in his eyes.

"Are you missing Melissa?" Emily asked as Sean looked back to the baby.

"It's hard not to think about her," he admitted quietly. "But I know it's right."

"That's good, then," Michael said. "So, why the tears, kid?"

"Oh," Sean chuckled with emotion, "I was just thinking about something that happened a long time ago, before my accident. It's not important, really."

Michael and Emily exchanged a disappointed glance as it became apparent that he had no intention of telling them. But they quickly forgot about it as Emma yawned noisily and Sean laughed.

"You have a beautiful family, Michael," Sean said, then glanced at Emily. "Not to mention an incredible wife."

"I can't argue with that." Michael's voice rang with sincerity.

"When I *do* get married," Sean said, looking again at the baby, "I want a woman just like Emily."

"Oh?" Emily chuckled. "How do you figure?"

"There must be lots of girls wandering around BYU who grew up on a farm. Adorable, spiritual, intelligent girls." Sean lifted his eyebrows comically, then glanced at Michael. "It's too bad she's already taken."

"You'd better believe it," Michael said, pretending to be offended. "And it's only because you're young enough to be my son that I'll forgive you for saying that."

Emily looked demurely at the floor. Sean and Michael exchanged a brotherly glance, then their attention returned to little Emma.

As Michael felt the struggles of the past few years slipping gradually into perspective, he had a strong desire to go to the temple. Again, he wished that Emily could be with him. But he knew it wouldn't be long before she'd be up and around, and they could be together within temple walls.

He sat in the celestial room longer than he ever had, just pondering and praying to understand why his life had taken these paths. As he thought of Emily, wishing she were by his side, Michael felt the entire spectrum fall into place instantaneously. One second it was not there. The next it was. He could only describe it as knowing without any doubt that the words of Emily's story were true, and the words spoken by the stake president were, also. In a single moment, Michael understood why he had been born into a particular place and set of circumstances. He understood why Emily couldn't have married him initially, and the part Ryan played in all of this. And he even understood why it was necessary for him to go through these years of fear and confusion—a situation that could only have been resolved fully by something as drastic as nearly killing the woman he loved. But now, his heart, his mind, and his spirit were completely at peace with one another. Yes, Michael thought as he stared into the crystal chandelier above him, absorbing the peace and beauty of this room that symbolized perfection, he understood.

Suddenly, Michael couldn't wait to get home. For no apparent reason, he laughed several times as he drove toward home. He ran through the door and heard Jess and James arguing in the family room. He hurried down the stairs and hurled himself to the floor between them, tickling them both at the same time until he left them laughing. Amee and Alexa came out of their rooms to investigate; he picked them up one at a time and swung them around, laughing and spreading kisses over their lovely young faces—those faces that resembled their father. He left them looking dubiously at each other as he ran upstairs and danced with his mother in the kitchen, ignoring the flour she had all down her front from rolling out cookies.

"Michael!" Emily called. Her ordeal had not damaged her vocal cords. "Is that you causing all the ruckus?"

Michael ran down the hall and bounded carefully onto the bed. He took Emma from Emily and held her tiny form close to his face, then he carefully set her beside him. He laughed as he took both of Emily's hands into his and kissed them over and over ridiculously. Her eyes went wide with an amused wonder, then widened further when he kissed her as if he never had before.

"I take it you enjoyed yourself," she said when he finally set her lips free.

"Oh, Emily," he said in a hushed expression of joy, "I love you. I love you more than life. And if you were to die tomorrow, which you won't, of course, because we have been promised that you would be here for many years yet; but if you were to die tomorrow, Emily, everything would be all right. Because God promised me that I could have you. He knew what I needed to go through to learn that for myself. He knew my weaknesses and gave me what I needed to make them strengths. Satan knew my weaknesses, too, and he tried to use them against me. But God gave me something that Satan couldn't take away. He gave me *you*, Emily."

The emotion finally bubbled out with a stream of tears. "God gave me you, Emily," he repeated. "A woman with such faith, such perfect conviction, that I only had to love you and God knew I would find a way. Emily, I'm going to ask Allison to make sure it's done. After I die, she can see that you and I are sealed. But even if she didn't it would be okay, because God can take care of it. He's God, you know. He can do anything. And he promised me that I could have you . . . not only now, but forever. And I will, Emily. Oh, I will! I will spend every day for the rest of my life fighting to prove to you and to God that I can be worthy of that blessing. And all of the children will be there, Emily. All of them. And Ryan is welcome to visit any time he wants. He's really not such a bad guy, you know. He just didn't understand. But God understands, Emily. He understands *me*, and you—and Ryan. He knew what we needed in order to accomplish what he asked us to do. Oh, Emily, isn't it the most incredible thing? Will you forgive me for all the hurt I caused you? Will you stay with me forever, Emily? Will you stand by my side as we create our own worlds? Will you spend the endless eons of time being my lover and my friend?"

While Emily laughed and cried and listened to Michael's impassioned speech, Emma lifted her little arms and stretched heartily, as if she was responding to his vision of all they would share. Emily became so caught up in the warmth surrounding them, that she didn't realize he'd asked her a question until she saw a flicker of doubt in his eyes.

"Emily." He took her by the shoulders and looked into her face. "You and I are supposed to be together—forever. I know it with all my heart and soul, and *no one* is going to take that away from me."

Emily's warmth increased as she realized he was trying to convince her, not himself. She was quick to assure him, "There's no need to tell me that, Jess Michael Hamilton. I've known since the day

I married you that we were supposed to be together forever. I tried to tell you, but I guess you had to figure it out for yourself."

Michael pulled her close to him, cradling her tender body that was slowly recovering from childbirth, kissing her brow and murmuring over and over that he loved her. When Emma began to fuss, he lifted her into his arms.

"Is everything all right?" Allison asked timidly from the doorway.

Michael turned and reached out a hand toward her. She eased close to the bed and put her arms around both him and Emily.

"Everything is perfect," Michael said.

Following Allison's example, the other children moved eagerly in from the hallway, as if compelled to be a part of the warmth surrounding their parents. They eased onto the bed and huddled close together, grasping hands, touching faces, exchanging kisses and eager embraces. LeNay appeared in the doorway, smiling at the scene before her, contentment glowing in her eyes.

"Look, Mother," Michael said, reaching out a hand toward her. "Look at my beautiful family."

"We're going to be together forever," James said with perfect innocence, and Michael chuckled.

"That's right, James, we are," he agreed. Michael touched his mother's face and tightened his arm around Emily. "Forever," he added firmly.

* * * * *

When Emma was two weeks old, Michael sat close to Emily on the couch while she nursed the baby.

"Maybe we should talk," he said quietly. "I sense you're lost in thought much of the time. Do you want to tell me about it?"

Emily sighed and closed her eyes. "I know I should be grateful that I have a thriving, healthy baby, but I . . ." the tears came, "I miss Tyson."

"I know," Michael whispered and brushed his lips over her brow, "I do, too. But we know where he is, Emily, and we know we will be with him again. We will all be together—now and forever,

Emily."

Emily looked up at him, admiration glowing through her tears. "You can't imagine what it does to me to hear you say that."

"I know what it does to me," he smiled. "But more importantly," he put a fist to his chest, "I *feel* it."

Emily leaned her head against his shoulder. "I don't have any trouble understanding, Michael. I don't. I feel peace." Her voice broke. "I just miss him."

They sat together in contemplative silence for several minutes before Emily said, "You know, Michael, I had that dream about Alexa and the baby over four years ago. But it didn't really make sense until now. I mean, it did, but I can see now that its meaning was something deeper than I'd first comprehended. And yet, if it hadn't been for that accident and the treatment I'd had, the doctors believe that Tyson's heart would have been sound."

"I don't think I like the way you put that," Michael said too severely.

"Oh, no, it's not that . . ." she said quickly. "Don't you see, Michael? The Lord knew long ago this was the way it would be. Tyson was only meant to be here a short time. If it hadn't been that, it would have been something else." She sighed again. "I suppose it's just nice to know we have the Lord in our lives, and the peace of knowing that it's all meant to be."

"It certainly is," he agreed.

"You know, Michael, when I think of everything that's happened these past years—and even before that—I marvel at how close God has been to us, helping us through, guiding us even when—or perhaps especially when—we've struggled. Perhaps if people stopped more often to comprehend that he is there, just waiting to bless us; that we have the power to accomplish so much more than the mediocrity of life; perhaps this world would have so much more peace."

"I know you're right," he said and held her close.

When Emma finished eating, Michael held her against his shoulder and patted her little back. He met Emily's eyes, and for a moment he could almost feel the reality of eternity. This peace, this ability to share and create life . . . this *was* life.

* * * * *

The week that Emma celebrated six months of life, Emily received her master's degree. The following week Michael put the house up for sale and made flight reservations to return his family to Australia.

Two weeks before their planned departure, Michael and Emily stood on the rim of the Grand Canyon, discussing its vastness. Emma was sleeping in a pack against Michael's chest. Sean was standing nearby, holding hands with Jess and James. He had admitted his dread at their going back to Australia, but they had promised to keep in touch. Penny and Bret had also admitted to dreading the separation; but they already had plans to come to Australia for a month after their youngest son graduated from high school.

The girls called to Emily, and she walked down the trail a bit to see what they wanted. Allison slipped an arm around Michael's waist and said quietly, "Dad, there's something I need to ask you."

"Okay."

"Sean and I have been talking a lot lately, and . . ."

Michael lifted a curious brow, wondering if something deeper was developing between them. But she surprised him.

"He's encouraged me to do this, but . . . well, I know it will take some time, but I want to work toward going on a mission. Do you think we can afford it?"

Michael threw back his head and laughed. "Yes, sweetie," he said, hugging her tightly, "I think we can afford it."

After several minutes of comfortable silence, she asked, "Is it possible that our being here now has anything to do with my wanting to come here as a child?"

"Well," he said casually, "your father wanted to bring you here, but . . ." He grinned and hugged her. "I thought you should see it before we go back."

"I love you, Dad," she said and rested her head against his shoulder.

The Friday evening following their vacation, Michael sent

Emily to the store for a few things. He was admiring the newly-developed pictures of the Grand Canyon, and others of Emily, wearing her cap and gown, when he heard the car pull in. He hurried to light the candles, douse the lights, and switch on the stereo. When she came in, he was situated in a chair as if he'd been there for an hour.

"What is this?" she asked, standing dazed in the dining room, where more than a dozen candles were glowing on a table set for two.

"This is a graduation party," he stated, taking the groceries from her and setting them aside.

"A party for who?" she asked suspiciously.

"Just me and you." He pushed an arm around her waist and urged her into a gentle dance step in time to the music.

"Just me and you?" she echoed.

"We can have lots of fun," he smiled. "We used to have lots of fun," he kissed her, "just the two of us."

"Where are the children?" she asked. "You didn't tie them up or anything, did you?"

"They are having a sleep-over party at Sean's."

Emily laughed in surprise. "Even Emma?"

"*Especially* Emma." He laughed back then brushed his lips over her brow. "Allison can take care of her. Besides, I bribed Sean."

"With what?"

"I gave him my Blazer."

"Oh," Emily smiled, "I see."

"By the way," he added, "I sold the house."

"Really? To who?"

"The Petersons," he stated.

Emily pulled back briefly. "You mean the seven-kids-in-that-little-tiny-house Petersons, who live down the street?"

"That's who I mean."

"But surely they can't afford what you—"

Michael quickly kissed Emily to silence her, then he whispered near her ear, "They had an offer on that little tiny house—a retired couple who wanted to live near their daughter. I asked Brother Peterson what he got for the house. He told me, and I said that was exactly what I was selling my house for."

Emily met her husband's sparkling eyes, marveling once again at his goodness. Did he realize the impact of what he'd just done for a good family that had always struggled with money and space? He smiled and she felt certain he did, but he was too humble to admit it.

"I love you, Michael," she said, pressing her fingers to the back of his neck.

"I love you, too . . . Emily Hamilton." He drawled her name as if it were poetry.

Their eyes locked, and Michael was surprised by the sudden warmth that rushed through him. He knew this feeling. It was one of those rare moments when the truth of heaven was manifest to earth through the heart of man. He saw it reflected in Emily's face and knew she felt it, too. In that moment, there was no question that he would be with her forever. As long as he continued on this path and endured to the end, he had no reason to doubt it.

Emily was surprised at the tears brimming in Michael's eyes, until she felt the reason for them in her own heart. The Spirit touched her with such strength that she nearly gasped from the rush of warmth and the swelling of tears into her own eyes.

She continued to dance within Michael's embrace while she concentrated on his eyes. Not only was there a complete lack of pain, but the peace and hope he felt was evident. She knew they would always be together.

She felt a giddy rush somewhere inside when he pressed his mouth over hers, kissing her as if they were newlyweds with their whole lives ahead of them. Somehow she believed it would always be that way when Michael Hamilton kissed her.

"Wow," she said when he finally eased his lips from hers, only to rummage them through her hair. "That was nice. Candles. Soft music. Dancing. Peace and quiet. I must be in heaven."

Michael drew back just enough to look into her eyes. "Yes, my love," he whispered, kissing her softly. "We just keep getting a little closer to heaven."

Photograph by Karl Roylance

About the Author

Anita Stansfield is an imaginative and prolific writer whose first published novels, *First Love and Forever* (winner of the 1994-1995 Best Fiction Award from the Independent LDS Booksellers) and *First Love, Second Chances* have been outstanding successes in the LDS romance market. She has been writing since she was in high school, and her work has appeared in *Cosmopolitan* and other publications. She is an active member of the Romance Writers of America and the League of Utah Writers.

Anita and her husband, Vince, live with their four children in Orem, Utah.

The author enjoys hearing from her readers. You can write to her at:

P.O. Box 50795
Provo, UT 84605-0795